The Dower House

Annabel Davis-Goff

St. Martin's Griffin
New York

THE DOWER HOUSE. Copyright © 1997 by Annabel Davis-Goff. All rights reserved. Printed in the United States of America. No part of this book may be used or reproduced in any manner whatsoever without written permission except in the case of brief quotations embodied in critical articles or reviews. For information, address St. Martin's Press, 175 Fifth Avenue, New York, N.Y. 10010.

Design by Ellen R. Sasahara

Library of Congress Cataloging-in-Publication Data

Davis-Goff, Annabel.
    The dower house / Annabel Davis-Goff.
        p. cm.
    ISBN 0-312-17028-9 (hc)
    ISBN 0-312-20645-3 (pbk)
    I. Title.
PS3554.A9385D68   1998
813'.54—dc21

                                                    97-33065
                                                    CIP

First St. Martin's Griffin Edition: May 1999

10 9 8 7 6 5 4 3 2 1

Praise for Annabel Davis-Goff's
The Dower House

"Class welfare has rarely been depicted with such eloquence, lucidity, and humor; Davis-Goff is a modern-day Mitford (as in Nancy)."
—*New York Post* (one of ten fiction "greats of '98")

"Fine and poignant."
—*Kirkus Reviews*

"Davis-Goff is very skilled at quick characterizations...and at capturing the finest distinctions of manners and convention."
—*The Washington Post Book World*

"The prose is so evocative that I blinked occasionally when I realized the page in front of me was white, and not the faded green of velvet curtains and overgrown gardens....A sympathetic, convincing portrait of a conflicted woman whose choice brings no one any real happiness."
—*The New York Times Book Review*

"Davis-Goff has an exquisite eye and a wonderful memory for the vagaries of adolescent girlhood, and it is a pleasure to watch her heroine experience new emotions, discover sex and sensuality, and accept responsibility for the direction of her memorable young life."
—*Publishers Weekly* (starred review)

"*The Dower House* has something of the flavor of a memoir as it evokes people and places with an elegant specificity. Davis-Goff also remembers well the emotions of a girl on the brink of adulthood—vulnerability, confidence, hopefulness, and desire all mixed together at any given moment."
—*Orlando Sentinel*

"Irish-born Annabel Davis-Goff beautifully describes the postwar world of the Anglo-Irish as they struggle to hang on to their estates by selling the family diamonds and marrying well."
—*Detroit Free Press*

"A carefully crafted depiction of a nearly extinct society."
—*Booklist*

"Davis-Goff...fills her characters with humor, charm, and a moving wistfulness for a vanishing lifestyle."
—*Library Journal*

"[A] careful, well-shaped narrative."
—*St. Louis Post-Dispatch*

"Anglo-Irish Ireland forms so rich a setting...that it becomes a powerful theme in its own right....This novel is about the furnishings of a vanishing way of life, told with expert authority."
—*The Baltimore Sun*

Also by Annabel Davis-Goff

The Literary Companion to Gambling (editor)
Walled Gardens: Scenes from an Anglo-Irish Childhood
Tail Spin
Night Tennis

For William Maxwell

Acknowledgments

I am grateful to Cynthia O'Connor, Julia Barker, Shirley Hazzard, Susanna Moore, Robert Gotlieb, Lizzie Grossman, Laura Van Wormer, Elinor Arneson, Jenny Nichols, and Max Nichols for their help and advice, and to Ingrid and Felix Mechoulam, in whose house I wrote part of this novel.

How much time does love take?

—E. M. Forster, *Aspects of the Novel*

We are no petty people. We are one of the great stocks of Europe. We are the people of Grattan; we are the people of Swift, the people of Emmet, the people of Parnell. We have created the most of the modern literature of this country. We have created the best of its political intelligence.

—W. B. Yeats

The Dower House

*M*OLLY'S FIRST MEMORY of her mother, and it might be argued of herself, was a reflection.

Over the mantelpiece in the drawing room of the house in which Molly had been born there was a looking glass with a thin, carved frame. The glass was old, and what it reflected was yellow tinted and somewhat flattering. In the corners the glass was mottled and unevenly darker where the oxidized silver paint had worn off. At Christmas and for some time afterward a twig of holly, cut from a bush behind the stable yard, would be stuck through the carved frame, and a few sprigs would rest on the mantelpiece itself. Gradually the berries would dry and shrivel, although the leaves would remain green. Wedged between the frame and the looking glass there would be invitations, sometimes engraved, sometimes written in ink, to parties and dances and hunt balls.

Although the house contained many photographs, few were now taken. The drawing room bore silver-framed witness to more affluent and, it appeared, happier days; there were albums of photographs of a time when Molly's father had been young, and the house—and the houses of his friends—had been full of laughing, smiling people who were, it seemed, in the habit of posing for photographs in clothes that, although they seemed

1

strange and in some way wrong to Molly, were clearly more festive than the lumpy hand-knitted sweaters and baggy tweed skirts that never kept Molly's mother, Morag, quite warm enough. The camera had been lost or broken, and the purchase of a new one, or even of a roll of film, was unlikely ever to be added to the list of things needed to alleviate the endless discomfort of the lovely but crumbling house.

Morag was a beauty, a great beauty, but a beauty in a time and a place where it could do her very little good. Her beauty had earned her a husband of great charm, but with a disinclination to face inconvenient realities, and a house that, although Georgian and architecturally perfect, was damp and old and dying. There was not, and never again would be, the money needed to keep it alive.

It was in front of the looking glass that Molly had watched her mother form memories. Memories for herself and memories for Molly. She and Molly would gaze at the soft, idealized version of themselves. Each would look at herself, the other. Occasionally Molly would meet her mother's eye.

In that first memory, or perhaps in one instance of that blurred collective series of memories—which came to form one milestone memory, tangible enough to have, in part, formed Molly's nature—she watched her mother draw a finger over the flakes of white and gray ash on the marble mantelpiece and sigh.

Morag would have considered admonishing the poorly trained and badly paid maid responsible for dusting the drawing room, and would have decided against it. Not only from apathy; there were practical reasons for not doing so. She understood that in the minds of these country girls there existed a statute of limitations on any instruction not reiterated at regular intervals. Any new demand could shorten the period during which a previous instruction might be held valid. The timid, overweight girl whose duty it was to dust the drawing room was also responsible for the buckets and containers that had to be expertly placed throughout the house during any but the lightest rainfall. The *ping* of a large drop falling from a high flaking ceiling into a metal bucket was a sound louder and more chilling to a householder than was the click of the deathwatch beetle. There had been no moment when Morag had been young enough or inexperienced enough to imagine that Dolores would compare the importance of a leaking ceiling and a dusty mantelpiece and necessarily make the correct choice.

Molly understood very early that the level of depression in the kitchen was almost as high as that in the drawing room. She also saw, and wondered at it, that the maids struggled to escape the lot of an unmarried domestic servant without appearing to notice the implications of the alternative. Maids who had left the house and married would come back for a kitchen visit. Molly could see that these girls looked tired, strangely older, thinner in a way that suggested the wrong kind of food and too little of it. She also often noticed the thin, mean smell of poverty when she was invited to hold the baby that usually accompanied them. Sometimes the girls would disappear into the drawing room, the door closed, to speak to Morag. That meant that Molly's mother was being appealed to for a small sum of money. This request, not often made, was never refused, although even such a modest sum could not easily be spared. There was very little money anywhere in Ireland; those who owned large houses and horses, and even those who had inherited English or Norman titles and land, were short of cash in the putting-one's-hand-in-one's-pocket sense of the word. Most of the money in Ireland had been drained out during the eighteenth and early nineteenth centuries, when tenants paid rents to landowners who, in turn, had been heavily taxed by the English government and too often spent their money in England.

Fern Hill was empty, dark, and shuttered before Molly told anyone about her memory of her mother's reflection. Although Morag had not died until Molly was eight, her death had erased from Molly's memory everything except the reflection in a looking glass.

Chapter One

*T*HERE WAS ROAST lamb for lunch. Roast lamb with mint sauce, newish potatoes, and carrots. The mint, potatoes, and carrots came from Lady Marjorie's garden.

Molly glanced nervously at her father as Mr. Paget carved two slices of lamb, each heavily streaked with fat, and laid them on Molly's plate. But her father did not intervene. He had one hand curled comfortably around a glass of claret and was listening to a racing anecdote, one with which even Molly, who had not yet been born at the time of the incident, was familiar. From her father's smile, Molly could tell that, far from being bored, he was listening to the story with pleasure.

Tibby Hassard was enjoying himself. Sunday lunch at the Pagets', although the household was not luxurious nor the family famous for its wit, gave pleasure to Molly's father. Shared memories—there were photographs of a younger Frank Paget among those in the Hassard albums—of a time when life had been easier gave Tibby a safe feeling, a feeling that had started with the glass of sherry before lunch. The modest lunch party was a small respite from the worries, largely financial, never far from the minds of all the adults present.

Molly was eight years old, and although not old enough to be able to describe her father's attitude in words, she recognized it.

Mr. Paget was also enjoying himself, was maybe even happy. His wife (not called Mrs. Paget but, as Tibby had reminded them in the car, Lady Marjorie, since her father was a duke) did not share her husband's light spirits.

If Molly's mother had been at lunch, she would have smiled, too, but she, unlike Tibby, would have prevented their host from serving Molly with a piece of meat that, although a treat for Tibby (and an extravagance for Lady Marjorie, one of five daughters brought up on a heavily mortgaged Scottish estate), Molly was unable to eat. Even if she could have forced herself to cut off a small piece and put it into her mouth, Molly could not have swallowed it. But Morag was not at lunch. She was at home, resting. Morag's resting was why Molly and her father and her ten-year-old cousin Sophie were visiting the Pagets instead of eating Sunday lunch at home.

The lamb—pink, greasy, and oozing a tinted liquid that ran into the mint sauce—prevented Molly from eating the vegetables—the safe part of the meal—with any enthusiasm. Playing for time, she cut her potatoes into small pieces, lifted them to her mouth, and chewed them until she felt able to swallow. The plate in front of her was part of a Mason's ironware service. There was a small chip on the side of the plate. The fork in her hand and the spoon and fork above her plate were silver, so old and worn that the tines of the forks were a little shorter than they were meant to be, and not quite even. Since silver is too soft to cut meat, the large knife in Molly's hand was of steel, too old to be stainless, and turned black where it had touched the juices on her plate. She laid down the knife and fork and looked despairingly at her father. Mr. Paget's anecdote was finished, and he was refilling Tibby's wineglass. The glass was Waterford, and it was beautiful but not large; Tibby's relief was apparent to Molly.

"Eat your lunch, child, it's getting cold." Lady Marjorie had been partially deaf since childhood, and her voice, in which her Highland origins could still be heard, was loud and somewhat strident.

Molly felt her face turn red. She was afraid that she would begin to cry. Her lip began to quiver.

"She's not hungry." The Pagets' nineteen-year-old son, Desmond, had not spoken since the beginning of lunch, although Molly had noticed that he, too, had appeared entertained by his father's steeplechasing story. Molly looked at him with her complete attention for the first time. Before lunch while the adults had drunk the traditional Sunday after-church glass of sherry, Molly and Sophie had been sent to admire a mother cat and her kittens in a basket beside the fire. Since Tibby did not permit animals in the house, the kittens had been of greater interest to Molly than had been the young man in a tweed suit whom she knew to be attending an agricultural college in England. She now realized from the way he spoke to his mother that he was not quite a grown-up but, although he belonged to the younger generation, his voice suggested that his opinions carried weight in the family.

"Don't be silly, Desmond, Molly needs her lunch. I've never heard of such a thing," Lady Marjorie said.

The rest of the table was silent. Molly glanced at her father, who seemed mildly put out by the interruption of the more entertaining reminiscences. Sophie, from whom Molly hoped for nothing more than sympathy, was looking thoughtfully at the velvet cuff on her dress. She, too, had been silent during lunch. Although children, when they sat with adults at a dining table, were not encouraged to speak unless spoken to, Sophie did not usually take that convention to apply to herself. Unless Tibby were present. Her uncle Tibby was the one adult whom Sophie treated with respect. Even by the age of ten she seemed to give his good opinion more value than Molly had ever seen her give anything else. Today, content with the knowledge that she was by far the prettiest and the best-dressed person in the room, she was acting the part of a demure princess. The sudden silence was, however, too much for her.

"My mummy says that I—" she started when, to Molly's

amazement, Desmond pushed his chair back from the table and stood up, smiling.

"She doesn't feel well; look how pale she is. I'll take her to the greenhouse and show her the *fleurs du mal*. Be sure to save us some gooseberry fool." With a gesture of his hand, he indicated that Molly should follow him.

As they left the room, Molly heard Lady Marjorie say: "The child is worried about her mother."

Desmond closed the dining-room door behind them. Molly felt a wave of embarrassment overtaking the relief she felt at leaving the plate of congealing food behind her.

"On second thought, I think it might be wise to make sure of the gooseberry fool now. Why leave anything to chance?"

Molly followed silently as Desmond left the large paneled hall and turned right through a swing door into a long, bare corridor. Just inside the door, which was lined on the back with green baize held in place with brass studs, was a large gong. Desmond pointed to the gong stick, a piece of polished wood with a bulbous end covered in worn chamois. It was hanging from a piece of equally worn leather.

"Like to have a go?"

Molly shook her head.

"Mind if I do, then?"

Molly was fairly certain that Desmond was not really asking her permission to strike the gong, but she was unsure how to answer. She remained silent as Desmond took the gong stick and, holding it in both hands, raised it over his shoulder and slowly swung it toward the gong. As the discolored chamois met the metal, it produced a low, deep, booming sound. Molly hoped that no one would think that she had been responsible for the noise, but at the same time she hoped that Desmond would repeat his invitation.

But Desmond, turning right again, led them into the butler's pantry. Not since a brief period around the time of the First World War, when the Pagets had received a large payment under

7

the Wyndham Act and had dipped into what was intended to be capital, had they employed a butler, but, as in the house in which Molly lived, many of the rooms bore obsolete names, evocative of the days when some of the Anglo-Irish landowners had not only the money and power to live in a feudal manner but the necessary proportion of cold blood to carry it off.

From behind the door leading from the butler's pantry to the dining room could be heard the low hum of conversation and the *clink* of glass and silver. Desmond raised a warning finger to his lips, and he and Molly moved carefully to a table on which had been set the gooseberry fool, a large Stilton almost entirely hollowed out, and a salver with a decanter of port.

Molly was now quite hungry. While Desmond helped them to the smooth, pale-green pudding, Molly looked into the Stilton. At the bottom of the cheese a small, fat, white maggot crawled slowly over a blue vein. Molly looked away. The decanter contained only a couple of inches of port. Her father had once complained on the way home from a previous visit that he had been given the smallest glass of port that he had ever been offered without humor having been intended.

"We'll eat this in the greenhouse."

Desmond handed Molly her plate and led the way through the hall, not pausing, as Molly would have liked, for a better look at the polar bear skin on the polished floor. Molly had in the past been encouraged to pat its huge head and gaze into its yellow glass eyes. At the far end of the hall, Desmond pulled back a heavy baize curtain and opened a glass-paneled door. A border of stained glass, wine red and a faded green, surrounded the larger opaque central glass panels.

Desmond led them into a small, unused conservatory; ferns and one lichen-covered wall all that remained of what had once been a palm-filled male sanctuary where Desmond's grandfather had been in the habit of smoking an Egyptian cigarette each day after lunch. The conservatory smelled of mold and damp, and Molly was glad to reach the open air through a peeling white door at the far end. Outside, a eucalyptus and a jungle of bamboo served, more than the pantry named for a long-departed manser-vant, as tangible reminders of a time when Desmond's grandfa-ther could afford—or, rather, not afford but had access to enough money—to collect exotic trees and shrubs and plant them in the mild, moist, hospitable climate of the south of Ireland.

Desmond led Molly into a large, domed greenhouse in the center of which was a lily-filled pond. Molly was happy to sit be-side it and take tiny bites of her gooseberry fool.

"Look," Desmond said. A large pink goldfish was nosing the underside of a lily pad on which sat the smallest frog Molly had ever seen.

"Sophie's your cousin?" Desmond asked.

"Yes. She stays with us when her parents are away. Some-times I stay with her. She's an only child, too."

"But your mother's having a baby?"

Molly looked at the dark-red tile at her feet. More than thirty years of mud and grit had coated and scratched it.

"Yes." Molly was old enough to understand that her mother was pregnant, but she had never been told that this was the case. She worried that this meant she wasn't supposed to know. The idea embarrassed her, and she put it out of her mind much of the time. She knew that her mother was at home with a nurse and there was a reason why she and Sophie had been taken out for the day by Tibby, but she didn't want to think about it.

"I suppose they're hoping for a boy?"

Molly supposed so, too. If she had it to choose, she would have preferred a girl. She and Sophie could dress up the baby in the old lace dresses and embroidered shawls that were kept be-tween sheets of frayed, crumpled tissue paper in a chest of draw-ers in an unused bedroom. But she knew that each family needed a son to inherit the property and encumbrances and to carry on the name for at least one more generation.

"If I ever have children, I want them to be girls," Desmond said.

Molly looked at him in surprise. It was not a view she had ever heard expressed before.

"Why?"

Desmond was silent for a moment. Molly had the impression that he knew what he wanted to say but was trying to find a simple way of explaining it.

"The wine glasses at lunch. Did you notice them?"

Molly nodded. She remembered them not only because she had been watching her father but because they were similar to some that were kept in a glass-fronted cabinet in the dining room of her own house.

"When I was a child there were eleven wine glasses left. There had originally been twenty-four of each kind. Now there are seven, and one has a chip in it. They set that glass in front of my mother because she doesn't drink. The glasses can't be replaced. They're original Waterford, not the stuff they make now and sell to Americans. We couldn't afford to replace them, anyway. Everything's like that—we're living on leftovers, preserving and patching and making things last. There's not quite enough to last my parents' generation, and there really won't be enough for you and me, but we'll probably do it anyway. But after that . . . If I have children I hope they're girls and grow up to marry Catholics or have jobs."

"Sophie's going to be a film star."

Desmond laughed, and Molly wished that she had not proffered this information in quite so reverential a tone.

"A film star. It's perfect. The healthy impulse to swim away from a sinking ship, modified perhaps genetically by the Anglo-Irish compulsion toward the impracticable. I admire the longshot aspect of it, of course. How's she going to go about it?"

Molly didn't know, and she suspected that Sophie didn't know either, and she wanted to protect herself as much as Sophie, to change the subject.

"Where are the flowers you were going to show me?"

"They're in the other greenhouse."

Desmond closed the door of the second greenhouse behind him, and Molly noticed that the temperature was a little cooler and that air was moving through openings where panes of glass had been removed and stacked, grimy and a little green around the edges, against a wall. Molly also noticed that the window frames had grooves of soft lead, less than an inch wide and shaped like blunt hooks, into which the glass could be slotted at night or during inclement weather.

Her family had briefly employed a Swiss au pair, and Molly, if pressed, knew enough French to understand what *fleurs du mal* meant. But when Desmond had first spoken of the flowers, Molly had been occupied with the food on her plate. Nor did she remember the implications of the phrase now that she saw them—irises in stained, lichen-covered clay pots; pansies in flat wooden boxes; tulips in a freestanding trough. All of them black. The darkness of the flowers did not seem sinister to Molly; what surprised her was the absence of warm color. In a greenhouse or garden, she expected her senses to be a little more stimulated than they were indoors.

"They're black," she said.

"We're still working on getting them black. They're really only a deeply compromised purple."

"Mummy read me *The Black Tulip*. It doesn't say how he did it. I thought maybe he soaked the bulbs in black ink."

"That's not the way it's done. Do you know who Charles Darwin was?"

"Daddy says that what he said wasn't true. It's in the Bible what really happened."

"Ah." Desmond smiled. Molly was shocked. It was the first time that one of her father's opinions had not been enough to clinch an argument.

"Let me put it another way. If you wanted to breed a Dalmatian with more spots, you would choose the most spotted male you could find and the most spotted bitch. When they had puppies you would take each puppy and count its spots." Molly laughed. "You would discard the less-spotted puppies from your breeding program and breed the more-spotted dogs with other highly spotted Dalmatians. You can see that that would work?"

"Yes," Molly said. She could see where this was leading; it

11

made such sense that she wondered how her father could disagree.

"You do the same thing with a tulip. You breed for darkness—sometimes you breed in a related species to accelerate the process. These things happen in nature, only there it is more random."

"But there aren't any black flowers in nature."

"I was thinking of people. You import a fairly large number of English people into Ireland. The strongest, richest men and the prettiest women tend to get first choice of who they'll marry. From the strongest, richest, prettiest pool they look for other desirable characteristics: a good seat on a horse, wit, nerves of steel about unpaid bills, the ability to hold large quantities of alcohol, a way with words, good enough circulation to live in large, cold houses, and the ability to eat awful food. Pretty soon you've got the Anglo-Irish. They're not exactly not English, but they're different."

Molly's mind was racing. She wondered if her father would like the black flowers. They had an air of restraint that her father, who despised excess, might have admired. He would have liked, too, the greenhouse oddly drained of color. Except for a strand of wisteria that had forced its way through a broken pane on the roof, the grayish-green foliage of the black flowers was the only color in the glass building. Molly wondered if the vine had broken the pane to get inside.

AFTER LUNCH ON Sundays, unless the rain was heavy (the occasional shower not considered a deterrent), Molly's father would take her for a walk on Woodstown beach. If Sophie were visiting, she would, a little less enthusiastically, come, too. Walking was a large part of Tibby's life. He wore old knickerbockers, hand-knitted stockings, and brown laced shoes that had been very expensive twenty years earlier. He walked for reasons he knew about and for reasons he did not understand but never questioned. In winter, if there was still enough light, he might carry a gun in hopes of putting up a couple of snipe, but game was not the purpose of his walk, either. Tibby walked over the field, not looking for something, not thinking of buying the land, not to flatten his stomach or to work off a heavy lunch, but because it gave him pleasure. It would be a rare afternoon in which he did not see, or remember, something of interest. One of the most admirable aspects of Tibby's character was his ability to remember without bitterness or regret.

After lunch—a little later than usual; Tibby had lingered at the Pagets'—her father took Molly and Sophie for their usual Sunday walk. The heavy jacket and matching trousers that Molly had changed into in Lady Marjorie's bedroom were recent hand-me-downs from Sophie. Molly felt none of the resentment that children usually feel while wearing clothes that had been chosen and bought for someone else. She attended a school in Waterford, where her fellow pupils—largely the children of Church of Ireland tradesmen and farmers from the surrounding counties—admired her clothes and their London department-store labels with the same frankness with which they let Molly know her deficiency in so many more important areas. The material of the jacket was thick enough for her to feel warm on the deserted beach. A thin mist blew in from the Atlantic. Molly felt nervous and guilty. She was not sure whether there would be repercussions from her behavior at lunch. Tibby seemed preoccupied. She was fairly sure that she was not the object of his thought, but she hoped that Sophie would not introduce the uneaten meal into the conversation.

Rush, the aging black Labrador that had waited patiently outside during lunch, ran joyfully on the beach, splashing in the water, making ineffectual attempts to catch a seagull. Sophie bent and picked up a small piece of driftwood and threw it into the water. Rush dashed after it and returned, shaking doggy water on them. He laid the piece of bleached wood at Tibby's feet.

"Good Rush. Who's a good boy?" Sophie said in a tone somewhat like that of Belinda, her mother, as she crouched down to hug the dog.

"Don't make a fool of that animal," Tibby said, not unkindly.

Sophie leaped to her feet, a little pink, remembering that what was considered charming in her own family was, by Tibby, thought affected and confusing for a dog that was supposed to earn its keep.

"Look! Look!" Molly shouted, pointing to the far end of the gritty beach where, partly concealed by the gusts of light mist, a small aeroplane was about to land.

"Heel, Rush," Tibby said, leading his small party up onto the low dunes that were held in place by clumps of beach grass. There were small sheltered pockets of clean, warm sand where Molly's family sometimes ate picnics.

They stood and watched in a silence broken only by Rush's panting as he sat on his haunches, mouth open. Molly watched as the plane, still tiny in the distance, touched the sand, bounced lightly but unevenly once, and came toward them. There was no sound. As the plane—its silver metal shining from the thin rays of sun penetrating the sea mist—came closer, they could finally hear the sound, not loud, of its engine. The colors, too—yellow wings, silver body, mahogany wing struts—became brighter as the plane came level with them, then rolled to a halt about seventy yards down the beach past them.

Molly waited to see what her father would do.

Unlike Molly, who was often unable to voice her simplest needs, Sophie had no difficulty in stating her wishes. "Let's go and see," she said.

"It's Mr. Hannon. From Knockboy." Tibby was walking toward the small plane, from which a man was alighting. Sophie, without hesitation, put herself at his side. Shy, nervous of the unknown, Molly made a pretense of calling Rush. The dog, obedient to a command from Tibby, ignored her, choosing instead—tail wagging and nose to the ground—to make his way back to the water.

Molly came to the tracks in the sand made by the aeroplane. Water had begun to seep into the four ridges, two wider than the others. Following the tracks, Molly walked slowly to where her father was talking to the man who had just climbed from the plane. Sophie was holding Tibby's hand.

"Mr. Hannon is going to take me for a ride. Do you want to come? There's room for two," Sophie called out. Her excitement made Mr. Hannon laugh.

"Two very small girls, if one sits on the other's lap," he said.

Molly looked at her father.

"Would you like to, Molly?" he asked, his smile encouraging, although his tone did not give the question any particular weight. The light craft appeared insubstantial, fragile, but not so small as it had appeared when she had been watching it land. She saw, with some alarm, that the section of plastic that served as a roof to the cockpit was transparent, and it was even more fragile than the rest of the aeroplane.

"No, thank you, Mr. Hannon," she said, not meeting his eye.

For a moment she thought that Sophie would try to persuade her. Then she realized that Sophie, who was clambering into the passenger seat without a backward glance, had been counting on Molly's timid nature. She was pleased to sit, like a grown-up, beside Mr. Hannon, without the disadvantage of a small girl on her knee. Molly felt sad. She slipped her hand into her father's; he had no way of knowing that for her to do so was a tiny act of courage.

Molly and Tibby drew back as Mr. Hannon switched on the engine. The propeller began to turn. The noise of the engine was loud, and there was a smell of fuel. They watched as the plane moved along the sand and then, gradually, lifted off and rose over the small tree-covered headland at the end of the beach. Tiny again, it circled out over the sea and then turned landward behind them. Soon it was out of sight.

Tibby and Molly continued their walk along the beach. Having the complete attention of her father was a rare pleasure for Molly, and she felt as though she should say something to please him, but she was considering the easy way in which Sophie had taken Tibby's hand. If her mother really was having a baby, might not that baby also want to hold Tibby's hand? Molly did not for a moment imagine that Sophie would graciously withdraw her hand, either literally or metaphorically, to allow Molly her place at Tibby's side.

"Mr. Hannon's father was the agent at Carrig when old Mr. Butler was alive. I went to school with the Butler boys; they were about the same age as Hannon. He went to Newtown. Old Mr. and Mrs. Hannon were very good sorts—he'd been in my father's regiment in the First World War and she was the rector's daughter from Dungarvan."

Tibby's conversation was full of biographic and geographic references. Being an agent on a large estate such as Carrig was one of the few acceptable forms of employment for an Anglo-Irish male, but Molly inferred that the Hannons were socially modest. Tibby and the Butler boys had gone to school in England at Repton, which was where Anglo-Irish families of their sort sent their sons. Mr. Hannon, however, had been educated at Newtown, a Quaker school in Waterford.

"Hannon used to come home from school sometimes at the weekend and his parents—well, the Butler boys were away at school, and I think they wanted their son to have friends that he'd have more in common with—told him if he wanted to bring a friend home with him that he could. He was a shy boy, and I suppose they thought it would be something pleasant he could offer another boy of his age: real food, only going to church once on Sundays—you know. So, early on in his second term he said he would like to bring a friend to stay. Old Mr. Hannon went to collect them after school on Saturday, and there was young Hannon with a little girl from two classes below his."

"A little girl?"

"Her name was Irene. Her father was a solicitor in Cahir. The Hannons were surprised, but they hadn't specified a boy and they didn't know what to say. Later, that was; of course, they welcomed the little girl. Mrs. Hannon quickly made up the spare room—they'd assumed that young Hannon would share his room with his guest—and neither of the children seemed embarrassed by the mistake. The weekend went off well enough, although the little girl hardly spoke a word. Then the same thing happened two weeks later."

"What was she like?" Molly asked.

"I saw her one weekend when I was visiting the Butler boys. She was little and thin. She had ginger hair, and she was wearing a dress I imagine was a hand-me-down. She was almost silent. I was mystified, the Hannons were mystified, but the Butler boys didn't go in for being mystified, and they tried to tease Hannon about the girl. He didn't rise to the bait. One afternoon that weekend the Butler boys were off at a tennis party—they were beginning to have places to go that I hadn't been asked, and they and I were invited to parties that young Hannon wasn't; we were getting to that age—I walked over to see Hannon. I took the path past the vegetable garden and along the lake." Molly nodded. She had a clear although not necessarily accurate image of how the house and grounds looked. She had never been to Carrig, now a hotel, the Butler family long gone. "When I got to the old boathouse—even in those days it was crumbling; now I suppose it's gone—I heard voices coming from the reeds. They didn't see me. The path was in the shade, and they were in the sun. They were sitting in the old punt in the reeds, young Hannon listening to Irene. I was too far away to make out what she was saying, but he was listening and nodding. She had a little book in her hand. After a while I called out to them, and she stopped speaking. They brought the punt in and got out. Irene didn't say a word except hello all the way back to the house."

"What was the book?"

Tibby smiled. "I thought you'd ask that. She slipped it into her pocket as she stood up. As though it was something private."

"And then what happened?"

"Well, nothing. The family got used to having her around. George Butler nicknamed her 'The Wife,' and it stuck."

"And what happened when they grew up? Did they get married?"

"Oh, yes. I never doubted it for a moment after I saw them in the punt, although I still have no idea what she was saying or

17

what the book was—it could have been Latin verbs or her diary. It was the way he was listening to her."

Molly was silent for a moment, trying to imagine Mrs. Hannon, whom she knew by sight, as a girl her own age. Her father lifted his head, and she saw the aeroplane was returning. It appeared against the white herring clouds and pale-blue sky as a dense black insect, then it grew to the size of a bird. The sound of the single engine, choppy but not unpleasant, became audible, and Tibby tightened his grip on Molly's hand and drew her up to the dunes. For the second time that afternoon they stood in silence as the small craft landed on the beach below.

Sophie was exultant. "You can see everything! We saw the cook at Woodstown House picking raspberries and Mr. Mulcahy walking his greyhound and an old woman feeding hens and some little girls skipping rope. You should have come, Molly."

Molly hoped that Mr. Hannon would repeat his invitation. She wanted to see what Sophie had described, to look down into the walled garden at Woodstown House. And she wanted an opportunity to look at Mr. Hannon, now that she felt some curiosity about him. But after a moment her father thanked Mr. Hannon for his kindness to Sophie, glanced at his watch, and said it was time to go home.

LATE-AFTERNOON SUN reflected on the upstairs windows of Fern Hill as they approached the house. A well-tended lawn, weed-free gravel, and syringa bushes in bloom under the library window suggested peace and order. A frightened, inarticulate maid weeping in the hall was their first intimation that something was wrong.

"Go into my study, Maisie," Tibby said quietly. "Girls, go upstairs and change for tea."

Maisie, responding to Tibby's tone, stopped crying, and Molly hurried upstairs followed by Sophie, who had opened her mouth as though to ask a question and had then thought better of it.

Molly, scared, although her fear had no name, did not want to be left alone with Sophie and to bear her curiosity and speculation, and when Sophie went directly to the night nursery, Molly continued along the corridor to the nursery bathroom. Next to the nursery bathroom—the house had been built along simple plumbing lines rather than for comfort—was the bathroom that served the guest rooms. The door stood ajar, and Molly could see, lying on the tiled floor, next to the lion's claw foot of the bathtub, a pile of stained sheets. Appalled, fascinated, she stopped and looked, trying to understand. There was blood on the sheets, of that she was certain. But pale blood, diluted with some other liquid and darker at the edges of the stains. Understanding that the stained sheets and Maisie's tears meant that something terrible had happened to her mother, Molly slowly closed the bathroom door.

Chapter Two

*I*T HAD BEEN generally agreed in the Hassard family that it was safe to read the tales of Beatrix Potter to Molly, although there were those who even now wouldn't feel up to taking a chance on *The Tailor of Gloucester*, with its references to the poverty of the tailor and the possibility of his cat doing without his supper. Molly had been happier with the stories in which nothing threatened the heroes and with the cheerful, rounded illustrations of beautifully dressed hedgehogs.

Sentimentality, particularly about animals, was not encouraged in the Hassard family. Dogs lived outdoors, most kittens were drowned, foxes were hunted, and old or injured horses were shot. Molly's soft heart was so full of pity for the whole world that even at the age of nine she slept with every doll and stuffed animal she possessed. Fearing the good-natured ridicule with which it had been decided her oversensitivity should be treated, she never revealed that her overcrowded sleeping arrangements were for the consolation of her entourage, not for herself.

A lack of sensitivity is not implicit in a distaste for sentimentality. Cruelty and sentimentality are often quite closely related. Molly had rarely witnessed acts of deliberate cruelty, and her most haunting memory was one in which her father had acquitted himself better than many a more sentimental man might have done. A cat had leaped out of a hedge in the narrow, winding road leading to Fern Hill and was struck by the car that Tibby Hassard was driving. The fatally injured animal dragged itself as far as the opposite ditch and vainly tried to struggle up the stone-faced bank into the hayfield at the far side. Tibby, with an oath, stopped the car, got out, and caught the terrified, agonized, cat hissing in the ditch and after a moment, bitten and scratched, managed to wring its neck. Molly was horrified, and admiring. She knew that she would no more have been capable of killing the injured cat than she would have been able to wring the neck of the plump cockerel they had eaten for lunch on Sunday.

Although in children's stories the fox usually appeared as the villain, and rabbits were mischievous heroes such as Peter Rabbit, Flopsy, Mopsy, and Cottontail, in life rabbits enjoyed none of the privileges that foxes did. Despite their raids on chicken houses and the outrage of farmers, foxes were protected when they were not pursued by a pack of hounds; rabbits were pests, fair game for boys still learning to shoot.

A fox engaged in any activity short of leaving the nursery with the male heir between his jaws was inviolate, while the most unassuming, law-abiding rabbit was fair game. This made the episode in the greenhouse all the more mysterious to Molly.

An unusually bold female rabbit had not only managed to penetrate the walled garden, but with a single-minded and apparently suicidal determination had burrowed a deep hole under the wall of the farthermost greenhouse. Presumably it was Tibby, one evening planting out seedling lettuce, who had seen the rabbit. Had it been the gardener, Madigan (addressed by Molly as Mr. Madigan, since she played with his children; the groom, who was childless, she emulated her parents in calling Rowe), his reaction would have been McGregor-like—except that he would not have considered eating his victim—and the foolish rabbit would have been swiftly executed. Tibby had been entertained by the sight of the determined doe digging a burrow in the middle of a bed planted with lettuce. He declared the greenhouse off limits to the gardener, the maids, and Molly.

Molly was too young to wonder how the decision to spare the rabbit had been arrived at, too young to remember the weeks of gestation, birth, and a period of grace for the baby rabbits to develop survival skills. She remembered no announcement of the event she finally witnessed.

Madigan was equipped with a large brown sack. Molly stood in the warm, humid greenhouse, pressed against the end door with its peeling white paint, and watched as her father, his sleeves rolled back to the elbow, plunged his arm into the burrow. Although Molly knew that there was nothing more sinister beneath than a family of rabbits, she watched with horror. She could not have plunged her arm into the dark unknown; at the same time, she imagined the fear of the rabbit family huddled in the dark. She gasped as the mother rabbit shot out of a second hole, evading Madigan, who waited with the sack, and ran frantically back and forth on the pathway between the two raised lettuce beds. Back and forth between Madigan with his sack and Molly, who, shrinking against the door, was almost as frightened as the animal.

"Leave her; we'll catch her last," Tibby said, his hand bringing up a small bundle of brown fur.

"Look, Molly." Her father held out the baby rabbit in his hand.

Molly nodded, but the presence of the increasingly frantic doe on the greenhouse floor prevented her from coming close enough to touch the tiny creature.

Tibby reached into Madigan's sack, which the gardener held open, the base resting on the earth and laid the baby rabbit at the bottom. Molly watched as her father reached into the burrow five more times, each time bringing up one more rabbit.

"Baby rabbits are called kittens or bunnies," he said, laying the last handful of fur at the bottom of the sack. He then reached out swiftly, grabbing the doe as she scurried desperately below. He lifted her, feet kicking, and reunited her with her offspring in the coarsely woven, potato-scented sacking.

Tibby lifted the sack, its contents not moving—it seemed to Molly, hardly breathing—and carried it through the greenhouse.

Molly followed him into the cooler air of the garden, breathing in the scent of the rosemary bushes that flanked the door, hearing the hum of the pollen-bearing bees circling the lavender flowers.

They walked along the worn paths—once, years ago, covered with gravel but now the tiny stones sunk into the earth and surrounded by moss and small flat weeds—until they reached the heavy wooden gate at the back of the garden. Madigan opened a small door set into the gate, and all three stepped through. The wood at the base of the door had been worn away by time and the uneven stones over which it had been dragged.

An old black Labrador bitch, overweight and lazy, returning from an illicit scavenging trip to the stables, approached them, attracted by the interesting sounds and smells coming from the sack in Madigan's fist.

"Sit, Bess," Tibby said, and the dog reluctantly sank first to her haunches and then, with a sigh, flopped over on her side.

Later, after Madigan had released the rabbits at the end of the paddock close to the woods and Molly had stood guard over Bess while he did so, she and her father returned to the greenhouse. Bess, whom Molly did not trust not to hunt the rabbits, accompanied them. It was the first time Bess had ever been allowed into the garden, but she showed no curiosity, following them slowly, tail wagging, belly swaying, into the greenhouse. She stood between the two beds of ragged lettuce stumps, her nose over the brick siding, watching as Tibby dug into the soft dry earth. Molly stood beside Bess, watching just as keenly. Years later she could remember the washed-out blue cotton dress she had been wearing, the sandals, one strap almost worn through at the buckle, and the brown pattern where the sun had tanned her foot.

Tibby's spade reached the base of the burrow and uncovered the nest. He leaned in and lifted out the lining of matted fur. Bess cocked an ear as he held out the nest for Molly to inspect.

Molly, overcoming a not quite understood reluctance, reached out to touch it. It was the softest thing she had ever felt, still warm, each strand of hair short and delicate. There were many colors, many thousands of strands.

Molly looked at the lines on Tibby's hands, emphasized by the black dirt, and she realized for the first time that her father was no longer young, feeling the pain, the fear and anticipation of loss, which was, for her, ever to accompany love.

Chapter Three

*N*EITHER OF THE Hassard cousins was educated in a manner designed to allow her to earn a living that did not involve some form of manual labor. The way each family went about attaining this disadvantage for its daughter differed.

Sophie, in a sense, had the better of it. Her lack of education was at least achieved in comfort. First there were governesses. The original governess, Miss Curtin, was qualified to the extent that she could read and write, do simple arithmetic, and play the piano with accuracy if not in a manner that gave much pleasure to those who heard her do so. When these simple skills had been passed on to Sophie, there was very little left to offer. Sophie and Miss Curtin went for walks, Sophie learned to darn a sock neatly and to embroider. Miss Curtin would have liked to teach her basic dressmaking, but Sophie's mother, Belinda, did not envision a future in which Sophie would wear homemade clothing. After Miss Curtin, there was a year during which Belinda tried a temporarily fashionable system of home education, which depended on self-motivation and the postal system. The post office did its part, but the day when it became apparent to Belinda that Sophie wasn't entirely clear about the difference between Charles I and Charlemagne marked the end of alternative education in the nursery at Dromore. Letters were sent to schools in England.

Brochures arrived. Belinda made a quick decision. The school chosen was for girls whose aims were social rather than academic and promised that the friends made there would be useful in later life.

Belinda ordered from Harrods a uniform suggestive of a trousseau. Every female member of the family was press-ganged into sewing on name tapes. Trunks were packed. Sophie, with the calm of one cognizant of her destiny, boarded the train at Rosslare. She spent the night on the Irish Sea, woke the next morning at Fishguard, and took the train to the Hertfordshire station, where the assistant games mistress from her new school was waiting to welcome her.

The brochures were slipped into the bottom drawer of a bureau and forgotten by everyone but Molly. She would pore over them, studying the photographs of chapels and tennis courts and healthy, confident girls, trying to imagine Sophie's life. She never considered that it might also have been her life if her father had not been born a younger son.

Separated from Sophie, on whose familiar if not always comfortable presence she had depended, Molly continued her own inadequate education at the cheerless Church of Ireland school in a nearby town. The school, although founded in the early eighteenth century, was as deficient of edifying tradition and academic excellence as any described by Dickens. Since public education was emphatically Catholic and largely devoted to reviving the Gaelic language, Protestants made financial sacrifices to send their children to private schools. Their choices were few and their expectations low.

Molly's misery was defined by smells, none of them pleasant. Scared, depressed, wearing a school uniform—navy blue, chosen not to show dirt—she spent her first term at the Talbot Street School gazing out the window of a classroom that smelled of ink and gas from the glowing blue and orange filaments of the overhead lights. She would imagine Sophie in the schoolroom at Dromore, looking out the window at the croquet lawn and the field sloping down to a stream where bullocks grazed and where a solitary cat might be seen purposefully setting out on an errand, picking its way high footed through the damp grass. Molly learned nothing of use. Her mind shied away when either Gaelic or mathematics were taught. What she did learn was fear—fear of the other children, of the coarse rigidity of the teachers. After a few painful mistakes, she learned that girls who sought confidences usually did so in order to betray them. Often within a breathtakingly short period of time.

Gas and ink were far from the most unpleasant smells Molly endured, and the misery of the classroom, although the most boring, was the least dreaded aspect of the school. She feared more the gritty playground, backed by the girls' cloakroom and the mossy, dank lavatories, the antiseptic smell of Jeyes Fluid only partially masking the damp filth of the interior. Most of all, Molly dreaded school lunches, the rancid smell of which made her feel sick as she walked, usually alone, up the narrow lane that led from the classrooms to the building where the less fortunate children boarded. Days would go by without Molly swallowing a mouthful of school lunch. She was frightened that one day the teacher at the head of the table would demand that she eat the gray meat, the watery cabbage, and the tepid potato, streaked dark where her fork had mashed it. Molly could not imagine either disobeying the teacher or swallowing any of the disgusting food on her plate.

Bewilderingly, Molly was never made to eat her lunch. After a while she understood that her disgust had not gone unnoticed, but the teacher who headed the table chose not to enforce the rule. Because of something about her, something that made her different. Molly worried about this difference, despite its convenience, which separated her from her more resilient fellow pupils—girls who ate school lunches without a shudder and who responded to betrayal and insult not with tears, but with a greater insult and more brutal invective.

Juliette Walker, the eldest daughter of the Protestant dentist, was the most popular girl in Molly's form. It was she—one cold, wet autumn afternoon as the day girls were preparing to go home—who enlightened Molly. Mavis, a short, red-haired farmer's daughter, not herself popular but emboldened by her perceptions of Molly as fair game, came in to attack.

"Will you look at her raincoat?" she said.

For a moment, Molly considered pretending that she hadn't heard. After all, she had not been directly addressed. The coat was a hand-me-down from Sophie, an expensive but inadequate substitute for the uniform raincoat. Molly had known that it would not pass unnoticed at Talbot Street, but she had listened, silent and helpless, as Belinda had decided that purchasing the regulation coat was an extravagance. Now was the moment of truth. Either she would carry it off in a manner confident enough to make it a single incident, or she would establish the offending raincoat as a legitimate object of teasing on which there would be no time limit. Molly knew that she would not be able to tell Tibby that the coat, already a little short in the sleeves, needed replacing. She knew also that she would have to wear it to school every wet day for the next two years.

"What?" she asked, playing for time. From a distant music room, she could hear someone making a game attempt at *Für Elise.*

"You're rude," the red-haired girl said, reveling in her moment of power. "Did your mother never teach you to say 'I beg your pardon'?"

There was an awkward silence while all the girls remembered that Molly had no mother. Some inhibition, founded more in superstition than kindness, made the subject of dead mothers taboo.

Juliette broke the silence, sweeping the ambitious red-haired girl back into the ranks.

"She's upper class. They say 'What?' It's only the likes of us that has to be polite. Don't you know anything?"

FERN HILL, a late-eighteenth-century house overlooking the River Suir, was the Hassard dower house. Built to accommodate a series of Hassard widows displaced by the deaths of their husbands and marriages of their eldest sons; grandeur to be replaced by comfort, splendor by elegance, power by convenience.

Dower houses no longer played a large part in the lives of the Hassards or their friends. Like shooting lodges, servants' halls, undergardeners, and ladies' maids, they were more often associated with the nineteenth-century novel than they were with day-to-day life. Primogeniture, along with death duties and entailment, although equally rich in literary association, still influenced the way they lived and planned. There was no Hassard family title to inherit, so the privileges of primogeniture were largely material. Miles, Sophie's father, was the eldest son, so he lived in Dromore and, despite the occasional financial panic, could afford to maintain the small island estate. Fern Hill cost less to maintain than the house, gardens, and grounds at Dromore, but more than Tibby, the younger son, could manage. So the avenue at Fern Hill, although a fifth of the length of that at Dromore, was pitted with holes. The roof leaked. Only the stables—designed to accommodate not only the horses of the dowager Hassards but also hunters from the island—maintained at Miles's expense, reflected the standards of previous, more affluent generations.

In winter, in a vain attempt to keep the damp at bay, a fire would be lit on alternating weeks in the library and Tibby's study; the drawing room, too large to heat with a single fire, was ignored. The door was kept closed, the patch of damp over a window unaddressed. Tibby would read by the fire after dinner during the autumn and winter. In spring and summer, he spent his evenings working in the greenhouses.

Each evening after she finished her homework, Molly would visit her father in the library to say good night. He would ask about her day; she would kiss his cheek and then leave. It was a tender moment, although neither was capable of showing either physical or verbal affection. Molly would have liked to comfort her father, but she did not know how. The best she could do was to reassure him about her well-being, a tactic that precluded her ever being able to ask for anything, either emotional or material.

Tibby always sat in the same chair, a little higher and stiffer than the other armchairs or sofas, a tall reading lamp behind him and to one side, on the other side a small table on which rested his glass of whiskey and water. He would have a book in his hand and a small strip of newspaper, to be used as a bookmark, which he occasionally brushed idly against his face. Often, when Molly entered the room quietly, she would see him, his reading glasses slipped a little way down his nose, gazing out the window past the weeping ash that reigned over the carefully mown lawn. He would blink and with an effort bring himself back to give a sad, kindly smile to his daughter.

Not the same day, but not many days after the incident in the girls' cloakroom, Molly lingered a little longer in the library. She was already later than usual, having loitered in the kitchen. The pope was dying—of hiccups, according to the cook—and Molly and the two servants had listened to the news on Radio Eireann. Molly was curious and silent, the maids' pious grief modified by the pleasure of drama and noisy emotion.

By not stepping closer to kiss her father, Molly prolonged the moment. Taking a deep breath, she asked, "Daddy, a girl at school said we were upper class. Are we?"

A flicker of what appeared to be pain crossed Tibby's face.

"The entire upper class perished in the First World War," he said, seemingly oblivious to whom he was speaking.

July 1959

SOPHIE'S GRANDFATHER—Belinda's father—sire to five daughters and no male heir, had been in the habit of proclaiming his displeasure, when one or more of his daughters offended him, by roaring, "You'll drive me as mad as Lear."

According to Tibby, Miles—Sophie's father—thought that *King Lear* was a cautionary tale for those who try to avoid death duties without seeking competent professional advice. Death duties and entailment were subjects to which Miles Hassard had given a good deal of thought. Too much, it had at times appeared. Sophie had confided in Molly a family secret—a family secret only in the sense that it was not spoken of within the family, since almost all members of Anglo-Irish society who might be interested or amused were well acquainted with the details. The traditional length of an Irish curse is seven generations and—since there is no statute of limitations on a joke at the expense of a well-known family—General Hassard's will, having provided inexpensive entertainment for three generations, showed no signs of shorter life expectancy.

THE OLD GENERAL had four children and a wife, who, at the onset of menopause, made a decision to enjoy ill health for the remainder of her life. Miles was the eldest son, the heir; Vera, eighteen months younger, was allocated a role as clearly defined as that of Miles. She was to be the daughter who stayed home to care for her aging parents. Tibby was brought up in a manner that encouraged the self-effacement appropriate for a younger son. His part was made clearer by the character of his younger brother, Jack, who played not only the role of baby but that of black sheep. Sent to a colony that had not been the recipient of a Hassard reject for a generation or two, he was rarely heard from, apart from a card at Christmas and periodic querulous letters of complaint concerning the terms of a small trust fund.

With the colonies already represented, and the Church of Ireland a depressed institution preaching to ever-dwindling congregations, Tibby assumed that an undistinguished military career would be his lot. He had not been brought up to question the justice of primogeniture, and he did not think in terms of the Brigade of Guards or the cavalry.

Fortunately for Tibby, his older brother, Miles, had a highly developed sense of family. So did the General. Since both were eldest sons, for each the idea of family was inextricably entwined with self-interest. The day after the family gathered to celebrate

31

the General's sixtieth birthday, Miles decided that it was time for an informal discussion of death duties with his father, to be followed by the presentation of a formal scheme, which he had roughly drafted, for the avoidance of such a tax. It was when Miles produced the piece of paper on which he had drafted his proposal that the General imagined himself a potential Lear. What Miles had intended to be a behind-closed-doors discussion became a family free-for-all.

When the General's wife, Adele, felt in need of cosseting, she would have her daughter, Vera, read aloud to her; *Sense and Sensibility* had been read recently enough for an analogy to be made. Miles's suggestion—that the bulk of the General's estate should be made over to him in order to avoid death duties—reminded Vera unpleasantly of the vulnerable situation in which the Dashwood widow and daughters had found themselves. In their case, entailment had been an unavoidable evil, but Vera saw no necessity for a daughter who was even then sacrificing her life for her parents to have her future left to the further discretion of her elder brother. Heated words ensued. Tibby made no claims for himself; but a poorly timed request from Jack for funds, with the suggestion that an inadequate or less than immediate response would damage the family name, added to the tension.

The Hassards were decent people, kindly and with a sense of honor. Even those petty flaws with which each member of the family was afflicted were modified by a sense of humor. None of these qualities helped. The General was at first hurt and then enraged to discover to what extent his family had imagined or even, in his darker moments he thought, planned their lives after his demise. The General was in excellent health. He still hunted once a week during the winter and held his own on the tennis court during those rare moments each summer when it stopped raining long enough for the court to dry out. It did not seem unreasonable that he might outlive his wife since she was a mere five years younger than he and, by her own account, a chronic invalid. Now it appeared that she intended not only to outlive him but to continue as mistress of Dromore until such time as Miles married. Miles, it seemed, was planning to marry Belinda Plunkett and to move not only his mother but his father into the dower house. Vera chimed in that at the age of thirty, she did not intend to be beholden to Belinda Plunkett for dinner invitations to her family home or for produce from its vegetable garden. Since it was only four months until Vera's birthday, the General inquired in a dangerous voice whether she did not expect him to last the summer. Tibby did nothing worse than laugh, but it was enough. As for Jack, his father suspected—perhaps unfairly but maybe not—that he was only waiting for his father to die before he came home to lean on a new generation.

By the end of the birthday weekend, few meals were completed without someone abruptly leaving the table while the rest continued to chew in a silence that defied digestion. A silent week after the General's birthday, Miles received a letter from his father's solicitor containing the terms of the General's new will. Miles's suggestions were being implemented after all. The entire estate, apart from a comparatively small sum set aside to allow the General and his wife a comfortable but modest old age, a smaller sum designed to keep Jack in place, and the normal small bequests to servants, would be made over to Miles. After the General's death, however, Dromore was to be blown up. The General had already signed a contract with a demolition company, who would set the dynamite one week after the General's demise. Miles was advised to plan for the moving and storage of the more cumbersome and valuable pieces of furniture and the paintings.

"Has money passed hands?" Belinda asked when Miles showed her the letter.

"I don't know."

"Well, find out."

Miles thought, not for the first time, that Belinda's tone was more evocative of his regimental sergeant major than of love's young dream, but since, all things being equal, he would back this strong-willed twenty-year-old virgin against the man who had survived Gallipoli and fought in the battle of the Somme, he did as he was told.

When Miles reported that the General had parted with a discouragingly large deposit to a demolition company, Belinda realized that further argument with the General at that time would be, at best, counterproductive. While she felt a mildly irritated affection for Miles, Belinda loved Dromore. Despite her youth and the limitations of her sheltered life, she understood the considerable price she was prepared to pay for it. Her love for Dromore and, to be fair, her feelings for Miles were unselfish. It was not just a wish to be mistress of Dromore. She wished to live in the house, but she also wanted to protect and preserve it, to pass it on to her children with a sound roof, and having won her generation's battle with the damp.

Dromore was a house worth fighting for. It had been built by Francis Hassard—cartographer and the most cold-blooded colonel in Raleigh's army in Munster—on an island that was part of the forty-two thousand acres granted to Raleigh by Queen Elizabeth. The house had been enlarged in the eighteenth century, and the more comfortable rooms were Georgian. Overlooking the river from a height, the house had an octagonal ballroom. To save the ballroom, if nothing else, Belinda was prepared to take on the General.

Belinda was twenty; the General, sixty. She had, she knew, time on her side. She also had a plan in the event of a sudden deterioration in her father-in-law's health.

A less determined woman might have hesitated before marrying Miles and facing the prospect of inheriting a pile of rubble; rebuilding—or even removing the rubble—would be impossibly expensive since the only access to the island was by boat.

Belinda might have argued, although she did not, that the boatman who rowed her, in her wedding dress and the Hassard pearls, to the island was not a small part of that for which she was fighting. The well-being of the employees and their families who lived on the island was implicit in her ambition. It was her unstated and perhaps not even conscious intention that the boatman's son—at the oars of a rowing boat in the small flotilla of wedding guests—should, if he wished, inherit his father's job and the small stone house that overlooked a half mile of the river Suir where local fishermen cast their nets for salmon.

"Miles . . ." Belinda's tone was soft, thoughtful.

"Yes, darling?"

"What is the name of the Tyrells' little girl?" Belinda asked.

"Why on earth do you want to know?"

"Maeve, Deidre, Cathleen—something Celtic Twilighty."

Mrs. Tyrell, wife of Owen Tyrell, the solicitor who had written the General's will, had never seen the inside of Dromore or received an invitation from the Hassards. Neither had anyone she knew, nor had they expected one. Mrs. Tyrell assumed the invitation to be the result of a misunderstanding but nevertheless spent sleepless nights and her whole family's clothing ration on a dress and hat with which she was less than happy. Belinda's wedding marked the pinnacle of her social life; it was an opportunity that she did not expect to have repeated.

Belinda intended to be by Moira Tyrell's side as the doctor's daughter from Kilmacthomas entered the octagonal ballroom for the first time. Although it looked as though it would rain later, the thin sunlight of the late afternoon, the windows open above the river, the candles in daylight making the Waterford chandelier sparkle, the white flowers and the family silver were all part not only of Belinda's wedding day, but of her plan to save Dromore.

It was not, of course, her primary plan. Belinda fully intended to produce a son within a year and to name him after the General. Ambrose. In case that didn't do the trick Belinda intended to corrupt Mrs. Tyrell.

MOLLY WAS GIVEN her first long evening dress for Eithne Tyrell's coming-out dance. She was fifteen and still two years away from the age at which she was entitled to come down for a dinner party and be seated between two young men or to go to a dance.

None of these privileges was unqualified, of course. Molly did not expect them to be. She was realistic about her place at the dining-room table and her chances of waltzing with a man between the ages of eighteen and thirty. She understood, even before she arrived at the island the morning of the dance, as Christy rowed her across the river, her feet tucked up to avoid the muddy brown water at the bottom of the boat, that a great, perhaps even the greatest, part of the pleasure would be describing the evening when she returned to school. It would not be necessary to mention that her dress had belonged to Sophie (it had been seen just once at a distant hunt ball). She would, if asked, say that it bore the label of a London department store, but she would not volunteer that it was dark blue, a color with associations of school uniforms and lint. Her fellow pupils would not understand that the blue illuminated Molly's pale face in a way that diamonds never could, and not one of them would have chosen the beautifully cut dress of rich taffeta over Eithne Tyrell's confection of pink and white.

"How is Mrs. Doyle?" Molly asked the boatman.

"Grand. She'll be home next month, God willing."

Christy's wife had been at Ardkeen Sanitarium for six months. Every Sunday after Christy had rowed the Hassards back from church and, half an hour later, the maids from Mass, he would row his children across to the mainland. Wearing their Sunday clothes, they would walk up to the main road and wait for Kenneally's bus, which would carry them to the gates of the sanitarium, where the greater part of the passengers would alight. Awkward families. Awkward in visiting the sick, awkward with their packages, brown paper and twine, newspaper and string, containing more often necessities from home than gifts. The man, in his worn black Sunday suit and white collarless shirt fastened at the neck with a brass stud, the inadequate ironing telling of his absent, sick wife and a household run by his too-young eldest daughter. The woman passenger, her prematurely aged face set in an expression of worry. Her thin, whining children. The sadness on the faces of the families in which neither the mother nor the breadwinner was absent, families in which a missing child's return home was not soon expected.

As she sat in the boat, Molly thought that Mrs. Doyle, whose youngest child was barely four years old, must miss her family and long to come home. She also thought that Mrs. Doyle must have been warmer and more comfortable during the winter in the sanitarium than she had been in the cottage, whose water came from a dripping outdoor tap and whose lavatory was in a small shed.

The boat reached the ridged, wet slip, and Christy handed her out, then pulled the boat a little farther up the steep incline. The morning was warm. In her excitement Molly barely noticed the light drizzle. Her dress was already safely at Dromore, as it had been since Sophie brought it back from the Limerick Hunt Ball. Molly's aunt Vera had made the necessary minor alterations.

When her parents had moved to the Queen Anne house in which her mother still lived, Vera had chosen a renovated cottage fewer than a hundred yards from her mother's front gate. The cottage had a small but beautiful garden, where Vera spent a large part of her summer days. "All part of the deal" was how Sophie, with a mysterious smile, had explained it to Molly, refusing to answer the questions that her loaded partial explanation begged.

Three weeks before the dance, Molly had been summoned by Belinda to spend a weekend on the island and to have her dress fitted and altered. "No point in leaving things to the last moment," Belinda had said briskly when Vera had grumbled that if the delphiniums were not staked that weekend, she would not be answerable for them. Belinda's words would have been, had she had one, her motto. Everything that could be taken care of in advance was. This left her largely unencumbered when a real crisis occurred. She was not interested in allowing Vera or Molly to engage in dressmaking the week before the dance, when they would be more usefully employed in the kitchen, or washing the three Waterford glass chandeliers and polishing silver, or filling with dependable geraniums the terra-cotta pots on either side of the front door.

Washing the chandeliers was an operation that Belinda had conducted with military precision and with the implicit suggestion that it was a tradition and skill not only singular to her family but one handed down from generation to generation. Molly, a maid, and two men from the farm, most of the mud wiped from their boots, listened solemnly while Belinda told them that anything broken was irreparable and irreplaceable. This was largely addressed to the men, although Molly and the maid were included. Nor, Belinda had continued, now addressing the two girls, was there an expert to whom they could appeal if either forgot the correct placement of each tear and pendant detached.

The chandeliers had been taken down from the ballroom, the dining room, and the hall. The men carried them into the conservatory and suspended them from a pole between two large sawhorses, beneath which a worn and yellowing blanket had been laid. The men, visibly relieved, returned to the hayfield, and Belinda and the two girls set to work. Two large basins of water, each with a piece of frayed towel at the bottom, sat on the table. Molly, Belinda, and the maid carefully unhooked each piece of glass and carefully washed it clean of smoky dust. The tear was then rinsed in the second basin, dried with a lint-free towel, held up to the light to make sure that it was unmarked by soap or fingerprints, and hooked back into place on the chandelier. Every so often, the maid would empty the basins of water into a bucket and refill them with clean warm water carried from a distant scullery. By lunchtime Molly's hands were wrinkled and her fingernails soft, and she no longer wondered why Sophie had been exempted from the task.

Washing the chandeliers had taken a full day. By the time they were finished, the men had gone home to their tea, and the rehanging had to wait until the following morning.

MOLLY, CARRYING A small suitcase containing her nightdress, a shabby teddy bear, and *The Constant Nymph,* walked up the avenue. Apart from a tractor, there were no motorized vehicles on the island. Miles's motorcar was garaged by the mainland landing slip. During the day, unless it was raining, visitors usually walked the half mile of the avenue to the house, but if it was an evening party, one of the men from the farm would harness a lazy cob to a sidecar, and the guests, a little windswept from the river crossing, would clamber up on either side of the old-fashioned conveyance and rattle up the avenue. That evening, when the guests arrived, they would be met at the ferry by two sidecars. The sidecars, freshly painted, were under cover in the stables, and the two cobs who would pull them were resting before their long night.

Apart from the previous night, Molly had spent the week at Dromore. Eithne's coming-out dance was hard work; with Belinda's efficient and economical direction, the ball would be almost as magnificent as the extravagant spectacles given by past Hassards on the island.

The dance for Eithne was the price paid to allow Dromore to survive the General's death. The practical Belinda intended it also to serve as a dress rehearsal for Sophie's coming-out dance in the year to come. For the one held at Dromore, not the one that would be held in London, which could cost ten times as much and which, if everything fell into place, might not be necessary. The money would, in that event, be spent on a wedding.

As with the dress, Molly benefited from all these plans. Belinda knew that if she didn't watch out for Molly, no one would. She also liked it that Sophie had a cousin to fill the role of lady-in-waiting. It even occurred to her that when Sophie was successfully married off (the preposition sometimes omitted verbally, but always implicit), she might make something of little Molly. Although she avoided thinking about it, Belinda knew that once she had launched Sophie into the dazzling career she planned, her daughter would be largely lost to her. Molly, on the other hand, could be installed in a country house with good shooting, sensibly situated for hunting and race meetings. Always an asset.

Belinda, lists in hand, greeted Molly in the hall. Belinda favored the backs of envelopes for the lists and sublists with which she ruled her empire. Belinda did not delegate. She worked her family and staff hard, but she neither burdened nor trusted them with responsibility.

"There you are, Molly. Good. Miss Hearne is nearly ready for you—she's set up in Uncle Jack's room."

Miss Hearne, borrowed from the closest hairdressers, had over the years been trained almost to Belinda's exacting standards. Told where to find her, Molly did not imagine that her uncle Jack was returning for Eithne's party. The bedroom that had once been his had, for more than twenty years—longer than Belinda had lived at Dromore—been used as a spare room. Nor did it seem that he would be the only member of the family absent that night.

"Vera, let me know as soon as possible if Adele is coming this evening. I have to do the placement," Belinda said.

Molly waited at the foot of the stairs as Vera, her hair in rollers tied firmly into place with a net, came down. "I think it might be a little much for her. Mrs. Gleeson will give her supper, and I'll tell her all about it tomorrow."

Molly left her suitcase in the night nursery. The door of the next room, Sophie's, was slightly ajar, and as she passed, her cousin called her name.

"Molly? Is that you?"

Molly pushed open the door.

"What are you doing?"

Sophie was lying on her bed. To lie idle above the hum of the downstairs activity suggested an aplomb that Molly could not imagine possessing.

"Hiding out. What's happening?" For Sophie this was never a rhetorical question, it was a demand for information. Or to be entertained.

"Granny's not coming tonight."

"Hmm. Vera?"

"Yes."

"So Mummy's relieved and Daddy'll think it's Granny's decision. He'll be relieved, too, but he won't know it since he won't admit anything's wrong."

For years, Adele had demanded sympathy and attention be paid her imaginary physical ailments. Now, ironically, although her body remained as healthy as any woman in her early seventies could expect, her mind had started to fail. It appeared to be the onset of senility, but since Miles would not admit the deterioration of his mother's mind (and sometimes, even more startling, of her discretion), no formal diagnosis had been sought.

"Just as well," Sophie added. "She's quite capable of pointing at the Tyrells and asking in a loud, clear voice who those common people are and what they're doing in her dining room. Vera'll describe the dance to her tomorrow, and she'll probably think she was there."

A sound from downstairs reminded Molly that she was supposed to be elsewhere.

"Don't forget to save your bathwater for me," she said, closing the door. The reserves of hot water at Dromore had been calculated to the last drop by Belinda; Molly had been instructed to take her bath before she left Fern Hill that morning.

Molly had noticed that rules often changed without notice. Sophie, expensively dressed in children's clothing until the age of seventeen, had suddenly been promoted to womanhood. For several years she had not been a child; it would be some time before she became a woman. Long after her hips had rounded and her breasts developed, Sophie had been treated as a schoolgirl. Any tentative curiosity she expressed toward boys her own age had been waved away in the singularly expert way in which the Anglo-Irish dismiss the inconvenient. Now that she might have enjoyed feeling her way toward love and sexuality, she had been given a deadline to hunt down and marry a man of birth and, it was devoutly hoped, wealth.

Molly found it confusing and unfair. What Sophie thought she did not know. Already Sophie was part of the adult conspiracy to keep Molly a child. A conspiracy that would be lifted, for one evening, to allow her a glimpse of the future.

ON EITHER SIDE of the fireplace in the octagonal ballroom hung a large, oval, Venetian looking glass.

The looking glass in front of which Molly stood was only

long enough for her to see her reflection from the waist up. The mirror was generous in the way that old glass is. Below, their reflection obscuring the waistline of Molly's dress, were roses, large, open, likely to drop petals onto the small Sheraton table. Earlier in the day, Molly had helped Vera arrange the flowers. The silent conservatory had become a richly scented hive of activity. Bowls of china and glass had been taken from glass-fronted cabinets, dusted, washed, and filled with water; sharp scissors and secateurs lay beside discarded leaves and short pieces of thorned stems on damp copies of the *Irish Times*. Molly had helped carry the bowls, balancing them carefully as she moved, not spilling a drop of water on the polished floors. Not allowing the informal yet carefully arranged flowers to shift from their intended places.

Molly had been gazing into the looking glass for some time. Not because she was vain, not because she was unsure of herself, although that would have been more likely than conceit, but because the atmosphere of the house, of the week of preparation for the dance, had made her nervously aware of the value of female beauty. While she knew that she was by far the least significant of the three girls being launched at Dromore that evening, she also knew that Belinda had given some thought to her, Molly's, appearance. It was the first time that she was aware that her appearance might have any importance to anyone other than herself. Certainly the first time that it had been suggested that it might have any value worth enhancing.

Molly's hair was brown and her eyes were blue. Her normally pale skin was flushed with excitement. Sophie's dark-blue dress and the weaker blue of Belinda's moonstones lit up Molly's eyes and illuminated her face. The looking glass provided an oval frame to the picture Molly made of herself. She was not a confident child, but thanks to the skill of Miss Hearne, Sophie's hand-me-down dress, and Belinda's necklace, she thought it possible that she could be admired. Maybe loved.

"Molly, Belinda thinks it is time for you to light the candles in the hall."

Molly was relieved that it was Miles who had entered the room. Miles showed very little curiosity about the behavior of those around him. He could be counted on not to notice that she had been posing in front of the looking glass.

Molly looked at the evening watch her father had given her the night before. The watch had been her mother's; delicate, silver, with a narrow band of diamond chips surrounding the face. It had once belonged to her grandmother. Tibby had arranged for a watchmaker in Waterford to clean it and set it onto a wristband of thick, ridged black silk. Grosgrain, Molly thought.

The hall was cooler than the ballroom. As Molly lit the candles, they flickered a little in the draft from under the front door. Molly's excitement rose with every candle she lit, especially as the ones in the sconces, on the wall opposite the fireplace, lit the huge hall a little more. A large log threw warmth and light onto an area that Molly had never before seen lighted. She noticed for the first time that the carpet covering the greater part of the hall was of a rich red and blue, although the full beauty of the colors and the intricacy of the pattern were fully visible only close to the fireplace.

The smell of the oak logs was less powerful than the scent of stock from the two large arrangements of flowers. White stock, pale-pink lupines, and light and dark delphiniums were arranged in tall glass cylinders. Each bloom had been planted, tended, and, that afternoon, cut and arranged by Vera.

Molly lit the last candle and shook out the stub of the match just before it singed her thumb. She was ready. She stood by the front door and looked out on the avenue through one of the glass side panels. Soon she could hear the faint sound of hooves. By the time she could see the sidecar bearing four guests in evening dress through the soft light, Belinda, who must have been watching from her bedroom window, was coming down the stairs. From the service door in the dark area beside the stairs, Norah, the parlor maid, who had been keeping watch at the kitchen window, scurried through the hall, making a last-minute adjustment to her apron. As she followed Belinda into the drawing room, Molly could hear the crunch of wheels and hooves on the gravel outside.

IT WAS STILL light as they sat down to dinner. Molly could see cattle grazing in the field at the end of the lawn; the giant ilex at the top of the avenue in silhouette. As she took her place at the dining table, she could hear the screech of a guinea hen from the yew trees.

Miles, Belinda was aware, thought that sitting down to dinner at half-past seven was, as he was quite capable of putting it, letting the side down. The side, she was uncomfortably aware, was easily identified that evening. Fourteen people sat at the highly polished table to which an extra leaf had been added. The side was represented by Miles, Belinda, Sophie, Vera, Tibby, and Molly and, as visiting players, Lady Marjorie, Frank Paget, Desmond, and a grandson of old Lady Carew, a schoolboy stuffed into a borrowed dinner jacket with strict instructions to limit his alcoholic intake.

The others were represented by Eithne Tyrell and her parents, Moira and Owen. There was one other guest, David Spencer, who sat between Eithne and Sophie. To the Tyrells, who were aware that Spencer was young, rich, well educated and good-looking, Eithne's dinner partner looked like side. To the others, with the possible exception of young Carew, who didn't like the look of the first course—trout pâté—Spencer appeared a parvenu. On this they were unanimous, although they might disagree as to the degree to which this defect diminished his other advantages.

Belinda had seated Spencer between Eithne and Sophie. Eithne smiled and attempted to flirt. Even though it was her coming-out party, she knew that David Spencer was far more interested in Sophie, who wouldn't officially be out until after her birthday. Belinda chose not to think about Spencer's admiration for her daughter until dinner was over. Even then, her first task would be to prepare a defensive position in case Miles, too, no-

44

ticed. She would deny David's interest and more vehemently, but less convincingly, deny that David Spencer was an unsuitable suitor for their daughter.

Miles needed to be handled delicately. He was intolerant of any deviation from the rules by which he lived, although he accepted the behavior of any bone fide eccentric provided the eccentricity was exhibited by a member of a family equal to or more distinguished than his own. The dance, the need for his wife to launch the Tyrell girl, his uncertainty of just how many people suspected the reason for this breaking down of carefully maintained class boundaries, Belinda's determination that Mrs. Tyrell should be seated on his right at dinner, his equally strong determination that his best port should not reach Owen Tyrell, all preoccupied and worried Miles.

Belinda had done her best not to add to Miles's inarticulate but visible discomfort. Even at the end of the long tiring days before the dance, she had never said aloud what she had often thought: *All this for an ordinary girl with a Waterford accent and poor posture.* To do so might have precipitated the conversation that had never taken place between Miles and Belinda. Sometimes Belinda wondered about the conversation that must once have taken place between Owen and Moira Tyrell. The conversation in which she had persuaded or, perhaps, bullied her husband into destroying or amending the General's will.

"His great-great-great-grandmother danced at the Duchess of Richmond's ball," Desmond, singing for his supper, said to both Molly and Eithne, neither of whom had spoken a word for four minutes.

"'There was a sound of revelry by night,'" Molly said, looking at the Carew boy with curiosity. "You'd never know it to look at him."

"Pardon?" Eithne pronounced the word to rhyme with "burden."

Molly glanced toward Belinda, who did not seem to have heard Eithne committing social suicide. Fortunately both Miles and her father were at the far—the grown-up—end of the table.

She, too, occasionally made errors, though not so extreme as that just made by Eithne. Tibby did not seem to notice, or perhaps did not care, that Molly spoke with a slight Waterford accent, but when she used a word that seemed ugly to him, he would correct it; if Molly said "note paper" or "mirror," he would look a little surprised, although in an absentminded way, and would supply instead the word that he himself used. Molly wanted to please him, so she did not question his old-fashioned vocabulary. She was, besides, grateful that he helped her to avoid the occasional hurtful disapproval of Belinda or Miles.

"The Duchess of Richmond's ball, on the eve of the battle of Waterloo. Byron wrote about it—young Carew's great-great-great-grandmother danced at it," Desmond said again.

Eithne was silent, her expression suggesting that she thought Desmond had gone off his head.

"It's in *Vanity Fair,* too," Desmond added, although without much hope that it would help. It didn't and he turned to Molly.

"During the ball," Molly said, "the word comes that the battle will be fought the following morning, and, one by one, the young officers quietly leave. Some of them fought in their evening clothes." She did not add that a nearby regiment of young officers, doomed or otherwise, would have made the evening a good deal more promising for herself and Eithne. It was a moment when, but for the presence of Desmond, each might have found a temporary ally in the other. But Eithne sighed, and Molly gave her attention to Desmond.

David Spencer, on Eithne's right, was describing a high point in that afternoon's tennis game. Eithne turned her attention to her food. Roast guinea fowl. She ate carefully, not impressed by the unaccustomed fare. At home, her mother served (as did Tibby's cook) a set meal for each day of the week. Roast beef on Sunday, cold on Monday, and so on. The main meal, the one that included meat, vegetables, and a pudding, was served at midday. Eithne's parents called it dinner.

Unlike her parents, Eithne entertained no unreasonable expectations for the dance. Her parents naively thought that Eithne was being launched into Anglo-Irish society. Eithne knew only that the dance would make her a little more valuable in the eyes of Raymond Cafferty's parents. The Caffertys owned a large drapery shop on the Quay in Waterford and were Catholics. Mr. and Mrs. Cafferty were not likely to be a great deal more enthusiastic about a mixed marriage than were the Tyrells, but Eithne suspected that they would be more welcoming to a pet of the Anglo-Irish upper classes than to one of their rejects. They need never know that she had not fit in at her own coming-out dance.

Molly, although happy to be talking about books and history with Desmond—feeling herself on firmer ground than she often did—kept one eye on the food being served. The hard work that Belinda and she had shared in the kitchen had not been in vain. The guinea hens, cousins of those now almost silent in the yew trees, were plump and golden. They were served with both Espagnole and bread sauce and with peas, broad beans, and thinly sliced, very crisp, fried new potatoes.

Miles had refused when Belinda had asked him to shoot the guinea hens. When she had tried her famous firm line, he had drawn himself up and, without resorting to the actual words, managed to imply that his honor had been impugned. Belinda had had to instruct the gardener to snatch four guinea fowl off a tree and stuff them into a sack. This plan turned out to be a little more difficult to execute than it had sounded when Belinda had airily described the operation to the dubious gardener and turned on her heel. The guinea fowl, it was discovered, slept a little higher in the trees than it had been thought. The gardener was literally working in the dark and was, it would seem, admirably deficient in poaching skills. Eventually four of them had been captured and slaughtered. Miles, mollified, had offered his advice on how they should be hung. Far too long in the opinion of Sophie and Molly, who used to look with disgust at the almost rotten game that hung, during the winter, in the tack room. Belinda, never squeamish, had plucked, cleaned, and trussed the guinea hens and had given Molly instead the pleasurable task of shelling peas and podding the broad beans.

As the second serving of the guinea fowl came round the table, Molly glanced at the plates in front of the guests. The adults had eaten heartily, and some were helping themselves to a substantial second helping. Eithne had left most of her food untouched for reasons, Molly thought, of suspicion of the unfamiliar rather than nerves. Sophie, across the table, fiddled with the watercress that had garnished the guinea fowl. She did not eat at all. Vanity, it seemed to Molly, although it might have been fear. Watercress grew wild in a stream on the island. Hemlock, similar in appearance but deadly poison, also grew in streams. Vera was the only member of the household trusted to pick watercress.

Molly relaxed a little. The pudding was cold and, she knew, delicious. She had dipped her finger into it in the larder. It had stood on a cool marble slab in the dark room that smelled of milk and cold meat, lit and ventilated by a small high window open onto a wilderness of rhododendron. Diplomat pudding was made largely of whipped cream, broken sugared sponge fingers, chopped fruit, and brandy. There were other ingredients, but Molly did not know them; the pudding, famous throughout the south of Ireland, was made from Belinda's secret recipe. After the pudding, savories would be served— devils on horseback, simple enough for the cook to handle on her own. Even now, pitted dates wrapped in strips of thinly sliced steaky bacon secured by a toothpick were sizzling in the oven of the Aga.

Sophie appeared not to notice the maid refilling her empty glass with red wine, looking instead at David Spencer, smiling in anticipation of the laugh with which she would reward his story about a London nightclub brawl. Belinda, at the other end of the table, wearing a dark-green velvet dress and the Hassard pearls, seemed not to notice either the wine or the flirtation.

Outside in the hall there was a noise, less a sound of revelry by night than a thump, as though someone had dropped a heavy

48

object, followed by a muffled yelp and a curse. Molly thought, for a moment of panic, that some guests had arrived early for the dance. The alarm must have shown on her face because Desmond said, "It's only Archy and the band."

"Should somebody . . . should I—?"

"No, it's another of Archy's talents, keeping his professional and his social life apart. When he greets my mother after church on Sundays—"

"He's a Protestant?"

"Major Archdale? Late of the Irish Guards?"

"But I didn't think—"

"You didn't think that if you were a Protestant you were allowed to have an infra dig job like playing in a dance band?"

"Well, yes."

"Much the view Mrs. Archdale took. When she couldn't stop him, she got two Pekinese and took up Theosophy, but I think Archy has more fun. There's certainly more money in it."

"And the other members of the band?"

"Local boys."

"So they're—?"

"Catholics. Which is one of the reasons Miles won't go out and ask Archy to join him for a glass of port. It wouldn't be fair."

"And the rest of the time, when he's not playing, what happens then?"

"Same as with any retired British officer—Kildare Street Club, red face, whiskers, tendency to pinch waitresses when he's had too good a lunch. Terrible shot, easy to tease about the loss of the Empire. People like him, find her a bore."

"Do you remember . . ." Molly hesitated. "In the greenhouse—the day my mother died?"

Desmond nodded.

"When you told me that the Anglo-Irish had no future and that our generation should try to integrate. Isn't Archy—Major Archdale—doing that?"

"Yes, he is—and doing it with grace. The Irish—the Catholic Irish—have a surprisingly subtle sense of humor. They can see

49

that the purple-faced former English officer earning a living playing with a dance band, and playing quite well, is a far less ridiculous figure than one who gives himself airs and is always late with the butcher's bill. And he's having fun. Sometimes I think the thing that loses their respect more than anything is that they don't see us having fun. And the glamor is gone. The wild, eccentric style, the originality and the humor."

"The 'Good Old Days'?"

Desmond laughed. "I sound just like my father. Although I was, of course, born just after the official end of the Good Old Days."

From the ballroom came the sound of the piano. Soon a second instrument tentatively joined in, and Molly felt an urge not so much to dance as to move with the music. Dancing—or ballroom dancing as it was called at school, where it was an "extra" after school on Wednesday afternoons—had so far consisted of dancing with another gym-slipped girl or being led around the assembly hall clasped to the torso of the dancing mistress, an elderly woman who did not wear a brassiere and who had a squeaky thumb. They danced to music from a decrepit gramophone upon which one of a half dozen worn and scratched records were played. Sometimes when the windows were open and the lilac was in bloom, Molly could imagine how it would feel to dance with a man.

Molly looked at the diplomat pudding and the Waterford glass bowl, full of plump strawberries and dark raspberries, beautiful with sprigs of pale-green mint, and found, to her astonishment, that she did not wish to eat it.

The band in the distant ballroom started to play "Blue Moon," at first just a thin melody and then one by one the other instruments joined in so that the sound pervaded the empty, still corridors and upstairs rooms of the large house and floated out the French windows onto the Suir below, where swallows darted to and fro over the brown water. Molly closed her eyes and Desmond took her hand.

"Come on," he said. "First dance, before anyone gets here."

Molly glanced at Belinda, although she was already getting to her feet. Belinda smiled and Molly left the room, her hand still in Desmond's as she followed him across the flower-scented hall, through the open double doors, into the ballroom.

Desmond returned Archy's wave of greeting as he took Molly in his arms. She felt Desmond's hand on the back of her waist. She laid her left hand on his shoulder, and Desmond drew her closer to him. Molly had never before experienced such intimacy. She was too young to remember the last person who had held her so close. It was hard for her to breathe. It was not Desmond's fault that she fell, that moment, in love. Nor was it surprising that she assumed that the touch of her body, far less clothed than his, felt as charged to him as his did to her. Molly, who had been nervous about dancing, melted into Desmond's arms, allowing him to move her across the deserted floor.

I am completely happy, Molly thought. *I will never forget this.*

Chapter Four

" ' DON'T ENCOURAGE MICE,' " Sophie repeated with a laugh, just before the door was safely closed behind Norah, the elderly parlor maid. "Oliver Ross told me that she says it to all our guests when she takes up their early morning tea. She even said it to his mother when she came to fish last year. Can you imagine? Mummy doesn't know, and I wouldn't tell her for worlds."

Breakfast at eleven o'clock in the library, on a table by the window. The meal was light: coffee (for breakfast, an unaccustomed luxury), wholemeal soda bread, butter, and thick, chunky marmalade. The wholemeal bread, whose possible crumbs had worried Norah, was slightly warm. Molly could not imagine that breakfast in bed, which she only knew about from novels, would have been more unusual or luxurious. Molly helped herself to the marmalade, which she had helped Belinda make during the one week of the year when the shops stocked Seville oranges. For two days, Dromore had been filled with the rich, sweet and slightly citric smell of simmering and cooling marmalade.

Sophie leaned back and sipped her coffee. As at dinner the night before, she seemed uninterested in food. She wore a light summer dressing gown and had kicked off her bedroom slippers.

52

Molly, who owned only one dressing gown—a garment designed to combat the cold of Fern Hill winters—was dressed in a soft, baggy tweed skirt, a blouse, and cardigan.

Molly wondered if Norah minded carrying the heavy tray up from the kitchen for the two young and healthy girls who had been allowed to sleep late after a dance. Molly knew better than to ask Sophie. Desmond would know, and she longed to ask him. She did not know when she might see him again, but she was not yet anxious about how long it might be. Her memories of the dance were in some way preferable to the almost unbearable pleasure she had felt when she danced with Desmond. Unlike Sophie, Molly was not greedy. She was content to think and dream for some time before she next saw him.

"When you were little, did you ever churn butter?" Sophie asked, watching Molly spread butter and marmalade on her bread.

"Yes." Molly was surprised by the question, having assumed that Sophie was reliving the triumphs of the previous evening. "I still do sometimes. At home."

"And make butter balls in the kitchen?"

"Sometimes I can make them curl as well."

"Do you love it?"

"Yes, and topping and tailing gooseberries."

"And picking black currants. And raspberries. What else?"

Molly understood that Sophie's question was limited to activities that a child might perform in the country, to childhood itself.

"Picking up sticks for kindling. Chestnuts. Looking for walnuts in the leaves. Helping make the Christmas cake."

"Norah telling us not to encourage mice. I'm going to miss that." Sophie's voice had become quiet and sad.

Molly said nothing, but she stopped breathing for a moment.

"David asked me to marry him. Last night, after the dance."

"Does Aunt Belinda know?" Molly asked instinctively before asking the more appropriate "Did you say yes?"

"Oh, Molly," Sophie sighed. "He's rich, and he lives in England, and here it's all, well, you know, hopeless." She shrugged and after a moment laughed. "And now I won't have to go to that finishing school in Switzerland."

Sophie wanted to discuss logistics, not emotions. She did not want to answer inconvenient questions. Like about love. So Molly waited.

"I told him he would have to speak to Daddy and that it would have to be a long engagement. I can't get married until I'm eighteen. It would be ridiculous. I told David that Daddy will be furious but to hold firm. When he's come round, he'll have a simply lovely time with his will and making things over to avoid death duties." The preoccupation with wills, Molly considered, might be hereditary. For the first time Sophie's voice was enthusiastic. "I'll have to make a will myself when he does that, or when I get married. I'll be a woman of property. Potential property, anyway. Guess what I'm going to leave you?"

"I can't," Molly said, quickly embarrassed.

"You have to."

A seasoned, two-years-younger victim of Sophie's intransigence, Molly understood that she would have to guess. She thought about possessions of Sophie's that she would like to have, carefully eliminating items of too great value such as Lil, Sophie's graceful and sweet-natured mare.

"Your charm bracelet?"

Sophie shook her head.

"The dress I wore last night?"

"It's already yours; try harder."

"Your coral necklace? Stamp collection?"

"No, silly, I'm not planning to die tonight. Most of that stuff you'll get when I am married, anyway. I'm not, for instance, planning to take my hockey stick to London in my trousseau, and you can have my clothes if you can still fit into them, which you won't do if you keep filling up on that bread and butter. No, something real, something grown-up, something that isn't mine yet. Something in this room."

"A book?"

54

"The Book."

Molly's gasp was not quite silent, and Sophie smiled, stretched, and reknotted the sash of her wrapper. She padded across the room to the bookcase, opened the door, and pulled out a book.

The Book was a family treasure, rediscovered by Tibby when he was sixteen. Home from Repton for summer holidays, he had been poking about in the library for something to read. Secretly interested in poetry, he had pulled a leather-bound volume of sonnets from the shelf along which Sophie was even now running her slim, pink-tipped fingers and, opening the book carefully, tilting it so that the spine was not at a right angle to the pages, he noticed colors—not quite a pattern—on the gold edging of the paper. He gently increased the angle and saw the colors shift and form the illustration of a Venetian scene. The Grand Canal, palaces, gondolas. It had seemed like magic to Tibby; a generation later, it still seemed like magic to the two girls looking at the treasure.

"Are you sure?" Molly asked.

Sophie laughed.

"You can always change your mind."

"I won't. Anyway, I'll be dead and I won't care."

"But . . . there's David and, anyway, you'll have children."

"Oh—" Sophie paused as though searching for a way to explain a thought too complicated for words. "They'll be David's children, too, and they'll think of The Book as nonrevenue-producing capital. They'd probably want to sell it."

Molly realized that it was not only the wish for power and to control the family's present and future, although these were undoubtedly the predominant emotions, that made her family's preoccupation with wills understandable. The idea of owning the book that she held reverently was a thrilling one—even if her ownership was predicated on the death of her cousin and best friend. She liked the idea that an object of value had an existence of its own. The fore edge–painted book existed. Wills only designated who would own it and care for it for a time. Ownership might be temporary, but the book was permanent. What Molly really meant was "immortal," but brought up as she was, such a dramatic word would be censored before it reached the level of conscious thought.

Molly's overexcited spirits suddenly sagged as she experienced a sharp feeling of loss. Sophie's death was unimaginable, and the will talk merely titillating, valuable only in that she would now be more sympathetic to Miles and Belinda's preoccupation. The real loss, the one that would never be acknowledged—would, in fact, be celebrated—was Sophie's marriage. Sophie going to London, leaving behind her ponies, piano lessons and French conversation, obligatory church attendance and licensed eccentricity, Christmas mornings in the hall and summer evenings lying in the long grass looking down at the Suir. Leaving her cousin. Molly.

"Don't go, Sophie."

"I've got to. Dromore is heaven for children, but for grown-ups it's different."

"Molly, Sophie, what are you doing?"

Both girls turned, startled. Vera, dressed in an odd but nevertheless somewhat familiar assortment of unseasonal clothing, was standing in the doorway.

Molly did not for a moment contemplate telling the truth, admitting that she was holding a family treasure with the pride of anticipated ownership, and in a low tone she knew to be childish and a little sullen said, "Nothing."

"Well, put it back. Where you found it."

Molly did so, carefully. With her back to her aunt, she reflected that Vera had not reproved Sophie. Even Vera seemed to know that Sophie's status had changed, that it might be wise no longer to treat her as a child.

"Why are you dressed like that?" Sophie asked, not quite aggressively. Asking Vera to account for herself.

Vera was not wearing the worn slacks and frayed shirts usually worn for summer riding, but, despite it being the end of July, she appeared to have started to dress in her hunting clothes and was carrying a bowler hat. She was also carrying a pair of large gauntlets and what seemed to be one of the motoring veils that Molly had seen in photographs of her grandmother riding in the General's first motorcar.

"I'm going to take the honey from the hives in the black currant garden. Time for life to get back to normal."

"Aren't you afraid of getting stung?" Molly asked, thinking of Vera invading the hives of angry territorial bees. Another of the dangerous or disgusting responsibilities that came with adult life. Plucking game, cleaning chickens, and now robbing bees. All female responsibilities; the male ones seemed more to do with death. Shooting pheasant and snipe and occasionally putting a small animal out of its misery.

"No," Vera answered. She turned to Sophie. "You'd better run along and get dressed if you're to be in time for lunch."

Sophie rolled her eyes back as Vera left the room.

"That's her idea of normal life. You see what I mean."

But she went up to her room to get dressed for lunch. Molly stacked the breakfast cups and plates on the tray and carried them to the kitchen.

August 1959

MOLLY WENT TO Ballinacourty that August, and Sophie, with unconvincing promises to write, went to the Dublin Horse Show. Every year since Morag's death, Molly had gone to stay with her grandparents. At Ballinacourty, Molly was treated as a child, and it was hard to make the necessary adjustments after the heady taste of adult life at Dromore. It was the summer of her sixteenth birthday.

Ballinacourty was a windswept, mid-nineteenth-century house surrounded by fields. It had been built by an affluent but unpretentious farmer. To drive up to the house entailed stopping twice to open and close gates, a traditional childhood duty for Molly. The house overlooked Dungarvan Bay; twice a day the tide, with short, choppy waves, swept up the narrow inlet, and twice a day, bearing the debris of the town and harbor, it swept out again. In the morning the fishing boats would set out to sea, and in the evening, followed by flocks of urgent white gulls, they would return. Closer to home than the gulls, whose shrieks could only be inferred, were the contentious rooks. They nested in the tall elms that sheltered the symmetrical high gray house. The third floor, where Molly slept, was on a level with their nests. She loved the raucous noise they made, a little louder at nightfall. In August it was not dark until ten o'clock, and she would lie in bed reading and listening to them settling down to sleep. The elms, which the rooks had made their own, leaned inland, their shapes determined by the salt-laden wind.

Molly drifted up and down the wide, graceful staircase, in and out of the sad, silent house. At Ballinacourty it was the memory of the Great War rather than the Second World War that prevailed. Rationing of petrol and butter had been part of Molly's early childhood. There were other reminders of Hitler's war in the form of older women who wore black and a friend of her father's whose right jacket sleeve, empty, was tucked into his pocket. More powerful by far was a portrait of Molly's great-uncle on the dark staircase. Her grandmother's only brother, he had been killed in the late summer of 1918 and mourned ever since. The stylized portrait showed a young man, fair haired, blue eyed. Shockingly beautiful and shockingly young. His death, his sister's love for him, the loss more than thirty years later of Morag, her only daughter, were all merged into one emotion for Molly's grandmother. Her grief was no longer violent; instead, a gentle melancholy. Melancholy and a sad pleasure in memories pervaded the house. Molly's grandmother was kind and vague, spending fine days in the garden accompanied by a pet hen. The hen, too old to lay eggs, had not only escaped the pot but was the only one allowed to enter the walled garden by the small latched gate cut into the high redbrick wall.

Inside the garden it was warm and quiet. Sheltered from the constant rain-bearing wind from the Atlantic, it was far enough from the rook-filled trees for the birds' cawing to be remote and pleasant. Fruit trees lined the interior wall. A third of the garden was purely decorative. Here Daisy—a name Molly's grand-mother had acquired when young and beautiful, when it had seemed impossible that she should ever become, although still handsome, white haired and arthritic—had gradually made a garden so strangely proportioned that it seemed a series of small separate gardens unified by the symmetry of the straight, narrow paths and the old apple trees. The rest of the garden was devoted to vegetables and fruit, tended by a boy from the village who also milked the cows and wrung the neck of the hen destined for Sunday lunch.

Molly, longing for someone to talk to, would follow her grandmother around the garden, watching Daisy snip the dead heads from flowering plants, straighten stakes, and rip up any weed impertinent enough to try to grow in her garden. Molly had not seen Sophie since the day after Eithne's dance.

Sophie was enjoying the attention of young men and the dis-approval of dowagers in Dublin. Only a hundred and fifty miles away, but so far as Molly was concerned, Sophie might have been in China. Sophie's letters were infrequent, hurried accounts of her triumphs. Some instinct, probably not discretion, precluded a reference to either her engagement or marriage plans. In the minds of both the girls, these were separate if related institu-tions. Molly's letters were more frequent but even sparser. Her swings from euphoria to despair, from hope to hopelessness, could not be committed to writing. Although there was a tele-phone at Ballinacourty, it was not regarded as a social instru-ment. It stood at the foot of the dark staircase in the drafty hall, in earshot of both the kitchen and the drawing room. Seeing Molly on the telephone, any adult would have paused to ask what was wrong; if the witness were her grandfather, he would also have inquired who was paying for the call.

Molly dogged Daisy's footsteps as she pottered in the garden and considered a morning not wasted if she managed to slip Desmond's name once into the conversation. She was reassured when Daisy referred to the past and the future as part of an un-broken pattern. Her sixteenth birthday imminent, Molly needed to know that her life would not always be the same. She feared becoming thirty without anything happening, still living at home with her father, visiting her grandparents for a month each summer. There were enough examples of women with such lives to make the fear real, so she was reassured when Daisy spoke of her own far distant girlhood with an assumption of Molly's almost unimaginable future as a married woman.

Even after she had had the pleasure of saying Desmond's name aloud in the presence of another human being, there were secondary benefits to be obtained from conversation with Daisy. If Daisy embarked on a sufficiently evocative train of thought, she would occasionally forget that she was speaking to a child. Valuable and sometimes surprising pieces of information were thus gleaned. Although as a young married woman Daisy would have been invited to tennis parties at Dromore, she would not have been asked to some of the more exclusive, largely English, house parties where the Hassards had been welcomed. This slight social inequality had made Daisy both more curious and more perceptive about the somewhat older, noticeably richer family, even before her daughter had married Tibby, the second son. And Daisy would wistfully, usually as a digression, tell Molly small details of Morag's childhood. A bantam hen taken by the fox whose chicks Morag had raised, a cat who delighted her by chasing cabbage whites in the garden.

Molly's grandfather Nicholas was, in contrast, no use at all. His interest in the past was confined to an epoch referred to as "my young days in New Zealand," and his anecdotes, although coarse enough to engage a child's attention, were well known to Molly and tooth-grindingly familiar to Daisy. Part of every summer day was spent in an attempt to develop a Protestant work ethic in Molly. Nicholas would evict Molly from the house if he found her reading or gazing dreamily into the distance, although of Molly's two preferred activities, reading was the more heinous. His insistence on the benefits of fresh air had connotations less of health than of moral preference. Nor was exercise his goal. Work was the activity in which he liked to see young people engaged. Unimaginative, unacquainted with the work of Freud—a familiarity with which would have by no means guaranteed respect—Nicholas, more than his wife, afforded Molly some relief.

Driven reluctantly from the house, handed a pitchfork, and sent to join the boys recruited from cottages along the lane, Molly would spend the morning turning hay. By lunchtime, tired and sunburned, she would arrive at the table with a feeling of achievement that allowed a temporary respite from her emotions. By nighttime she would be, once again, struggling to reconstruct the memory of Desmond holding her in the ballroom at Dromore until, just before she slept, she was able to experience the moment in a way that her fear and excitement had inhibited while it was actually happening. Then the next morning, wanting only to huddle with her memory, she would be chased out again by her grandfather to collect eggs. If Molly was preoccupied and did not react quickly enough, she might be treated to a lecture on the hardships of Nicholas's youth. It usually included an account of having his tonsils removed on the kitchen table. Again, robbing the existing nests, searching for new hiding places in the barn and outbuildings, returning with her eggs lying on straw at the bottom of her basket, Molly would find a little peace.

Tibby came to visit. Molly had been at Ballinacourty for a week. He arrived a few moments before Daisy and Molly returned from church. Nicholas, whose interest in the Church of Ireland was limited to teasing its clergy, was at home. He and Tibby had little to say to each other; were Nicholas capable of introspection he would have known that he blamed his son-in-law for Morag's death. Both, however, shared a taste for a second large glass of sherry before Sunday lunch and were capable of maintaining a companionable silence while drinking it.

Molly kissed her father a little awkwardly—she was carrying her prayer book and gloves. She knew that she was too old to embrace him. The casual setting down of one's possessions in the wrong place was a sure way to incur Nicholas's wrath, and after a moment she went upstairs to take off her hat and leave her gloves and prayer book in her room.

Molly paused for a moment on the staircase and looked at the portrait of her great-uncle. He had been christened Sainthill. The name had been shortened to Saint. Had he lived, such a name might have proved a burden, but young, dead, mourned, it fitted him perfectly.

" 'They shall not grow old, as we that are left grow old,' " Molly quoted very quietly. " 'Age shall not weary them.' " She could not remember how the line ended. She read poems in her anthology at school while she was meant to be doing her homework, but she had never heard anyone speak of poetry as anything other than lines to be memorized and then recited in class, flatly and with hesitation and embarrassment. She did not consider her enthusiasm a secret, but she had never considered talking about it with anyone. She wondered if her grandmother knew Binyon's lines and thought that maybe, if the time were right, perhaps alone with her in the garden, she might ask.

A door opened downstairs, and Molly, two steps at a time, rounded the corner onto the landing, passing her grandparents' bedroom, her grandfather's dressing room, and a spare room. She resumed her contemplative pace as she reached the steep, narrow staircase that led to the top floor and her own room.

" 'Age shall not weary them,' " she repeated a little louder. Age would not weary them as it had her father. The portrait of her great-uncle Saint made her think about her father, and she understood that he mourned not only her mother but the passing of a time in which his existence had made sense. She could see that he felt his life inconsequential in the new Ireland. He belonged to a generation whose role was now redundant and who, when the last of his contemporaries had died, would become an extinct species.

There was wine for lunch. Nicholas opened a bottle when either Tibby, who enjoyed it, or the rector, who did not drink, came to lunch. On days when there was no guest, Nicholas would open a bottle of Guinness. Molly would sometimes, at his request, pour the stout into his glass. No matter how carefully or how slowly she poured, holding the glass at as extreme an angle as she dared, she never managed to pour the whole bottle into the glass before the pale brown foam would rise to the top and threaten to overflow.

"You'll never make a barmaid," Nicholas would say, shaking his head as though it were a vocation he passionately wished her to follow. Daisy would purse her lips, whether bored with the often-repeated line or dismayed by the suggestion that any member of her family might be employed in a public house, Molly could not tell.

"Our Lord turned water into wine, not the other way round," Nicholas said, sharpening the carving knife and sizing up the chicken. "Told that vicar chappie that when he wouldn't have a glass. Didn't know what to say."

Tibby merely nodded, not taking his appalled eye from the thick slice of breast Nicholas was hacking off the chicken.

Daisy unpursed her lips. "Since he was our guest, maybe he thought it might be bad form to say something about the devil quoting scriptures for his own purpose."

Molly smiled nervously. This kind of exchange was as far as she ever saw the mild irritation between her grandparents go, but she didn't like it. She wanted Nicholas to be in an expansive mood during meals so that he would not criticize her or insist that she eat something she dreaded. The safest meals, on both counts, were those when the rector came to lunch, usually twice a summer. The food was delicious, and her grandfather needed her, if not as an ally, certainly as a reliable foil. After attempting to pour a glass of wine for both the rector and the rector's wife, and after exaggerating his amazement that neither drank, he would pour a small glass for Molly, who knew enough of what was good for her to sip it appreciatively. She noticed that when her father was present, Nicholas felt no need to waste even half a glass of wine on a child.

"It's Molly's birthday soon," Daisy said, and Molly experienced simultaneous waves of anxiety and relief. She was relieved that the day was not to be forgotten; so far her birthday had never gone uncelebrated, but she always feared the possibility of it passing unnoticed and agonized whether it would be more tactful to remind her father or to pretend that she, too, had forgotten. The anxiety was the familiar one that any event calling for the expression of emotion raised in her. Molly's birthday was not a day that she anticipated with much pleasure, but, as with Christmas, she felt it important that they all got it, to some extent, right. Fortunately, an August birthday did not come under the same scrutiny as one celebrated during the school year. Even so, it would be necessary by the time she returned to school to have some evidence of a present and a mildly enhanced description of the festivities that had surrounded its presentation.

Tibby, too, felt relief. In his case, the relief was that he would not have to decide alone an appropriate form of celebration. At the very least he might manage to get a sense of what was expected of him, both by Daisy and his daughter. From Nicholas he expected nothing more than a lurid account of an appendectomy performed by an amateur on some long past but key birthday.

None of the three asked Molly what she might like to do.

"She's getting a little old for the circus," Daisy said.

Molly listened. Her relief that she would not be taken to the circus as a birthday treat was modified only by her anxiety about alternatives.

"It is the week of Tramore Races," Tibby said, a little tentatively.

"I suppose we could go to Cork for lunch and a visit to a cinema." Daisy, too, sounded tentative, but for a different reason. Tibby feared sounding self-serving, but Daisy had no particular wish to go to the cinema. Her hesitation was entirely to do with concerns of health. She considered the cinema a breeding ground for germs.

There was a short pause. Without knowing that she was about to do so, Molly broke the silence.

"I'd like to go racing," she said, and then seeing their mildly surprised faces, added, "If that's all right."

The three adults, relieved of the decision of how to celebrate Molly's birthday, began to discuss a new scheme to make money devised by some neighborhood Anglo-Irish families: a cooperative market, open once a week in Dungarvan, where members could sell vegetables, fruit, baked goods, eggs, and honey. Tibby himself thought that he might join the scheme, although he was hedging his bet by speaking of the venture ironically.

"We're thinking of calling it the Very Common Market," he said.

Nicholas, who did not feel himself to be part of the Anglo-Irish gentry, narrowed his eyes. His disdain did not imply that he felt any solidarity with the Irish working man.

"I suppose there'd be no harm in sending eggs, and I've got more Michaelmas daisies than I know what to do with this year," Daisy said quickly to deflect his jibe.

Who exactly, Molly wondered—for a moment diverted from considering what she would wear to go racing—did Daisy imagine would spend money on flowers? In Dungarvan? In that moment she foresaw the life and death of the Dungarvan market and, as she now almost automatically did, considered what Desmond would have had to say on the subject. She found herself again wondering what she would wear to go racing.

Clothing, as always, presented two problems—availability and suitability. Molly's wardrobe contained either the hopelessly inadequate or the unnecessarily lavish. Her worn and outgrown winter coat hung alongside an ice-skating dress that had once been Sophie's.

Apart from shoes—her feet were already larger than Sophie's—Molly thought that she could be becomingly dressed for the race meeting. But she did not wish to go to Tramore Races as a well-dressed child. It would be her sixteenth birthday, and society would, were she not careful, keep her in ankle socks and sensible shoes for another year. It was, however, equally important that her emergence from the chrysalis of childhood be achieved in an inconspicuous manner. Never had she needed the absent Sophie more.

IT WAS the week before Molly's birthday. She was once again home at Fern Hill.

65

Since Fern Hill was the Hassard dower house, Adele, Molly's paternal grandmother, as the General's widow, would in the normal course of events have lived there. But when the never-alluded-to deal had been struck during the final weeks of the General's life, Adele had been reluctant to live by herself, and her daughter, Vera, adamant that she would not leave her cottage and garden on the island. Belinda was happy to delegate both the credit and the responsibility for the Dromore gardens, lawns, and shubberies to Vera. Perhaps more significant, she decided that Tibby and Morag should live at Fern Hill. She understood that to save Dromore, every interested party had to be paid off as fully as the limited Hassard war chest allowed. Jack, the most dangerous, was the one Belinda feared most. As a result, while every other member of the Hassard family found himself shunted further into the twentieth century, Jack continued his even-then-dated career as a remittance man. He settled for a small lump sum and a slightly increased monthly allowance. Since there was very little cash to spare, Tibby and Morag were given Fern Hill but, of course, only for the duration of Tibby's life. The house, like Jack's minuscule trust fund, was entailed. It would someday return to the main line of the family. Only one generation, Belinda's, would suffer because Miles had locked horns with his father.

Molly sat down to dinner with Tibby. Tea had been served at half-past four, and dinner was, as usual, a light meal. Molly was delighted to be promoted from the kitchen to the dining room. She was unsure whether the change was permanent. She was, of course, unable to ask Tibby but thought that she might, the following morning, while avoiding a direct question, find out from the cook.

Molly and Tibby sat at what, strictly speaking, was the foot of the table. On more formal occasions, Tibby sat at the head of the table with his back to the fireplace. The foot of the table was in the part of the room where three windows set into a curved wall looked out over the river, each at a slightly different angle.

Molly could see a woodbine in pale warm flower on the distant dark brick of the garden wall. Behind her, a long Irish Chippendale sideboard with carved lion masks and hairy paw feet stretched almost the full length of the wall. A Victorian filigree fruit basket stood next to a large salver, an inscribed trophy of a long-ago steeplechase; beside them, an owl of polished boar tusk, its head, claws, and wingtips of silver. A small plume set in the owl's head could be pulled out, and Molly knew that it had something to do with cigars. Trophies and extravagances from the Edwardian Hassards. On the table, equally polished, stood a three-branched candelabrum.

When Tibby and Molly were seated, Eileen, a new maid, nervously set their supper in front of them. Kidneys on toast, with large, dark mushrooms from the pasture behind the stables. Molly's napkin, though frayed around the edges, was of heavy linen and bore the initials of her mother. The napkin ring, late Victorian and undistinguished, was engraved with the family crest. There had been no reason why Molly's great-grandparents should have hesitated before imposing family identity upon every piece of silver they owned. They had assumed their way of life would last forever.

Molly carefully cut her kidneys. She was happy to eat the outer portion, and she knew that Tibby would not comment on the hard whitish core she left on the side of her plate. Nevertheless, she wished that the food had been something she could have eaten without appearing childish. She wished, too, that she and Tibby could slip easily into conversation. The silence, along with her aversion to the food, made her feel even more childish.

"I'm looking forward to going racing on Saturday," she said tentatively.

Her father looked startled for a moment. With an almost visible effort, he gave her his attention. "I hope it won't be dull for you. I'm senior steward—it may take up some time."

"There'll be lots of people I know." She suddenly couldn't think of one except for Desmond. "Like . . . Lady Marjorie."

"Odd the way some people never learn to sit on a horse properly. Like Frank Paget. Marjorie can ride. No problem there, if they'd feed their horses. Frank's a perfectly competent steward;

got common sense, sticks to the point. But on a horse he's an embarrassment."

Molly recognized the opportunity to introduce Desmond's name into the conversation, but she thought that he didn't ride and feared an unconsidered out-of-hand condemnation.

"Funny thing is, he was bred to ride." Tibby paused. Molly thought his thoughts had drifted away again, but a small smile, the smile that told of a memory recalled, indicated that he was about to embark on an anecdote that amused him.

"Frank Paget is a younger son. So was his father. Both generations went into the army—his father was stationed in Cairo during the first war. Tommy Paget taught a camel to go over the jump course at Cairo racetrack."

"He taught a camel to jump?"

"After a fashion. Can't have been much fun for either of them. I suppose he had a fair amount of time on his hands."

Molly tried to imagine the scene. Desmond's grandfather, dead before she was born. Sand and palm trees, hot sun and small, dark men in white. Frank Paget was tall, thin, and a little stooped. Perhaps his father had been also.

"What did he wear?"

Tibby laughed.

"You mean a top hat and pink coat as though he were hunting with the Kildares? Or maybe a topee and some kind of tropical gear? Probably his uniform, don't you think?"

This time Molly could see it. Early morning, the deserted racetrack, a young man far from home. Did they have mist in Cairo?

Eileen, breathing adenoidally through her mouth in a manner that Belinda would not have stood for, took away their plates and brought the fruit from the sideboard. Molly took a peach from the basket. The peach came from the espaliered trees on the north wall of the smaller greenhouse. Pink, yellow, unbruised—it was easily peeled, the skin coming off in three or four lengths held between her thumb and the slightly discolored fruit knife.

"They managed to have a fair amount of fun in Cairo in

spite of everything. Your uncle Jack was there for a time and your great-uncle, my mother's brother, on his way back to India from leave. He was on the same boat as a pack of hounds being brought out for some regiment with more money than sense. Christmas Eve, going through the Suez Canal, they unloaded the hounds and hunted jackal by moonlight."

AFTER DINNER, Tibby came downstairs in the clothes he wore to work in the greenhouse. An earth-stained pair of gray flannel trousers held up by an equally worn school tie and a frayed, collarless shirt. His clothing smelled of sweat and more strongly of the tomato leaves and shoots he had nipped from the mature plants.

It was half-past eight, the evening light soft with a warm breeze from the river. Molly, restless and full of longing, walked to the end of the lawn and through a field in which half a dozen bullocks grazed and an old mare stood on the bare, dusty earth under an oak tree, head bowed, tail swishing away flies. Molly was glad to see the cattle on their feet; had they been lying down, it would have foretold rain the following day.

At the end of the pasture, she climbed over a stile and, following a stream fed by a waterfall from the large pond, pushed her way down an overgrown path that led steeply to the river. Brambles fought for space and light with rhododendron and azaleas, imported shrubs once planted by an English landscape architect and a Scottish gardener who'd had an endless supply of cheap labor from the local lunatic asylum. Following the path, she walked until she could see the river divide on either side of the rich, dark mud and stiff rushes at the northern tip of the island.

Leaving the path at a point where she had both Waterford and the island in view, Molly climbed down to a patch of thin, pale grass. She and Sophie had spent long idle afternoons there, searching idly among the sparse green blades for wild sorrel in the spring and beechnuts in the autumn. She became aware of music—carried by the wind over the flat surface of the river from a fair on the outskirts of the city, the tinny sound of English and American popular music. Molly's exposure to music was limited to the wireless in the maids' sitting room at Fern Hill. Although there was a gramophone in an upstairs room used for ironing and storage, there were only three or four worn records. And it had been a long time since anyone bought a new needle.

"Cherry Pink and Apple Blossom White." "Red Sails in the Sunset." The songs of Alma Cogan and Pat Boone. Part of the limited repertoire of the fairground music. Molly sat on the grass, hugging her knees and listening. The breeze carried a phrase or even two or three lines of a song, and waves of desire filled her. She felt nostalgia for events and feelings not yet experienced; she longed for Desmond, craved the warmth of another body. She wished there was someone she could talk to about love. But love, sex, even romance, seemed to be the only adult privileges to which Sophie not only laid no claim, but which she ignored.

She heard a shot. Some distance away and from a direction other than that from which the music floated. *Someone shooting pigeons,* she thought, and a moment later her barely conscious thought was validated by the clattering of twenty or thirty pigeons, in a hurry, over her head.

Looking up, Molly realized that night was at last falling. The birds and trees were silhouetted against the fading sky. It was time to go home. She remained a little longer, experiencing a hope engendered by the restlessness and desire implicit in the music. Why should she not be loved by Desmond? She wondered if anyone could love another as much as she loved Desmond without the object of that love feeling something in return. If he were at Tramore Races—and surely he would be—it might be possible in some small way to set in motion the course of events that would allow her to follow Sophie, more modestly, but surely more happily, more gratefully, to the altar.

Picking her way through the bushes, she could hear the rustling of some small nocturnal animal. It was almost dark, and a sickle moon shone over the stables. Soon she could see Fern Hill, now in complete silhouette against the sky, to the left one of the greenhouses and the weeping ash standing free on the lawn in front of the house.

To Molly's surprise, many of the downstairs lights were on. She quickened her pace. She wondered if her father had missed her and worried. She had no sense of how long she had been gone and thought, a little sadly, that the first day in which she had attempted to be perceived as an adult had ended in an act of childish thoughtlessness.

There were two motorcars in front of the house. She could also see lights in her father's study and the corridor leading to the billiards room. Molly hurried up the shallow steps to the front door. She felt a small twinge of fear.

Eileen was in the hallway. The maid was weeping and Molly felt sudden terror. She was afraid of the implications of Eileen's grief and an even stronger fear that she did not understand. She no longer remembered the weeping maid in the hall on the afternoon when she, Sophie, and Tibby had returned from their walk on the beach. The afternoon of Mr. Hannon's aeroplane.

Chapter Five

*D*ESMOND PAGET HEARD of Tibby Hassard's death in the members' bar at Tramore Races.

"Poor Molly," he said, surprised by the depth of his feeling. He'd known Tibby all his life. A carefully worded letter of condolence was all any of them could do. Desmond was aware, although not in any way that he could have articulated, that his feeling for Molly was not only pity but a tenderness in some way connected to the slightness of her body in his arms when they had danced at the Tyrell girl's coming-out party.

"Cleaning his gun? In August?" Pauline McBride prided herself on her frankness. Desmond sometimes thought that frankness merely the arrogance of a girl with a small trust fund in a cash-poor society.

"Apparently." Desmond's voice was cold, forbidding any further discussion.

He did nothing to interrupt the silence that followed, feeling at that moment dislike for Pauline, the girl he supposed he would someday marry. Suicide was condemned by both the law and the church. Discretion would make it easier for a sympathetic coroner to bring in the expected verdict of accidental death. Although beyond the reach of the legal system, a suicide could not be buried on consecrated ground. This gave great pain to the survivors; fortunately this additional shame was rarely added to the tragedy. The native Irish—with the instinctive tact that the Anglo-Irish envied, emulated, and never achieved—produced an endless stream of doctors, policemen, and coroners gullible in the face of death occurring late at night while an experienced shot had apparently been cleaning a loaded gun. There was, of course, a price paid for this generosity; those left to grieve, as Molly was, were forced to do so under false pretenses. Tibby had not, of course, left a note or letter. But it was far from clear that he would have done so even had he lived in a society in which suicide was a less unacceptable choice.

Desmond allowed the sulky and unchastened Pauline to lead him to the paddock to view the horses parading before the third race.

MOLLY STOOD, her back to the Dromore nursery that for the time served as her bedroom. She was looking out the window and trying not to cry. Soon Belinda and then Sophie would come in to say good night, and she both wished to spare them her tears and allow herself, if she could wait, to cry for as long as she needed once they had gone.

The moon, yellow and pale, showed through the ilex at the top of the avenue. Soon the stars would appear. She had once—it didn't seem so long ago—spoken of the stars "coming out," and Tibby had reminded her that stars were always there, but she could only see them when it was dark. Molly began to cry.

The door opened. Molly moved a hand in greeting but she did not turn her head, hiding her tears. Sophie crossed the room and stood beside her.

"Mummy wonders if you would like to go away to school. She's coming up later to talk to you. I thought I'd lay the ground so she doesn't take you by surprise."

Molly, her head averted, nodded. So long as she did not show her tears or audibly sob, both girls could pretend that she was not crying.

"Not if you'd hate it, of course. You know you're welcome to stay here as long as you like. Forever." Uncharacteristically, Sophie laid a hand on Molly's shoulder. She rarely touched another human being if she could help it.

From the corridor outside the nursery—Sophie had left the door ajar, betraying her intention not to stay long—Molly could hear the sound of a maid's footsteps. Distant, then muffled as she trod on a small, worn carpet, then louder, on wood, as they came closer. Black laced-up shoes with slightly raised, thick heels. A tentative knock, and then the door pushed open.

"Miss Sophie, there's a telephone call for you. From London."

Sophie moved lightly toward the door.

DURING THE FIRST WORLD WAR, Miles had been sent to prep school in North Wales. He was seven years old. Many Anglo-Irish families had, for several generations, sent their children to Arnold House. The remainder of the pupils were English and came from sometimes richer but usually less distinguished families who lived in the neighboring counties of Cheshire and Lancashire. The Irish and English boys did not easily mix, the Irish boys finding themselves sometimes professing nationalistic views that they would neither have expressed nor held at home. The rivalry was ritualized in the Irish-English football match played each St. Patrick's Day. Neither the English nor the Irish boys could have failed, however, to notice that when parents of the Anglo-Irish boys dined at the headmaster's table, dinner jackets were worn by the masters, but when the guests were English, a suit was all that was required.

Three years after Miles had been sent away to school, Tibby joined his brother. Tibby's first term had barely begun when the influenza epidemic reached the small school. The early Victorian building was cold, drafty, and, during the greater part of the school year, very damp. More than half the boys were sick; the dormitories became wards, ministered to by the local doctor—

too old to serve in France—the school matron, and two house-maids. Tibby, ordinarily a robust child, succumbed to the flu and soon afterward developed pneumonia in both his lungs. It took a little longer than it should have to diagnose the deterioration of his condition. In terms of treatment this made little difference, but the telegram to Tibby's mother was sent rather later than it should have been.

General Hassard had been fighting in France. Adele Hassard took the night ferry from Rosslare to Fishguard and continued by train to North Wales, arriving late the following afternoon. Miles, frightened and helpless, waited for his mother, fearing that Tibby would die before she arrived.

Miles had so far escaped the flu, and he loitered in the corridor outside the sick bay where Tibby lay barely conscious. He stood at the window that overlooked the cold, bare, leafless avenue up which the dogcart bearing his mother would come.

When Adele had arrived—her silver foxes in place, her hair neatly up under a small, smart hat, and, inexplicably, a bunch of fresh, sweet-smelling violets pinned to her lapel—Miles found that his fear did not abate. He had believed that if Tibby were still alive when Adele arrived, he would survive. Two boys had already died quietly of the flu and, even more quietly, had been taken from the school.

Moments after his mother's arrival, Miles realized that she was as powerless as he was to save Tibby. She did not pause to reassure or comfort her eldest son. It was only after Miles had left Arnold House for Repton that he understood that Adele had expended all her energy on controlling her emotions. Her unspoken message, in lieu of a reassuring embrace, was that he should act like a man. It was not until he knew that Tibby would live and Adele had left for Ireland that Miles was able to cry. Sobbing, he allowed the school matron to hold him to her bosom. Comforted by the smell of talcum powder and starch while Clockwork—as the boys had nicknamed her—patted his shoulder and said, "There, there." He understood vaguely that there was some connection between the dinner jackets donned for visiting Irish parents, his mother's violets, and her refusal or, perhaps, inability to comfort him.

Miles, now older than Adele had been at the time of the epidemic, understood how paralyzing his mother's fear had been. Fear that Tibby would die. Fear for her husband fighting a war that had already slaughtered a generation of young men. Fear that she would, alone, have to bring up Miles, Tibby, and the two other children she had left at Dromore. Although she had failed him then and continued to fail him, Miles bore his mother no resentment. He understood her helplessness. A helplessness he now—Tibby dead—felt himself.

It was not only Morag's death that had defeated Tibby. It was also his lack of a purpose in the new Ireland, and, it was this that caused Miles the greatest sorrow—Tibby's place in the Hassard family. Tibby had been the most intelligent of the General's children; the most handsome of the sons. He rode better than either of his brothers, and his wit and charm had made him the most sought-after young man at parties and hunt balls. None of which could compensate for his position as younger son.

Mourning the death he had dreaded more than thirty-five years before, Miles decided to protect his family in a manner in which he had not, as a child, been protected. He was determined that Molly, now an orphan, should never feel as bereft as he, both his parents alive, had felt in childhood. So it was with surprise that he heard that Molly was to be sent to a boarding school outside Dublin. Belinda presented the plan as a fait accompli, and when Miles failed to detect any reluctance in Molly's demeanor, he acquiesced. Disappointed that he could show nothing more in the way of affection, he wrote a surprisingly large check for the school fees.

September 1959

THE AFTERNOON BEFORE she went away to school, Molly visited her grandmother Adele. Molly's new, ugly, and expensive uniform (Miles had written another check) had been packed in the old trunk, the name Hassard painted across the top in yellow

76

with a brown border—which had accompanied first Miles and then Sophie back and forth across the Irish Sea. Molly felt fearful, impatient, and depressed. Her last hours of home life passed slowly; Sophie was in London, and time spent with Miles or Belinda was, in different ways, heavy with unexpressed emotion.

Molly took a shortcut through the woods—never quite out of sight of the river—to her grandmother's house. When she had been a small girl, Tibby had taken her for walks there on summer Sunday afternoons. The path was called the Fox's Walk, and Molly had carried a stick in case they met the fox.

Walking noiselessly through the woods, hearing the calls of the late-summer birds and the sound of the small river waves hitting the mud at the point of the island, Molly thought of Tibby on the strand at Woodstown, waiting for Mr. Hannon's aeroplane to bring Sophie back to them. Her father, himself a boy, had walked along a similar path and come upon young Hannon and his sweetheart in a punt. Molly thought that she might some day ask Mrs. Hannon what book it was that she had been reading that afternoon.

The path led past the garden behind Vera's cottage. Her aunt was in the garden, bending inelegantly to cut back a plant. Aware that she should say good-bye to her aunt also, Molly hesitated. A trellis covered with sweet pea separated them. As Molly was about to speak, Vera straightened, wiped her brow, and scratched her bottom. Molly stepped back, thinking that to wait a moment before announcing her presence would be tactful. There was a sharp crack as she trod on a piece of dry wood, and a guinea fowl, napping in the shade of a large yew tree, screamed.

"Shut up, you stupid creature," Vera snapped. She was looking almost in Molly's direction.

Molly froze, heart pounding, until her aunt resumed her labors. She then turned and silently padded down the fern-bordered path to her grandmother's house.

On the worn gray flags of the veranda, a cat lay asleep in the sun. Molly paused to scratch the back of his head and under his chin. He rolled over in sleepy pleasure, hypnotized. White butterflies danced above the low lavender border surrounding the veranda. A French window into the drawing room was open, and Molly stepped inside.

Although Adele's drawing room had two smaller windows facing west with a view of the river through trees, Molly had to pause while her eyes adjusted to the dark interior. The room smelled pleasantly of furniture polish and the scent of a large bowl of pink, blue, and white cut flowers. It was late enough in the afternoon for Adele to have risen from her afternoon rest and to be ready for tea, which she might take in the garden or at Vera's cottage or, during the colder weather, in the room in which Molly now waited.

After a moment, Molly heard a low sound, unmistakably a sob. Blinking, she could now see the figure of her grandmother, dressed in black, sitting in the corner of a faded sofa. Adele looked tiny, reduced by the large, extravagant flowers of the chintz.

"Who is it?" she asked.

"It's me. Molly," Molly answered nervously. She had never seen an adult shed tears. It was an unnerving sight. Part of the strain of spending time with Miles or, when he had been alive, her father, was the fear that an adult would show himself unable to control his emotions. What the result of such a lapse might be Molly did not know, but she felt that the consequences would undermine the shaky foundations of a society already in its last days.

"Who are you?" Adele sounded querulous.

"Molly," Molly said, suddenly desperate.

Her grandmother said nothing.

Molly moved closer. The old lady sniffed, and as Molly sat beside her, Adele shuddered as a small child does minutes after it has ceased to cry. Molly felt a nervous respect for the old lady, more recently modified by fear of her uninhibited comments and startling non sequiturs. Now she realized that her grandmother was irrevocably bereaved.

Molly took Adele's hand in hers and stroked the swollen,

arthritic fingers on which two rings, enlarged to pass over the crooked joints, fitted loosely.

"What is the matter, Granny?" she asked.

Adele looked at her, bewildered and, Molly thought, a little frightened. "I don't know," she said and started to weep again.

Molly realized that Adele, whose deteriorating mental capabilities had been irreparably damaged by the shock and grief of Tibby's death, had forgotten the death and perhaps even the son for whom she was mourning. Even as she felt pity for her grandmother and shame at having witnessed her loss of control, Molly felt a surge of anger. For a moment she had thought that she had found someone to whom she could talk about her father.

Unsure of whether she should explain who she was, which would be difficult to do without mentioning Tibby, and unsure of whether it would be either kind or safe to remind Adele of his death, Molly was relieved to see the door to the drawing room pushed open by Mrs. Gleeson, carrying a tea tray.

"Ah, Molly. Fetch yourself a cup and I'll see to herself."

Gently disengaging Adele's hand, Molly rose. As she reached the door to the kitchen, she glanced back. Mrs. Gleeson, who had herself raised six children and lost one, was sitting in Molly's place, holding Adele's hand.

"Whsht, now, don't you cry. You'll have a nice cup of tea, and haven't I made you a fine sponge cake with raspberry jam from your own garden."

Adele reached out a shaky hand for the tea Mrs. Gleeson had poured for her. Mrs. Gleeson took a not entirely clean handkerchief from her apron pocket and applied it to Adele's nose.

"Blow," she said.

December 1959

MOLLY CAME HOME from school to her first Christmas at Dromore—her first Christmas living at Dromore; Christmas Day had been spent there each year since Morag's death. She spent most of the short, damp days in Miles's study in a sagging armchair beside the fire, reading his copy of *Some Experiences of an Irish R.M.* She read out loud the parts that made her laugh. Miles, who knew the book well, would laugh, too. Belinda, never much charmed by the more feckless aspects of the Irish, would smile. Molly never read anything aloud if Sophie was in the room. Sophie, thin, irritable and impatient to be away, was sitting out the long engagement decreed by Miles.

Christmas was, of course, subdued. Tibby was never far from anyone's thoughts, although his name was rarely mentioned. When it was, the reference was always to an amusing incident. The humor of the anecdote reminded them of their loss without the embarrassment that would have otherwise accompanied the evocation of any strong emotion.

Belinda's talents had rarely been more tested. Or less noticed, except by Molly. However little any of them might feel like celebrating, ritual and form could not be abandoned without a high price being paid. Molly was grateful to know what was expected of her, to obey the unquestioned rules, to follow time-honored and undemanding traditions. She understood that if each member of the family did what was expected of him, time would pass and the period when Tibby's death hovered like a tangible presence over the room would eventually be over. Then her grief, perhaps already a little less sharp, would be personal and private.

Christmas Day was cold but sunny. A white frost left the lawn crisp and the air sharp and clear. Presents were opened before breakfast. A tray with a pot of tea and thin slices of bread and butter had been set on the hall table. "Early morning tea, but in the hall," was what Belinda, leaving nothing to chance, had said to Norah. A Christmas tree that had come from the Dromore woods stood, a white sheet at its base, in one corner of the hall, its scent blending with the smell of the turf fire. The tree was modestly decorated. Sprigs of holly lay along the mantelpiece and tucked behind the frame of the painting above.

Although Sophie's presents were more sophisticated than Molly's, they were not visibly more expensive nor were there more of them. Molly felt the comfort that material objects can give one whose life has contained subtle but constant deprivation. A moss-green Shetland cardigan, some books, and, even more welcome, book tokens. Also a watch and some clothes that she knew Belinda did not consider attractive but that were currently the rage at school. The pleasure that these presents gave Molly was not entirely acquisitive. The felt skirt and pastel twin set would provide protective coloring and allow her a little status at Kingstown House.

The presents the adults exchanged seemed dull to Molly. Adele had made a cream-colored twinset for Belinda, the pattern complicated and the garment soft. For her son, she had made two pairs of chamois gloves and knitted a pair of the long, thick socks he wore with his knickerbockers when shooting. There was no way for Molly to tell whether any of them was pleased or disappointed. The thanking was in the low-key manner in which all the not actually insane Anglo-Irish that Molly knew conducted their social life.

Christmas lunch, too, was traditional and well cooked. Since Tibby's death was so recent, there were no guests. Molly had never before been part of so festive an occasion that did not entail entertaining guests, and this added to her sense of well-being. Turkey, chestnut stuffing, Brussels sprouts, roast potatoes, gravy, and bread sauce. A Christmas pudding decorated with a sprig of holly, and brandy butter. Paper crackers, red and green with gold decorations, lay in front of each place. Wine, not usually served with lunch if there were no guests. Sophie, silent, fiddled with her food but drank her wine, and soon Vera's critical eye was upon her. Molly began to regret the lack of an inhibiting guest.

"So, when are we going to see that young man of yours again?" Vera asked.

"Whose young man?" Adele asked.

There was a flicker of tension around the table when Adele spoke. Since the afternoon when Molly had visited her and found her weeping, she had seen Adele only once. Earlier in Christmas week she had gone to tea at Adele's house. Vera had been present and had either, depending on one's point of view, dominated or borne the brunt of the desultory conversation. Adele had been finishing one of Miles's Christmas socks, and Molly had held a skein of wool for her grandmother to wind. The simple ritual, one of the first useful tasks she had performed as a small child, had given her pleasure, and, returning in the late afternoon dusk, a hint of frost in the air, she decided that on her earlier visit she must have witnessed a temporary lapse, a not unreasonable reaction of grief. Her grandmother's behavior on Christmas morning, opening her presents, thanking and receiving thanks, had been what one might have expected from a shaky old lady enjoying her moments of attention and the festivities. Until she sensed the nervous reaction to Adele's question, Molly had had no reason to believe that her grandmother's mind had further deteriorated.

"Fiancé." Sophie's tone was short but she spoke quietly.

"What?" Vera asked.

"Fiancé. His name is David and he's my fiancé."

"Nonsense. Puppy love. You're far too young to think of an engagement."

Sophie opened her mouth, then changed her mind. A short silence increased the discomfort at the table.

"It's no good making sheep's eyes at that curate." Adele seemed to be speaking to Vera. "He's not, I'm afraid, the answer to a maiden's prayer."

Molly looked at Vera. She wondered if her aunt had been disappointed by a not entirely heterosexual curate or whether the whole thing was a figment of Adele's imagination.

Miles spoke before Vera had time to collect herself. However much he disapproved of David and the engagement, he loved his daughter. And he wanted to eat his Christmas lunch in peace.

"When are we going to see him, Sophie?" he asked. "Maybe he could come over for, ah, for the West Waterford Hunt Ball. We could give him a little hunting." He glanced at Belinda for help.

"I don't see why not," she said. "I don't think we could give a dinner party for it this year, but I don't see why you and he shouldn't go."

Vera sniffed, but Belinda ignored her, her smile, loving and indulgent, remaining on Sophie. "I'm sure Violet Banville would be happy to have you—should I ask her? Why not?"

"Why not?" Sophie asked, rolling her eyeballs in simulated incredulity and glancing pointedly at Vera and Adele. Her voice was loud enough for everyone to hear while low enough for them to pretend otherwise. "Maybe. We'll see. I'll ask David."

Vera sniffed again. Adele twitched her nose as she did when she disapproved. Whether her disapproval was a reaction to her daughter's interference, or Belinda's seemingly casual attitude toward mourning, or Sophie's glowering face, or some other real or imaginary failing on the part of any one of them, Molly could not tell.

They finished lunch awkwardly. Belinda kept the conversation going without much help from anyone apart from Molly, but since both Vera and Adele believed that children should be seen and not heard, Molly knew that only a minor conversational contribution would be useful.

During lunch, the wireless from the servants' hall had been carried up to the drawing room and tuned to the BBC. As they drank their coffee, the family listened to the Queen's speech.

Miles was moved, Sophie bored. Vera and Adele twitched and sniffed. Molly watched Belinda, wondering if she was upset. If Belinda was annoyed to have had Christmas—in which she had invested a good deal of work and organization—marred by the ungenerous spirit of her sister-in-law, she didn't show it. Molly understood that self-control was the basis of Belinda's power. It also seemed possible to her that Belinda didn't particularly care if the day was a happy and affectionate one; it was more important that the traditions of how Christmas Day was celebrated at Dromore should be followed. If the others chose not to enjoy themselves, she could not concern herself with that. She knew that they had been well and properly fed, and that appropriate presents had been exchanged. The rest of the day would follow time-honored tradition. That was what was important.

In accordance with these principles, the Christmas-afternoon walk took place after the Queen's speech. Gumboots and dogs, cold air. Exercise to work off the effects of the heavy meal. Even the dogs, used to a good walk every day, sensed that this was a special occasion. Nell, Belinda's cocker spaniel, ran in circles and darted away on the trail of mysterious game. Mingo, the black Labrador that once had been Tibby's, stayed close to Miles's heels as though to impress his new master, or perhaps even himself, with his allegiance.

Rush, Tibby's other dog, older, slow, and a little deaf, trailed behind the others. Sophie and Molly waited for him to catch up. Pausing by the ferry, they watched Nell run about on the frozen grass. The reeds beside them were dry and brittle; a thin line of ice on the mud marked the high-tide line.

"She looks as though Vera had slip-covered her." Sophie's smile was, for the first time that day, unforced. "Those feathers make her look like an armchair. An elegant armchair. In a boudoir, perhaps."

Molly laughed, but Sophie fell silent again. She stared across the river, her eyes fixed on the still, stiff landscape. The only movement a thin curl of smoke from one chimney of a gaunt Victorian rectory. Below them, Nell ran onto the wet mud closer to the water, coating her long coat and feathers with river-smelling dirt.

"If they think they're going to get David over so they can laugh at him falling off a horse in front of the West Waterfords, they've got another think coming," Sophie said savagely. She threw a stick for Nell, who had shown belated signs of obeying Belinda's whistled summons.

Waiting for her dog, Belinda watched Sophie. Worried about her daughter's sullen distance, irritated by her untrainable dog, Belinda addressed another not immediately soluble problem— Rush.

"Poor old boy, Tibby should have put him down."

Miles made a helpless gesture.

"Not yet. Maybe when she's away at school."

Belinda watched Rush limp up to the girls, who had begun to walk again, in no hurry to catch up with her and Miles.

PULLING OFF GUMBOOTS in the porch and coats in the hall, the two girls remained a little behind the rest of the family, who, pink-nosed and virtuous from their walk, had gone on to the blazing fire, tea, and the Dromore Christmas cake in the library.

Molly had watched Belinda supervise the making of the cake. Although Sophie was her daughter, it was to Molly that Belinda taught the workings of a well-run house. It was Molly who learned the secret recipes. It was not Sophie who would mark linen or visit the kitchen in her future life. It would not be necessary for her to know how to make barmbrack, the traditional Halloween cake, adding the wedding ring, a sixpenny piece, and the dreaded piece of wood condemning the finder to the despised fate of old maid. It was not necessary for Sophie to know that the fruit for the Christmas cake had to be thoroughly dried after washing and shaken in flour—otherwise it would sink to the bottom. She would never need to know how to make marmalade. Hers would be ordered from Fortnum and Mason's or Harrods.

Molly wondered at Sophie's distance from all these fragments of knowledge and ritual, which not only made her life safer and richer but also seemed to have an intrinsic value of their own. They never spoke of that feeling, but she knew Belinda shared it, although she probably gave it another name. Small secrets. Mysteries of a tiny race.

Molly understood that Belinda had marked her to maintain the tradition and, in her turn, to pass it on to the next generation. Or, as Desmond had suggested, the perhaps greater responsibility of breaking that very tradition. To be the last female Hassard to consult Mrs. Beeton. The last to make the Christmas cake. The last to preserve eggs in water glass each autumn; to make chutney from the small green tomatoes left at the end of the season. The last to insist that the Wren boys, each St.

Stephen's Day, sing the Wren song instead of the popular American ballad they would prefer. Sophie seemed willing to abandon these traditions; how could she bear to? Although Molly rarely felt happy anymore, she would be unable to contemplate, as Sophie seemed able to do, the possibility of never again waking up in the morning to the sound of horses' hooves on the cobblestones of the stableyard behind the house, of seeing the early morning mist lift off the river.

With an irritated glance at the Christmas tree as she passed it, Sophie finished the thought she had started standing by the Suir.

"Or maybe they think they'll mount him on that half-broken brute the Banvilles unloaded on Daddy last season and break his neck. If they're planning to kill David, I'd be grateful if they'd at least wait until after I've married him."

February 1960

TWO SUNDAYS every school term were deemed "Long Sundays." Parents traveled from all over Ireland to collect their daughters as soon as prayers and choir practice were over. Each term, Miles drove up for one of the Sundays, sometimes two. Belinda, when she came, was hard-pressed to fill the day, but Miles grasped the essentials. Food and indulgence. And he had the advantage of the Kildare Street Club.

The Kildare Street Club had once been the bastion of the Anglo-Irish upper classes; now it was sanctuary for the landed gentry. Without it, a visit to Dublin would have been for Miles, and many like him, a confusing journey into an almost unimaginable future. The club had once had its own oyster bed in Galway and the exclusive use of two pews at St. Anne's, the nearby Protestant church. Now it offered less exclusive fare, but its members, who found the dues harder to come up with each year, needed it even more than had their confident, powerful forebears.

Tibby had been a member. Molly had once eaten lunch with him in the ladies' dining room when he brought her up to

Dublin to have braces put on her teeth. Now Miles, having collected Molly from her school in Dunlaoghaire, drove her along the coast road to the large Victorian redbrick building on Kildare Street. Seating his niece in front of the coal fire, he ordered coffee and biscuits, knowing food to be the first requirement of an outing from school.

Old copies of *Punch* and *The Illustrated London News* lay on the tables against the walls of the large, dim room. Molly looked at the cartoons and pictures, happily bored, until it was time for lunch. The magazines were subscribed to at Dromore. They had not been taken at Fern Hill.

As soon as the dining room opened, Miles and Molly went down to lunch. Since it was Sunday, Miles ordered roast beef. It came rare, with Yorkshire pudding and horseradish sauce. Molly ordered the same, choosing the comfort of the familiar over the lighter, less-institutional food she preferred. She asked that her meat be served without gravy. Although she was less squeamish than she had been at Ballinacourty (and much less afraid of Miles than she was of her grandfather), she still liked to have a good look at her food before she ate it.

The greater part of Miles and Molly's time together was spent in companionable silence, but during meals they would talk, often about Tibby. Molly particularly treasured those details that Miles would occasionally add to her knowledge of her father as a young man or as a boy. At dinner, they would more often talk about Molly's school, the anxiety both felt at her incipient return making the subject uppermost in their minds. Miles did not understand why she had to be at boarding school; Molly did, but it did not alleviate the misery it caused her.

"I thought after lunch we might go to the cinema. Eugene"—Miles was referring to the club hall porter, to whom he deferred on most urban matters—"tells me that *To Catch a Thief* is 'a grand fillum.'"

"We're not supposed to—" Molly started half-heartedly. Miles knew that a visit to the cinema was against school rules, but he did not consider most rules to apply to him. He could see the sense of forbidding other people to take their children to the cinema, where they might pick up infectious diseases, but when it was Molly and himself, he couldn't see the harm.

Molly didn't argue. She very much wanted to see a film that offered not only Grace Kelly and Cary Grant but a glimpse of high life on the Riviera. Miles ordered Stilton and water biscuits and a glass of port, which reminded them both of Tibby. Molly ordered a Knickerbocker Glory. Miles watched her eat it, his expression equal parts amusement and concern.

He cleared his throat. "Have you heard from Sophie?"

"She wrote to me from the Spencers. She was staying for the weekend and thought it would be funny to say she had letters to write after breakfast."

Miles looked blank, so Molly explained. "Like characters in Jane Austen—you know. She told me all about the family and the house. It's in a place called Virginia Water."

Molly stopped herself. She imagined that Miles already knew everything she did about the Spencers and their house. If he didn't, then she would feel odd letting him know that Sophie told her things she didn't tell her parents. Although that clearly was what Miles was asking.

"Large place, I hear. Stockbroker belt. Spencer Senior made a fair amount of money out of the war."

"The black market?" Molly asked hopefully. Miles had never before seemed a potential source of information.

"Of course not." Miles laughed. "It was all perfectly aboveboard."

Molly continued to look expectantly at him.

"Perfectly legal," he said. "Only—lots of chaps fought. Some of them were killed or wounded. Then there were the chaps who stayed home and got rich. Not quite the thing." After a pause, he added, "Fellow plays golf."

If Mr. Spencer played golf, provided he did it out of doors and didn't make other people—like Sophie, for instance—play with him, where was the harm? Molly wondered. *Must all sporting events be blood sports or involve some physical risk? Did Miles feel that golf would be an acceptable pastime if every now and then the ball hopped off the tee and bit a player in the ankle?*

March 1960

SPRING CAME EARLY that year. Violets and primroses were already in full bloom when Molly came home from school for the half-term holiday. She found Sophie at Dromore.

Sophie's hair was a little shorter, and she smoked. Otherwise she was unchanged. If anything, she had become more herself. As though her months in London had refined and distilled her essence.

The day nursery had become Sophie's boudoir; the transformation effected by the commandeering of two paisley cashmere shawls, some cushions, and an ashtray; Sophie's attitude and demeanor did the rest. She had been in the habit of holding court in the nursery, Molly as a solitary lady-in-waiting, when they were children. But there was little that was childlike about Sophie now. She had a new way of sitting in a chair, her legs tucked up beside her, an elbow propped on the arm, making her seem lithe and sophisticated.

Sophie greeted Molly affectionately, reassured herself about her well-being, and dragged her upstairs. She was not even slightly interested in hearing details of day-to-day boarding-school life. Sophie had not found a confidante in London and had eagerly awaited Molly's return from Kingstown House. Molly listened as Sophie told her about life in London, about living with their great-aunts in a large flat beside the Albert Hall, about shops and fashions, nightclubs and parties, about David and his family.

It was not until Molly's second day home, when the girls were sitting by the nursery fire, rain beating against the windowpanes, that Sophie spoke about her first weekend at Virginia Water.

"Virginia Water is where the Spencers live; it's in the stock-broker belt, which means it's full of men like David's father

89

who have lots of money, drive Jaguars, and belong to golf clubs. The house is large and quite ugly and not at all old, and the gardener seems to have done his training in a municipal park. But the house has central heating, and they have it on flat out all winter. Even in the bathrooms. And all the beds have electric blankets . . ."

Molly listened, fascinated by Sophie's description of a world that she had not only never seen, but hadn't even read about. She hoped that Sophie would describe the food. Her stomach was comfortably full of the treats with which the Dromore cook was trying to "feed up" two girls, one fashionably thin, the other simply badly fed. She wanted Sophie's descriptions of excess: cakes and puddings as rich and unsuitable as the decor of Mrs. Spencer's bathroom.

"Did you get breakfast in bed?" she asked. "You didn't say in your letter—"

"There were a few things I didn't say in my letter. I wasn't quite sure how secure the post was."

Molly raised her eyebrows in inquiry and pleasurable anticipation.

"If it weren't for the electric blanket and wine at dinner, it would never have happened. David'd been pleading with me to go to bed with him and sulking when I wouldn't and—well, he came into my room after everyone was in bed and tried to get into my bed. I wouldn't let him and we were arguing in whispers and then we heard a creak outside the door and I got the giggles and David put his hand over my mouth. I bit him and he got cross and in the end—it'd never have happened in a cold bedroom, I can promise you that."

"You mean—"

"Yes."

"Well?"

"Well, what?"

"Well, go on, what was it like?"

"You're much too young to—"

"No, I'm not. It's all they ever talk about at school."

90

"It's not all it's cracked up to be. Blood all over the sheets and so forth. David didn't really know what he was doing. And, would you believe it, Mrs. Spencer—she's called Angela—knew about the sheets the next morning. Probably smelled the blood like a shark. Either that or she was snooping around my room, checking up on the maid. Or me. Who can say, except you can be sure it had nothing to do with hospitality."

"Golly!" Molly said. "What happened then?"

"There was a godawful row, and lunch was a tad chilly. I think she even extracted some kind of bogus promise from David that we wouldn't do it again until after we were married. Which was fine by me."

"How did you get through the rest of the weekend?"

Sophie shrugged.

"I could have cared less." Her face broke into a smile and she laughed. "I had the hell of a time, though, writing my bread-and-butter letter when I got back to London."

"But you do love him. David?" Molly, encouraged by Sophie's face relaxed in laughter, forced herself to ask.

"Of course. It's just that—it hurt, and it was so, well, messy."

Molly believed that Sophie was fond of David, maybe even loved him. But she knew now that she could not, in turn, confide in Sophie, her guide to the adult world. She, Molly, already knew more of passion and desire than Sophie ever would.

April 1960

MOLLY WASN'T ANY good at games. She was tentative, awkward, and uncoordinated and it maddened her. Cynthia Sweeney was athletic but, in her words, "bloody minded." Cynthia gloried in her disdain for the entire Irish Protestant educational system. Her father was English, part of "the flight from Moscow," as the Anglo-Irish described the new wave of rich English immigrants who had arrived during the first years of the postwar Labour government.

As the weather grew colder, Molly became adept at finding

91

ways to avoid the playing fields. It was easier than she had imagined. The games mistress had no interest in enforcing the presence of girls who might not someday play for Kingstown House on the first eleven. The school had such an investment in denying the sexual maturation of the girls that all references to menstruation were oblique. Any girl who had the wit to debit her account two shillings and eleven pence in the nurse's book, denoting the purchase of a package of sanitary towels, could, if she so wished, instead of playing hockey in the drizzling rain, stretch out on her dormitory bed and peruse a well-thumbed copy of *Woman's Own*.

Molly was thin. Her breasts were small, and she had not yet started to menstruate. Uncharacteristically turning this source of shame to her advantage, Molly pleaded cramps when she could not face an afternoon on the playing fields. Cynthia did not always bother to make up an excuse. She merely failed to show up, taking pleasure in the general reluctance to confront her. Eventually, inevitably, the two girls were detailed to take a walk together. Molly overcame her initial reaction—to change clothes quickly and make for the hockey field—and instead put on her navy-blue overcoat and the maddening little Juliet cap that was meant to sit on the crown of her head, but only did so if anchored with hair clips.

Cynthia was one of two girls who, although they were in the sixth form, were not prefects. Taking a perverse pleasure in her struggle with authority, Cynthia refused to accept any of the compromises that would have allowed her the privileges of the other girls in her form. She seemed to take no pleasure in the admiration she elicited from many of the younger girls, but she was, nevertheless, a disruptive presence.

The first walk upon which Molly and Cynthia were sent was intended to be, in differing ways, punitive to both girls. They walked down the graveled avenue in silence. It was not Molly's place to speak first. They left the school grounds and turned into the public road. Cynthia casually took her cap from her head and stuffed it into a pocket. She unbuttoned her overcoat, letting it hang from her broad, thin shoulders. Molly, after a moment, unclipped her own cap. It made an unsightly bulge in her pocket. Cynthia's seemed to have been subsumed into the fabric of her coat.

"It's not that I'm bad at hockey, you know," Cynthia said.

Molly sighed with relief. It had seemed possible that the entire walk might have taken place in excruciating, unbroken silence.

"I'm pretty good at games." Cynthia continued, "They could use me on the first eleven, and they know it. But I'm not interested in playing games unless I can take a hot bath afterward. Every time I play."

Molly caught her breath; the idea was revolutionary.

The school had been a large, suburban, late Victorian house. It might have been built for a prosperous merchant or for a senior English naval officer stationed at Kingstown, as Dunlaoghaire had been called for the hundred years prior to Irish independence. The house had been enlarged, and an ugly wing had been jerry-built, exposed to the cold on three sides. There was a large dormitory on each floor; each dormitory had one lavatory and one bathroom. The old part of the house contained only two bathrooms. Hot water was limited, and washing took place at a row of basins filled with tepid water carried upstairs each morning from the basement. The emphasis on modesty made this ablution even less efficient than such an unsatisfactory arrangement would otherwise be. Baths were allocated, fifteen minutes apart, twice a week. Sometimes the scheduled time necessitating a leave from the evening study hall. Each girl was allowed to wash her hair on alternate Saturdays, drying it as best she could in front of dimly glowing, heavily banked coal fires. While bathing at Fern Hill and Dromore had always been an uncomfortable and chilly experience, Molly suffered now from the feeling of rarely being quite clean.

"I often take the opportunity to have a nice long soak in the afternoons. I like to lie there and listen to the shouts and whistles from the playing field."

"But if you were caught—"

"Then what?"

Molly was silent. She nodded slightly to herself as she realized how Cynthia managed to avoid the greasy hair and spotty complexion of the other girls.

"Then what?" Cynthia repeated. "What would they do? Expel me? For taking a bath? I don't think so. I'd get a dorm mark or have to sign Biddy's book. They might write to my parents." She laughed. "That'd be a mistake."

"I didn't think—"

"Exactly." For a moment Cynthia sounded depressingly like one of the staff. "That's what they count on. If you got in the habit of asking, 'So what?' to everything, you'd soon see what was important and what wasn't."

At the end of the road, not glancing to right or to left, Cynthia turned into a small sweet shop. Going into a shop was a crime even more heinous than taking off one's school cap. Not only was shopping forbidden, but the girls were not allowed to have cash. Things were happening fast. Molly tried to assess them in light of Cynthia's attitude. An attitude that made all of Molly's previously accepted ideas due for reassessment. Cynthia, as the senior girl, was in charge and responsible for Molly. Molly watched as Cynthia casually bought a chocolate bar. After slightly too long a hesitation, Cynthia broke off two squares of chocolate, retaining six for herself, and handed them to Molly.

"Consider yourself lucky to get anything. I come from the most selfish family in Ireland."

"Thanks awfully," Molly said, nibbling the chocolate, making it last. She was often hungry. "If we're caught shopping, so what?"

"Exactly."

"There'd be an awful row, and we'd have to go for walks in the junior school crocodile."

Since Molly had arrived at Kingstown House as a senior, she had never had to walk, one of a pair, with the younger girls. It was hard to imagine Cynthia as part of a pedigerous, navy blue, serpentine undulating through the suburban streets of Dunlaoghaire. Perhaps the younger Cynthia had avoided walks in the same cavalier manner in which she now eschewed organized games.

94

"Which would be a dreadful bore, but still worth the risk."

"I'm bad at games, so what?"

"You give up a certain amount in the way of popularity. On the other hand, you don't get muscular calves. I saw Meryl de Courcy running up the front stairs using her hands. Being captain of the hockey team may be worth less in the real world than she imagines. On the other hand"—and Cynthia looked at Molly severely—"there's no point in being wet on general principle."

"Yes, I can see that," Molly said doubtfully, some of her confidence already seeping away. "What about honor? We're on our honor not to go into shops."

"Says who? Honor's a bigger word than that. I'll be the one to decide what I'm on my honor for. Probably nothing that makes a third-rate school cheaper to run."

"Where do you want to go?"

"When?"

"Now."

Molly hoped that Cynthia would choose to walk down the steep hill and along the pier at Dunlaoghaire. The breaking waves and the smell of the sea reminded Molly of Sunday afternoons with Tibby. Or that they take a less populated route and walk to the Martello Tower. Although most people Molly knew could name Joyce as the author of *Ulysses*, *Ulysses* was banned in Ireland, but even the possibility of pornography did not stimulate an Anglo-Irish interest in his other work. No one Molly knew had read anything by him.

"I don't know about you, but I'm planing to post a letter, go back to school through the side gate, and catch up on my rest."

In one sentence Cynthia had stated her intention to break three other school rules. Snubbed, but with her admiration increasing by the minute, Molly silently followed her fascinating new acquaintance—she had wit enough not to assume friendship—to the end of the road and watched her take a letter, probably not addressed to her parents or any other member of the most selfish family in Ireland, and slip it into the post box set into the wall. The plate on the front of the post box bore a crown and the letters *V.R.*, the letters rounded by many coats of green paint.

THE NEXT TWO afternoons, despite a cold wind and intermittent rain, Molly played hockey. She wanted some time before another outing with Cynthia. Her instinct told her that Cynthia was at her core treacherous and anarchic and that even were a subservient friendship possible, a high price would be paid for it. Molly was beguiled but wary.

Each morning, during the moments between the wake-up bell and getting out of bed, Molly would chart the day ahead of her. She would try to find something to which she looked forward. Sunday, unless one was a communicant, there was an extra hour in bed. Tuesday, a riding lesson in the afternoon. It was her favorite day. Thursday, the curate came to lunch and roast pork and stuffing were served. Friday, school fruit was delivered. Like the pork on Thursdays, school fruit was not only a treat but a necessity. Molly's revulsion to most of the meals served caused her, although she was still growing, to lose weight each term. The fruit and riding lessons, subscribed to without discussion by Belinda and Miles, filled her with inarticulate gratitude.

Molly would then consider the darker moments of each day and prepare herself for them. Thursdays apart, lunch was a constant source of anxiety. The evening meal was merely unappetizing—macaroni and cheese or Russian salad—but lunch was frequently a meal that Molly knew herself unable to eat. As many as three times a week, the meal would be roast beef, boiled cabbage, and boiled potatoes. Shepherd's pie, made from the leftovers of the previous day, would also be served. Although she did not like shepherd's pie, Molly could eat some of it. The portions of shepherd's pie were offered in order of seniority. Often several of the senior girls at the table refused the pie, and Molly would find herself with a meal she could eat. Her fear was that one day she would be given the fatty, tough, overcooked beef, the gray potatoes, and the watery, dirty cabbage, and the mistress at the head of the table would insist that she eat it. Molly knew that even were she able to put a forkful of the repulsive food into her mouth, she would not be able to swallow it. Three days after her walk with Cynthia, Molly came face to face with her fear.

Miss Simpson taught Form II and tended to treat all the girls, regardless of seniority, as though they were the same age as her pupils. Like all the women who taught at Kingstown House, teaching was neither a vocation nor a choice. For most of them, something had gone wrong in their lives. More than one had been the daughter chosen to stay home and care for her parents; the parents now dead, she sought shelter and a minimal salary at a school where her lot was only marginally more comfortable than that of her pupils and her future vastly less hopeful. Miss Simpson had the added humiliation of a hormonal imbalance. Her voice was deep, her features craggy, and hairs, stiff and unchecked, grew from her chin. Each day she wore the same tweed suit—a light sprinkling of chalk dust on her right sleeve— wrinkled lisle stockings, and laced-up shoes. Startled at first, the girls soon got used to Miss Simpson. The school staff was for them a series of temporarily powerful, eccentric characters and unexplained rules. Experience had taught them that Miss Simpson could rarely be appealed to, as could some of the younger teachers who still hoped for a different life. Miss Simpson had had no luck since the day she was born.

Each week the girls sat at different tables. That week Miss Simpson sat at the head of Molly's table. Molly had eaten shepherd's pie twice that week. Thursday she had breezed through with two helpings of the curate's special lunch. Friday, the last day to dread, she found herself fiddling with a particularly unappetizing plate of food, aware that Miss Simpson was watching her.

"Eat your lunch, Molly." Miss Simpson's deep voice suggested that she expected to be obeyed without hesitation. Molly glanced down at her plate and cut a potato in half. It was not quite cooked, and the center was hard and damp.

"Stop playing with your food. Everyone else has finished."

"I'm not hungry, Miss Simpson," Molly said in a small voice.

It was not an adequate excuse, but she knew herself unable to eat the food on her plate.

"Don't be ridiculous. You're a growing girl. Eat your lunch. Now."

The table had become silent. Molly could feel tears welling in her eyes. She simultaneously tried to employ every method that had ever been even partially successful in warding off tears. She bit the inside of her lip. She counted silently and fixed her gaze on one of the prints of Flemish interiors on the dining room wall. A small metal insert in the bottom of each black frame bore the name of the former pupil who had donated it.

"Molly, I'm waiting."

Molly concentrated on the small dog in a van Eyck reproduction. She took a very deep breath. Sometimes, not often, that helped.

"Very well." Miss Simpson's unimaginative eyes were cold. "You will stay here until you eat your lunch. Daphne, please clear everybody's plate except Molly's."

The junior girl at the end of the table, whose turn it was to clear the table, started to take the plates out of the dining room. Another girl brought bowls of steamed pudding with yellow custard. Molly remained silent.

"I'm not about to allow you to waste good food," Miss Simpson said. "It's good enough for the rest of us. I don't know what's so special about you."

Molly tried to imagine how it could end. She imagined herself sitting all afternoon in the dining room, her untouched plate in front of her. When the other girls returned after games for tea, she would still be there. What would happen then? She did not imagine that Miss Simpson would relent, but she was not, by now, able to eat even one mouthful of potato.

"I can't eat it," she said, her voice shaking.

"I beg your pardon?"

Molly was silent, unable to speak without sobbing. She wished there were someone to tell her what to do. Sophie would have been her first choice, but Sophie would never have found herself in a situation like this. But if she had, what would she have done? Cynthia would know, of course. Cynthia would have asked herself, "So what?"

Molly took another deep breath and, fairly sure that her voice would not break, said, "I can't eat it." Her voice sounded ridiculously high; she paused and took another breath. "I won't and you can't make me."

There was the sound of a sharply inhaled breath. One of the younger girls allowed her mouth to drop open. The girls at the nearest table had fallen silent, listening. Molly realized that Miss Simpson was out of her depth. For the first time in her life, Molly sensed the joy of power.

Suddenly aware that she still held her knife and fork, she placed them, very deliberately, side by side in the center of her plate. She put her hands in her lap.

"We'll see about that." Miss Simpson had angry red blotches on her sallow, dry cheeks. "As soon as lunch is over you will go to the headmistress's study. I'm going to recommend that she write to your parents."

Molly paused to savor her moment of triumph.

"I'll be interested to see just how she goes about that," she said.

May 1960

"I'M AFRAID THERE'S been a bit of trouble at school."

Molly would have been more proud of herself if she had been able to introduce the subject before Sunday lunch at the Kildare Street Club had reached the cheese-and-biscuit stage.

"Oh?" Miles seemed unsure whether he was listening to a confession or being offered a minor item of school gossip. His mild confusion was understandable; Molly had never been in trouble before.

"I couldn't eat my lunch."

Miles waited, as he often did when Belinda started to tell him something, reasonably sure that with a little additional information, he would understand what she was telling him.

"I couldn't eat my lunch, and they told me—at least Miss Simpson told me—that I had to."

"That doesn't sound so terrible. You need to eat, Molly. You're a growing girl."

"Uncle Miles, I couldn't. It was disgusting."

"I see." Miles paused.

Molly knew that he was giving her his full attention, even though his thoughts had before been far away. He seemed quietly, deeply sad. "Well, there doesn't seem to be anything wrong with your appetite now."

Molly hesitated.

"The other girls, do they eat the food?" Miles asked.

"Well, yes, but they don't like it much."

"Nobody likes school food."

Molly was silent.

"Why do you think you're the only one who won't—can't eat it?"

Molly had given this question much thought, and she had not come up with an answer. She hesitated again.

"I'm not like the rest of them." She smiled, her smile was not to soften her answer but an acknowledgment that she knew how she sounded and meant what she said.

Miles chewed silently for a moment, then sighed. "No, you're not, are you? And nor is Sophie."

Molly knew that now was the moment to say that she was unhappy at school, that she was learning nothing, and that she wanted to leave. But Miles seemed so sad, she said nothing. It seemed more decent for her to go directly to Belinda.

"Well, I'm glad you sorted it out. Belinda's got a lot on her mind at present. I know you don't want to worry her."

Molly assumed that Miles's distracted unhappiness and whatever it was that Belinda had on her mind pertained to Sophie. She wondered what it might be without considering, for even a moment, asking Miles.

"Sophie wants to get married. Aunt Belinda and I are worried about it."

Molly looked sympathetic, assuming there was more to come. Sophie's wish to marry was not a new development.

"She wants to get married this summer."

Molly understood Miles's disquiet at Sophie's wishes, but she was puzzled by his helplessness. She had the impression that Belinda, for whom she thought helplessness an alien state, was as distressed as Miles.

Molly ate tiny forksful of chocolate cake, spinning out the pleasure, and wondered why Miles, or, rather, Belinda, didn't just tell Sophie that she would have to wait. Sophie wouldn't be eighteen until the end of the summer. Why, for that matter (this was probably Molly's first conscious rebellious thought), should she allow Miles to be so preoccupied with Sophie's whim that she should be unable to tell him how unhappy she was at school? She wanted to ask his help in finishing her education somewhere else. To exchange misery for quiet unhappiness.

"I don't know anything against the young man, of course, but I wish I liked his family better."

Molly wished that Sophie liked David better than Sophie seemed to, but she was glad that Miles had not broached that particular aspect. She wondered if he'd even noticed.

"But Sophie isn't marrying his family."

"She is, to some extent. Her children will be half his blood. If she were a thoroughbred mare you wouldn't, ah, marry her to a cart horse."

Molly nodded.

"Would you?" he asked, seeming to need more confirmation that she was following his argument.

"No, but Sophie probably isn't planning to race her children."

Miles looked startled. He wasn't used to flippancy from Molly. Molly was even more startled that Miles was perhaps more open to the theories of Darwin than had been her own father.

"Nowadays, people tend to laugh at the English upper classes."

Molly allowed Miles's statement to go unchallenged. Although she had never heard the class system questioned, let alone considered an object of hilarity, she supposed the English post-war Labour government might have seemed, to Miles, a jocular version of the guillotine and tumbrels.

"But," Miles continued, "if you look at history, it works. It's no accident that Winston Churchill is a descendent of the Duke of Marlborough."

"Do you think that that was breeding or upbringing?"

"The two go together, that's the point. It's not just the way the original Duke of Marlborough was brought up, it's also the way Winston Churchill was brought up and all the generations in between. Leadership. Privilege and responsibility. These ideas work. That's why the idea of the aristocracy has lasted."

"But don't some of the men who work at Dromore live by the same ideals?"

"Yes, that's the same thing," Miles said. "When young Fagan took over from his father as vet, I thought that he'd probably inherited his father's touch with animals. I knew that he'd be gentle with the dogs and see a horse as a living creature and not as a livestock investment. The same way that I know that Bridie will give Belinda's dog a real walk if we are away and not help herself to the best sherry—because her mother worked for my mother and married the gardener, and they're both decent people."

"And you don't think that David—or his family—?"

"I don't know. I'd be happier to see my daughter married to someone I could be sure would do the right thing."

Molly knew, at that moment, that Miles would have been far happier to see Sophie married to Desmond than to the richer, more powerful, and more expensively educated David. She thought that Miles, whom she loved but knew to be slightly ridiculous, would understand the value she gave Desmond. That he, Miles, understood the courage it took to continue in the life and traditions of the already almost extinct Anglo-Irish. That what seemed to others passive and unimaginative in Desmond's gentleman farmer existence was, to Miles, duty uncomplainingly performed. Rather like her father's life, she thought, and remembered Tibby entertaining her with a description of

Desmond's grandfather riding the camel, only a couple of hours before he shot himself.

"Like the time Daddy ran over the cat in the lane and it wasn't dead and he got out of the car and got scratched before he could wring its neck?"

"Exactly."

"And didn't say anything to Mummy when we got home?"

Miles nodded. Molly wondered how she knew or remembered that Tibby had spared Morag the details of the incident. She certainly hadn't consciously remembered the fact until she had, without premeditation, told Miles.

"Of course, it doesn't always work that way. Every family has its poor characters and its way of dealing with them—"

"Like Uncle Jack being sent to shoulder the white man's burden?"

"The British Empire was, if not built, maintained by the sacrifices of younger sons."

Molly knew better than to press the Uncle Jack joke and much better than to suggest that the involuntary sacrifices of the colonized might have been greater even than those of the younger sons. Like many of her generation, the first to be born in an Ireland not under British rule—born after the post boxes embossed with the British crown had been painted green—Molly's loyalties were to her country *as opposed* to England. Miles and Tibby thought differently; their loyalties were to Ireland *and* to England. There were, of course, a portion of the Anglo-Irish who thought of themselves as English and of the Irish as an ungrateful, colonized race. Sophie was the only example that Molly knew of a fourth category. She wished to be free of the sinking ship of her Anglo-Irish destiny and to throw in her lot with the unsubtle security of an England where she imagined the trains ran on time and where there was plenty of cash and hot water.

THE POST WAS delivered at lunchtime. During the second half of the meal, a prefect would go from table to table distributing let-

103

ters, usually from home but with a sprinkling of missives from grandmothers and an occasional pen pal. As with all things at Kingstown House, there was a strict standard of what was correct. A letter a week was the norm, a second letter made a girl envied in an admiring sort of a way. Three or even four suggested very clearly that the girl in question was "wet" and her mother probably the one who had made her that way. One unfortunate girl had a father who, when he needed to convey a single piece of information—such as on which Sunday he would take her out—would send a postcard. The general feeling was that he should have spent the extra penny on the stamp for a letter and have added an item of news and a more affectionate salutation. The girl was pitied, her father despised.

While the prefect moved from table to table—there were never so many letters that sorting was necessary, and on rare occasions she would return to a table with a second letter for someone who was already reading one—Molly would watch her. Not openly, not longingly like Belinda's dog, but out of the corner of her eye, feigning indifference.

It had been two weeks since Miss Simpson had ordered Molly to eat her lunch. There had, mysteriously, been no repercussions. Miss Simpson ignored Molly, and the rest of the staff appeared ignorant of what had happened, although Molly knew that even if Miss Simpson had not reported her defeat at Molly's hands, there was no one in the whole school who had not discussed the incident at length. No one who wasn't waiting to see what would happen next.

This notoriety was not comfortable for Molly. She still had no friend at school with whom she could talk, and she lived in fear of some new confrontation. It seemed unlikely that the headmistress would wish or could afford to have an act of defiance perpetrated with impunity. The other girls watched her every move, hoping that Molly might become a Joan of Arc and lead them to anarchic freedom, and she missed the time when she had felt herself to be invisible.

She went out of her way not to court trouble. She played

hockey or lacrosse every afternoon it did not rain and joined, un-happily, the Irish dancing in the gymnasium on wet afternoons. She was aware that Cynthia watched to see if Molly planned to usurp her power. For want of a better plan, Molly kept her head down and longed for some new drama to take the focus away from her.

Two younger girls at the table were already reading letters from home, calling out news that might interest or stimulate the envy of friends, when the prefect's hand, bearing a letter with an English stamp, reached over Molly's shoulder. A letter from So-phie. Molly took the letter and felt it between two fingers, try-ing to gauge how long it was. She did not open it, saving it for a moment when she would be alone to read it.

"Our cat's having kittens, and Mummy says I can pick one out for my own."

"Lucky dog."

At another table the headmistress rose to her feet, and the roomful of girls followed suit, chairs and benches making a scrap-ing sound as they were pushed away from tables as the girls stood to say grace.

"For what we have received, may the Lord make us truly thankful."

Miss Bowers, who had once played hockey for Ireland, strode out of the dining room. Handsome rather than elegant, in one of her two suits, a silk blouse with a cameo brooch at the neck. Nylon stockings. Flat-heeled shoes whose polished finish would have satisfied any military standard. Miss Bowers's room was at the top of the front stairs. No girl had ever seen inside. Molly wondered what Miss Bowers did there to fill the hours between dinner and breakfast. Molly often paused for a moment when passing to listen for the sound of a wireless or conversation or the polishing of shoes, but it was so quiet, it seemed as though Miss Bowers ceased to exist as soon she closed the door behind her.

Lack of information did nothing to curb speculation among the girls about their headmistress's private life. Her only friends seemed to be a middle-aged couple named Flanagan. It was on

105

them, faute de mieux, that myth was built. The Flanagans happened to be acquaintances of the parents of a girl, no longer at Kingstown House, who had divulged that Mr. and Mrs. Flanagan's Christian names were Dennis and Noreen. Even the most junior girl at Kingstown House referred to Miss Bowers's friends as Dennis and Noreen.

The myth was a primitive one, not based on any evidence and with complete disregard for the age and lack of physical charm of any of the protagonists. The girls chose to believe that Miss Bowers and Noreen had been best friends. Dennis had once been engaged to Miss Bowers but had fallen in love with Noreen. After a period of agonizing soul-searching, he had confessed to Miss Bowers and married Noreen. All three remained close friends, although a high price had been paid for the friendship. The only variation in the myth was the degree to which Dennis regretted his choice. Many of the girls considered the story to be fact.

Molly had, one Sunday morning in the car on the way to church, described to Belinda and Miles the painful, passionate life of her headmistress. To Molly's surprise, Belinda had laughed, remarking that she would have thought Noreen was more Miss Bowers's speed. A startled glance from Miles was followed by a brief silence and a change of subject. Molly gave much thought to what Belinda had said. She never discussed it with a fellow pupil. It did, however, suggest a flaw in one of the girls' basic beliefs: that every teacher, or, for that matter, woman without a man, was thus other than by choice. Belinda's irresponsible remark also cast light on the mysterious emphasis on some school rules: no girl was allowed to visit a dormitory other than her own, close friendships were discouraged, and dancing was monitored. The latter somewhat complicated by the lack of alternative partners who would perforce have had to be male and even more threatening, although in a more easily verbalized way. During her time at Kingstown House, Molly had never seen any evidence of a friendship even potentially unhealthy ("unhealthy" being the euphemism for overemotional or lesbian). Thanks to

106

Belinda, she now understood the watchful preoccupation of the staff.

A short interval followed lunch before the girls were expected on the playing fields. This half hour devoid of scheduled activity was used by the girls to change into games clothes and to digest their heavy lunch. Molly used the time to go outside to read her letter. She waited until she was seated on a bench under a chestnut tree to open the envelope. The paper was thick and expensive, and Sophie's handwriting large. The short letter covered both sides of two sheets of paper.

Dearest Molly,

I am getting married in July, and I want you to be a bridesmaid. David's dreary sister seems to insist on being the other, but I have chosen a shade of pale orange—light and rich like a ripe orange mixed with cream—that will look super on you but will make Priscilla look as though she's in the last moments of some not quite respectable disease.

The wedding is going to be on the island, and Daddy will pull out all the stops. Lots of people from England. David's ghastly family, of course, millions of them, but lots of fun new friends. I offered not to wear white to tease Angela (she asked me to call her "Mother" like some kind of demented nun, ignoring the fact that I have a perfectly good mother of my own. She'll go on being Mrs. Spencer right up to the moment she asks me to call her Angela and maybe, if I'm feeling my oats, a little after), but actually I'm going to have the most divine dress. A girl who used to be a deb and makes madly expensive things is designing it.

Longing to see you, tons of love,

Sophie

P.S. If you hate the idea of orange, we could do something else—green or dark blue, which would look even better on you and really deal a low blow to Priscilla. Bit odd for a wedding but I hate to miss a chance to *épater la bourgeoisie*.

Molly read the letter twice. Although excited by its contents, she wished that since Sophie had gone to the trouble to write a letter and had organized herself enough to find the address, stick on a stamp, and post it, she had taken a little more time and explained how she had so quickly broken down the objection by both families to an early marriage.

There was no pocket in Molly's gym slip, and she held her letter in her hand as she started back to change for games. To return to her dormitory, beneath whose windows she now passed, it was necessary, if she were to obey the rules, to travel the length of the building, ascend the stairs, and return the same distance along an upstairs corridor. The front stairs, the direct route to her dormitory, were forbidden to anyone other than staff and prefects. No reason was given for this rule. Perhaps it had to do with the preservation of the stair carpet, the permitted route being covered with well-worn linoleum. Perhaps to create an artificial privilege for those permitted to ascend to the upper floor by this both more aesthetically pleasing and direct route. No punishment was given if the rule was broken, although there was always the possibility that Miss Bowers would step out of her study and find a girl halfway up the stairs, frozen like a rabbit. The girl would then, as the headmistress looked on, have to retrace her steps, scurry past Miss Bowers, and continue her journey by the legal route.

"Molly."

The voice was cool, interrogatory, ironic. Molly turned. Cynthia came out of the garden, which lay between the school and the playing fields. Again, except for prefects, the girls were forbidden to take a shortcut through the garden. Molly imagined that the reason for this rule—apart from the petty joy of curtailing liberty—was to prevent the girls from helping themselves at the end of the summer term to the fruit from the red currant bushes that were planted on both sides of the path. Although many girls, late for games, ran through the garden, few were confident enough to pick the currants.

Cynthia emerged from the garden, in her hand a small bunch of half-grown, slightly muddy carrots. After a moment's hesitation, similar to the pause before she had given Molly a share of the chocolate during their walk, Cynthia held out her hand. Molly shook her head. While the headmistress's door merely opened onto the foot of the front stairs, her window looked out onto the garden. She had lacked the money to buy chocolate but she could, by taking a risk identical to the one Cynthia had just taken, pick her own carrots.

"Shepherd's pie and tapioca didn't quite do it for me." Cynthia was one of the few girls who didn't call the milk pudding "frog's eyes." "I thought I'd take matters into my own hands. What are you doing?"

Molly, still excited by her letter, held it up to show Cynthia. "My cousin, Sophie—I think I told you about her—she's getting married in July, and I'm going to be a bridesmaid."

Cynthia looked at her sharply. It was as though she was waiting for Molly to complete a thought.

"This came as a complete surprise to you?"

"Yes, Sophie just wrote. From London."

"She's having a baby, then, is she?"

Molly was silent. Although Cynthia's pronouncement seemed unthinkable, she could not find another explanation for the dramatically imminent marriage. There was no one she could ask, and, for the first time, more than a week went by without a letter from either Miles or Belinda.

109

*A*DELE HASSARD HAD two widowed sisters, and it was with these women, her great-aunts, that Sophie lived in London. Their flat was in one of the two buildings close to and similar in architectural intent to the Albert Hall. Although they lived halfway between Knightsbridge and Kensington High Street, the sisters made few concessions to the time or the place in which they lived. Their apartment, unusually large with a generous hallway and a wide corridor, had the atmosphere, as well as the furnishings, of an Edwardian country house.

One sister was rich and the other wasn't. Charlotte had married well, and she had the better bedroom and more expensive clothes. Isabel, the beauty, had married for love and been left a widow at thirty. Both sisters had been widowed young, and each was the mother of an attentive and dutiful son. Charlotte, the younger, had a married daughter who lived in Kenya. Sophie thought that both women must have had opportunities to marry again and had chosen not to. She also thought that they were probably happy. Dignity and elegance, rather than luxury, embodied the Edwardian atmosphere of their flat. High standards and a relentless vigilance toward minor self-indulgence or laziness kept them from "letting the side down."

Every day the sisters sat down to breakfast, hair pinned up, faces lightly powdered, each wearing a black dress—on Charlotte's bodice, a diamond brooch; on Isabel's, in smaller stones, the crest of her late husband's regiment. At the end of the ten o'clock evening news, Charlotte rose and turned off the wireless (to call the wireless a "radio" would be an example of letting the side down), and the two women made their way along the corridor to the kitchen for their bedtime cups of Ovaltine. It would have been as unthinkable for one of them to appear at breakfast in her dressing gown as it would have been to sit listening apathetically to the program that followed the news or to have left the cups for their daily maid to wash the following morning.

Charlotte and Isabel had been excited by the idea of Sophie living with them while she attended the Constance Spry Finishing School. They anticipated with pleasure the addition of a young girl at breakfast and dinner and had, after discussion, gone to some trouble to make the guest room less a temporary resting place for a friend up from the country and spending the night and more a bedroom suitable for a girl Sophie's age. Without discussing it, the sisters worried about social life and chaperones, looking closely at photographs in the newspapers of young girls of good families smoking cigarettes in nightclubs with young men. The old ladies were prepared for Sophie to go out sometimes with her friends and expected her to visit the Spencers on the weekend, either to stay (or "stop" as they would have put it) or to eat Sunday lunch. They were ready to take a tactfully firm line about makeup and church attendance and wondered if Belinda would provide guidelines on more complicated issues. These issues they imagined would only pertain to where and when Sophie saw David.

Almost immediately the great-aunts became aware that life with Sophie would not be as simple as they had anticipated. The first problem to manifest itself was Sophie's attendance record at Constance Spry. As soon as Sophie told them of her not-yet-official engagement, she to all intents and purposes ceased going to the school. Her position, when questioned, was that she was about to be married. Charlotte pointed out that the finishing

111

school, with its classes in cooking, flower arrangement, and social skills, was surely the perfect place to prepare for married life.
Sophie dismissed this argument with her soon to become familiar, "Oh, Aunt Charlotte . . ."

Isabel, separately, and after a few days' interval, did no better.
Sophie offered her an "Oh, Aunt Isabel . . ." and some broken
sentences in which the phrases "hopelessly boring," "quite common," and "utterly vulgar and stupid" were repeated several
times. Retiring to confer, neither sister heard Sophie leave the
flat. She returned just before lunchtime, her hair shining and
with a little color in her cheeks. She said she had been to the
hairdressers in Knightsbridge and had walked home through the
park. She brought the women a bunch of violets, the flowers surrounded by dark green leaves and firmly tied with raffia. She
had bought them from the swollen old man who sold them from
a doorway close to the Knightsbridge underground station. After
she had paid for them, he had tried to kiss her. She waved away
her great-aunts' outrage with the explanation: "He'd been drinking; I could smell it on his breath."

She was sweet, affectionate, and entertaining during lunch,
and Charlotte and Isabel, who disapproved of charm when they
recognized it, fell once again under her spell.

Soon, without anyone saying anything more, finishing school
was forgotten as the preparations for Sophie's wedding became
occupation enough. Although the wedding was to take place at
Dromore, there was plenty to do in London. The wedding was
being arranged on an inconveniently brief schedule. Sophie's
wedding dress had to be made. The material for Molly's dress and
those of the two smaller bridesmaids had to be bought and sent
to Ireland in the suitcase of a reliable, geographically suitable
friend, together with a pattern to ensure that Molly and David's
sister, Priscilla, would look somewhat the same. There were guest
lists to be drawn up and negotiations about who should be edited
from them. Sophie registered her bridal list at Harrods, and in
Dublin at Brown, Thomas. There were additional complications
about what could be safely and inexpensively transported back to

London after the wedding and what gifts, if any, could be sent from London to be on display at Dromore. Sophie sometimes joined the bickering and discussion and at other times seemed too bored to speak. There was the engagement photograph for the front page of the *Tatler* and a decision as to how Sophie would be dressed. Should she wear the Hassard pearls? Or a not quite beautiful necklace that David had bought her at Asprey's? Was it even suitable for her to wear a necklace that was intended for a wife before she was actually married?

"Typical," Sophie remarked to her great-aunts at dinner the night before she was to be photographed. "The Spencers think jewelry is something you *buy*. They're immensely proud of a stockbroker friend of Mr. Spencer's who *bought* a castle in Ireland. I told them it doesn't count if you buy it. David was furious and beastly to me afterward. He thinks that if his parents don't like me, they won't give us that divine house as a wedding present."

Charlotte and Isabel, speechless and disapproving, noticed that Sophie seemed more animated than she had been in a week.

The following morning Isabel came into the drawing room, where she expected to find her sister reading the *Times* or the *Telegraph;* taking two newspapers was an extravagance of Charlotte's, which Isabel enjoyed while retaining the additional pleasure of mild disapproval. Instead, she found Charlotte standing at the window.

"Isabel, do come and look."

On the wide steps behind the Albert Hall a photographer was taking a photograph of a beautiful young woman wearing a little black dress and what appeared to be a great deal of diamond jewelry. An assistant held a board covered with a metallic substance that reflected the dim sunlight onto the model. Every now and then, at the photographer's instruction, another young woman stepped forward with a hairbrush to rearrange the hair of the lightly clad young woman in order to show the long, dangling earrings to a greater advantage.

"I wonder she isn't cold," Charlotte said. Her sister silently agreed with Charlotte's disapproval of the girl's neckline. A revealing décolletage, like scent, would have been acceptable after dark.

"It's for a magazine."

Both sisters stood watching for some time, deeply interested. In the evening, they often watched the crowd entering the Albert Hall, and, with greater fascination and a kind of admiration, they watched the queues form, sometimes the night before, when tickets for a particularly popular concert were to be sold. Often they would speculate about the small group, largely students, who would arrive with camp seats and sleeping bags and wonder at the camaraderie that seemed to grow from the shared passion of young people who would so cheerfully spend a night on the pavement in order to buy tickets to listen to classical music. During the more than twenty years they had lived in Albert Court, neither of the sisters had attended a concert at the Albert Hall. They were not particularly fond of music, and both sisters were now deaf—Charlotte wore a hearing aid, and Isabel missed a good deal of what was said to her—but that was only part of the reason. Sophie had the impression that the sisters had not been to the theater for some years before the evening, her first week in London, when they had taken her as a special treat to *The Mousetrap.* They had been vague about their tickets and confused by the programs and intermission. Charlotte had undertipped the taxi driver who drove them home.

"I took Sophie a cup of tea," Isabel said to her sister, her tone a little defensive. "She's not feeling well."

"Again? Should we send for Clark?" Neither sister would have stayed in bed or, for that matter, allowed someone to bring them a cup of tea there, were she not ill enough to warrant a visit from the doctor.

"I asked her. She said no, she'll get up soon."

Sophie worried her great-aunts. In varying degrees, they attempted to discuss their concerns and her perceived shortcomings. For some of these they neither had the wish nor the ability (nor even, sometimes, the vocabulary) to communicate their feelings. The first time Sophie did not appear at breakfast had elicited chilly disapproval. When Sophie slept through the breakfast hour and rose too late to go to her classes, they were a bit chillier. Now that she didn't get up for breakfast at all, sometimes feeling sick in the mornings, she said, the old ladies had nothing to say. Despite their lifelong intimacy, conversation between them had always been correct and discreet, and neither, from superstition as well as a reluctance to be the one to voice a slanderous thought, would be the first to say she thought Sophie was pregnant.

Both sisters dreaded the inevitable scandal, drama, and unhappiness that would ensue if Sophie really was pregnant. Where they differed was in their private attitudes toward how and why Sophie had attained this condition. Charlotte thought of sexual intercourse as a necessary but unpleasant duty rewarded by the privileges of marriage and the pleasure of motherhood. Isabel's brief marriage had been filled with sexual passion, and she suffered from the absence of physical love. She had not allowed herself the thought that she could enjoy similar pleasures with a subsequent husband. She might, mistakenly, have assumed that desire had been the reason that Sophie had slept with David, but Charlotte would have been baffled—and disgusted.

Seeing that Charlotte's distress was even greater than her own, Isabel said generously if somewhat dishonestly, "I think it's nerves about the wedding."

"Do you really think so?" Charlotte's plea for reassurance was shameless.

"Yes," Isabel said firmly.

Below them, the model perched on a balustrade, back arched, hands clasped over one knee. She was showing a good deal of leg, but the old ladies barely noticed her. They turned back into the room. It was time to put on their coats and take their walk to Harrods. They did it twice a week.

"YOU LOOK LIKE death warmed over," Caroline Penrose spoke as though through clenched teeth, the effect of half a dozen pins held between her lips. "Turn."

"Thank you. Thank you very much." Sophie, standing on the small, dressmaker's footstool, rotated another forty-five degrees. She felt a little giddy, and her mouth was dry.

"Hangover?"

Sophie nodded, then realized that Caroline, pinning the hem of her dress, could not see her face.

"Well, yes, a bit, you know."

A hangover was a perfect explanation for the way she looked and felt. Too bad she couldn't offer it to her great-aunts.

"Do you want anything? Alka-Seltzer? Fernet Branca?"

"Maybe a cup of tea when you've finished this bit."

Sophie hoped that Caroline would offer her a biscuit with her tea. To ask for one would cause suspicion. A cup of tea and a dry biscuit spelled morning sickness as clearly as bailiffs in the kitchen indicated insolvency.

"I assume you didn't look like this when you had your photograph taken."

"No, I didn't. I looked very nice. Jersey and pearls. You could just imagine the sensible shoes and a Labrador at my feet."

Caroline nudged her leg and Sophie shifted a few inches farther in the circle she was describing. Sophie looked down at Caroline's well-cut hair, her expensive cashmere cardigan, and her, in fact, rather sensible shoes. Aloof and evasive, Caroline was a mystery to her. She kept her friends at arm's length. They, in turn, hoped that there was some good secret in her life that she kept from them. That which was visible seemed thin and sad, although in no way pathetic. Strength of character was not at issue, but Caroline's choices and what she wanted were hard to understand. After her debutante season, Caroline, who had learned to sew at school and was good at it, took a humble, low-paying job at Hardy Amies, learning everything she was taught and a good deal more. Then she left to make to order, one at a time, beautiful and expensive dresses. Nearly always for girls she knew socially. She rarely went out and had almost never been seen dining with a man. She lived alone. Her flat was larger and more ex-

116

pensive than the shared quarters of most former debutantes, and furnished as though she intended to stay. She was a girl who either did not wish to marry or who knew that she would not.

Usually Sophie's curiosity about her friends was limited, but Caroline was an exception. During the previous fittings, Sophie had discovered two facts that had made her even more curious. Caroline owned rather than rented her apartment. And she was a Catholic. Had she been feeling stronger, Sophie would have attempted to find out where the furnishings had come from—to her eye they had an inherited look.

"There." Caroline stood and took a pace or two backward. "Turn around. Slowly."

Sophie turned obediently while Caroline watched. When Sophie had completed her turn, Caroline gripped the gathered material at Sophie's hips and gave it a gentle tug downward.

"Hm. You've lost weight. Let me just put a pin in here."

"Don't take it in."

Caroline raised an eyebrow.

"I'm thinner than I want to be, and I'm sure to put on pounds before the wedding with all the fattening meals I'll have to eat, you know, with David's family."

Caroline was silent.

"Better than being too fat. When Olivia Ponsonby got married, her mother shut her up in her room for two weeks and fed her Ryvita and lettuce," Sophie went on nervously.

"Olivia Ponsonby?"

"Girl in Ireland."

Sophie watched Caroline lose any interest she was prepared to entertain about Olivia Ponsonby. Sophie was usually rather good at remembering not to talk about Ireland. People weren't interested, or, if they were, it tended to be in an ignorant or sentimental way.

"Look, if I don't gain any weight you can put a dart in the day before, and if it doesn't fit I'll carry a huge bouquet and no one will notice." Sophie realized that she was gibbering.

117

Caroline regarded her with an odd expression. "Do you know you're actually a little green. Let me unpin you and get you out of that dress."

Sophie nodded, not trusting herself to speak as a wave of nausea swept over her. Despite four aspirins that morning, her head still hurt, and she now felt a sharp pain in the pit of her stomach.

July 1960

"YOU'VE LOST WEIGHT. I hope you're not banting."

"I'm not. School food is disgusting."

"Move," Vera said, impatiently tapping Molly's ankle. She took another pin from her mouth. "It's ridiculous for someone your age. It'll ruin your health."

Molly shuffled round. She didn't feel thin. Her stomach was distended. At lunch she had eaten two helpings of each course. Tea would be in an hour, and she thought that Bridie would send up potato cakes or drop scones in honor of her return from school. During the day and a half she had been home, she had understood that the kitchen and household staff had allocated to her the place previously held by Sophie as daughter of the house. Once more, Molly's privilege came from Sophie's promotion.

"Stand still."

Molly, who was standing still, said nothing. She looked out the window. At the end of the lawn, the large, limp leaves of a pocket-handkerchief tree were stirred by a breeze off the river. Molly felt calmer watching the tree and wondered why Vera was so irritable. Maybe she resented being pressed into service for the niece who was the only member of the family with less power than herself. Molly had plenty of time to consider this since Vera was aligning the hems of two layers of material. Molly's position was the only one in the family not fixed. She would remain junior and subservient to Vera unless she married, but if she married well, she would move past Vera and

118

could conceivably take precedence over even Sophie or Belinda. But Molly wanted to marry only Desmond. The prospect of a privileged life as the wife of an elderly earl did not interest her, but knowing that she had so little control over her own destiny made her thoughtful.

"It's very kind of you to make my dress," she said, shifting an inch or two in anticipation of Vera's signal. "It's going to be lovely."

The dress was pale orange crepe de Chine over a slightly darker silk skirt, the bodice two layers of the paler crepe de Chine. Vera could hem the underskirt in the usual way, but the crepe de Chine would have to be rolled.

"Four bridesmaids and half the county to the reception afterward. I wonder at Sophie having so large a wedding."

"Well, she had to have David's sister and I suppose she thought that Melanie and Sarah would look awfully sweet carrying her train. But Aunt Celia's having their dresses made, isn't she?"

Vera sniffed and did not reply, confirming what Molly already knew but had chosen not to address. Her aunt's complaint was not about dressmaking. Molly was curious about any factual details Vera might divulge and wanted to see how far her aunt would go in either confiding in or questioning such an insignificant member of the family.

She turned again, now facing a long bookcase. The books, more of them leather bound than covered with promising dust jackets, were behind glass doors. A full shelf was devoted to the works of Charles Lever, and another shelf was largely filled with the works of Surtees, the cheerful red bindings full, so far as Molly was concerned, of empty promise. Molly had often visited this bookcase when looking for something to read. Few new books were bought, and Molly was dependent on the library of a previous generation. For an adolescent girl, the pickings were thin but not, as she had feared, nonexistent. In the same way that she had unearthed *The Constant Nymph* from the library at Fern

119

Hill, she found *Seven for a Secret* by Mary Webb. Molly was amazed to find two novels, neither of them of huge literary distinction, that addressed, at some length and with clarity, passion and longing and which suggested that neither emotion was unnatural in a young girl. The books evoked tears in Molly, not only for the plight of the heroines but because she recognized, in someone else's description, the painful feelings that she constantly, privately, suffered. Belinda was the only other person at Dromore who might have read either book, but Molly did not question her, fearing that Belinda might scornfully dismiss the books as "shopgirl romances." Molly also feared that she might expose a little more of her own nature and feelings than she chose to. That her grandmother Daisy had read neither book Molly discovered with no risk, casually asking the question while Daisy recalled Ouida, the forbidden novelist of her own girlhood. While the plots of Ouida's novels with their emphasis on high life were dissimilar to the rural settings and themes of Mary Webb's work, Molly could see that the romantic longing of both generations was similar. She was young enough to believe that the feelings to which her grandmother alluded with a mildly nostalgic smile would only have been a pale shadow of what she, Molly, now felt. It seemed possible that her constant state of longing might be the unique manifestation of a hitherto literary convention.

"The aunts haven't been heard from, have they? I wonder if they'll come over for the wedding?"

"It might be a little much for them." Molly was glad to feel the conversation on slightly safer ground.

"And they might not want to." Vera paused, and Molly knew that she was expected to ask why that might be. Nervous and out of her depth, she decided to remain childishly, passively silent. Moving around so that she now faced Vera, she saw the door open and Belinda, on her rounds, pause a moment. "They have to feel some responsibility for what happened while Sophie was under their care," Vera said. "And I imagine they're disgusted."

Molly, horrified, watched as Belinda stepped energetically into the room.

"Disgusted by what?" she asked in a pleasant tone.

There was a moment's silence, during which Molly met Belinda's eye and then glanced away. She felt a jolt of fear in her stomach.

"A shotgun wedding celebrated on such a large and, under the circumstances, vulgar scale."

Belinda seemed lost in thought, but not unpleasant thought.

"I see," she said finally, her tone mildly amused. "Molly, when you're finished here, I'd like you to come and see me. I want to open Fern Hill for the week of the wedding. There'll be more people coming from England than we can put up here, and maybe you can get the house in order—Norah says she can get you a girl from the village. You'll act as hostess. The major meals will be here, of course."

Molly gasped. At her feet, Vera twitched in imitation of her mother.

"I'll be doing the flowers, so you'll find me in the pantry or the garden." Belinda turned to go but then, as an apparent afterthought, turned back. "Were what you implied true, Vera, surely the decent thing to do would be to close ranks."

And she was gone. The silence left by Belinda was painful. Molly cast her eyes around the room. On the desk there was a letter from the Irish Distressed Ladies, a charity that both Vera and Adele supported. Although the subject seemed safe enough, Molly couldn't frame a question or find a comment that did not seem ridiculous. Completing the circle and attaining the position from which she had started, she found herself looking once again out the window onto the lawn. Under the pocket-handkerchief tree, glossy against the rich green lawn, there were now two magpies.

One for sorrow, two for joy, Molly thought. Tibby had always saluted a magpie when he had seen one. Molly raised the hand farthest away from Vera, the first two fingers extended, and inclined her head to the sleek, arrogant, black-and-white birds.

"WHAT WAS I to do?" Sophie asked, almost a year later. Ten months had passed since Sophie's wedding. Eleven months since Vera had pinned the hem of Molly's bridesmaid dress. Sixteen months since Sophie had surrendered to David's urgent gropings and petulant pleadings and had relinquished her virginity in the guest room of the Spencer house in Virginia Water. Twenty months since Tibby had died at his own hand. "What was I to do? The invitations had been sent. Caroline had finished the dress. People had sent presents."

Molly stood at the window of Sophie's tiny perfect London drawing room, looking out onto the tiny perfect garden in Trevor Square. The garden was surrounded by a freshly painted black wrought-iron fence. It was half-past six. Residents of the square were given keys to the garden, but Molly did not think that Sophie had ever walked on the narrow gravel paths or sat on the carefully mown lawn.

Sophie lay on a small sofa, pillows behind her head. She was applying a second coat of polish to her nails.

"Light me a cigarette, darling, would you?"

Molly lit the cigarette, drawing the smoke experimentally into her mouth. She placed it between Sophie's lips, carefully avoiding the hand Sophie was waving in order to speed the drying of the polish.

"And maybe a drink while you're up."

There was an open bottle of white wine on the drinks tray, cool rather than cold. Molly filled Sophie's glass and, as an afterthought, poured for herself what remained in the bottle, a little more than half a glass.

"There's a bottle in the fridge. Would you be an angel? Take the evidence down with you, if you don't mind."

Carrying the bottle down to the kitchen in the basement,

Molly wondered if she should go home. Sophie had given her no clue to how long she was expected to stay. David was not home from work, and Molly did not know when he was expected. Nor did it seem that dinner had been planned. The kitchen had a depressing, neglected atmosphere and smelled of the overripe banana in the bowl of tired fruit.

"What's the package in the hall?" she asked, returning with the wine.

"Oh, that. Open it. It's something sort of wonderful. You'll see."

Molly carried the carefully wrapped box into the drawing room and set it on the floor by the window. Sophie watched as Molly, heeding the warnings of FRAGILE, GLASS, HANDLE WITH CARE, THIS SIDE UP, cut the string, tore off the brown paper, and opened the box. Lifting some crumpled newspaper and an underlayer of tissue, Molly could see a wooden handle. She lifted the bulky object. As the packing fell away, she saw that she was holding a miniature greenhouse, made of wood with leaded-glass frames. The proportions were perfect, and the workmanship, although simple, was fine. The white and green paint was somewhat worn, the wood showed through. Molly felt a strong, not completely understood, emotion—it seemed like admiration and melancholy.

"It's beautiful. What is it?"

"Eighteenth century. A botanical specimen case. Carried to the foothills of the Himalayas or on a voyage to the South Seas. I got it at Mallett's."

"It makes me want to cry."

"I know," Sophie smiled. "Me, too. It cost a fortune."

But why? Molly silently thought and longed to ask, *Why did you marry David? To have enough money to buy a toy greenhouse to remind you of the greenhouses at Dromore? If you hadn't married him, you'd still be there and not need reminding.*

Instead, she remained silent and started to stuff the packing materials back into the box.

"You know the way a certain kind of boring woman says, 'I like dogs better than humans, they're more trustworthy'?"

"Yes," Molly said slowly, anticipating an idea a little more complicated than those usually propounded by Sophie.

"Nobody says it about *things*. If you like dogs better than humans, you tend to congratulate yourself on it; if you take comfort in a diamond bracelet, you'd be well advised to do so silently."

Molly smiled and nodded, not much the wiser.

"Things. Certain objects help me remember stuff I thought I'd forgotten. Remembering something that happened when I was little or a detail about a place seems more important than anything that happens now. Even things that didn't make me happy."

"I thought it was supposed to be the senses, not things, that remind us."

"Yes, but the sensation comes from an object—you know, like in Proust—the taste, the sound, the sight, the feeling. It all entails an object."

"I didn't know you read," Molly said, astonished. Sophie laughed.

"I can read, you know. But like my errands of mercy and my drinking, I do it secretly. Like when I was sick. There wasn't much to do, and I was in disgrace. The funny thing is that we'd finally had to tell both families I was pregnant—so they'd have to let us get married—but afterward we all pretended that there was nothing unusual about the wedding. It was the only way we could all go on. So when something went wrong, David was hopeless. He didn't want to call the doctor, and then the pain got worse. There was blood all over the sofa. He panicked."

Sophie stopped, aware that Molly was not listening. Impatient, she got up from the sofa, blew briefly on her perfectly lacquered nails, crossed to the drinks tray and picked up the corkscrew.

Molly still sat on the floor, lost in thought. She gazed into the square and wondered at what Sophie had told her. The miscarriage was a story she had heard many times, but the news of Sophie's attempt to recapture memory would require hours of consideration. Greenhouses and walled gardens, she thought, could evoke nostalgia only in someone brought up in a country where it is never quite warm enough.

"So we got married anyway. What else could I do?" Sophie said, her tone uncharacteristically defensive. "I threw my bouquet right at you. It's not my fault you muffed it."

Chapter Seven

July 1960

*T*WIGS AND BLACK soot lay on the thin layer of old ashes in the library fireplace, debris from an abandoned bird's nest in the unswept chimney.

Molly wrote "chimney sweep" on her list. Before leaving the room she opened each of the heavy windows. A sash on one of them was broken; for a moment she considered adding the broken sash to her list and then refrained, reminding herself that she was only preparing the house for the overflow of guests for Sophie's wedding. The house would be occupied for not more than three or four days; broken sashes would be repaired by whomever lived next at Fern Hill. Or, quite possibly, not.

This house is not my house. This house does not belong to me, Molly silently reminded herself. Even when alone she tried to control her bursts of energetic happiness as well as the sadness, the sense of loss that the house evoked in her.

Molly went upstairs to change her clothes. A visit to the chimney sweep's house was clearly the first task to be performed that morning. Until he finished his work, the dust sheets should remain over the furniture.

Molly had lighted a small fire in the grate in her bedroom. Although it was July, the house was damp. She planned to light a fire in each room. She had started with her bedroom. The day before

126

she and Theresa, the silent and evasive girl whom Norah, the oldest and senior maid at Dromore, had recruited to help, had lighted the Aga stove in the kitchen. The stove heated the kitchen—as a small child Molly had often sought not only comfort but warmth there—and provided hot water for the entire house. The two girls had made tea, and Molly, if she so wished, would be able to cook some kind of a meal for herself that evening. The water heated by the Aga was held in a tank in the dark linen cupboard next to the kitchen. Three walls of the room were fitted with wide slatted wooden shelves on which linen was stored. On the unpolished wooden floor stood the large, creaky wicker basket with the words GOOD SHEPHERD LAUNDRY stenciled on it in black. Sophie and Molly had spent long winter afternoons lying on the shelves like cats, enjoying the warmth, talking, breathing in the dry, dusty air. At the back of the top shelf they had found Harlequin costumes. Yellow and black diamond-printed material, made for an amateur theatrical production or a fancy-dress party. The costumes, in good condition, looked as if they had been worn only once or twice. They smelled of dust.

Theresa disappeared for her dinner soon after the Angelus sounded, and reappeared an hour later. Molly did not ask where she lived; she assumed it was nearby. Molly suspected that Theresa was comfortable with the house—there would always be difficulties with maids and sightings of ghosts, given the nature of Tibby's death—because she had slept or sought sanctuary there in the past, fearing something more immediately threatening than the ghost of a mild Anglo-Irish householder. Molly had decided not to inspect the short corridor at the top of the back stairs where there were three maids' rooms and a dilapidated bathroom. She knew instinctively that if Theresa had sought refuge at Fern Hill, she had done so in the kitchen and servants' quarters.

Telling Theresa that she would return soon, Molly left the silent girl, who could not quite meet her eye, scrubbing the heavily ridged kitchen table. Theresa would next scrub the wooden shelves of the storage cupboards and the marble shelves of the larder, the large, deep, veined and stained sinks in the scullery, and, last of all, the black and red tiled floors.

Molly walked up the short lane that ran between the high stone walls of Fern Hill and the property next door to the main road. While she waited for Kenneally's bus to take her into Waterford, she wondered if the linen in the airing cupboard should be sent to the laundry or whether the heat from the Aga would be enough to air it. Her own bed the night before had been warmed by two glazed earthenware hot-water bottles. The linen had not, she thought, smelled damp or musty. Maybe the sheets should be spread over the bushes in what had once been the bleaching garden behind the now unused laundry. Molly liked the idea of reverting to the customs of previous generations. She would ask Belinda's advice. They would speak on the telephone that evening, the resumption of telephone service to Fern Hill being one of the conditions Belinda had made to Molly being allowed to stay alone in the house. That Belinda had been able to have the telephone reconnected in a matter of days had been impressive. Inquiries about how she had achieved such a miracle were waved away; Molly assumed that Belinda had, as usual, made it easier for someone to accede to her wishes than not to do so. Molly had not known that this talent could extend even to postal office bureaucracy.

Molly gave the conductor her fare, the large copper penny engraved with a hen on one side, the Irish harp on the other. The bus carried her the mile and a half into the city, passing familiar houses, and occasionally people she knew. One of the Miss Butlers walking a pair of greyhounds. A boy with whom she had been at school, riding a bicycle. The bus bore her on into the city—a city because it contained two cathedrals, one Protestant, one Roman Catholic. In most countries, Waterford would have been a medium-sized town. The bus carried her along the quay, over the bridge, and into the poorer outskirts beyond which the countryside began again.

The chimney sweep lived in one of a row of small, attached

houses on the main road and facing a steep, rocky hill that provided shelter and privacy but reduced the light that penetrated
the small windows of the houses. Molly noticed a poster for
Duffy's Circus on a telephone pole on the far side of the road.
Since there was no footpath on that side, anyone wishing to read
the details would have to take his life in his hands. The bright, familiar red, orange, and green poster did not need words, however.
Its message was in its colors: Duffy's circus is coming to town.

Molly glanced at the sky as she knocked on the door of the
chimney sweep's house. Soon it would rain. The door was
opened by a small boy, barefoot and wearing clothes that appeared to have been passed down by a brother. In his hand was
a thick slice of soda bread spread with jam. Some of the dark-red
jam was smeared around his mouth. His hair was cropped close
to his head. *Ringworm or lice?* Molly wondered.

"Mam," he called over his shoulder into the dark interior of
the house, "there's someone at the door."

A woman, red-faced, her sleeves rolled up, came to the door.
She smelled of washing soda and carbolic soap; her hands were
coarse and red. Behind her, Molly could see the kitchen, and in
it, a galvanized tin tub with a washboard. A baby crawled on the
dirt floor.

Molly left a message for the sweep and received assurances
that he would be at Fern Hill the following morning. Carrying
her shopping basket, she walked back to the part of the city she
knew better. She strolled along the quay, past a boat unloading
coal and another loading grain. The sky grew darker while Molly
paused to look in the windows of the department stores, and
soon it started to drizzle. She hurried past clerks returning to
their offices from lunch, old women concealed in their heavy,
dark shawls, the occasional farmer in mud-stained gumboots,
until she rounded the corner, passing Reginald's Tower, the
eleventh-century Danish fort, and found herself on the Mall. A
moment later she was in front of Merry's, the shop where her
family bought their groceries and where Belinda had arranged
for her to charge goods to the Dromore account. The name

MERRY'S was painted over the front door in gold on a red background, followed in smaller letters by GROCERIES, FRUIT, AND VEGETABLES and, in even more discreet letters, LICENSED TO SELL WINES AND SPIRITS.

The interior of the shop was cheerfully, luxuriously Victorian. The walls and central pillars were paneled. A marble counter ran the length of the shop, and a long mirror reflected the merchandise stacked in colorful profusion on the shelves and floor. There was a small bar in the rear, patronized by the males of any visiting Anglo-Irish family who did not wish to go to the length of eating lunch at the Waterford Club. The bar provided a social aspect to shopping at Merry's. The sound of the machine slicing rashers of bacon mingled pleasantly with the laughter and conversation from the rear of the shop. The smell of the bacon and freshly ground coffee blended with the fainter scent of new sawdust on the floor. Baskets of tomatoes and green vegetables added to the cheerfulness of the scene. Molly felt her heart lift, filled with confidence by her new, although temporary, responsibility to make Fern Hill comfortable for the guests who would come to stay for Sophie's wedding.

She shyly presented her new red account book to the assistant behind the counter. In it were listed her purchases for the day. They were few and would easily fit into her basket since milk, eggs, and butter came from the farm next to Fern Hill, and meat, bread, and, had anyone wanted it, fish were delivered. Fruit and vegetables came from the garden. Even now, Madigan, although his role had become more that of caretaker than gardener, maintained the peach trees and vines in the greenhouses, the espaliered pears and the raspberry and currant bushes in the walled garden. He had planted a section of the garden with vegetables, and there was lettuce in the greenhouse—less, Molly assumed, for his own consumption than for a modest sale to a greengrocer in Waterford.

Molly bought half a pound of streaky rashers, tea, sugar, and whole-meal flour. Her supper that evening was to be bacon, new potatoes, and peas. The tea and sugar were mainly for Theresa. In the morning Molly would make bread with the flour and the milk, which was, even now, turning on the not quite cool enough marble in the larder. She waited at the counter while the assistant took a pen from the pocket of his long white overall, entered the total in her account book, and handed it back with a smile and a flourish.

It had started to rain. Molly hesitated in the doorway. The sky was uniformly gray, relieved only by the white of the scavenging seagulls circling above the river. It seemed futile to wait. She hurried across the Mall and took shelter in a doorway close to the bus stop. The bus came once an hour but did not adhere to a rigid or, in fact, predictable schedule. The day was not cold, and the doorway provided partial shelter; Molly rearranged her basket to protect the spoilable goods from the rain and, far from miserable, settled down to wait.

Keeping one eye on the Mall, from where the bus would turn, Molly considered her plans. The following morning the sweep would come on his bicycle, his extendable brush over his shoulder and his dust sheets on his back. Once he left, Molly planned to light fires in every fireplace in the house. If it had stopped raining, she would open every window and let in the warm late-July air. Molly's great-aunts would arrive in two days' time, and Molly was determined that Fern Hill should come alive again, that she would make it part of the last magical and traditional event in the Hassard family. The generations to come would live in a flatter, duller world. Molly reminded herself that two days after Sophie was married, Fern Hill would be closed again, the furniture covered with dust sheets, the shutters closed and barred.

"Molly."

Not startled, but for a moment confused, Molly saw that a car had stopped on the side of the street, a little ahead of her. Desmond Paget leaned out the window of his muddy and far from new Rover. Molly smiled and hesitated, not quite sure what she was supposed to do.

"Get in. I'll take you where you're going."

"Oh," Molly's instinctive wish to demur, not to take him out of his way or to be any trouble was overridden not so much by her desire to be with Desmond, but by her habit of not arguing with adults. She got into the car, which smelled of gun oil and the border collie sleeping on the backseat, and set her basket down on top of two old race cards.

"Dromore's on my way—you're soaked." He looked with surprise at Molly's basket of damp provisions. "What on earth are you up to?"

"I'm—" She hesitated, not sure whether to say "living at," "staying at," or "sleeping at," and avoided all three by saying, "I'm going to Fern Hill. I'm getting the house ready for people staying for Sophie's wedding. On Saturday. You're coming."

Desmond smiled. "Indeed I am. I hear you're to be a brides-maid."

Molly felt herself blush. For a year, since the night of Eithne's dance, she had been rehearsing her next conversation with Desmond, and now she felt herself slipping back into the role of a child. Fern Hill was only minutes away, and she could already feel the regret of lost opportunity. Further moments were lost in an awkward silence while Molly watched the ineffectual wiper blades push the rainwater back and forth across the muddy windscreen.

Desmond stopped the car in front of the house and turned off the engine.

"Would you like to come in?" Molly asked.

"Yes."

Despite the rain, he stood for a moment looking at the house and the pastures at the end of the lawn.

"You've let the grazing?"

"Yes. Or rather, Uncle Miles has. Except for what he needs for his hunters."

"The place is entailed?"

"It's really the dower house for Dromore. It belongs to Uncle Miles."

Desmond nodded and they went indoors.

"I don't think there's anything to drink. I haven't got that far yet. Would you like some tea? I could make us something to eat."

Desmond shook his head. Molly worried for a moment that she was failing as a hostess and then felt a much stronger fear that if she failed to anchor Desmond with food or drink, he might soon leave.

"Shall we sit in Daddy's study? It's the only room with the dust covers off."

Desmond seemed barely to be listening as he looked around the hall, his eye lingering on the green-veined Connemara marble mantelpiece and the fine but dusty moldings on the ceiling.

"It's a lovely house," he said, following Molly into Tibby's study. The rain had eased and Molly opened a window. The room was filled with the smell of phlox and the pleasant warm damp of an Irish summer's day after rain. Desmond sat himself comfortably in Tibby's worn armchair. Molly took her usual place in the corner of the sofa, drawing up her bare brown legs under her cotton skirt. Desmond did not seem as though he were about to leave, and suddenly she felt happy.

"Are you staying here?"

"Yes."

"By yourself?"

"Yes, but only for a few days. After the wedding I'll go back to Dromore. There's a girl who comes every day to help."

"You're not afraid?"

"Of burglars? Ghosts?"

Desmond said nothing.

"When I was little, I was afraid of the dark. The maids had filled me up with stories of the headless horseman in the lane. I told Daddy that I was afraid, and he told me that there probably weren't such things as ghosts, but if there were, they wouldn't harm me."

Desmond seemed to be waiting for her to tell him more, so,

although she had completed her thought, she continued. "I'm still afraid of the dark sometimes." And after a pause: "I don't think I'd be afraid of Daddy's ghost."

She thought for a moment of Heathcliff's desperate attempts to conjure up Cathy's far from benevolent ghost, but since her association—that of obsessive love developed during childhood—pertained more to Desmond than to her father, she said nothing. It was also possible that Desmond had not read *Wuthering Heights*.

"I don't think I would be afraid of your father's ghost either. He was always kind. I liked his sense of humor."

"He was funny even when he felt sad. That is why it's so hard to understand him killing himself."

Desmond looked surprised. She could see that his surprise was not that Tibby had taken his own life, but that Molly should have said so. Her father's suicide, like the General's will, was a family secret only in the sense that within the family it was treated as a secret.

"I was here," she said quietly. "It was the day I came back from my grandmother Daisy's house. We had dinner, and then he said he was going to work in the greenhouse. I went for a walk, and when I came back—"

She smiled to reassure Desmond that she was not going to cry.

"What were you doing in Waterford?" she asked, fearing to embarrass him further.

"Oh, the usual. The bank. They like you to come in and have a chat—not that anything changes. We borrow money; when we sell the bullocks in September, we pay it back. Or most of it. I know, and Hennessy at the bank knows, that we are both marking time, hoping we can keep it going for my parents' lifetime. After that, it just won't work. My mother was unwise enough to announce stuffed vegetable marrow for lunch, so I told her not to wait for me—if I was late I'd eat at the club. But I couldn't face that, so I had glass of stout and a sandwich at a pub and then I met you. Look how well it turned out."

Molly could see lines on Desmond's forehead that had not

been there when she first met him, eight years before, the day he had shown her the *fleurs du mal* in the greenhouse. The day her mother had died. Desmond was twenty-six years old and already he had a few gray hairs. Molly thought his face and hands looked as worn as his tweed jacket did. The cuffs of his shirt—flannel with dark blue pinstripes—were a little frayed. On his wrist a plain watch with a time-darkened leather strap. Since Desmond's father was still alive, Molly decided that it had belonged to his grandfather.

The top of Tibby's bureau was rolled back, and Molly could see, attached to the time-darkened key to an inner drawer, a folded piece of white silk faded to a dirty, pale yellow. She could read the words: LORD, I SHALL PASS THIS WAY BUT ONCE, LET ME BE—Although the silk had hung there for as long as Molly could remember, she had never lifted it to see how the prayer ended. Apart from conventional attendance at a Church of Ireland service each Sunday, this was the only evidence, if it were in fact that, of religious faith that she had ever known her father to display. A wave of sadness came over her again, evoked by the sight of the once-familiar object.

"Do you know what you're going to do now?" Desmond asked.

"This afternoon or for the rest of my life?"

"You're finished with school? Or are you going somewhere to be finished off?" Desmond stressed the final preposition to emphasize the jocular nature of his second question. The first appeared to be rhetorical.

Without a moment's thought, Molly decided not to correct his impression that she was a year older than she actually was, that she was already, if only just, an adult.

"I don't know. I probably won't think about it until after Sophie's wedding."

Desmond's face registered mild disapproval.

"The entire world seems to stop for that young lady's convenience," he said.

Molly felt guilty. Unlike Desmond, Miles and Belinda knew

that Molly had another year of school, and neither had been negligent in regard to her future.

"She's an only child, and this is her wedding."

"Just make sure that it is your turn next."

"I don't want what Sophie wants. Anyway, my father was a younger son, so . . ." She shrugged.

"What do you want?" Desmond smiled lazily. Molly wondered if such a conversation was as rare in his life as it was in hers.

She was silent; what she wanted was so specific that it allowed no room for mere fantasy. Since she could not tell the truth, she was at a loss for words, unable even to imagine what a girl might wish for, were she not in love with Desmond.

"I don't know," she said carefully. "The usual, I suppose."

Desmond raised an eyebrow.

"You know. A husband and children. A home, a family."

Since Desmond nodded, rather than smiled or teased her, she feared that she might have sounded pathetic.

"It's not just because my parents are dead. It's also because I'm part of Uncle Miles and Aunt Belinda's family. Sophie was sort of a sister even before—I'd like to have a family of my own like that—I mean a smaller house, of course. Not like Dromore."

"I'm sure you will," Desmond said gently, sparing her his lecture on the lack of any imaginable future for the Anglo-Irish. "Choose carefully. Not that there's much choice. It's a very small pool."

Molly reminded herself to breathe. She was self-consciously aware that Desmond could—should—see that since she and he were part of that very small pool, anyone would logically consider each of them as at least a possible mate for the other.

"Unless you're planning to cast your nets a little farther out," he continued, "make a timely exit from the sinking ship. Like your cousin, Sophie."

Molly shook her head.

"I can't imagine it," she said.

"I can't either. I'm stuck here. Too many ties and not enough energy."

Molly smiled in seeming agreement. She did not lack energy and the paucity of her ties might well have been the reason she would stay close to what she had.

"I thought about getting married once," Desmond said.

Molly's stomach lurched. She would not have wished Desmond to be completely inexperienced either romantically or sexually, but any specific information, even of the past, was painful. "I was a student in England. She lived in London—shared a flat with two other girls in Earls Court. A friend of mine from Cirencester took me there—a bottle party." He paused and smiled, Molly watching hawklike from behind the facade of her interested smile. She thought that Desmond smiled at the recollection of his own younger, naive self, rather than in affectionate memory of the girl, whoever she was.

"She was called Patricia—she was a secretary at the BBC. She was very pretty and a good sport. I never met her family, but when I thought that I might ask her to marry me, I invited her home. I decided I'd introduce her to my parents, and if she looked as good on my territory as she did on hers, I'd propose during the weekend. We arrived late, for some reason, after dinner. She met my parents, we had a drink, and it seemed fine. The next morning she brought her handbag down to breakfast." Desmond smiled again. "My mother didn't allow a flicker to cross her face. I knew, they knew, they knew I knew, I knew they knew. When I found myself alone with them, they said she seemed like a very nice girl. I said nothing. It was a long weekend and a longer trip back on the boat train to Paddington."

"It was bad luck for her. Did she know what had happened?"

"No, I didn't say anything, obviously. But she knew something had gone wrong. Of course, there's no reason to suppose she'd have said yes."

Molly would have liked a long time to think about Desmond's story. It did not reflect well on him, she was certain, but she would have to consider it later.

After a pause, she said, "Sophie's going to marry David Spencer anyway."

"Yes, she is. But she isn't going to take him to live with her family—or in Ireland. Although in time, I suppose, they'll have Dromore."

"I don't think that'll ever happen."

"Oh?"

"At least, I can't imagine it. I can't see Sophie sitting still while David takes her father's place on the island."

Following a train of thought, unspoken but clear to Molly, Desmond asked, "What's going to happen to this place? Do you have time to show me around?"

"I'd love to."

Molly led the way through the hall—a little dusty, the ink in the barometer dried up, a cobweb covering the top of one of the gumboots on the porch—out the front door, and down the shallow, worn gray steps onto the gravel, in which chamomile and a few dandelions had taken root. "Fern Hill is the dower house. I suppose, in theory, Belinda would live here after Miles dies and Sophie and David would live on the island. At least that's what would happen if Sophie were a boy. I'm not quite sure how it will work."

Desmond glanced at his watch and at the sky, which was growing dark again.

"I should leave," he said. "It's later than I thought. Maybe I can come again someday. No, you'll be back at Dromore."

"We could still come over here," Molly said hopefully.

"And you? Where will you be when they've all decided where they're prepared to live?"

"I don't know."

"I—" Desmond said, taking her hand.

Molly felt herself freeze with awkwardness, unsure whether he was holding her hand or if he were taking his leave and had forgotten that he held her hand in his.

"What?" she asked after a moment.

He shook his head slightly, as though returning from a daydream.

"Nothing." He placed his other hand over hers and lifted it to the level of the top button of his worn tweed jacket. Molly understood that this was not a handshake while still not daring to assume it was anything more. "It's just," he said slowly, "that sometimes I wish—"

When it became clear he would say no more, Molly, with a courage she did not know she possessed, looked him in the eye and smiled a slow, sad smile.

"So do I," she said.

Desmond nodded. After a moment, he released her hand and got into his car. As he turned the corner into the lane, he waved back to Molly, who stood on the steps of the empty house.

Chapter Eight

*M*OLLY MADE EACH bed in the Fern Hill guest rooms as though Desmond would sleep on it. She smoothed, with firm palms and outstretched fingers, each sheet as though he would lie on it. Each pillow, old, flat, occasionally slightly stained, was plumped up, its seams aligned with those of the starched pillowcase that enclosed it as carefully as if she would, for the first time, lay her head beside his.

Molly set the fire in each bedroom grate, crumpling sheets from the *Irish Times,* laying kindling from the Fern Hill woods under logs from a fallen apple tree as though each fire would, alone, light her bridal night.

Two days before Sophie's wedding, Molly cut and arranged the flowers for the house. Her guests—the great-aunts and Caroline Penrose, bringing with her the wedding dress she had made—were to arrive on the mail boat the morning of the day before the wedding. Molly planned to have the house in perfect order and breakfast ready when Miles arrived with the travelers. Although no annuals had been planted at Fern Hill since Tibby's death, the hardier perennials had survived. There was no shortage of flowering shrubs and wildflowers. The large vase in the library was filled with lilies—Molly had found them, unlikely survivors, behind a tangle of interloping brambles in a corner of the garden—and graceful branches of a shrub with dark green leaves and a small white flower whose name Molly did not know. The lilies were strongly scented, and Molly knew that Tibby would have objected to their sweet, decadent smell, but she liked the sensuous contrast with the mild ladylike flower arrangement she had made in the other rooms. She thought, with no tinge of resentment, that her father no longer had a say in the way she arranged flowers. In the hall, using a large luster jug, she constructed an ambitious but conventional arrangement using foxgloves and lupines as a base, filling the spaces between with stock, Canterbury bells, larkspur, meadowsweet, and two shades of astilbe, one a faint, pale pink and the other the color of raspberry fool. The flowers, with the exception of the foxgloves and the meadowsweet—which she had picked in the lane on the way to the farmhouse where she bought eggs—came from the overgrown garden. Belinda had taught her that she need never fear the clash of color in flowers if she excluded yellow and orange. Her grandmother Daisy believed that every vase of flowers needed at least one touch of yellow "to bring out the colors." Belinda's method was tried and true, so Molly confidently mixed pinks and reds and purples and then, out of deference to her grandmother and because she imagined her mother would have learned the same principle from Daisy, she added a few white flowers in whose center there was a just-visible dot of yellow. Molly was pleased with the result. For the dining room she chose white and pink roses in a low silver bowl, and for the bedrooms, small romantic bouquets of wildflowers. She made a posy of white field flowers for her own room, using cow parsley and some small flowers that she had found in the hedgerows of nearby fields. With the same surprise she had felt when she ignored what would have been her father's objection to lilies, she noticed that she had spent more time making the faintly bridal bouquet for her own room than she had on the delicate posies on the night tables of her great-aunts' and Caroline's rooms.

Molly spent those days alone, fearing even the company of the apparently—but perhaps merely politically—unobservant

Theresa. Aware that she was in an altered state, she turned her overexcited energy to making Fern Hill a welcoming (and temporarily functioning) small country house. Working alone, she could think about Desmond and replay every moment, every nuance, his every word, the memories bringing happiness of an intensity she had never before even approached. Her happiness would intermittently be pierced with small cold currents of fear that if there had been some mistake, if Desmond was not going to claim her, her despair would be so great and her loss so final that she could not imagine continuing her life. She did not think in terms of suicide but rather that she might sink into sonambulant apathy and—she thought in a moment of self-mockery—like Henry I, never smile again. Then she would remind herself of the way he had held her hand, of her sense that he was happy in her company, and she would be reassured.

MILES CAME IN and drank a cup of tea when he brought his aunts. He refused the place Molly offered him at the head of the table.

"I'm just stopping for a cup of tea. I wish I could stay. The island the day before a wedding is no place for a man. But Belinda has given me a list of people to chivy in Waterford before I meet the Spencers. They're coming on the Dublin train."

Aunt Charlotte sniffed—her reaction a pale shadow of Adele's method of expressing disapproval—and although no one at the table said anything or even caught another's eye, each knew what the others were thinking. That to fly to Dublin and come south by train was soft, bourgeois, and, well, English. In a way just as telling, neither old lady showed even a flicker of surprise that Miles had insisted that Molly should sit at the head of the table. After they had eaten the breakfast Molly had cooked and gone upstairs to rest after their long and tiring journey in the rooms she had prepared for them, her great-aunts began to think of her as no longer a schoolgirl but as a charming and unassuming young woman who had become an excellent housekeeper.

Molly showed Caroline to her room. Caroline was pale and drawn and had eaten only a piece of toast at breakfast. She brought her coffee cup upstairs with her. Molly, who had never before seen anyone leave the dining room with food or drink, looked at this strange and beautiful girl with nervous fascination. There were three hatboxes in Caroline's room.

"When you think of food, I think of dresses."

She laughed when Molly looked startled.

"I'm thinking about Sophie's train and how to keep it clean at the rehearsal this evening and whether one of those ridiculous dogs will tear it, and you are visibly thinking about lunch."

"I am," Molly said. "Belinda said a cold lunch and ordered a ham, but I picked some rhubarb, and I'm making a rhubarb crumble for pudding. With cream."

"Men would think that we're envying Sophie and thinking about getting married ourselves. I never think about what's really happening—I'm always stuck at the arrangements."

"Like me. And Aunt Belinda. But I do think about Sophie and—about getting married."

"Of course. I do, too—but only in my free time. Do you have any more hangers?"

Isabel and Charlotte, who had between them more than a hundred and ten years of both making and fitting in with domestic arrangements, descended the stairs minutes after Molly had placed the crumble in the oven of the Aga cooker and tidied herself for lunch. She came into the library with offers of sherry and white port as the old ladies were settling into their chairs and taking out their needlework. The window that overlooked the lawn was open, and the syringa in the flower bed below the window were in bloom.

At lunch, Molly's great-aunts nodded approval at the cold meal set before them. Caroline, who eschewed the ham and salad, ate two helpings of the rhubarb crumble and smoked a cigarette with her coffee.

Sophie's wedding was to take place at St. Olaf's, a church smaller, older, and darker than the cathedral. Had Molly been the bride, it was the church she would have chosen, but in Sophie's case it had been arranged when a small, quick wedding had seemed necessary. When it had turned out that Sophie had nothing to conceal, her ill-tempered lack of enthusiasm and an uncharacteristic firmness on Miles's part had prevented Belinda from orchestrating a more spectacular event at the cathedral. St. Olaf's was also cold.

It was raining when those members of both families needed for the wedding rehearsal came out onto the steps. Angela Spencer, who had hoped to see her son married at St. George's, Hanover Square, to someone other than Sophie Hassard, made no attempt to disguise the distaste she felt. Her nose was pink, and she had sneezed twice during the rehearsal. Martin Spencer hovered about her solicitiously, but Molly could see that Mrs. Spencer was used to a little more attention than that.

"The veil," Caroline said, shaking her head.

"I know," Molly said sympathetically, stepping back into the porch and helping Caroline fold the Hassard wedding veil. She wrapped it, for protection, in the sheet that had been pinned to the back of Sophie's skirt to simulate the train of the wedding dress that hung in Caroline's room. "I was wondering if the milk would turn in time for me to make bread for tomorrow's breakfast," Molly said.

"Instead of sizing up the perfectly all right best man?" asked Caroline.

"Were you?"

"It wouldn't do me any good. I'm a Catholic."

Since Caroline's arrival, Molly had tried hard to avoid her eyes-like-saucers look; this time she failed abjectly. "Oh," she said, stopping herself before she asked whether the great-aunts knew.

"And, anyway, I've got a boyfriend. But he's married. And—there's another reason."

Molly was at a loss to imagine what Caroline, who had airily announced herself an adultress as well as a Catholic, might feel warranted reticence. For almost ten minutes, Molly forgot about Desmond.

CAROLINE AND MOLLY returned to Fern Hill with the veil and changed their clothes before meeting the great-aunts and the rest of the party at Dromore for dinner.

A southeast wind blowing up the river made their umbrella useless, and the two girls huddled together under a large, thick black shawl that covered their heads and partially protected them from the rain as Christy rowed them across the river.

"If it rains tomorrow, Sophie might as well get married in a bathing suit," Caroline said crossly, thinking of her comfortable flat in Knightsbridge with a two-bar electric fire in both rooms.

"It won't rain tomorrow," Molly said confidently. Her imagination held such a clear picture of what the following day would bring that it was already almost a memory.

Caroline sighed. "If you say so. I hope Sophie's in a better mood—otherwise dinner at Castle Drama may be a bit too exhausting for me."

But when Molly and Caroline, leaving their wet macintoshes in the hall and wearing the dry shoes they had carried with them in a bag, entered the library at Dromore, they found Sophie and David in a pose that *Country Life* would have been proud to photograph. Sophie stood beside David in front of the fire, Belinda's dog, Nell, reclining at their feet like a carefully placed accessory. Each held a glass of sherry, and they were laughing at something one of the great-aunts had said. Molly noticed that not only had Sophie changed her clothes but that her hair was done in a softer and more becoming way than it had been at the rehearsal that afternoon. As Molly and Caroline entered, Belinda rose to her feet.

"There you are and not too wet. If I ever win the Sweeps, I'm going to build a bridge—that damned ferry gets less charming each time I cross. Sit down, Caroline, Miles will get you a drink. There's one more thing I'd like to do before dinner. I wonder if I could ask you, Molly—"

"Can I help?" Caroline asked.

"No, you sit down. It'll just take Molly and me a moment. Last-minute presents."

"Don't you believe it," Sophie said, "You know that tomorrow there'll be presents at the church just begging to be forgotten. What'll you bet old Mrs. Carrington-White tries to press a large and badly wrapped package—a fish or something—on me as I go up the aisle?" Turning toward David with an affectionate smile, she added, "Now, there's a family who's really made an art of eccentricity. I'll tell you about them later."

"Tell us now," Caroline said, understanding immediately what Belinda required of her. "I want to hear."

The wedding presents were displayed in the billiards room. Miles had originally caviled, but it was the only downstairs room that could be spared, and since he did not play billiards and didn't think to say that the loss of the billiards room left him with only the downstairs gents' as an exclusively masculine territory, he was overruled. Molly and Belinda quickly unpacked four boxes that had come by the afternoon post, and Belinda entered the name and a description of each gift in a small book.

"It's difficult to place them so that no one is slighted," she said, running a hand through her hair.

Molly, who was moving presents and cards to make room for the new gifts on the billiards table—the top of which had been temporarily built to a low, white-clothed pyramid in order to display the wedding presents to their greatest advantage—paused. "Is this all right for"—she peered at the card—"it looks like the name is Tarkington. It came from England. How do you decide?"

146

"They're not coming, they just sent a present. I mix bride's and groom's families and friends evenly and put things sent by guests who aren't coming toward the back. I hope I'll give you your wedding someday, Molly, but it may take me a year or two to get over this one."

Still Belinda lingered, fiddling with the edges of the large lace-trimmed tablecloth.

"That girl—David's sister, Priscilla—came to me before dinner," she said eventually. "She can't find her earrings and thinks maybe one of the maids . . . Can you imagine? Really, these people. Turn the lights off when you've finished."

Molly walked around the billiards table, looking at the presents. There was a second narrow table on which more gifts were displayed. Those that came from David's family and friends tended to be expensive, modern, and in conservative good taste; many of the boxes had borne Asprey and Harrods labels. The Irish presents were not so uniform. An eighteenth-century Irish silver tea service and a Waterford glass decanter were more impressive, but there was also a set of Beleek ornaments—the kind of present that a young bride has to remember to take out each time the giver visits. Smaller gifts from the staff at Dromore and from impoverished spinster cousins were carefully placed in prominent positions. Molly wondered, as she often now did, how it would be if it were her wedding and she were about to marry Desmond. There would be few if any packages from Aspreys, nor would there be family treasures except, perhaps, from Miles and Belinda. Molly could not imagine that she would miss acquiring three silver toast racks. Her life would hardly require more than one dinner service, but it would be lovely to have new and expensive linen and to step out of the bath into large, thick towels. The sheet under which she had slept the night before had a seam up the middle. Miss Shaw, Molly's last governess, had taken upon herself duties that were not strictly hers but that, but for her, would have gone unfulfilled and their lack unnoticed, and she had cut the worn sheets down the middle and sewn together the stronger material of the outer edge of each sheet, extending by some years the useful life of each. These sheets lay at the bottom of the pile of linen, brought into use only when the day the Good Shepherd Laundry should have delivered fell on a holy day or when the house was, as it was now, full. It required an act of will not to test the seam with a big toe, searching for a weak spot. It served to remind Molly that the comfort with which she was now surrounded was not her birthright but merely a result of being included in the richer Dromore Hassard family, and that even they, after the necessary expenditures of Sophie's wedding, would have to go into a period of retrenchment. This would mean a suspension of entertainment and a drop in indoor temperature. In the nineteenth-century novels that Molly read, families waiting for their coffers to refill would mark time on the Continent, a fate that seemed enviable to her. She had never left Ireland and would, unless she moved quickly and firmly, spend a large part of the retrenchment in an Irish boarding school.

DESPITE THE ADDITION of Vera and Adele, Angela and Martin Spencer, and David's sister, Priscilla—dismissed earlier by Caroline as "quite pleased with herself"—and the general nervous anticipation of one of Sophie's sudden changes of mood, officially described as prewedding nerves (an appellation that had covered some months of poor behavior), the pleasant atmosphere of the drawing room continued into dinner. David was clearly amused—his parents a little less so, Priscilla visibly bored—by the descriptions of Anglo-Irish eccentricity to which they were treated. Several members of the family had enjoyed the opportunity to display the gifts of the raconteur. The stories were long familiar to every member of the Hassard family with the possible exception of Adele, whose memory was now erratic and to whom Vera had given a double portion of the mild tranquilizers prescribed by the family doctor. Familiarity was part of the pleasure, and the anticipation of the punch line was greater than if the stories had been new.

The multitude of anecdotes about Mrs. Carrington-White having been exhausted, another family was now under discussion. Distant cousins of the Carrington-Whites who were also, it appeared, distant cousins of the Hassards.

"A Miss Carrington-White married a younger son of the Percevals and your aunt Elizabeth Osborne's husband—" Miles was comfortably settling down to a description that to be followed would have required a pencil and paper and a good deal more interest and patience than Molly saw evident in any person at the table. Sophie cut him off firmly.

"Never mind that now, Daddy. David already thinks we're the result of centuries of reckless inbreeding, so don't you encourage him. Severin Perceval had a ghastly American wife—"

"Yes, well, he married that woman who came over to hunt with the Kildares. Lots of money, widowed or perhaps divorced. She came from, I think, Chicago and cut quite a dash—more courage than sense on the hunting field. Anyway, she took a shine to old Severin, and before he knew it, she had him married. At first it all went swimmingly, married at the end of the hunting season, and all summer it was racing and the Horse Show and then there was cubbing. But I don't think she'd reckoned on a winter at Roche Hall."

"It's built on the side of a hill—" Belinda did not trust Miles to describe the full horror, but she herself was corrected by Sophie.

"More a small cliff, really."

"The stables were above the house," Belinda continued, "so there was a constant sort of invisible stream running under the house and you didn't know how much of it was drainage from the stableyard. My mother used to say that she was always afraid of typhoid when she went to stay during summer. The house doesn't get any sun until the afternoon, and it's cold. Cold and damp and unhealthy."

"The Percevals never spent any money on the house," Miles continued, used to being interrupted. He had the demeanor of a man wishing to be scrupulously fair. "They spent it all on keeping up the shooting—a gamekeeper, keeping the woods stocked."

"He kept his young pheasants warmer than his guests." Adele was often clearer about the past than the present, although, as every other member of the Hassard family was uncomfortably aware, her taste and discretion were no more dependable when recalling her youth than when she commented on the events in hand.

"With her money—what was her name?" Miles asked.

"Rhoda," Belinda said.

"Rhoda. With Rhoda's money it became possible to heat the place properly for the first time. She had some company down from Dublin and spent a fortune putting in central heating. She sent Severin up to stay at the Kildare Street Club for a month, and she stayed in the house while these chaps tore it up. She was paying through the nose and kept on top of them and the whole thing was done by early spring. Severin was back by this time, and they turned on the new heating. He complained a bit. He was used to damp drafts and a big log fire to thaw out in front of. It was not until summer that he discovered the dry rot. It had been dormant for years—only because it was pretty well frozen in place for half the year. Now it began to sprout beside the new radiators all along the front of the house. He was beside himself with rage. His father died of an apoplectic fit—burst a blood vessel when a tenant farmer of his shot a fox the day before the lawn meet at Roche Hall, so it was in his family."

"And he drank like a fish," Belinda added gently.

"Well, he did tend to keep warm with a fairly steady diet of Paddy, and he liked his glass of port. It turned out that she could put it back with the best of them. They started to have the most appalling fights—she broke the looking glass behind the bar at Lawlor's after Punchestown."

"The pub people go to on the Naas road on the way home after racing," Sophie explained to David. She appeared not to be addressing her future in-laws. Priscilla retaliated by betraying not

150

the slightest flicker of interest. Although Molly knew that Priscilla's behavior had been provoked by the way Sophie treated her and the entire Spencer family, she felt a strong dislike for Sophie's future sister-in-law.

"But the fights they had at home were the ones that finished it off. Old Severin was a pretty good shot, his father had left him a set of Purdys, and he'd collected a few along the way himself that weren't strictly covered by his gun license. When . . . whatshername—?"

"Rhoda," Belinda said. "You've forgotten to say that he stammered," she added.

"Yes. Severin had a desperate stammer. When—er—Rhoda pushed him too far . . . He wasn't really a violent man, but he would take her arm, grab a gun, and drag her to the front door and open it. Then he'd give her a shove and shout, 'W-w-w-one . . . t-t-t-t-w-w-w-two . . . t-t-t-three . . !' shouting so she could hear as she took off down the avenue. Then he would start shooting."

"The avenue's half a mile long and full of potholes. But there are plenty of shrubs—mostly rhododendrons," Belinda said pleasantly.

"Convenient for the pheasants," Sophie said.

"I used to dance with Severin Perceval when I was a young married woman," Adele said thoughtfully. With the exception of David, Martin, and Priscilla Spencer (Angela had come downstairs braced), everyone braced himself. But Adele's recollection was harmless. "He danced the fox-trot better than any man in Tipperary." For a moment it seemed as though she might say something more, but the recollection, if indeed there had been one, evaporated.

"Fairly standard way of treating unsatisfactory wives in Ireland, is it?" David asked, his voice too bluff, too English. "I'll stand advised."

There was a moment's pause while those breathing a premature sigh of relief turned their attention from Adele to the cold look of dislike in Sophie's eyes.

151

"He's got no one but himself to blame," she said, possibly to Caroline, as though she were putting the clinching argument to an existent and extensive discussion. Then, with a turned shoulder, excluding the rest of the table, she asked her father about one of his horses.

Since it was a family meal, and since there was the usual shortage of males, Belinda had arranged the seating so that Adele had been buffered between Miles and Vera. Caroline had been seated beside David in case of a spat between the betrothed couple, and she now leaped forward with an inquiry about a mutual acquaintance in London. Belinda easily engaged Martin Spencer in conversation. Nothing could be done for Angela Spencer on Miles's right since Sophie showed no intention of allowing her into the evaluation of the new vet's treatment of a lame mare.

Angela had the look of a woman who has severely miscalculated the appropriate clothing for an important social occasion. That her dress was a little too stiff and formal and not quite warm enough was not, however, all that was troubling her. She had been, and still was, disappointed that David was marrying Sophie rather than a more conventional English girl from a good family with a little money of her own. Implicit in her disappointment had been a sense of superiority, and she had, rather later than she would have wished, worked out that the Hassards were perhaps even less enthusiastic about her than she was about them. An afternoon and evening at Dromore had left her, for the first time in many years, unsure of herself. She had a sickening suspicion that she had pursued the wrong prizes, aspired to the wrong goals, and that it was apparent to the Hassards that everything about her was false, shiny, and nouveau riche. She looked with an uncharacteristically critical eye at her own daughter and knew her to be pretty, young, expensive, and very ordinary.

David, who already knew what his mother suspected, chose either through stubbornness or stupidity not to talk to Caroline about the one rather dull man they both knew slightly.

"I want to ask Molly about the curse," he said, turning to her. "Before dinner they were telling me about an Irish family that has a curse." He made it sound like yet another amusing foible.

"Catholic Irish or Anglo-Irish?" Molly said, playing for time. She had been up since half-past six and longed for her bed.

"I don't know. Apparently an old woman put a curse on her landlord after he'd hanged her son. For seven generations no father would live to see his son reach the age of twenty-one."

"The Delafields. No Lord Delafield—no head of the family—would live to see his son reach the age of twenty-one."

"Yes," he said expectantly, and when Molly said nothing more, he continued, "Do you believe it?"

"That the old woman cursed them or that the curse worked?"

"Both."

Molly was aware that the other conversations at the table had died out. A large part of her upbringing had been predicated on not showing or, better yet, not quite experiencing extremes of emotion, but she felt a quiet, hard anger at this man who with unearned superiority was condescending to a culture too subtle for him to understand.

"Yes, I do." She spoke quietly, aware in the silence around her that even Adele and Vera were supporting her.

David laughed. So did Priscilla. Molly felt her eyes fill with tears. She dug her nails into the palms of her hands and told herself that if she cried now, she did not deserve the grown-up status she was temporarily enjoying and that she planned to claim permanently. Nevertheless, she knew that she could not speak and that her condition was apparent to at least Sophie and Belinda.

"Molly's superstitious," David said and laughed again. His laugh was forced, and at that moment Molly hated both him and his sister.

"What about you, Sophie?" he asked, turning to her. "Is my future wife superstitious?"

"Of course not."

David turned to Molly, either failing to see or choosing to ignore the tear running down her cheek.

"You see."

"You didn't ask what happened." Sophie said quietly. "Six generations of Delafields died before the eldest son came of age. The present Lord Delafield, who's a friend of Daddy's, has cirrhosis of the liver. He's not going to get better. His son, Teddy, is eighteen. You'll meet him tomorrow. I'm not superstitious. But they're all dead."

Molly wondered if any member of the family had actually begged Sophie not to marry David. Then she wondered if anyone had told her that even at this late moment she didn't have to.

"What did she say?"

"She said she had a pain."

"Like Nina—in *Vile Bodies.*"

"Nina was addicted to ether. That was different."

"Was she? How do you know?"

Molly and Caroline were in Caroline's bedroom, their hair in rollers, Caroline's face made up. Their dresses for the wedding hung ready for them. Like two colonels in the advance party of Francis Hassard's bloody Munster campaign, they awaited the arrival of the main army. Ready for action, killing time, Molly gingerly smoked one of Caroline's cigarettes and admired Caroline's lean body and expensive slip. The great-aunts, with the practical good manners of their generation, had inquired whether the girls needed help and had then retired to the drawing room.

"Conrad—my boyfriend—told me. It's in the book once you know—there's a bit about how there's always a slight smell in her room."

"My father and Uncle Miles were at a prep school in Wales where Evelyn Waugh taught."

"Decline and Fall?"

"Maybe. I like to think so, but he taught at another school, as well. But—you told her she didn't have to marry David if she didn't want to, and she said she had a pain?"

"That's the long and short of it. Why don't you have a go?"

154

Molly shrugged. Since Sophie was due to arrive at Fern Hill in five minutes to put on her wedding dress, she thought that Sophie probably now did have to go through with it.

"Lots of presents to return," Molly said and, after a pause, added, "Caroline?"

"Mmm?"

"Listen to this and tell me what you think. A young man, the son of the house, brings a girl home to meet his parents before he asks her to marry him. The parents like her, the first day goes well, but the following morning she comes down to breakfast carrying her handbag."

Caroline laughed, Molly knew that she did not need to finish the story.

"What do you think?"

"What do *you* think?" Caroline asked. "It's an Irish story of course. Anglo-Irish. Country house, I assume?"

"Of course. I don't know. I've been thinking about it. I understood why she wouldn't *do,* of course. Bringing your handbag down to breakfast is the sort of thing David's sister might do."

"And take out a compact and apply too much lipstick after she'd polished off her bacon and eggs."

"Yes," Molly said. "But the story really isn't about the girl, it's about him. I can't decide whether he is merely snobbish, or whether he is sparing both of them an uncomfortable future. I forgot to say that he wasn't an aristocrat or the heir to a huge estate or anything. He was like, you know, us."

"It's odd how indigestible the bourgoisie seem to be," Caroline said thoughtfully, drawing on her cigarette, "The turn-of-the-century habit of poor aristocrats marrying American heiresses and rich aristocrats marrying Gaiety Girls often turned out better. I suppose extremes are easier to assimilate than subtle differences."

"I ended up thinking that he couldn't have really been in love with her. If he had, he would have married her anyway or moved to England or something," Molly ended lamely. If Desmond had been considering marrying a girl with whom he

155

wasn't really in love, a whole new batch of questions were raised. Molly did not want to think of him as lacking in depth of feeling. It was a troubling thought that he might have chosen the girl for practical reasons rather than as a soul mate.

"Were they sleeping together?" Caroline asked.

"I don't know—that's not the point," Molly said faintly. It was not a question she had asked herself.

"It's always the point," Caroline said and glanced out the window. "Here they are."

Molly went to the window and looked down at the two cars coming up the avenue. The solitary magpie on the lawn cocked his head and then, leisurely, flew away.

EVEN ANGELA SPENCER, now suffering from a real cold and having overestimated the hot water supply at Dromore, had to admit that St. Olaf's looked both impressive and beautiful in a way she was just beginning to understand. She clasped her mink stole tightly around her shoulders, her smart silk dress doing little to save her from the damp cold she could feel rising from the worn stone flags beneath her feet.

Sophie, on Miles's arm, walked up the aisle of the crowded church. Molly and Priscilla Spencer—Priscilla a little pink in the face and inclined to giggle; she had had two glasses of champagne before the wedding party left Fern Hill—carried flowers, and the two younger bridesmaids held the train of Sophie's dress. As Sophie drew level with the front pews where the Spencer and Hassard families sat, retaining her father's arm only with the tips of her fingers, she paused to speak to Vera.

"The church looks more beautiful than I could have imagined, and so does my bouquet. Thank you, Aunt Vera."

Vera flushed with pleasure and shifted in her seat. A small, almost painful smile appeared on her lips. Molly, although in a trance of excitement and anxiety, suddenly understood that Vera's life might have been different. Vera was a spinster, an "old maid," not by nature or choice, but through circumstance. If she had

156

been more fortunate—if, for instance, the curate had returned her affection or had had more courage—Vera might have become a different woman. Molly wondered if Vera had ever been a bridesmaid, if she had ever anticipated her own wedding. It seemed likely; Molly had seen photographs of Vera. She had been pretty in an old-fashioned way.

Slipping into the pew beside Belinda, Molly felt a shiver of fear. There was no reason to believe that Vera had been less pretty, less accomplished, or less deserving of a husband, children, and a home of her own than she herself was. Molly had not seen Desmond come up the aisle. Longing to seek him out but fearing he might catch her doing so, she had not dared to glance about her. Now she was in the front and would have to wait until she followed Sophie and David down the aisle. She sat up straight, extending her neck and turning her head slightly so that if he glanced at her, she would be shown to advantage.

When Sophie paused before repeating the words "love, honor, and obey," Molly was not the only one in the church to hold her breath, nor was Angela Spencer the only one to experience a chill. But a second later, in the playful tone she had chosen to make her vows, Sophie repeated the rector's words and, moments later—those who knew just cause having held their peace—she and David were pronounced man and wife.

MOLLY HELPED SOPHIE into the rowing boat, arranging her train and the hem of her dress so that they lay clear of the small puddle of muddy water at the bottom. She watched David, a little clumsily, step into the boat and seat himself beside his new wife. Molly, Priscilla, and the two little bridesmaids waited for Sophie's boat to be pushed away from the slip so that they could climb into the second boat. The parents of the bride and groom would take the third boat. Most of the guests would have to wait for the first boats to return, and many would have to watch the small flotilla cross and recross the brown river.

The rain had stopped during the night, and the sun had been

shining all morning. Radio Eireann had been switched on for the weather report, the gardener had been appealed to and, after gazing at the completely blue sky, had pronounced that the rain "should hold off until morning." Miles had paced the lawn after breakfast and, though gloomily aware of the damage high-heeled shoes would later inflict, thought that there was no reason to fear that his guests would, like cars in the parking field at a wet point-to-point, sink slowly into the mud.

"If your father was here, he'd have quoted *Lord Ulwin's Daughter*," Sophie said to Molly as Christy gave the small boat a push and stepped into it. Molly smiled. Priscilla and David looked inquiringly at Sophie, who said nothing.

"Victorian poem," Molly said quickly. "Elopement, boating accident, somewhat sentimental. My father was fond of quoting it."

David and Priscilla looked at Molly as though she had taken leave of her senses.

"My grandfather used to quote Longfellow in the mornings when he came to wake us up," Molly added, slightly desperately.

"A literary family," Priscilla said after too long a pause.

"Depends, really, who you compare us with," Sophie said with a yawn. "All right, Christy."

Christy dipped his oars, and the boat moved slowly away from the slip.

In the bow of the boat, white hydrangeas had been stuck into a jam jar wedged into place and concealed by the large veined leaves, the heavy blooms acting as a base and a support for some pale mauve flowers. Salvia, lavateria, and a flower that looked like a miniature gladiola, but which Molly knew had another name, showed between the large, dense white hydrangea blossoms.

The boat carrying the bridesmaids was bedecked with nasturtiums, the orange and dark-yellow flowers still attached to their long trailing tendrils. Molly could see the colorful patch from which they had been picked on the farther shore, edging the low stone wall that separated Christy's garden from the river-bank.

York and Lancashire roses—remnants of a more affluent time when the Dromore Hassards had employed six gardeners, a time when the landscaped grounds at the end of the croquet lawn had been maintained—now grew wild, struggling to survive in the long grass. The small-bloomed roses decorated the third boat, into which Belinda and Miles and the Spencers were climbing. No two boats were decorated alike; the flowers and shrubs had been picked from the grounds of Dromore, the small gardens of those who worked and lived on the estate, and from the fields and hedgerows.

"Seat yourself there, and you'll have a grand view of the whole proceedings," Molly heard Christy's second son, Declan, say. She could see Angela Spencer gratefully accept his worn, red hand as she stepped uneasily onto the wet, unsteady planks at the bottom of the boat. Although Angela was the first to board, Declan settled her in the stern. Miles and Belinda, requiring no assistance, followed her. So did her husband. The boat in which Molly and the bridesmaids were seated had just set off on its short journey across the river, and she saw Angela say something to Belinda, which caused Belinda's face to light up with pleasure. It seemed that Angela, an unlikely candidate, was succumbing to the dangerous, dubious charm of the Anglo-Irish.

The atmosphere in Molly's boat was less cheerful. One of the smaller bridesmaids, Melanie, had wept during the wedding service. The words "in sickness and in health" had cause morbid tears in an already overexcited child. Molly had watched her struggle to control herself and understood that sympathy would be neither kind nor helpful. The previous night she, too, had been unable to prevent one solitary tear escaping and running down her face. Had it been acknowledged by anyone at the table, she would have wept without control, and the shame would have always been a humiliating memory. Melanie's father, Molly's first cousin once removed, had handed his daughter his top hat and a silk handkerchief, and she had calmed herself by polishing it and smoothing out the beaver. The child concentrated on her task, the crisis had been averted. Molly, who watched Melanie's father behave much as she imagined Tibby would have done, had felt her own tears dangerously close. Melanie was now embarrassed and subdued. Sarah shivered in her thin dress as the sun was obscured by clouds, and Priscilla looked unhappily at the small choppy waves that the cool west wind was slapping against the sides of the boat. As Liam rowed, the rowlocks creaked.

Since Molly sat facing the shore where the wedding guests were waiting, she was able for the first time that afternoon to look for Desmond. The boat was more than halfway across the river when a Rover, not the muddy, green car in which Desmond had driven her home from Waterford and for which she had been watching, rounded the corner and parked on the grass beside the narrow road. Almost the full width of the river separated them when she saw Desmond, his parents, and another couple get out of the car. She was too far away to be able to see clearly, and had she not had such a sense of the easy, confident grace of his stride, she might not have been sure that it was him. Aware that his eye would be drawn, if not to her, at least in her direction, she sat up a little straighter. Turning to Sarah, she put an arm around the child, rubbing a little warmth into her bare arms.

"We're almost there."

Sarah smiled weakly and, remembering that the afternoon promised many excitements, beginning with a ride on the sidecar up the avenue to the house, started to squirm in her seat.

"Look at the heron," Molly said to Melanie. "He's always there at this time of day."

Priscilla chose not to glance at the solitary heron who stood, his head and neck hunched against the wind, immobile at the tip of the island. The bird faced upstream, the brown water of the receding tide passing to either side of him. It seemed to Molly that Priscilla had chosen not to take any responsibility for the events of the wedding weekend. She had refused to smooth over any awkwardness and seemed to despise her mother's sudden loss of confidence in the values by which they lived. Priscilla seemed to see, as clearly as did every member of the Hassard family and as her parents did not, that the moment that money had passed hands and David had been sent to a far from minor public school, he had been pushed farther up the social ladder than his parents could climb. It was as though Priscilla was smart enough to recognize the snubs that would await her if she chose to aspire to a higher social position than her parents' money could guarantee. She had decided, in a manner similar to the one in which Sophie had decided her own future, that she would consolidate her position and enjoy it rather than commit herself to the anxieties and humiliations of advancement. When she married, she would marry someone at least her equal, financially and socially. There was no reason why their children a generation later might not enjoy some of the pleasures and privileges for which, she suspected, David had paid too high a price.

Something—a creak of the rowlock, the melancholy cry of a curious seagull circling overhead, the not entirely unpleasant smell of the mud exposed by the falling tide—caused Molly to remember sitting on the bench of the rowing boat the morning after Eithne's dance, her small suitcase beside her, looking over Christy's shoulder at the approaching landing slip where her father waited for her. She felt a fresh wave of sadness—sadness caused by Tibby's death and her own loneliness. She was afraid that she would always feel that sad.

She knew, too, that she had exposed herself to a new kind of unhappiness by depending on Desmond to save her, but she did not know how to do otherwise. Holding Sarah a little closer and smiling at Melanie, she scanned the receding bank of the river, trying to keep Desmond in view. It would be, she thought, at least twenty minutes before he and his family crossed the river to the island.

Just ahead of them, Sophie's boat was drawn up to the slip, and Christy, standing in shallow water, placed a hand on either side of Sophie's waist and lifted her and the bundled train she

161

held in both hands onto dry land. It was not by chance that it was Christy who had rowed Sophie and David, the bride and bridegroom, to the island, nor that his eldest son had taken the bridesmaids across. The hierarchy of the men whose boats carried the guests to the island—as that of the groom's sons waiting with the sidecars and the relatives of the maids in black dresses and white caps and aprons, carrying trays of glasses or filling bridge rolls in the kitchen with egg and cress—was as carefully stratified as the order in which the bridal party had come down the aisle.

Molly, with years of practice, jumped neatly from the bow onto the slip while Liam, Christy's elder son, helped Priscilla and the two little girls ashore. Holding her long skirt just clear of the ground, Molly ran up the slight incline to join Sophie and David by the sidecars. Sophie was standing in front of Miranda, a fat mare taken from her summer field for an afternoon's work. Sophie scratched Miranda's neck and kissed the old horse, twitching at flies, on the nose.

"For goodness' sake, Sophie, don't let her slobber on you," David said. Molly noticed that he kept his distance from the horse.

"She won't."

Sophie laughed as Miranda attempted to nibble her bouquet, and did not pull it away from the old mare's greedy, inquisitive muzzle until Molly protested.

"Sophie. Don't let her."

Sophie laughed again and, placing one satin shoe on the pedal step, jumped lightly up onto the sidecar. Like the rowing boats, the sidecars and the horses had been decorated with flowers. Posies of forget-me-nots and of love-in-the-mist had been attached to the horses' bridles and tack. Children dressed in their Sunday best hung back close to the boatman's cottage, watching Sophie and the bridesmaids arrive. As the first sidecar started up the avenue, the children, no longer silent, ran after them. Their voices and the clattering of the horses' hooves on the stones frightened the guinea fowl deep into the yew bushes and the dark undergrowth, not visible but making their presence known with the occasional outraged shriek.

The octagonal ballroom looked over the river on three sides, but since it also had double doors opening onto both the hall and the lawn, Miles and Belinda did not have to depend on a tent in the garden to shelter their guests. The receiving line was leisurely, since the arrival of the guests was regulated by the river crossing, and allowed for conversation. Once Sophie had taken her place between her new husband and her father, Molly helped place her train so that it was shown to advantage. Priscilla made her way toward the stairs, and Molly followed her.

" 'Go when you can and not when you have to,' " Sophie said, mimicking the tones of a long-departed governess.

David looked at her inquiringly. After a moment, Belinda, realizing Sophie was not going to explain, said, "Sophie had a governess—Miss Curtin—who used to say that to the children. She claimed it was a guiding light for royalty."

"The guiding light for royalty," Molly added, wondering how David would fare when he had no one to explain Hassard family jokes.

Molly did not catch up with Priscilla, who had preceded her up the staircase and had gone into her room. Molly passed the guest rooms and, going through the green baize door at the end of the corridor, went into the nursery, closing the door behind her.

The familiar objects reminded her that this, rather than the room at Fern Hill in which she had spent the past few nights, was now her bedroom. She felt exhausted and longed to stretch out on the bed. That she did not do so was less from anxiety about her dress than the fear that someone would enter and find her, supine, staring at the ceiling. Instead she sat in the rocking chair, put her head back and closed her eyes. The nursery clock ticked; Molly concentrated on its calming sound and wondered who had wound the clock. She could hear the sound of guests arriving, excited voices and the crunch of wheels on gravel.

Since Molly had come to live at Dromore, the three nursery rooms had become her territory, although Sophie still wandered through them with the confidence of an owner. For Molly, Belinda had removed the abandoned debris of childhood, leaving only what was decorative: the entire collection of Beatrix Potter in the bookshelf; a dolls' house; a rocking horse, its paint faded and chipped, the horsehair from its mane largely missing. Her father had ridden on its back as a small boy. Vera had moved her dolls through the wallpapered bedrooms and down the tiny carpeted stairs of the dolls' house. Would Sophie's children play with the toys of their grandparents' generation? Molly thought not. What, then, would become of these family treasures? What would become of her? Molly wondered if she would live with her aunt and uncle, sleeping in the nursery of the large empty house, for as long as Miles lived. And then what? Instead of an orphaned niece would she become a maiden aunt? A poor relation? Assuming, that is, as Molly did not, that the social order of Anglo-Irish life and Dromore itself would survive another two generations. She felt as though she were disappearing, fading away, becoming invisible. She felt as though she knew how it would feel to be a ghost.

Molly took a deep breath to calm herself and went into the nursery bathroom to look in the mirror over the basin. The bathroom was small, functional, linoleum floored, the only touch of comfort a towel rail heated by the sparse supply of hot water. During the winter, after a shallow bath, Molly was grateful for a warm towel and a bathroom in which some of the nip, at least, had been taken from the air. Molly valued the privacy of her own bathroom. There were tribes who ate their dead whose taboos were less rigorously observed than the rights accorded to certain bathrooms and, to an even greater extent, lavatories at Dromore. Miles, as the only male, enjoyed the greatest privilege: dominion over the downstairs gents' cloakroom. An exclusively masculine preserve, it consisted of a washbasin and lavatory, the latter enclosed in a wooden cubicle whose door had frosted-glass panels, and a narrow, dark room in which guns, fishing rods, macin-

164

toshes, and gumboots were kept. The varnished paneled walls were hung with framed photographs of horses, races, and winning posts, and a large mounted salmon. The smell of perished waterproof was almost masked by the stronger and pleasanter smell of gun oil. On a cold day, Sophie and Belinda were sometimes brave enough to use this only downstairs lavatory. Molly would not even consider it. When she had been very small, she had once accompanied Sophie as far as the door, where she had been instructed to stand guard. Sophie had crossed half the distance to the closed door of the lavatory when the floor creaked. She had frozen in her tracks, Molly had retreated a step or two. There was a repetition of the creak and a shadow crossed the frosted glass. Sophie whirled, tiptoed in haste back the way they had come, and both girls fled along the corridor, up the front stairs, and into the night nursery. Only then, the door closed beside them, their faces stuffed into the satin eiderdown, did they give way to uncontrolled giggling.

Hierarchy and caste rather than fear ensured that the nursery bathroom was not used by adult members of the family. Had there been eight children, two nannies, and a governess, they must have shared it as best they could. Nursemaids used a bathroom in the staff wing. Now that Molly was the only inhabitant of the nursery, the rules still held. It was all hers. Neither Belinda nor Sophie enjoyed a similar privilege. They shared the main bathroom. There was, in addition, a guest bathroom and a separate lavatory across the landing. It was from there that Molly could hear Priscilla now emerging. She suspected that Priscilla was appalled by the ornate Victorian lavatory that seemed to glorify its function. The bowl was decorated with a floral design and proudly bore the name of its maker. The seat was wooden and, standing a little higher than usual, thronelike. A chain, ending in a wooden handle, hung from the large tank just below ceiling level. For as long as Molly could remember, the slot above the doorknob had read *Engaged,* the mechanism that should have changed the legend to *Vacant* when the door was unlocked having been broken.

Molly's headdress was made of the same material as the over-skirt of her dress. The soft, pliable fabric had been gathered into tiny rosettes and attached to a stiff hairband. Molly carefully smoothed the surface, fearing to undo Miss Hearne's work, which involved hairpins.

As Molly descended the stairs, she saw her grandfather and her grandmother Daisy. A maid carrying a large silver salver was offering champagne to the guests who strolled through the hall on their way to view the wedding presents. Rather to her surprise, Molly saw Caroline standing with her grandparents. Daisy embraced Molly.

"How pretty you look," Daisy said as she released her and stepped back to look at her dress. "Your dress is lovely. You need fattening up, though."

"Don't go too far away with that," Caroline said to the maid carrying the tray. "'Needs fattening up.' Nobody ever wants to fatten up a boy. Girls are fattened up like pigs going to market. And none of them wants to be fatter. Does that mean they don't want to go to market?"

Daisy looked startled, but Nicholas, who had planted a damp kiss on Molly's forehead, now put his arm around her. "This lit-tle piggy doesn't have to go to market if she doesn't want to. Not while I'm alive."

Although the prospect of living in her grandfather's house, bullied by him and terrified at meals, was even less appealing to Molly than that of living as a maiden aunt at Dromore, she was grateful to her grandfather. He had never before suggested that she held any value to him, or a place in his affections.

Caroline caught the eye of the maid with the salver and beck-oned to her. Nicholas and Caroline took fresh glasses of cham-pagne. Daisy had not touched hers, and Molly declined, planning to save her limited champagne-drinking for later, possibly in a more romantic setting. Nicholas and Daisy moved into the draw-ing room, and Molly and Caroline drifted toward the receiving line at the front door, both feeling somewhat responsible for Sophie and for those whose paths she crossed were neither girl there to act as a buffer.

"I like your grandparents and your great-aunts."

"You do? Grandpa doesn't have much of a following in this family. The great-aunts talk about Daisy having made her bed and now having to lie in it, but my father used sometimes to say something about outcross and hybrid vigor."

Caroline looked bemused.

"Horses. Breeding in a new strain. Taking a risk to revitalize."

"Your grandfather came back from the First World War—he's a survivor in other ways, too, of course—made it through the Crash, supported a family. They're all survivors."

Molly was feeling well disposed toward Nicholas, grateful for his affectionate gesture and the suggestion that she possessed some inherent rights as well as being the recipient of the generosity of her relatives. The gratitude she felt at Dromore sometimes exhausted her. She was heartened by Nicholas's recognition of her value and by the security of not only being under his protection but having his blood in her veins.

"Don't you think the rest of us will survive?" Molly asked a little nervously, granddaughter of Nicholas but daughter of parents who had not proved so resilient.

"Some of us will, some won't. Way too soon to know which ones will."

Molly didn't like the idea that her chances in life should be measured by comparison with those around her who were so clearly in control of their destinies. During the year she had been in love with Desmond, she had often thought of their conversation in the greenhouse looking at the black flowers, with its implication that she, as a member of the dwindling Anglo-Irish population, was, in addition to any unfortunate hereditary tendencies, culturally and racially headed for extinction.

As they passed through the front door, Molly saw Desmond, the instigator of her feeling of living in the shadow of a volcano—doom inevitable but not immediate and largely ignored by those struggling for day-to-day survival—enter. She introduced him to Caroline, aware that she was blushing as she did so.

"I was looking for you," he said.

Molly, who had hoped that her blush was fading, felt it deepen again and found herself unable to look at either him or Caroline.

"Oh," she said weakly. She had in her mind rehearsed meeting Desmond at Sophie's wedding, but she had not expected it to be so immediate, that he would seek her out in so public a fashion, or that there would be a witness. Caroline, who appeared to have noticed nothing, continued out onto the gravel in front of the house, where guests had arrived in large enough numbers for the reception to have become festive.

Molly moved instinctively toward the library to draw Desmond away from the stream of guests coming in the front door. Mrs. Archdale led the way, wearing a stole that Tibby had once described as "boiled mink," accompanied by Major Archdale, clearly less happy in a too-tight morning coat than in the attire he wore when playing with his dance band. Desmond allowed himself to be led into the library. To her surprise, he drew her to one side instead of making for the French windows as she had imagined he would.

"I just needed to ask you," he said, rushing his words, "someone's made a baggins of the sleeping arrangements—probably my mother. The thing is, Belinda said you might be able to help—we've had three English guests billeted on us, and we were only expecting two, and there's really not room. Belinda thought you might be able to squeeze one more in at Fern Hill. Just for the night."

"Of course," Molly said with a sinking heart. It was to solve this domestic problem that Desmond had sought her.

"Thanks, I'll introduce you to him a little later."

There was a pause while Molly silently willed Desmond to say something, anything, to restore the intimacy that had seemed almost tangible between them a few afternoons ago at Fern Hill.

168

Instead, he gave her a friendly smile and returned the way he had come. Molly, unable to detain him, watched him go and felt a heavy despair in the pit of her stomach.

Moving with the air of one on an errand to prevent anyone engaging her in conversation, Molly went through the French windows onto the lawn. A breeze was blowing from the river, and small white clouds shunted unthreateningly across the sky. Molly told herself that nothing bad had happened. Desmond had been preoccupied with the awkward business of laying off a guest; an encounter between them along the lines of her fantasies had not necessarily been ruled out. Though in her heart she suspected this not to be the case, she knew that in order to keep going for the rest of the afternoon, she had to reassure herself as best she could.

Vera, followed by a small troupe of middle-aged and elderly women, led the way to the herbaceous border. Molly's grandmother Daisy was among them. One of the older ladies was carrying an earth-stained canvas bag and a businesslike pair of secateurs. In return for tribute in the form of flattery and for a moment of power, Vera would dispense cuttings from her prized and sometimes rare plants to the acquisitive women whose passion for gardening left them as lacking in pride as a drug addict in need of a fix.

Molly reduced her pace to avoid a meeting with the Butler sisters. Even on days when she felt more sure of herself, the Misses Butler provided more pleasure and amusement at a distance than they did at close range. Constance and Muriel Butler lived in a faded redbrick Queen Anne house on the Dunmore road. They had endeared themselves to the local population by breeding and successfully racing greyhounds and, by their habit, although they were not twins, of dressing identically. Striving for a mirror image was the full extent of their fashion ambition. That afternoon they wore blue-and-white silk dresses, navy-blue shoes with ankle straps, and, as a sensible precaution against the possibility of a wind off the river, white hand-knitted cardigans. Their clothing tended to be girlish. They wore tortoiseshell slides in their slightly too long, wavy brown hair and perhaps too much dark-red lipstick.

Molly made her way across the lawn to the front of the house where the sidecars circled to drop guests and return to the ferry. A fresh load of gravel had been raked over the avenue earlier in the week by the men who had filled in the puddles and ruts— visible signs of one of the bottomless pits into which the dwindling reserves of Anglo-Irish money were traditionally poured (the roof at Dromore was even more expensive, but unlike Fern Hill it was kept watertight and in good repair). Although a good lawn and thick layer of gravel were signs of affluence and a well-maintained house, the boundaries between the two had to be carefully monitored. Geraldine—the older sister of the Carew boy who had filled in at Eithne's coming-out dance, the grandson of old Lady Carew, descendent of the girl who had danced at the Duchess of Richmond's ball—had lost a far from superfluous suitor when her father, the Brigadier, had ordered the young man off the property after watching him drive up to the house at a speed that sprayed gravel onto the lawn.

As Molly approached, she could see Desmond talking to his mother—presumably reporting a successfully accomplished mission—and another couple. The young man, noticeably more attractive and better turned out than his companion, was laughing with an aplomb Molly had to admire. She would have found no humor in finding herself a guest farmed out to a neighbor, unsure of either her welcome or a comfortable bed. Without knowing much about tailors or men's clothing, Molly could see that the young man wore his morning coat with the same ease as did Desmond, although his was newer. Apart from Sophie's clothes and the possessions of a few of the richer girls from Northern Ireland at Kingstown House, Molly assumed, as a direct result of experience, that old things were of a better quality than new. Clothing, furniture, books; all these, if they had belonged to a previous generation, were substantial, durable, of good material. Their replacements tended to be thin and shoddy. Miles's twenty-five-year-old shoes from Lobb, carefully polished and maintained, would last him his lifetime; Molly's new shoes from a shop in Waterford would not last twenty-five months. The trunk she took to school had been Sophie's and Miles's before her; the new suitcase that accompanied it was already worn at the corners and looked as though it had been made of cardboard. A comparatively deprived Anglo-Irish upper class had made a snobbish virtue out of disparaging the new. Sophie had antagonized her father-in-law by being dismissive of new houses and new jewelry. Molly had been brought up with the same prejudices, but sometimes she thought that valued pieces of family jewelry had once been bought from a jeweler, houses had once been built, the trees around them newly planted saplings. Had new been different then?

"Molly, we were just coming to find you." Desmond joined her at the edge of the lawn. The young man, who was drawing looks of curiosity and veiled admiration from the other guests, followed him, smiling at Molly as though delighted to meet her. Behind them, the two women followed the guests trickling into the house through the front door. Molly assumed that Lady Marjorie would be conducting an intensive inspection of wedding presents.

"Molly, this is Gerald Sweeney. Gerald, this is—"

"Molly, my hostess and the guardian angel who is going to save me from a night in Desmond's intermittently haunted potting shed."

Molly felt her spirits lift, not only because Desmond, too, was smiling, his abrupt and harassed demeanor changed to one more relaxed, but because Gerald Sweeney was looking at her with unconcealed admiration. It made her aware of the soft, thin fabric brushing against her legs. It made her feel light and graceful. Molly knew little of flirtation. It was an art neither practiced nor prized in County Waterford. The closest she had come to it was the unexpected attention of a couple of jocular friends of Miles's who used to make Sophie and Molly giggle, both girls mystified that neither Miles nor Belinda was as amused as they were. Later Molly came to suspect that the attention paid to her or her cousin was less a tribute to their personal charms or their capacity for appreciating wit than an attempt by an inept performer, having failed with the orchestra and stalls, to play to the gallery.

"I'm—" Molly started, then caught herself. She had intended to say that she was at school with a girl named Sweeney but remembered that she had allowed Desmond to believe that she was no longer a schoolgirl. She started again: "I have a friend called Cynthia Sweeney."

"Brave girl. She's my cousin. Once removed. I like to stress that. And the fact that I take no responsibility for her actions. Close friends, are you?"

Molly backtracked before she got in deeper.

"I'm more a . . . sort of . . . lady-in-waiting than a best friend."

Gerald laughed. "Granddaughter of the Loose Canon, daughter of the Chancer, she's bred for—I don't know . . . something—to end up a duchess or on the gallows. I'm very deferential in her presence."

Molly felt her eyes begin to assume their saucerlike proportions and, as she often did, wished for a little time to digest this new information. It seemed to her that intelligence of this kind was rarely offered to her, but when it was, it came in bulk.

"Molly'll fill you in on the house rules," Desmond said. "Chapel at six-thirty—"

"I'm sure you have obligations of your own to fulfill," Gerald said, taking Molly by the arm. "This adorable girl will relieve you of the embarrassment of introducing me to your relatives."

Holding Molly close enough for her bare arm to feel the sleeve of his morning coat, he led her away from Desmond and back across the lawn. Molly looked back toward Desmond, appealing, laughing, helpless, for the first time in her life flirtatious, glowing with the reflected admiration of a handsome and entertaining man. Desmond's mouth was slightly open, his admiration and regret unconcealed.

"First, a drink," Gerald said. "You don't have one—I expect you did and you gave it away to someone whose need seemed greater than your own."

"I—"

"You're not going to tell me how old you are, are you? Please don't. If you're twenty, I'll be polite but disappointed; if you're thirteen, I'll reluctantly give you back to your nanny—and I don't want to do that."

Molly understood that Gerald was telling her that for this afternoon, or the next ten minutes, she could free herself of her puritanical adherence to literal-minded truth; that not all questions had to be answered, not all assumptions corrected. Compliments should be accepted; this was an interlude for fantasy, an initiation into a delightful adult game.

Allowing Gerald to lead her as though it were he, not she, who would conduct the tour of Dromore, Molly, already heady with the relief of Desmond's renewed admiration and Gerald's attention, accepted a glass of champagne from the elderly parlormaid holding the salver.

"Let's start with the gardens," Gerald said, "before the traditional Irish wedding rain starts. Or maybe you have an admirer waiting for you—standing in the corner of some romantic arbor, holding two glasses of tepid champagne?"

Molly laughed, knowing better now than to demur. Although she knew she should take Gerald's compliments with, as her grandmother Daisy would say, a pinch of salt, she suspected that he must find her attractive enough to expend this amount of energy flattering her.

"Let him wait; my need is greater than his, and it'll do him good to see you monopolized by an obviously stricken rival."

Molly wondered for a moment if Gerald suspected how she felt about Desmond; a perceptive sense of humor rather than experience made her decide that he did not and that his charm came more from how he perceived himself than the one whom he was charming.

Entering the gardens, Molly and Gerald gave the scavenging old ladies a wide enough berth to avoid their conversation but not to avoid their glances, not all of them approving. Molly had an admirer.

"I really am more grateful than I can say for you rescuing me. Lady Marjorie terrified me, and she was none too pleased to find me as a last-minute addition to what I suppose one would call her house party. I got a look at the bachelor's quarters—although there was no question of me getting to kip there. Edwardian and punitive, and it's not as though Lady M. has an unmarried daughter or even an eccentric sister in the attic that she's dying to get off her hands—it's more that unmarried men are deliberately kept in discomfort on general principle. Like at school. Although I assumed that economy more than character building went into cold showers."

Gerald paused. Molly elected not to pick up her cue, choosing not to remark that the Spartan conditions in the Paget household were caused solely by economy.

"Fern Hill won't be the warmest house you've ever been in, and hot water is just as scarce there as it is everywhere else in Ireland."

"I shall wash only at your suggestion," Gerald said loftily.

Although Gerald seemed perfectly content with her company—it was almost as though he had made his journey to Ireland with the express purpose of meeting Molly, viewing the gardens at Dromore, and spending a night at Fern Hill—Molly began to feel that she should return to the house. Although she had fulfilled her obligations as a bridesmaid, and for the time being as a hostess, she did not wish to appear delinquent in her unspoken role of lady-in-waiting to her cousin and dutiful niece to Belinda. She had spent a great part of her life making herself available to either of them, and although the time spent in the garden with Gerald was pleasurable, she was beginning to feel uncomfortable more out of habit than conviction. But Gerald seemed not to be in the habit of being either hurried or directed toward the convenience of others.

"First let's look at the river," he said. Molly allowed herself to be led out of the garden and onto the lawn, which stretched down to the banks of the river. A low stone balustrade, weather worn, marked the end of the lawn. In front of it there was a wrought-iron bench. Molly longed to sit down but feared for her dress. Instead she leaned on the balustrade and looked at the river. Gerald stood close to her and laid his arm across her shoulders. Molly shivered and he drew her closer, although not in a way that made her want to, or feel she should, draw away from him. She watched the cumbersome black dredger discharge a load of mud on the farther bank of the river and, below them, a moor hen going about its business.

After a moment, she asked, "Have you and Desmond been friends for long?"

Gerald glanced at his watch. "About two and a half hours—but it's not a really close friendship. You shouldn't, you know, ask one suitor about another."

Molly understood that it would be boring to react with a literal-minded protest, and though her stomach leaped and her superstitious instincts told her it was dangerous to allow the description of Desmond as a suitor to go unchallenged, she forced herself to laugh lightly.

"All right, how long have you known David, then?"

"David?"

"David Spencer. Sophie's husband. It's their wedding, you know, and I think we should get back to it."

"Oh, him." And he shrugged. Molly thought how convenient it would be never to have to answer a question and wondered how such a state might be arrived at—and what would be the price paid. She knew that it would never be a skill she could acquire.

"I've known David a little longer than Desmond, but we're not quite so close." Gerald said. Molly could detect a note of restlessness in his tone, and although her confidence sank, she took the opportunity to turn her back on the river and encourage Gerald to saunter back to the house and into the drawing room.

"There you are," Caroline greeted them. "They're just going to cut the cake."

"Already?"

"Sophie's conducting this at a fairly brisk clip. Maybe you can get her to slow down a bit."

Seeing Belinda's eye on her, Molly introduced Gerald to Caroline; she did not wish to give the impression that she had spent Sophie's wedding wandering in the garden with a young man she had just met. She was curious also to see if Gerald would bestow the same amount of flattering attention on pretty Caroline. Although Gerald was complimentary and Caroline polite, Molly observed a tension between them, a sensed recognition, although not of a kind that suggested that they had previously met. She understood that Gerald's flirtation with her had lacked this cynical and erotic charge. His tone assured her that it was a game in which she would come to no harm. This assurance he did not extend to Caroline, who was in return, while provocative, guarded. Molly's emotions were mixed. She felt a mild jealousy that Gerald should so easily turn his attention from her to Caroline—and a stronger feeling, also a kind of jealousy, a fear that there would always be Carolines between her and what she wanted. That, as Sophie had overshadowed her during childhood, there would always be someone prettier, more confident, more obvious, demanding of attention, who would effortlessly draw any man from Molly's side to her own. It was not so much the loss of Gerald's attention—for she still felt that Gerald, fickle as he might be, valued her more than he did Caroline—as the fear that the world was full of women and girls who could, at will, take Desmond away from her.

The wedding cake had been made by Maisie, the former cook coaxed back to the Dromore kitchens for one final bravura performance. Molly had imagined that the wedding cake would be a larger and more ornately decorated Christmas cake, but instead, a grease-spattered, yellowed *Mrs. Beeton* had been taken down from the kitchen shelf where it was kept beside Belinda's recipe and menu book and the tradesmen's red account books, held upright by a stoneware Varsity marmalade pot that contained a couple of short, blunt pencils and a few rubber bands.

Three pounds of currants and sultanas had been picked through for stalks and stones, three pounds of raisins stoned with a hairpin, the fruit, washed, dried, and tossed lightly in flour.

Half a small nutmeg had been grated, candied oranges and lemons chopped, two pounds of butter softened and then creamed with two pounds of castor sugar. Flour, eighteen eggs, lemon rind, blanched almonds, and half a pint of brandy had been added. The cake had been baked in a slow oven for five hours; when removed, it was allowed to cool and left to stand in its brown-paper-lined tin. The following day the recipe had been repeated, but since the batter was baked in two smaller tins, one half the size of the other, the baking time was somewhat less. A day later the cakes had been covered with almond paste, the ground almonds and castor and confectioners' sugar bound together with one beaten egg and four egg yolks—Mrs. Beeton having been abandoned and the traditional Dromore Christmas cake marzipan substituted—and the carefully smoothed surfaces coated with both royal and transparent icing.

Molly watched as Sophie cut through the thick icing, then the dense, rich cake. The white encrustation of decoration— the pink addition that graced the Christmas cake having been eschewed—was like frozen snow, not only in its stark whiteness but in the slight crunching sound it made as Sophie, David's hand resting on hers, cut the first slice. Sophie's ceremonial duty completed, her place was taken by Norah, who cut the rest of the cake into slices and set them on plates for the other maids to carry around to the guests. The following day, the second layer would be cut into smaller pieces, put into small boxes lined with crenulated paper, and posted to friends, relatives, and former employees who had not been at the wedding. In much the same way as the objects added to the Halloween barmbrack were believed to predict the future, girls slept with a slice of wedding cake under their pillows to dream of their future husbands.

Gerald was at Molly's side like a friendly shark accommodating the whims of a pilot fish. She could not see Desmond and did not want to crane her neck past the attentive Gerald to search him out. Grateful though she was to Gerald for her new image— no longer a schoolgirl but a young woman who attracted the attentions of a handsome stranger from across the water—she now feared that he might prevent her spending the longed-for time alone with Desmond.

"Molly, where did you disappear to?"

Instead of explaining her absence, difficult to do in Gerald's presence, Molly introduced Gerald to her cousin.

"Sophie, this is Gerald Sweeney. He's a cousin of a girl I . . . knew at school."

Smiling, without much interest at Molly's hesitation and use of the past tense, Sophie asked: "What happened to her?"

"Nothing yet, but plenty will, unless I'm much mistaken." Gerald said.

"Do you know what I'd really like?" Sophie asked Molly, ignoring Gerald.

"The head of John the Baptist on a charger?" Molly asked quickly, hearing the dangerous note in Sophie's voice and reacting with a sureness that surprised herself and earned a quick glance from Gerald.

"Well, that, of course. But more immediately I'd like a nice strong cup of kitchen tea. In a nice, big, thick kitchen cup."

"Here?"

"Hmm. Perhaps not. I'll tell you what—I'll meet you in the nursery in five minutes. I'll bring the champagne."

Smiling slightly at Gerald, who was worldly enough not to try to accompany her, Molly slipped through the crowded drawing room, across the hall, through the swing door, and along a short passage to the kitchen.

Entering the kitchen, Molly instantly became a child again, warmly greeted, her dress of silk and crepe de Chine, among the uniforms and Sunday best of the others, not causing the ripple that would otherwise have been felt when a Hassard entered a roomful of estate employees. Molly was not only a child but, as they were, dependent.

Two large kettles were already heating on the Aga. A silver teapot stood on the kitchen table, awaiting a refill. Seated at another table by the window, the large, brown, earthenware kitchen teapot in front of them, were men and women who worked at

Dromore but who were not needed in handing round tea, drinks, cake, or sandwiches.

Molly took down from the shelf the nursery teapot—broad blue and white stripes—and, eschewing the offer of two cups taken from the draining board and hastily wiped by a girl whom Molly recognized but could not put a name to, she warmed the teapot and put two kitchen cups and saucers on the nursery tray.

Carrying the tray and moving awkwardly to avoid treading on her skirt, Molly ascended the uncarpeted back stairs. At the end of the landing there was another baize-covered door. Passing through it, she trod once more on polished wood and Turkish carpets. The nursery door was slightly ajar.

Sophie, crushing the full smooth lines of her dress against Molly's bed, was smoking a cigarette. Her satin slippers, one on its side, were discarded on the floor beside her. Molly gave Sophie her tea and sat again in the rocking chair where she had tried to compose herself only a few hours earlier. Sophie did not speak, acknowledging her cup of tea only with a smile. She gazed thoughtfully at the ceiling and blew a lungful of smoke through her nose.

"Do you remember when Mummy read *Orlando, the Marmalade Cat* to us?" she asked eventually.

"Yes."

"Why did you cry?"

Molly hesitated. She knew the answer to Sophie's question, although the incident to which she referred had taken place ten years earlier. Her hesitation came from a reawakened sense of shame brought on by the memory of her tears.

"Come on. It's my wedding day—I get to do what I like."

"The logic of that escapes me," Molly said, using a phrase of her father's.

"Molly—"

"Because he left his family behind on the beach when he went up in the balloon."

Sophie nodded thoughtfully and continued her inspection of the tiny cracks in the ceiling.

"Think of one thing," she said, her voice in no way indicating a change of subject, "one thing that would make you completely happy. Make *you* happy, not high-minded stuff like world peace. Don't tell me what it is. All right?"

Molly nodded.

"Got it?"

Molly nodded again.

"All right. Now, if God or a genie or some other trustworthy omnipotent being were to tell you that you could have a happy life, no strings attached, but that you could never have that one thing that you were thinking of, would you accept?"

Molly looked at her, appalled. "No," she said slowly, understanding the willful implications of her stubborn reply. "Would you?"

"I don't know," Sophie said, her voice low and helpless. "I don't know."

During the silence that followed, Molly startled herself with two thoughts. First she wondered if Sophie had asked the question to see whether she, Molly, had a secret dream, a secret longing. Then, when her cousin did not pursue the topic, she wondered what Sophie, on her wedding day, had chosen for her source of happiness—and then it occurred to her that Sophie might not have been able to think of anything.

"It wouldn't, I suppose," Sophie said eventually, "be practical for you to sneak downstairs and bring us back two large slices of wedding cake, preferably with extra marzipan?"

"I probably could, but it would have to be three slices. One for Gerald. If you don't mind him sitting on the bed, dropping crumbs onto your dress."

"Encouraging mice. When you went to get the tea, I tried to palm him off on Caroline. He wouldn't go for it; said he'd met her kind before. Upper-class English families who invite you to stay and then, as they see you to your bedroom in the east wing, warn you, no matter what you hear during the night, not to leave your room."

"What did you do with him?"

"I introduced him to the Butler girls. I was almost sorry not to stay."

"Did he fall for it?"

Molly was referring to the trap that the Butler sisters with their matching clothing set for the unwary. Most strangers were startled by the no longer young, whimsically symmetrical pair into making some reference to their apparent twinship, allowing Muriel Butler to reveal in an affronted manner that she was three years younger than her sister. What was in it for Constance Butler was not clear, but she played her part with equal enthusiasm.

"Absolutely not. He listened to my introduction carefully and then asked: 'Butler? Are you two related?' "

"Fairly impressive."

"I thought so. I'm going to ask him to come and visit in London. He's not actually one of David's friends. He has an awful brother who is."

"Shouldn't you be getting back to your guests, awful or otherwise?"

"In a minute. Give me another cup of tea with lots of sugar and tell me one more thing."

Molly poured the tea and gave it to Sophie, who had pulled up the eiderdown as she huddled against the headboard. It seemed to Molly that Sophie was in shock.

"It's your turn to tell me something. I told you about Orlando, the Marmalade Cat."

"That's not such a big secret."

"Yes, it is—anyway, it's the one you asked."

"What do you want to know?"

Suddenly Molly didn't want to know anything that pertained to Sophie's marriage or her new life or her visible unhappiness.

"Tell me the first thing you remember. Ever."

Sophie nodded thoughtfully and sipped her tea.

"Do you remember Patience?"

"Of course."

Patience was the pony who had pulled the trap that the Hassards had used during the war and in the years afterward before cars were back on the road.

"The first thing I remember," Sophie said, "was my father showing me how to give Patience an apple. He cut it into quarters with that penknife he carries in his pocket and showed me how to make my hand flat so that she didn't bite my fingers by mistake. I remember how her breath was warm and smelled sweet, like clover. Her whiskers were sharp and tickled my hand, but her muzzle was the softest thing I ever touched. How about you?"

"Lying on a rug under a cherry tree in bloom. At Fern Hill. The grass under the rug was long, and the rug was bumpy. It was beige and brown with red stripes."

Sophie nodded, looking satisfied. Putting her teacup on the night table, she got off the bed and smoothed the creases in her dress with her outspread hands. She turned and moved to the mirror to adjust her hair and veil.

"What's that on your dress?" Molly asked, horrified by a brown-and-red stain on the cream satin.

Sophie stood transfixed, looking at the white counterpane on Molly's bed. It, too, bore a small red stain.

"Oh, hell," Sophie said, sounding tired and discouraged rather than appalled.

"Tell me what to do," Molly said quickly.

"Nothing. Pull the counterpane off and leave it to soak in cold water. I'll go and change into my going-away suit. Perhaps the dress can be saved. Caroline will embroider a flight of butterflies across the back—or something. Oh, damn it all."

And she went out, leaving her bouquet on the bloodstained bed.

CONTRARY TO HIS protestations, Gerald was deeply engaged in conversation with Caroline; in fact, had her leaning against a

182

wall beside a doorway while he stood in front of her, one hand on the wall just above her head, his arm and body keeping her captive. Molly found the sight disturbing and, for reasons she did not understand, erotic.

She glanced around for the Butler sisters, who had presumably withdrawn, defeated, some time ago. The idea that social life, or perhaps life itself, was a series of minor or major skirmishes, each with a clear victor and an even clearer loser, was not a happy one. As a dedicated noncombatant, Molly presumably lost each encounter by default. The sisters were chattering happily, even flirtatiously, with her grandfather. It was impossible for Molly to tell whether this was a first meeting or if the three were old friends. The tiny Anglo-Irish population—fifty thousand in the whole republic—made it probable that any two Protestants from the same county would know each other; equally probable was the likelihood that the nuances that defined and separated the tiny but rigid social structure would have kept them apart. Only a large, almost democratic, gathering such as a wedding or the hunting field could have been a meeting place. It was the first time Molly had seen her grandfather not at a disadvantage, even at his own dining-room table. Trapped in privilege he had neither sought, earned, nor deserved.

It took Molly a moment to get Caroline's attention—by bobbing up and down like a small child—and a slightly longer moment for Gerald to show a flicker of irritation.

"Sophie needs you upstairs."

"She's not changing? Already? Is she trying to get this wedding into the *Guinness Book of Records*?"

"There's a problem with the dress," Molly mumbled, feeling a humiliating blush rise on her face.

At the mention of the dress, Caroline lost all interest in Gerald; the same words extinguished in him the mild spark of curiosity that Molly's urgent interruption had kindled. As Caroline moved away, Molly observed Gerald adjust his demeanor to the less intense attitude he displayed toward her. She glanced around for Desmond. Had she been sure of her next meeting with him, she would have been content to leave the day as it stood—the early disappointment more than compensated for by Desmond's expression as Gerald had borne her away.

Although she would not have refused it, Molly did not require dramatic, immediate gratification. She did not crave the notoriety, or the struggle, that had marked Sophie's premature transition to the status of a married woman. Allowed to choose the tempo of her own fragile love affair, she would have developed a not necessarily spoken understanding that would have become gradually visible to the rest of the world over the next few years, ending in an inevitable and suitable marriage. The events of the afternoon would have kept her satisfied for quite a long time had she not known that it might be months before she again met Desmond. In a barely acknowledged recess of her mind lurked the fear that another exchange that afternoon might be in some way less satisfying—if he were, for instance, again preoccupied with arrangements. A less satisfactory encounter would spoil the pleasurable memory of his open admiration.

"You're far too young to be looking over my shoulder when you're supposed to be talking to me."

"I was looking for Desmond. We should remind him not to leave with your luggage. Is it in his car?"

"You'll find that where my immediate comfort is concerned, I'm not as vague as I look. I'd be happy to borrow a pair of pajamas from you tonight, but I really like a pair of clean socks in the morning. While you were away I ingratiated myself with your family. You'll find that your grandfather, far from being an impediment, will encourage you to elope with me."

"He will?"

"Absolutely. I was having a most enlightening conversation with a delightful pair of sisters about the mating habits of greyhounds when he strolled past whistling a song from *Ruddigore.*"

Molly looked interested rather than enlightened.

" 'She could easily be taken for forty-three in the dusk with a light behind her.' "

Molly gasped.

"Taking a bit of a chance, I thought," Gerald said. "I mean, the Butler sisters might have a passing acquaintanceship with Gilbert and Sullivan."

"He wouldn't care, and look how well he's getting on with them now."

The Butler sisters, it might be argued, were not in a position to pick and choose with whom they conversed at a Hassard wedding, but Caroline and Gerald, both of whom Molly considered fairly grand, found him charming. As they would have found her father. Once again she wished she could freeze the afternoon in time and return to it when she had considered and adjusted old beliefs and opinions in light of new and sometimes startling information. But since she could not do so, she tucked away this new image of her grandfather and gradually, towing Gerald behind her, made her way toward Desmond, who was gracefully leaning against the banister at the foot of the stairs. Since he was standing beside the girl with whom Gerald had arrived, she thought that she might have a chance to draw him away if Gerald fulfilled, at least minimally, his obligations.

Crossing the hall took a little longer than Molly imagined. Gerald had to be introduced to the gregarious and the curious, and even she seemed to earn a little more attention than she used to. Eventually they reached the small group around Desmond. Molly hesitated, but Gerald, lifting a full bottle of champagne from a passing salver, leaned into the circle and topped up the already half-filled glasses. Putting an arm around Molly's shoulders, he drew her into the group, but before introductions could be made, all eyes turned toward Sophie at the top of the stairs.

The staircase at Dromore dominated the hallway. Behind the first landing there was a large window that overlooked the stableyard and the river beyond, which provided the natural light for the hall. The stairs divided and continued from both sides of the landing and climbed to the second floor. The pale-green carpet was held in place by long, slender, three-sided stair rods. As small girls, Molly and Sophie had loved to help polish the rods. The

185

rods had to be slid out of the fittings on either side of the carpet and then carried to the housemaid's pantry. Each rod would be rubbed with Brasso, applied with the remains of a pair of Miles's old flannel pajamas. The liquid turned white on the metal and left dark stains on the cloth. The most satisfying part had been rubbing the dried polish from the rods and watching them become bright and shiny.

Conversation stopped as Sophie paused before the window, silhouetted in the light. Molly saw that Caroline had caught up the back of the wedding dress into a small bustle to cover the stain. The result flattened the front panel of the dress and gave Sophie a faintly regal air. Watched by the silent and admiring guests, Sophie moved quickly and lightly halfway down the stairs and, with a light, graceful, and beneficent gesture, threw her bouquet toward Molly.

Molly stretched up her hands to catch the falling flowers, but before she could reach them, the silent girl at Desmond's side, jumping onto the bottom steps of the staircase, stretched up and, one-handed, caught the bouquet. She turned with a triumphant smile and put a hand on Desmond's shoulder, looking into his eyes.

"Now you really will have to marry me," she said, a little too loudly.

Chapter Nine

MOLLY, UNLIKE SOPHIE, not only enjoyed but adapted to life at Albert Court quickly. It was midway though a mild September—about the time Molly would have returned to school—when she arrived in London. Although physical comfort had not been a motivating force in this radical and premature change in her life, she felt conscious gratitude for the centrally heated draft-proof flat and for tea with delicate sandwiches and cakes from Harrods every afternoon in front of a cheerful coal fire. Her sense of well-being would be enhanced during those minutes after tea, while the light outside grew gloomy although not yet dark, when Isabel would heat an iron spoon, long-handled enough for supping with the devil, over the coals, pour a few drops of scented oil into it and, straight-backed and elegant in her black dress, move slowly and carefully about the drawing room while the scent of the warm oil permeated the elegant atmosphere of the high-ceilinged room. Molly would rise and draw the long, faded green velvet curtains and light the lamps. She would carry the tea tray along the corridor to the kitchen, where she and her great-aunts, the division of labor decided by an unwritten but firmly memorized rota, would wash and dry the teacups and plates. Afterward Molly would go to her room to do homework or to write to Belinda and Miles until it was time for their light supper. On some but not all evenings, they would watch a carefully chosen program on the television before Ovaltine and bed.

Although Molly sometimes could not sleep and lay awake crying, she did so in a warm bedroom with a fat satin eiderdown, a carafe of water, and a small tin of biscuits on her bedside table. Although the flat was large by London standards, it was smaller than anywhere Molly had ever before lived. She knew where both her great-aunts were at any moment, and she found their calm and ordered presence comforting. When she felt lonely or afraid, she could reassure herself with an image of Great-aunt Charlotte buffing her nails in the next bedroom or of Isabel in the drawing room needlepointing a new back for one of the dining-room chairs.

Not surprisingly, since both Molly's parents had been much younger when they died than either of the great-aunts now were, she soon developed a fear of losing them. She watched carefully for signs of aging or ill health, and when she realized that both the old ladies might continue their lives as they now were for some time, she then understood that there was a conflict between their goal and hers—between that of their generation and her own. The old ladies worked, struggled, to maintain the status quo, understanding that small lazinesses such as eating lunch in the kitchen were really the *snip snip* of the tiny threads that still attached them to a life of dignity and independence. Breaking these threads would free their bodies and minds to drift into that dangerous area of diminished expectations and standards—into compromise, ill health, the squalor of old age, and eventually death. Her great-aunts were, each day, valiantly fighting for their lives. But Molly, once she had spent a period of recuperation, contemplation, and rest in the civilized comfort of Albert Court, knew that her life was predicated on change and that she, too, was fighting for her life. Not avoiding imminent death, but ensuring that she would not play, a generation too late, the role of Vera. The best interests of her great-aunts would be served if in two years' time the three of them were sitting by the fire sipping China tea, her aunts pressing a second slice of Fuller's walnut cake on her, looking forward to watching, on television, Sir Malcolm Sargent conduct the last night of the Proms at the Albert Hall. But Molly's own interests would be better served if she were sitting two hundred yards away in the audience—better still if she had been part of the motley troupe of students lined up for tickets the night before.

It was not only because she had arrived exhausted at Albert Court that it took Molly a little time to understand that, despite affection, in this she was at odds with her great-aunts. For change to seem possible, opportunity was necessary.

The old ladies liked to discuss, although a great deal less anxiously than they had when Sophie had been their ward, the fine points of the responsibility of having a young girl in their charge. Molly was too young to be "out," but since she was not to be a debutante, and since she had earned some adult status acting as their hostess at Fern Hill, she could not be treated as a child. And even a child is entitled to a small social life. Reluctantly forced to accept that *tea dansants,* the ideal solution, were a thing of the past, the old ladies agreed that it was desirable for Molly to spend time with people, by which they meant girls, her own age. From somewhere, probably a misunderstanding of an initially not quite accurate television portrayal, Molly's aunts knew of coffee bars, and Molly was pressed to visit these establishments; with whom and to what end never clearly expressed.

That coffee bars existed was undeniable; but so far as Molly could ascertain, their clientele did not come from the Queensgate Education Centre. Molly's fellow students almost all fell into one of three distinct categories: those whose idea of after-school refreshment was a champagne cocktail at the Ritz, those who believed that an unchaperoned visit to a South Ken coffee bar would condemn them to an afterlife in a Mideastern fundamentalist hell, and the lank-haired, black-stockinged, dark-lipsticked girls who, Molly assumed, drank absinthe with brutal but brilliant artists in some location unknown to her but probably on or close to the Kings Road.

Nor had Molly been invited to join the ranks of the culturally shocked daughters of oil-rich Arabs or diplomats who spent much of their time in their bedrooms; equally alien were the well-dressed and worldly not-quite-debutantes who missed classes to recover from a late night or to keep a hairdresser's appointment. The company of the seemingly disillusioned art students would have been a more natural milieu for Molly, but although they would have gladly accepted an out-of-work Apache dancer, they had no interest in the conventionally behaved and attired Molly, who knew, as they did not, that tragedy is rarely glamorous.

Although Molly was unhappy, it was not because she lacked friends or for want of congenial company at the Queensgate college. She fell asleep each night painfully missing Desmond and woke each morning as though she had that moment discovered that he was engaged to Pauline McBride. She missed her father, but her feeling for him was more helpless pity than sharp pain. Her father's death had accelerated her progression up the generational ladder. Rather than replace her parents with Miles and Belinda, she was just old enough to wish to rebuild her family by having a husband and children of her own. With Tibby dead, the loss of Desmond represented a loss greater than that of purely romantic love.

Molly, although quietly miserable, was grateful for her new life. She was more than fond of her great-aunts and took pleasure in her studies at the casual and comfortable house in Queensgate; that she was a student there rather than a schoolgirl at boarding school outside Dublin was a source of pride to her. The success of her confrontation with Miss Simpson, when she had refused to do something that she could not do, had led her to announce that she was not returning to Kingstown House. She presented this as a fact. It had been her intention, while she believed that Desmond cared for her, to leave school in order to clear the way for courtship. Deprived of that hope, in a moment of strength born of anger, she had decided to do something that would make her happier without regard for the convenience of others, even those to whom she was most indebted. She succeeded more easily than she had expected. Even Sophie's contribution ("A secretarial course is always useful") after the initial smile had found general agreement.

Molly had also found the courage, made necessary by her request, to broach one of the taboo subjects of Anglo-Irish society: money. She asked Belinda whether she, Molly, had any money and, if so, how much. Belinda's embarrassed hesitation was due not only to delicacy but because Tibby had not left his affairs in order. It was not so much that he had mismanaged a respectable sum of money than that he had not faced up to how even his modest style of living was nibbling away his inadequate capital. Belinda, in a kind and unsentimental way, told Molly that the difference between the cost of Molly continuing her education in London rather than at an Irish school was not an issue. With a single exception in the early seventeenth century, no Hassard had ever attended a university, so it was only a matter of one year's tuition. Belinda also told Molly that Miles, as her trustee, had decided that none of Molly's modest inheritance should be touched for her education or living expenses until she was twenty-one and that her income, such as it was, would be reinvested so that the trend of the past twenty years, although far too late, might be reversed. Belinda tactfully told Molly that she could not expect an income large enough to make her independent. She would be somewhat less well off than Vera, but since she would be just as welcome at Dromore, it was not grounds for fear. And Molly would of course, Belinda added with a smile, in the fullness of time, marry.

Molly thought that she would not marry, but she did not say so. Since she would not marry and since she did not wish to play the role of maiden aunt, it would be necessary for her to earn her living. Soon after she arrived at Queensgate, she realized that if she were to continue the course of studies she had started at Kingstown House, it would not qualify her for either interesting or well-paid work. Even if a university education had been available to her, the academic level necessary to graduate from

Kingstown House was not high enough for her to gain entry to a university. Seeking no one's advice, Molly canceled her geography course and, after a moment's guilty hesitation, French and German. She enrolled instead in shorthand, typing, and simple book-keeping. With a little more enthusiasm, she signed up for a course in the nineteenth-century novel. It seemed to her that she should be able to earn a living as a secretary, and she thought that the people to whose company she aspired (she had yet to meet one of them) would be less dismayed by her inability to draw from memory a map of the South Wales coalfields than they would be by an ignorance of the work of George Eliot. She did not, however, discontinue her math studies, both because she was irritated by the suggestion that girls were intrinsically inept with numbers and because she took pleasure in their order and logic. Molly grasped at certainties wherever she could find them.

Five days a week, Molly went to school (although school was a word she assiduously avoided using), walking on fine days and taking the bus if it rained, and came home to the pleasant routine of her great-aunts' lives. On Sundays, she accompanied them to church, ate a proper Sunday lunch (roast beef and roast potatoes, which had cooked slowly while they attended the service), and sometimes afterward walked to Sophie's house for tea. On Saturdays, she would visit Sophie in the late morning, chatting to her while she dressed, and, at a time when Molly would normally eat lunch, the three of them would drift over to a pub on the Fulham Road. It was there that David and Sophie seemed most like a married couple. The atmosphere of the pub, the open and pleasant emptiness of a day on which there was nothing to do except argue about where they should eat lunch when the pub closed or if they should go to the cinema later in the afternoon, seemed to calm Sophie's irritability. David, who seemed progressively less tolerant of Sophie's failings, was on those Saturdays pleased by his wife's beauty and by the admiration she elicited from the men whose friendship he valued. Alcohol soothed Sophie, while it made David expansive and his friends flirtatious. Molly was included as a scarcely visible little sister of Sophie's, and after a time it was accepted that her capacity for alcoholic intake was two half pints of shandy.

THERE WERE, it seemed to Molly, whole days when Sophie's descent to the ground floor of her house in Trevor Square was a mere scavenging mission and that one of the functions that her rare and, in a sense, privileged, visitors performed was to fetch and carry up Sophie's simple needs. A cold bottle of wine, the evening paper, and occasional small quantities of food.

How the steady stream of books arrived, Molly did not know, nor could she guess how they were chosen. That afternoon a copy of *The Great Gatsby* lay facedown on the floor. Caroline Penrose was lolling on the bed; Sophie, limp on her chaise longue. An already empty wine bottle stood on the table; the two young women were lazily waiting for Molly to arrive to break the spell, turn on the lights, and carry up tea and more wine. Empty the ashtrays.

Molly thought that Caroline probably left her own reclusive solitude out of respect for a friend further advanced in malaise, although if agoraphobia was one of the symptoms the two shared, the enclosed living quarters of Sophie's shrinking life should have posed little threat to her visitor.

"Gatsby," Molly said, settling into her small familiar armchair. "Have you got to the part—"

"The pearls in the wastepaper basket. How kind of you to ask and—yes, I did marry him without a shudder."

Caroline Penrose, curious and amused, raised an eyebrow.

"If you haven't read the book, I can't explain, although you were, of course, at my wedding, so you can probably work out the gist of it," Sophie said to her.

Molly and Caroline waited; Sophie's tone had an unusual intensity.

"He bought pearls for her. Mine came from my mother and will go to my daughter if I have one. I bet Daisy Buchanan's diamonds were real. I wonder if Caroline knows about pearls and paste—she's quite interested in our exotic, primitive ways. Molly, you explain."

That Sophie had delegated the explanation told Molly that Sophie was fading. "Fading" was a word Molly used to describe—only to herself, never aloud—what seemed to happen to Sophie soon after she had shown a moment of her old wit. An ill-chosen word or an invisible association of her own could send Sophie back into an exhausted, irritated state. Molly hastened to obey her cousin, but she instinctively took her explanation from the shorter version of the litany of Anglo-Irish customs and conventions.

"Anglo-Irish women have real pearls. Their diamonds are usually paste—eighteenth-century paste, preferably. Occasionally a family will still have entailed jewelry—jewelry that they may not legally dispose of. They may even have enough money to hang on to a diamond brooch or two. But the other way round is not all right. In the unlikely event that someone has real diamonds and decides to dress up her twin set with a string of artificial pearls, it doesn't do."

"Why not?"

"It just doesn't," Sophie answered, already bored.

In the silence following Sophie's dismissal, Molly reached lazily for a glass on the ottoman between her chair and the end of Sophie's bed.

"Hey, that's mine. Get your own."

"Sorry." Molly handed the glass to Caroline.

"She wants to read your thoughts," Sophie said, again suddenly animated. She laughed as Caroline looked puzzled.

"More folklore, but this time, strictly speaking, it's French, although since it involves a governess, it's also about us." The "us," as it now did more often than not, meant the Anglo-Irish and appeared to be less a device to include Molly than a barrier Sophie had erected to separate herself from her husband, his family, and his friends. "Molly and I had a governess once. The usual misunderstanding. She thought she was in Ireland to learn to speak

194

English—which, incidentally, she did very soon although with a strong Waterford accent—and my parents thought she'd teach us French. French was supposed to be spoken during our largely silent lunches for a few months each time a new governess came—hell for my father, of course. The governess I'm thinking of— What was her name, Molly?"

"Mademoiselle Cottard."

"Mademoiselle used to say that if you drink out of someone's glass, you can read their thoughts. So what was Caroline thinking, Molly?"

"That's easy," Molly said, smiling. "She's thinking about the dress."

"Are you, Caroline?"

Caroline nodded.

"Stop it," Sophie said. "What use is a used wedding dress, anyway?"

"You could have given it to your daughter—or to Molly."

"I don't have a daughter, and the way things are going around here, David may be the last of his line. And I don't think Molly would want my wedding dress. She spent her childhood in the kitchen with the maids, and she's superstitious."

April 1961

DESPITE GERALD'S ATTENTIVENESS at Sophie's wedding, he had neither called at Albert Court nor telephoned Molly. Molly knew that he was aware of her presence in London since Sophie, at whose house he was an occasional visitor, had told him. Molly was disappointed, more because she would have enjoyed the status and opportunities conferred by the interest of an attractive young man than because she longed for his company.

Inevitably, one Saturday midday, seven months after Molly had come to London, Gerald turned up, the latest addition to the group drinking in the Goat in Boots. Molly was happy to see him and interested to notice that the group around the bar greeted him as one of their own. His well-cut cavalry twills and chukka boots, as well as the right public-school tie, seemed all that was required.

"That settles it. If Gerald's here, we're going to the Indian," David said a little too loudly, his face flushed.

Gerald smiled modestly, the others laughed—except for Molly, who did not understand the joke.

"Gerald's famous for—" Sophie started, but was interrupted by Christopher, a friend of David's who, like most of his male friends, worked in the City.

"Don't tell her; it'll be more fun if she doesn't know."

"On one condition," Gerald said. "Molly has to sit next to me."

Sophie applied lipstick, Molly braved the Goat in Boots lavatory, choosing the evil she knew over whatever might be offered at the Taj Mahal, and a few minutes later, her arm firmly tucked under the sleeve of Gerald's British warm, they crossed the Fulham Road.

Molly sat between Sophie and Gerald. She and Sophie usually sat next to each other so that Molly should not be ignored, so that Sophie would not be shouted down when bickering with her husband. Molly used to wonder what the Indians who owned the restaurant thought of the boorish young men and the beautiful, arrogant, and doubtless, to them, immodest young women. The waiters, however, remained phlegmatic, even when one of the men would shout for them to bring more beer. Sophie and Molly alone in the group said "please" or "thank you"; Molly was the only one embarrassed by her companions' behavior and her implied complicity. Although it had seemed that the others were not only indifferent to but unaware of the impression they made, it now began to seem likely that at least subconsciously they knew how they were perceived.

There were six of them at the table: Molly, Sophie, Gerald, David, Peter, and Christopher. Christopher shared a flat just off the Earls Court Road with Peter, who was an articled clerk in a firm of solicitors in Greys Inn and attended the Saturday gath-

ering at the pub only when the former debutante he was court-
ing spent the weekend with her parents in Wiltshire. Molly noticed that the well-connected girl's filial duties seemed to have
become more pressing during the past few months. She suspected that Christopher, too, was suspicious since he was often
short with anyone who was not in a position to answer back. She
braced herself against his probable rudeness as the Indian waiter
approached to take their order.

"And how is our friend Caroline?" Gerald asked, breaking the
rather anxious silence that tended to fill the time between sitting
down and giving an order for immediate drinks and food soon
afterward, food for which they now found themselves ravenous.

"Why ask me?" Sophie asked. "She told me you were taking
her out on Thursday night. I haven't seen her since."

"Ah-ha," Gerald said and laughed, apparently not embarrassed. He turned to Molly, who was asking the waiter which of
two chicken dishes was the milder. "This young lady will have
the vindaloo chicken—very mild. And I'll have the same—hot."

He handed the menu back to the waiter, who hovered, uncertain. After a moment, Gerald glanced up at him.

"Oh, yes. I'll have a lager with it. Same for you, Molly?"

"The medium vindaloo is very spicy, sir."

Gerald looked thoughtfully at the waiter. The attention of
everyone at the table was on him—Molly's, too, although she still
didn't know why the others were smiling and muffling giggles.
She could tell, and it made her uncomfortable, that the waiter
thought they were laughing at him. He was unfortunate enough
to live and work in England at a time when Peter Sellers had
made his accent, previously unremarkable, seem funny.

"Thank you," Gerald said with elaborate courtesy, "but I like
it spicy. In fact, you might ask the chef"—his choice of noun
caused Christopher to attempt to supress a laugh while his mouth
was full of beer, and after that there was no curtailing the hilarity at the table—"you might ask the chef, if you would, to make
mine extra hot."

"Very well, sir," the waiter said, just as courteously, his expression a little short of inscrutable, as he backed away from the table.

The food arrived more quickly than usual, and as they were served, Molly could see several waiters and someone who looked as though he worked in the kitchen clustering behind the beaded curtain that divided the restaurant from the murky nether regions.

The waiters placed their food on the table. Molly helped herself to a small piece of chicken, avoiding the skin, and a larger portion of rice to dilute the spice of the curry. Gerald leisurely filled his plate and picked up his fork. Molly was aware of a heightened interest in the back of the restaurant, but Gerald appeared to be listening to a conversation between Christopher and Sophie about people whom they did not know but whose names and photographs appeared in William Hickey's column. Christopher and Peter shared a flat with a soft, unreliable young man who worked on the gossip column at the *Daily Express*. Christopher maximized the advantages accruing from his flatmate's indiscretion and was now disclosing some far from probable detail about why Olga Deterding, the oil heiress, had arrived at her decision to leave Dr. Schweitzer's leper hospital at Lambaréné.

Gerald loaded a fork with food, holding it in midair as he joined the conversation.

"It gives me a little sympathy for my pessimistic old pa," Gerald said, and put a forkful of his curry into his mouth, confident that he would not be interrupted as he chewed. After a moment, he signaled to the waiter. "When he was a young man, the world valued brave men and beautiful women—our clearly inferior generation puts more of a premium on rich women and feckless young men."

He glanced up at the waiter, who stood expectantly beside him.

"Everything all right, sir?"

"Yes, indeed, but I think we'll need a little more of your excellent mango chutney." Turning back to his fellow diners, he asked, "I mean to say, are Edward Langley and Dandy Kim Waterfield the kind of fellows who built the British Empire?"

Gerald's Colonel Blimp imitation was enhanced by the growing color in his face and by the tiny dots of sweat breaking out on his darkening forehead. The waiter, disappointed but not discouraged, went to fetch the chutney.

"But working in a leper colony—even if you change your mind—isn't that a good thing? Although you're rich and the papers make a big fuss about it?" Molly asked.

"Category mistake," Christopher said cheerfully.

"Fallacy," David reflexively added. Molly did not think that he had been listening when she had asked her question. "Not that Molly knows a lot about fallacies. She's from Ireland, where they don't have snakes—they have Saint Patrick, in his role of exterminator, to thank for that."

David rarely risked a public dig at Sophie; when he did so, it meant that he was very angry and had had too much to drink. The attacks usually came in the form of veiled references to sexual behavior or a sneer at the Irish.

"I don't entirely buy that stuff about phallic symbols," Sophie said, ostensibly addressing Molly. "It's not only women who have a fear of snakes. How about horses? Do you think that Cormac would be more frightened if David went into his stall and waved his phallus at him or if there was a boa constrictor curled up in his manger with its eye on him?"

Everyone laughed, and no one refuted the dubious logic of Sophie's attack. David, silent, was flushed almost as dark as Gerald had now become.

"You and I," Gerald said to Molly, "must have a quiet evening together so that you can tell me everything that has happened in Ireland since I left."

Now it was Molly's turn to blush. Fortunately, the combination of curry, beer, and the warmth of the airless restaurant had made the others both a trifle unobservant and a little pinker themselves. Peter and Christopher might not have noticed Molly's embarrassment, but they, and David, were curious to see how Sophie, clearly in a waspish mood, would react to flirtatious interest in her young cousin from a man whom she clearly regarded as too old and too experienced.

"Where will you take her, Gerald? You'll have a hard act to follow after this performance."

Everyone laughed. Gerald's face was puce, his eyes watering as he wiped his nose with a silk handkerchief; his plate was almost clean.

"I thought I would do the fire-walking and snake-charming festivals on my own, and if Molly would like it, I would take her to dinner at a quiet bistro and then drop in at the Blue Angel for an hour or two."

Molly was excited by the prospect of her first visit to a nightclub and pleased that attention was focused on Gerald and Sophie, even though it put her in the position of being the bone over which two powerful and well-fed dogs were fighting. She glanced toward the waiters at the back of the restaurant. The man in stained overalls holding a dirty dish towel looked reproachfully at the waiter who had served them and withdrew behind the beaded curtain.

"You'll enjoy our great-aunts," Sophie said. "You'll meet them when you take Molly out."

"I look forward to it," Gerald said, unruffled by Sophie's reminder that the great-aunts would, as Miles would have said, "vet" him before entrusting Molly to him. "That is, if Molly agrees to spend the evening with me. Would you like to, Molly?"

"Yes," Molly said faintly, crimson once again.

"Let's say Tuesday."

"That'd be lovely."

A simple night out on the town with Gerald was for Molly a major event, with nuances that she would need time to consider. Gerald would be less fazed by being introduced to the great-aunts than she would be introducing him or even, before that, telling the old ladies that she would be out for dinner and would be coming home very late since she might stop in at a nightclub. The most difficult thing she had so far had to tell her great-aunts was that she didn't like to eat most meats; that conversation had taken some hours of preparation, and although it had been intended only to explain her abstinence from some foods, it had embarrassingly caused a change in Charlotte and Isabel's carefully structured routine—perhaps the largest change in several years. The great-aunts, a little flustered, now confined their carnivorous behavior to weekday lunches, when Molly was at school. While Molly picked at her curried chicken, they were digesting an omelette or risotto, since it was a Saturday and Molly might have been, although she rarely was, home for the midday meal. Sunday's roast beef and Yorkshire pudding had not come up for review, such a break in tradition being unthinkable to either Molly or her great-aunts.

Molly did not know to what extent Isabel and Charlotte felt themselves responsible for her virtue and reputation. Since neither woman had brought up a daughter since women got the vote, she could not depend on even the standards of a previous generation. Sophie's shotgun marriage, even without the result of a baby, would not help Molly. Even the question of what to wear became complicated. Sophie could be trusted to advise her on what dress would be appropriate for an evening that would start at one of the new Chelsea bistros, its sparse decor dimly lit by candles stuck into wax-encrusted bottles, and would end at the more romantic of London's two most fashionable nightclubs. It would be necessary to borrow a dress from a possibly disapproving Sophie and to buy a pair of shoes. The dress would then have to pass the appraising eyes of her great-aunts, neither of whom wore glasses even for reading. Gerald would be the first young man who had taken Molly out to dinner and only the second attractive man with whom she had ever danced. She felt ashamed, since she was no less in love with Desmond than she had been five minutes before, that she was so pleased and so happy to be treated as a pretty and perhaps even desirable girl.

"And Lady Marjorie?" she heard Gerald ask Sophie. Evidently conversation had resumed while Molly had been worrying about the strategy she needed in order not to turn Tuesday's proposed pleasure into an embarrassing humiliation.

"Exactly the same as when you last saw her," Sophie said. "That's the point. Nothing changes; that's why Molly and I live here."

Gerald raised an eyebrow. David looked as though he was about to say something, then thought better of it.

"Is it? Is that why you're here, Molly?" Gerald asked.

"Save something for dinner conversation on Tuesday." Sophie felt that Gerald was paying too much attention to Molly and, consequently, not quite enough to herself.

"Is it, Molly?" David asked. "She's turning pink."

Molly knew that her complexion was alternating between her normal winter paleness and an unbecoming red.

"Take a look at your own face," she replied lightly and got, at David's expense, a laugh. "Or Gerald's."

Gerald hiccuped loudly, and everyone laughed again. He took a long gulp of his lager, finished the last morsel of food on his plate, and signaled for the waiter. Sweat poured down his face.

"You can take the plates away—it was very good. More drinks for everyone."

He hiccuped again, louder. The waiter permitted himself a small smirk and carried away the empty plates.

"Desmond Paget looked as though he might find himself married—that'd be a change."

Sophie laughed. "Oh—Pauline. That's been going on for years."

"Seemed like a fairly tough character to me."

"She caught a bit of bad luck—the Mau Mau."

Gerald looked not unreasonably surprised.

"She had them all set to emigrate to Kenya. Desmond wouldn't have had a chance."

Molly gazed at the flocked wallpaper. The part that had once been white was faded to a grayish yellow, and she wondered why the proprietors of an Indian restaurant should have chosen such an improbable decor.

"And now he can't bring himself to tell her that all bets are off?"

"It mightn't be the worst thing in the world for him if he did marry her."

Molly could not keep from listening, torn between curiosity and fear that she would hear something that would add to the pain that she had almost managed to integrate into her life.

"No one could make the Paget place pay, there's not enough land, but Pauline could make it last a little longer. She's got some money of her own, and she'd set a fire under Desmond and put an end to some of Frank Paget's schemes. I think Lady Marjorie likes her—the Colonel's lady and Judy O'Grady. Or something like that."

David didn't pick up the reference, but Molly had long since—sometime around the middle of January—stopped attributing quotations for him.

"The black flowers they grow in the greenhouse are beautiful," Molly said. She had been looking for a chance to say something in Desmond's defense that would not compromise either him or herself.

"There's not exactly a huge market for them in Waterford. Or for the sea kale or exotic goldfish or whatever it is Frank Paget fritters the family money away on. Anyway, Pauline may be slightly awful, but Desmond's no great catch himself."

"I should think there are lots of girls, nicer than Pauline, who would be happy to marry Desmond," Molly said.

"You're probably right—what a depressing thought. It says a lot about the eligible men in the south of Ireland."

"Would *you* be happy marrying him?" Peter asked, breaking his somewhat sullen silence to pick on the apparently vulnerable Molly.

For a moment Molly considered telling the truth. It would be satisfying to stop them all. To end the banter, the small snide observations, the not-so-clever cleverness, the petty competitiveness, the prurient gossip—to end it all with a simple factual declaration. To say: "There is nothing that would make me hap-

203

pier. I love him." Two things stopped her. Not timidity or fear of ridicule. She imagined the silence and then someone, Sophie surely, gently reminding her that Desmond was engaged to be married and, with genuine bewilderment, adding that she'd thought that Molly barely knew him. Molly would have had to admit both to be true. At night when she went over every moment she and Desmond had spent together, she had only four meetings to think about. The day her mother died, Eithne's dance, the afternoon at Fern Hill, and, briefly, Sophie's wedding. Molly knew there were two explanations for her love: either she had recognized her twin soul, the man she was meant for, or that Desmond was the only man who had stood still long enough for her to focus her need to love on him. She didn't even know if he took sugar in his tea. She assumed that he believed in God and voted Fianna Fail, but she didn't know on what day his birthday fell. She knew that he had a sister, much older, married and living in England, but she didn't know the sister's name or whether there were children.

"Sophie and I were too well brought up to consider such a question before a proposal," Molly said lightly, surprising herself.

"How do you do that—eat that stuff?" Peter asked Gerald, who was mopping his brow, his face still suffused with color.

"It's good for you." He blew his nose dramatically. "Gives the system a bit of a shock. Keeps it on its toes."

"But—"

"I know how he does it," David said. "I was crossing from Gibraltar once on a wretched little boat. Lots of Spaniards vomiting all over the place. I started to feel a little queasy myself, and I thought, 'You can't be sick in front of all these people, you're British.' And I wasn't."

Sophie, poker-faced, allowed herself to sigh—but quietly enough for only Molly to hear her.

I've got to spend time with smarter people. Molly's thought was so clear that it seemed possible that she might have spoken aloud. She glanced around the table guiltily, caught Sophie's eye, and smiled. Sophie was intelligent enough, but since she gave little value to her intelligence, it didn't seem to count.

"Wogs begin at Calais," she heard from the other side of the table. Either Peter or Christopher. She thought but could not be quite sure that the waiter, carrying another tray of lagers toward them, was still out of earshot.

"FINISH YOUR SPINACH. I promised your great-aunts."

Molly, who was slowly but happily eating a bowl of spaghetti, laughed. She was at ease with Gerald. As had been her great-aunts. He had given them the impression that he usually enjoyed a twenty-minute chat and a glass of sherry with the elderly relatives of every girl he asked to dinner. And he made Molly feel that although the encounter had been unique, it had been so in a completely charming and original way and that her great-aunts were an asset that she could, were she not so modest, exploit to her advantage.

It had been a long time since Molly had felt so happy. Or had had such a sense of relief. She had for some months enjoyed living at Albert Court in pleasant surroundings with affectionate and courteous companions. Now she had the new sense that everything would be all right. She felt confident she would be able to support herself and, in time, marry a man whom she loved and who loved her. It seemed possible to her that she could make Desmond love her or even, although she could not quite imagine it, that she would love someone else as much, though in a different way, as she now loved Desmond.

Gerald, with his attentive charm, was not the only reason for her rise in confidence, nor was the event that had occurred earlier that day. It was a pleasing instance of the whole being greater than the sum of two encouraging parts.

"You look very pretty—are you having a good time?"

The restaurant where they were eating was dimly lit. It had rained briefly while they ate, and through the window the street outside was wet and shiny, lit by streetlights. The name of the restaurant was painted across the window and its shadow fell against the pale-yellow interior wall. It made Molly feel as though she were in Vienna, although she did not know why. She had never been to Austria and at that moment thought no city superior to London. Or more magical. She smiled with pleasure and Gerald gently ran a hand along her bare arm.

"Yes. It's been a lovely day."

"Even before me?" Gerald asked the question in a gently teasing tone, allowing his hand to rest for a moment on Molly's.

"Even before you."

Gerald looked as though he really was interested in Molly's news, so she went on. "I was late back from lunch—I was having my hair done."

Gerald was attentive, waiting for Molly to describe an incident, unaware that she had already mentioned two things of significance. Molly had gone to Sophie's hairdresser in Knightsbridge. The hairdresser, of whom Molly was a little scared even though Sophie had told her how much to tip, had kept her waiting, been dismissive and a little irritated that she was not springing for, in his opinion, a much-needed haircut. He had then left her under the dryer for at least ten minutes more than was necessary. Although Molly did not take it personally—she had noticed with surprise expensively dressed and confident women with upper-class accents who were also his victims—and although she was very pleased with the result, she hurried back to the Queensgate school, aware that she was twenty minutes late for her English literature class.

"I came rushing in the front door, out of breath, and just as I got my foot on the first step of the stairs, the door to the principal's office opened."

It occurred to Molly that Gerald might consider this another moment that he would have expected her to dismiss with the arrogance that Sophie, Caroline or, indeed, Cynthia, the only other female acquaintances of his whom she knew, would employ. But Gerald raised an eyebrow in a manner that suggested that he re-

206

membered similar incidents in his life all too well, even though, Molly ruefully thought, he had probably been eight years old at the time.

"She said: 'Molly Hassard, could you come into my office for a moment.' I went in, rather nervous, and she asked me to sit down and offered me a cup of coffee. I was completely baffled; I couldn't imagine what was coming next except it couldn't be about being late for class unless, of course, she was planning to expel me."

"A cup of coffee in lieu of a stiff drink?"

"The thought did cross my mind. And then she told me that if I liked, she would send me on an interview for a job."

"Doing what?"

"Part-time work for a writer. Called Henry Latham—I hadn't heard of him, but I think he's quite well known by, you know, people who know about that kind of thing."

Gerald nodded. "I haven't read anything of his," he said, "but he sometimes does book reviews for—I don't know—the Sunday papers and the better magazines."

"I'm going to go and see him. Tomorrow after classes. For tea."

"Sounds promising."

Molly was unable to describe the full extent of her elation. She did not imagine that working two afternoons a week would constitute financial independence nor that typing for an established author would constitute an entrée into the world of art and literature, but it would be a move in the right direction. The prospect of having enough money to get her hair cut at Sophie's hairdresser and not to have to wear laddered stockings or to skimp on lunch at the end of the week made her feel more powerful than she ever had before.

One of the reasons Molly did not mention the financial implication of her not-yet-secured job was a conversation she had had with her great-aunts. She had forced herself to broach the subject of her evening engagement during Sunday lunch. Eschewing the temptation of either rushing through the door on

Saturday evening yelling, "Do you know what?" or casually on Tuesday evening saying, "By the way, I shan't be in for dinner— don't wait up," she spoke with a calmness she didn't feel while the three of them were eating apple pie in the dining room over- looking the fountain below the Albert Hall. To Molly's amaze- ment, the only advice or instruction she had been given was that she should be sure to pay for her own meal. Molly had allowed a silent attentive nod to be taken for acquiescence and waited until the next day, when she would be sure of privacy, to tele- phone Sophie.

Sophie, who had answered the telephone in an irritated and preoccupied manner, reacted with a brief bark of laughter.

"Don't be wet," she said. "Neither of the old girls ever went out on a date. They're probably thinking about traveling alone— on a stagecoach or something."

"Are you sure?"

"I suppose they warned you against letting him take you to dinner in a private dining room. Gerald's not dangerous, but"— her voice changed and she paused, adding emphasis—"he's not to be taken seriously, either."

Molly, preoccupied with the embarrassing aspects of money, had not paid attention to Sophie's warning, if warning it had been.

Molly's weekly income was such that she thought of it as pocket money rather than an allowance. As long as she could re- member, money, or more accurately the lack of it, had been a source of embarrassment. The buff envelopes accumulating and gathering dust on the hall table, the handed-down clothes, the leaking roof at Fern Hill, the holes in the avenue leading to the house. The whole question of who should pay for things was mortifying for Molly, even when, as was usually the case, the re- sponsibility did not lie with her. There was sometimes an awk- ward moment at the pub when they arrived Saturday morning. David, as the richest person present and the dominant male, bought the first round of drinks. Occasionally he would become engaged in conversation—Molly suspected sometimes deliberately—when they entered, and there was a moment, intensely awkward for Molly, although causing only impatient irritation in Sophie, while the other men stood around, hands in pockets, jingling change, waiting in passivity and parsimony for one or the other to crack. In the end David always paid.

Molly trusted Sophie's assurance and believed that it was not necessary to offer—let alone insist, as her great-aunts would have liked—to pay for her dinner. To offer to split the cost of the drinks at the Blue Angel afterward would be ridiculous. Nevertheless, as dinner drew to a close, Molly's sense of well-being was compromised by the familiar feeling of embarrassment.

"You've become very quiet. Is anything the matter?"

"No."

"You regret not having ordered the crème brûlée?"

Molly laughed and shook her head.

"You've eaten too much? You haven't had enough to eat? I've got spinach between my teeth? Gravy on my tie? You left the iron on, and your great-aunts are even now burned to a crisp? You forgot to feed your goldfish? I haven't said anything nice about your dress? That's it, isn't it?

Molly laughed.

"It's very pretty."

"Thank you."

"I believe it *is* the crème brûlée." Gerald raised his voice and waved his arm. "Waiter!"

"No, really. Please, don't."

"Well then, what is it?"

"I was just thinking . . ." Molly faltered and felt herself start to blush. "I was just thinking that all this . . . going out . . . is very expensive."

Gerald opened his mouth as though he were about to laugh and then checked himself.

"You were worried about how much it was costing me to take you out?"

Molly nodded, not quite meeting his eye. "Yes," she said, "and if I hadn't drunk all this wine, I wouldn't be able to tell you that."

"I see. Don't give it another thought. It's all right."

Molly looked doubtful.

"I don't imagine that your cousin Sophie spends a lot of time torturing herself about much she costs David or for that matter anyone else."

"Sophie's very confident. She was even as a little girl."

"Or Caroline. Do you think she goes out of her way to order the least expensive dish on the menu?"

"Probably not."

"And why do you think that is? Is she confident, too?"

"More than I am."

"Or is it a kind of let's-stick-it-to-them hostility toward men?"

Molly was silent.

"A lot of girls—most, really—feel like that. And men know it and they don't mind," he said calmly.

"It doesn't seem quite fair that girls like . . . who—"

"That girls like you who are nice to men shouldn't get some credit for their nature?"

"Well, yes."

"It's easier for men to deal with girls who feel that they're not on the same side. Easier in the sense that they're more comfortable with a conflict of interest. You and I are on the same side. We like each other. We're friends, we're having a good time together, and it would make some sense that I would ask you out again and that you would accept?"

Molly nodded.

"Well, suppose I was to take you out on a Wednesday night, and I called you on Tuesday evening and told you that I'd just met the most stunning girl at a cocktail party, and she'd invited me to the opera for the following evening—her father had given her his box—and asked if you'd mind postponing our date. You'd be nice about it?"

"Probably."

"But, for the sake of argument rather than conceit, you'd be disappointed?"

"Well, yes."

"And I'd feel bad. You'd feel bad. It wouldn't, I'm afraid—for the sake of argument only, you understand—change the way I behaved. With Caroline or Sophie, I'd lie through my teeth. They wouldn't believe me, but I'd go to the opera, and I—depending on the opera girl—I would call them the day after to make a new date. In the meantime, they would have calculated to the minutest degree just how hard a time they could give me without being more trouble than they were worth. The punitive spending of money and the withholding of sexual favors would be only part of it."

"I see."

"Of course, if a man has an ounce of sense, he marries your type of girl. It's odd how few seem to have that ounce of sense."

Molly thought of Desmond and how the girl he was going to marry suggested that he, too, lacked the necessary ounce of sense.

"Now you're silent again. I've depressed you."

"I was just thinking about what you said and wondering what I'm supposed to do."

"We'll talk about that later. What girls usually do now is go and powder their nose while I pay the bill."

ON FRIDAY MOLLY went to tea at the house in Trevor Square. It was half-past five when she arrived, and tea by that time usually meant drinks. Normally by then Sophie would be downstairs, but that day she was still in her bedroom, stretched out on top of the fitted bedcover, her head against a bank of starched, lacy pillows. She held a delicate green-and-pink teacup in her hand and sipped from it slowly. She looked uncharacteristically animated and almost triumphant.

Caroline was perched on low, full-skirted armchair. The chair

211

reminded Molly of the Christmas afternoon when, looking out over the Suir, Sophie had said that Belinda's feathered cocker spaniel looked like a slipcover armchair. The first time Molly had seen the chair, she had asked Sophie if she remembered, but Sophie had replied only with a faint smile.

Caroline sat with knees together and long legs splayed to either side. She had dark circles under her eyes and appeared irritable and discontented. Molly knew that her own news and preoccupations, her evening out with Gerald, and her interview with Henry Latham would have to wait, perhaps until another occasion, to be discussed and examined.

"The doctor said—"

Caroline interrupted before Sophie could quote the doctor. Molly was sorry, both because she imagined that what the doctor had to say might have dispelled the mystery of why Sophie seemed so pleased with herself and because she was not used to hearing Sophie invoke an authority other than her own opinion or the tradition by which the Hassard family lived.

"I was staying in Scotland once, and the younger daughters of the house were recovering from measles. The doctor prescribed flat champagne. I'm going to make a wild guess—neither their nor your tame doctor are on the National Health."

"So?"

"So if you lived in a council house and came to his clinic and your husband was unemployed, do you think he would tell you to lie around for the next eight and a half months, or do you think he'd tell you to get on with it?"

"Well, David isn't unemployed. Unemployable, maybe, but fortunately he works for his daddy. What difference does it make to you, anyway?"

Caroline lapsed into a grumpy silence. Sophie angled her hand a little to look at a ring that Molly had not seen before. She seemed pleased with it.

"Does this mean—" Molly asked tentatively.

"Yes, it does, and David is so pleased that he gave me this. Way above the usual Spencer taste, don't you think?"

Sophie held out her hand for inspection, and Molly went to the bed, taking Sophie's hand to look at the ring. A pale-yellow stone, like a tinted diamond—old and beautiful—was surrounded by modest but not tiny diamonds. The stones were set in gold, the color of which accentuated the richness of the pale stone.

"It's a citrine. Late eighteenth century. The first piece of Spencer jewelry I'd willingly leave my daughter."

"I think David sprang for that exquisite little job in anticipation of a son, not a daughter." Caroline seemed intent on souring Sophie's pleasure. "Of course, if you produce a son first and then a daughter, you'd only have to lie on that bed for eighteen months."

"You'd think David's father had a really old title or Blenheim to leave."

"Well," Molly said, with a vague attempt to keep the peace, "there is quite a lot of money."

"Thank God. So he'll leave it to David, and David'll spend it. Or leave it to this baby. Male or female, what difference?"

"These are the new empires." Caroline was beginning to sound more cheerful. "Spencer père wants to found a dynasty. He's not going to be content with one grandson. He'll need at least two. And a daughter to marry off strategically."

Sophie sighed, her habitual look of discontent creeping back onto her face.

"Where do you think half the aristocracy of England comes from?" Caroline asked, her pale face at last animated. "Titles handed out to whores and rich men who helped out whenever royalty was feeling the pinch. Your father-in-law is way above the average Tudor adventurer-favorite or Stuart mistress turned duchess in character, antecedents, and social responsibility."

"Caroline's feeling a bit discouraged," Sophie said conversationally to Molly. "Apparently Gerald stood her up this week with a cock-and-bull story about having to go to the opera." Sophie paused long enough for Caroline to experience discomfort but not long enough for her to frame a rejoinder. "Anyway, the

213

doctor said that I probably wouldn't have lost the last baby if I hadn't been tearing around getting ready for the wedding. And trying on dresses."

"Game, set, and match," Caroline muttered, just loud enough for the other two to hear but not so loudly that they had to respond. Molly wondered for which day of the week Gerald had canceled his date with Caroline.

May 1961

"WHAT ARE YOU doing, Molly, dear?"

"Oh, nothing. Just thinking."

Isabel looked inquiringly at her great-niece, the right to private thought for an unmarried girl not being firmly established in her mind.

"About this book," Molly said, lifting the paperback copy of *The Great Gatsby,* which she had laid on the satin eiderdown. Reacting to the look of concern on Isabel's face—caused by the hour or the potentially dubious content of paperback novels—she continued: "He's an American writer. He's—there's no one quite like him in England. There's a nice line I just read. Would you like to hear it?"

Isabel nodded.

" 'Don't be morbid,' Jordan said. 'Life starts all over again when it gets crisp in the fall.' Fall is what they call autumn in America."

"Very nice, dear. Would you like me to switch off your light? It's quite late."

"Yes, please. Good night, Aunt Isabel."

Molly slid down between the sheets. She had been thinking about *The Great Gatsby* and whether Sophie and David Spencer were not a little like Daisy and Tom Buchanan and about another line in the novel: "I had that familiar conviction that life was beginning over again with the summer." She felt that the lines described, although there was nothing cyclical or seasonal in her

214

own emotions, her new feeling of hope and, if not power, at least the diminution of powerlessness.

The breeze stirred the curtain, and the lights from the street danced in the looking glass of the Victorian wardrobe in Molly's room. She watched the crack of moving yellow light as she considered the events of the past week. Gerald, her job, Sophie's pregnancy. The last, although in the eyes of others and even Molly herself, the most significant event, she thought about least. Not because it would affect her least, but because it was a condition over which she would have the least influence.

The crack of light under the door disappeared and she could hear the faint sound of Isabel's bedroom door closing. Molly sat up in bed and drew her nightdress up over her head and set it at the foot of her bed where she could reach it quickly in the morning. The nightdress itself was pretty and light on her body—a present from Charlotte, who herself wore beautiful nightdresses and underwear without ever, it appeared, having considered that most women do so in order to appear attractive to a man—but the feeling of being naked between the much-laundered sheets was even more sensual to Molly.

Lying in bed, reviewing—as she had every night since her night out with Gerald—Molly remembered making Fern Hill ready for the guests who were to stay for Sophie's wedding. She had taken a pile of clean towels from the linen room. Thinking about the harlequin costumes she and Sophie had found and wondering, although she did not divert herself from the task at hand, whether they were still there, Molly had stood in the linen room, holding the stack of warm towels against her body, and had been shocked by how intense was the feeling of comfort they gave her.

It was the feeling she had had when she walked from the table to the dance floor at the Blue Angel. Flattered by Gerald's admiration and reassured by his understanding, Molly had been happy and excited when they arrived at the nightclub. Soon after they had arrived and Gerald had ordered drinks, the band stopped playing, and the cabaret began. A young man—or perhaps not so young—took a microphone and began to sing. He did so with an ease that led Molly to assume that he sang every night at the Blue Angel and, from their response, that his audience had heard him many times before. It seemed to Molly that they all knew one another. He sang sophisticated songs with wit and songs of love and longing as though he and those who listened to him had experienced those emotions. And that those emotions were valid enough for the pleasant but light songs to achieve a greater validity, to touch the borders of art. His dinner jacket, his white shirt and black tie, looked as comfortable and a part of him as did the complicity of the couples at the small tables. It made Molly feel as though her constant sadness was a part of what made her fine and would be found admirable by those around her. She glanced at Gerald, who was smiling slightly—a smile of recognition and pleasure—and she was happy that he was strong and masculine. Even his charm, which made her faintly uneasy, seemed within acceptable bounds when compared with the singer and his intimacy with the faces and bodies he could not quite see in the dark around him.

Later, Gerald, again taking her hand, led her between the tightly packed tables through the laughter and the cigarette smoke, to the dance floor.

"Smaller than a boxing ring," he said, "and only proportionately less dangerous."

Molly smiled, the wine she had drunk giving her confidence, reassured by the small, crowded floor where her dancing could be neither displayed nor judged.

"Yellow Bird." "Plaisir d'Amour." Molly could feel the thin silk that lined her dress brush lightly on her thighs, above her stockings and the skin between her brassiere and her panties. Gerald pulled her closer to him, folding her body into his arms and pressing his face into her hair.

"Love Me Tender." Elvis. Molly yearned for something to which she could not put a name. She was not so naive that she

216

did not know about desire, but the yearning was not only sexual. Her longing for love was almost as strong. And for fluidity and freedom. To move unencumbered by constrictive clothing, to leave behind the hunched stiffness of cold and damp, to take pleasure in her youth, to enjoy the measure of physical beauty she possessed. And to feel the warmth of another body. Not since Desmond had danced with her that summer evening at Dromore, the warm air from the river coming through the French windows, had Molly been held so close by another human being. Belinda and Miles kissed her good night affectionately, and Molly felt confident of their love, but it would have been unthinkable—except just after Tibby's death and his funeral—for either to enfold her in a close embrace.

"Le Jour ou les Pluies Vendraint." "Smoke Gets in Your Eyes." Molly—moving with the music, aware of her body, aware of Gerald's body against hers, aware of the glamor and romance and of the place and people who surrounded them—realized that glamor and romance and sexual desire are not merely attributes of love but have an intrinsic value of their own. Gerald released her hand and held her, instead, with both his hands on the small of her back, just below her waist. Molly laid both her hands on his shoulders. As he pulled her closer, she slid her arms around his neck. She noticed that other couples were dancing in the same manner. Gerald's fingers pressed lower on her back and, almost involuntarily, Molly, reacting to their pressure, pushed her hips closer to him. She remained thus, moving with the music and with Gerald's swaying body for a moment or two until she became aware of his erection. It took her a moment longer to understand what it was that she felt against her, and she hesitated for a further moment before pulling away, not wishing to acknowledge, by her reaction, that she had noticed.

Gerald held her less tightly, but no less affectionately, and when the music ended, he took her hand and led her back to their table. As they sat, he glanced at his watch.

"We might think of calling it a night. You have a big career move tomorrow."

217

He tried to attract the attention of the waiter, and Molly went to find the loo. In the taxi on the way home they sat, not awkwardly, a little distance apart.

"You're very quiet, sweetie, is anything wrong?"

"Something happened when I went to get my coat. I didn't understand it."

She paused and Gerald took her hand.

"The woman who looks after the cloakroom—you know, where you put your coat—there was a girl who had left something, a big hat, I think, and the woman had put it on the top shelf. When she went to get it—the cloakroom lady—her sleeve fell back and I could see a number on her arm, quite clearly marked. On the inside of her arm, just below the elbow—"

"It's a tattoo. She was in a concentration camp."

"But she looked just like everyone else. She smiled at me." Molly began to cry. "I don't know why I'm crying. I'm not crying for her." As she said it, it occurred to her that if she weren't crying for the middle-aged woman in the shabby black dress, it would be reasonable for Gerald to assume that she was crying for him, possibly even because of what had happened on the dance floor.

"I know."

Gerald tendered his handkerchief, and Molly took it gratefully, wiping her eyes and blowing her nose.

"Too much excitement, like an overtired child."

"Like I ate too much at a birthday party?" Molly managed a little smile.

"Exactly. And wine makes girls weep."

"It does?"

"Yes. And because the music was romantic, and I'm holding your hand, and you're in love with someone else."

"Why do you think so?"

"Oh, everyone is, don't you think?"

Molly was quiet.

"Don't come back to me with exceptions," he said. "I don't want to hear, 'Even Sophie? Even Caroline?' "

218

"But—"

"You're too good for me, Molly. Too good for the lot of us." Gerald raised her hand and kissed it, looking over it at Molly with a smile that held no trace of flippancy. "I'm going to be your Dutch uncle and guide you through the perils of being a beautiful young girl in a sinful city."

"You are?"

"Yes. Here is Albert Court and a cue for my first lesson. What girls usually do with the handkerchief they've cried into is to take it home, wash it and iron it, and return it to its owner. In this instance though, since I fear your great-aunts, I will go to the trouble and expense of having it laundered myself."

The following day Molly had arrived exactly on time at Henry Latham's house. The house, small and part of a terrace, was situated west of Kensington Church Street, a little south of Notting Hill Gate. It had a small garden in front, full of green plants in bud and a few small white flowers; a creeper whose name Molly did not know had reached the top of the front door and was advancing on a dark-green shutter. Molly lifted the old-fashioned door knocker and tapped it tentatively and then again a little louder since either or both the Lathams—she assumed that there was a Mrs. Latham—might, at their age, be a little deaf. The door was opened by a woman of the age that Molly had anticipated, but slim and very pretty. She greeted Molly with a good-humored smile.

"Molly? Yes. Do come in." She led Molly through a narrow hall and showed her where to hang her coat, then led her into a small, pretty room, three walls of which were covered with bookshelves. The fourth had two French doors that led to a small garden.

"Sit down, Molly. If you don't mind waiting for a few minutes, my husband is reading. He's almost done. Then we'll have tea."

Henry Latham was sitting at the window. He smiled and raised a hand in greeting. He held a book. Molly took a chair that placed her a little outside his eyeline if he were to glance up while he read. Mr. Latham read aloud and after a moment or two, Molly recognized the name Rawdon Crawley. He was reading *Vanity Fair* to his wife.

" 'Thus it will be seen that the parishioners of Crawley were equally happy in their squire and in their rector.' " Mr. Latham closed the book and took off his glasses. He looked at Molly, who edged herself to the front of her seat.

"I'm Molly Hassard. Mrs. Lewis at the Queensgate Education Centre sent me."

"Yes, yes. I'm sorry we made you wait. I read aloud to my wife before tea each day, and we weren't quite finished."

"I love to be read to, and you were at my favorite part."

Mrs. Latham stood and left the room. Mr. Latham looked inquiringly at Molly.

"When Becky goes to Sir Pitt Crawley's as a governess."

"And why do you think that is?"

"Because I'm entirely on her side. Later, you don't like her."

"Yes, the novel without a hero also lacks an adequate heroine. Tell me another favorite part of a favorite novel."

Molly thought for a moment and then smiled happily. She liked Mr. Latham and thought that he liked her and it made her confident.

"*Jane Eyre.* When she is a governess and comes down to dinner to make up the numbers and is snubbed by the girl everyone thinks Mr. Rochester is going to marry, and then, after dinner, the gypsy tells their fortunes."

"Yes. Yes." Mr. Latham seemed to be enjoying himself as much as was Molly. She knew that this was not part of the interview, that these questions were not a test. They seemed more like the beginning of a friendship. She glanced toward the door and asked, almost reluctantly: "May I help your wife with the tea things?"

"My wife is—ah—losing her sight. Slowly. She and I have agreed that it must not be allowed to limit her life any more than is strictly necessary. She likes to continue to do the things she always did. It's very important that everything in the house be in its right place and that nothing is done out of order. I'm sure you will get used to it very quickly."

Molly understood from this that Mr. Latham had decided to give her the job. Since she was by nature tentative and unsure, she would have liked him to spell it out more clearly, but she understood that it was not his way and it would be more graceful and dignified to accept his assumption that she was capable of communicating with nuance and tact. It was more important, she told herself, to pay attention to the details of the routine imposed for Mrs. Latham's safety and convenience than to seek reassurance for herself.

"It sometimes seems," Mr. Latham continued, "as though Alice and I have spent our married life preparing for old age. Although, of course, we didn't think of it like that at the time. We called it leading a life of the mind. Taking the longer view." He paused for a moment and smiled. "My wife is a musician. She plays the piano. What if I had been the one to lose my sight and she had developed arthritis? What then? It's all in the luck of the draw, isn't it? But I still think you're supposed to prepare."

Molly thought it might be easier to prepare for a happy, or at least contented and productive, old age if one were happily married, as the Lathams seemed to be. She considered her fear of later playing the part of her aunt Vera, and it occurred to her that that very afternoon, in making the acquaintance of Henry and Alice Latham, she might have taken one of the first steps toward a life of self-sufficiency.

" 'Work and love,' Freud wrote," Mr. Latham continued. "People tend to misunderstand those three simple words. They reverse the order, and they assume that love means romantic love. However, we shouldn't assume that you only favor the underdog in literature—maybe you are just partial to governess scenes. How do you feel about the Saki governess?"

"The lady who finds herself stranded in a railway station and is mistaken for the new governess—?"

"By some haute bourgeoisie and plays along with them. I forget what the story is called, but it's very satisfying. Comeuppance is a very effective literary device. There must be some other good governess scenes. Of course, Tolstoy reverses the convention in *War and Peace,* with the ugly princess's companion—almost the same thing as a governess, don't you think? Who flirts with Prince Anatole. What is her name?"

Mr. Latham frowned. Molly did not know the name for which he was searching. She wondered if he had forgotten why she had come—and whether she should remind him.

"She's really Becky Sharp in much the same situation, but Tolstoy needs her to be unsympathetic."

The door to the kitchen opened.

"Molly, perhaps you *could* help my wife with the tea tray. I'll clear this table. I know where everything goes."

Molly rose quickly and went into the kitchen. She moved carefully in order not to confuse Mrs. Latham. The tea, elaborate and varied, was set out on two trays. Molly realized that this was done to avoid either Latham having to carry too heavy a tray.

The tray that Molly carried—the heavier one—had a silver teapot, cups and saucers, milk and lemon, and two plates of sandwiches. Tomato and cucumber. The second tray bore the cakes. One, a sponge cake, had already been cut. About a third was missing, and Molly could see the dark-red filling. Raspberry, she thought. The second cake was oblong and covered with rough dark chocolate. Molly had gasped when she saw it—partly to be polite and partly from the anticipated pleasure. By now she was thoroughly enjoying herself, any anxiety about the interview long past.

Molly was hungry, and she ate many of the sandwiches. The quantity that had been made and the pleasure Mrs. Latham took in her appreciation encouraged her. The sandwiches had been spread with cream cheese and chives instead of butter, and the cucumbers had plenty of salt on them. When at last she paused, Mr. Latham indicated the chocolate cake.

"And now for the pièce de résistance."

"Shouldn't we—?"

Molly hesitated. The sponge cake was already cut into and

222

wouldn't last forever. In fact, were they not to eat it that afternoon, she doubted whether the two old people would finish it before it became stale.

"Absolutely not." And as though she were reading Molly's thoughts, Mrs. Latham continued, "I have the end of the sponge earmarked for trifle for Sunday lunch."

"My wife is an artist," Mr. Latham said gently, his tone completely serious.

Mrs. Latham cut Molly a slice of cake. Inside the thick, hard chocolate crust were three layers of pale, dense cake separated by two fillings. Molly's eyes widened.

"It's called a *marjolaine*," Mr. Latham said. "Alice, tell Molly how it is made—and, Molly, you must eat while you listen."

Molly took one of the small silver forks and ate a tiny piece of cake, making sure that she got a little of the chocolate and some of the filling. It was one of the most delicious things she had ever tasted.

"It takes several days to make," Mrs. Latham said. "First you make the crème fraîche. While that is sitting, you toast the hazelnuts, hull them, and grind them. When they are ground, you sieve them. You use the sieved hazelnuts as flour, and you add beaten egg whites and sugar to make a long, flat piece of cake. You cut it into three pieces and use them for the layers. The first filling is thickened crème fraîche—you have to add a little cooled melted butter to make it harder—and the second is praline and crème fraîche. You cover the whole cake with a chocolate and crème fraîche coating, and cool it until the whole thing is quite solid."

"A *marjolaine* is French, seventeenth century, I think," Mr. Latham said. "It's one of my wife's specialties."

"It's the best thing I ever ate," Molly said. "I love chocolate cake. And cakes that have cream and fruit in them. Or if they have some orange or lemon so there is a contrast with the richness and sweetness. We don't have them much at home. Irish cakes seem more, well, masculine."

Both the Lathams seemed very interested, so Molly told them

about the Dromore Christmas cake and Sophie's wedding cake and how one was decorated in white and the other had some pink curlicues and a sprig of holly on it. Then she told them about barmbracks and how she and Belinda made marmalade and the Christmas pudding and how Vera made green tomato chutney. With encouragement, she told them about Great-aunt Jarre's ear trumpet and how she had been allowed to speak into it as a treat when she was a small child. And how she had taken Belinda's dog, Nell, to the vet to have the stitches removed from a cut paw and the vet—the one her uncle Miles called "young Fagan"—had put Nell up on the table, looked at her paw and said, "Hmph. She's taken them out herself and saved you fifteen bob."

She was about to tell them about Mr. Hannon and the aeroplane and Mrs. Hannon when she glanced at her watch and saw that it was twenty to seven. With an embarrassed haste that would have done credit to Cinderella, she got up, both the Lathams insisting that she had not stayed a moment too long.

She was out the door and halfway down Kensington High Street before she realized that she did not know if she was now employed or not.

The next day Molly avoided the principal since she would not have been sure how to report on her interview. The day afterward, there was not only a telephone message at Albert Court from Gerald but a letter in a small envelope with tiny, stiff writing addressed to her on the hall table. Molly took it into her bedroom and closed the door.

Dear Molly,
    Mademoiselle Bourienne. The Schartz-Metterklume Method—I think I may be forgiven for having allowed the latter title to have dropped out of my mind. I have a friend, even older than myself who, each morning upon waking, runs through the names of his eighteen grandchildren and if he can do so, congratulates himself on having survived another night without becoming senile.

As you may have gathered, Alice and I would be very happy if you will have the time and energy to do a little work for us. Your predecessor used to come two afternoons a week, one of them early enough to go to the library and post office if necessary. We paid her two pounds and five shillings. Please let me know if a similar arrangement would be acceptable to you. If so, please come to tea on Tuesday, and we'll start work afterward.

Alice joins me in sending you love,

yrs. H. Latham

"I shall be working for Mr. Latham two afternoons a week," Molly excitedly told her great-aunts at tea.

The two old ladies paused and thought, but did not speak, seemingly unable to find anything untoward in the arrangement.

"Be sure to look up any word that you're the least bit unsure about in the dictionary," Isabel said at last.

Molly assured her that she would; it was a resolution she had already made herself.

"Gerald Sweeney telephoned this afternoon," Charlotte said.

"Did he leave a number?"

"No," Charlotte looked slightly shocked. "I'm sure he will call again."

But Gerald didn't call again, and before dinner Molly, with four coppers in her pocket, quietly left her room where she was doing her homework, let herself out, and descended to the ground floor and went to the second-closest pay phone—the nearest one being visible from the drawing-room windows of her great-aunts' flat—looked up Gerald's number, and dialed it. But there was no reply.

Chapter Ten

October 1961

HE AFTERNOON POST arrived while Molly was at school and Mrs. Conjoyce, her great-aunts' daily maid, set it out on a salver on the table in the main corridor. Her aunts would pick out personal letters if there were any and carry them to the drawing room to read; circulars and bills were left for the following morning, when they would be taken with the morning post to Charlotte's desk. Unlike Fern Hill, where the thin buff envelopes mounted up on the hall table, their demands met or reduced only when a large enough dividend arrived or the bullocks were sold, bills at Albert Court were paid promptly and the receipts filed away tidily. If either aunt were to die during the night, her affairs would be found in the same perfect order as her underwear drawer. This was not connected to old age or expectation of imminent death; both had lived like this since childhood. Nothing had ever been bought that could not be paid for—both women would have preferred to darn a dress or a pair of stockings, to dine on bread and cheese, than to incur the smallest unpayable debt. Of course, it was only since both had been widowed that either had any control of money. Bills and taxes had been paid first by their father, later by their husbands. Both women had borne children and lost a husband before either had possessed her own checkbook.

226

"Molly dear, I believe there's a letter for you on the table," Isabel said as Molly entered the drawing room. "It's from Belinda." Manners would have made it impossible for Isabel to have opened Molly's letter, but no inhibition or sense of privacy stood between her aunt and the anticipated pleasure of news from Ireland.

Molly was a little tired—she hadn't slept well and the bus had been slow and crowded. She would have preferred to have drunk a cup of tea and eaten something sweet before she embarked on an errand or even a conversation. But since Belinda's letter was a treat for her great-aunts, she went back along the corridor and fetched the letter. When she returned, she found that Charlotte had poured her tea and arranged a plate of three small sandwiches on a small table in front of the comfortable dark velvet chair, close to the fire and under a reading light.

Molly opened the letter. She could feel, rather than see, her great-aunts shifting in their seats, seeking greater comfort in anticipation of the treat. Molly sipped her tea.

"Dear Molly [she read],

"I spoke to Sophie on the telephone this morning, so I know you are well and so are the aunts. She has probably passed on our news, such as it is, but if I thought like that there would be no reason—except to send our love—for us to write to each other. She has probably told you that Granny's rheumatism is very bad. The weather has been cold, and now that it is getting damp, there are days when she doesn't feel up to getting out of bed."

Molly paused for a reaction. The aunts made sympathetic noises about their sister's ailments, and both sat up a little straighter. Neither commented on Sophie's new habit of telephoning her mother—and in the morning, no less, when the more expensive rates applied. It seemed Sophie, too bored and apathetic to write a letter, lay in bed telephoning her friends and, apparently, her family in Ireland. Needless to say, she had not mentioned Adele's aches and pains to Molly.

"Mrs. Gleeson looks after her very well, and it is quite cozy. A fire in her bedroom, two cats on the bed, and meals on trays. She has taken to listening to the wireless. Very loud since she is getting a little deaf."

Molly paused, allowing the great-aunts to be reassured by the care their sister was receiving, to register faint disapproval at the unhygienic feline presence on her bed, and to ignore completely—as though they themselves had not heard the words—any mention of deafness.

"Tom Daley is resigning from the West Waterfords. He never really recovered from his fall last winter and walks with a limp. They are, as usual, in the most appalling financial difficulties and there is hope that the soi-disant Baron de Lecky will take them over. He can afford to and, as Miles says, until he breaks his neck, he would make as good a master as poor Tom has since he got into the habit of taking an additional drop to keep out the cold. Miles has discovered Trollope and is reading his way through the Pallisers. He's got to the one with the good hunting scenes, so he's taking a keener interest in the doings of the West Waterfords than he used to, although I think he sometimes muddles up the problems of Lord Chiltern's pack with the inferior one we have to make do with. Anyway, in the heat of the moment the other night, he volunteered us to walk a couple of young hounds next spring. I don't know what poor Nell will think, but I was hoping it might bring you home for a visit. There was a time when it would have made Sophie happy."

"They wouldn't live indoors, I suppose?" said Charlotte. Isabel shook her head.
"Daddy used to read Trollope," Molly said.
"So did Father," said her great-aunt Isabel.
It occurred to Molly that the great-aunts' father, her great-

228

great-grandfather, had probably read Trollope as contemporary fiction. It also occurred to her that during Tibby's lifetime, she had seen no evidence of Miles reading anything that might be even loosely thought of as literature. He appeared to be adopting some of his dead brother's habits.

"Who is 'the Baron de Lecky'?" Charlotte asked.

"He's an American, very rich. He bought Fethard Castle—it's early Victorian but with lovely gardens. He's done it up to the nines and bought some horses. He's mad about hunting. Uncle Miles is funny about his riding clothes."

"Is he really a de Lecky?"

"Aunt Belinda says he is but that he has no real claim on the title. She says"—Molly paused, trying to avoid the word "bastard," which was the one Belinda had used, and continued— "there should be a bar sinister on his crest."

"And do people use his title?"

"It depends. I suppose some people take it at face value, and some people humor him. Some refuse and call him Mr. Lecky very firmly. He's not married, so Uncle Miles says that at present it's not much worse than a cynically bestowed life peerage. He— Uncle Miles—thinks it's all a huge joke, specially since it makes Aunt Vera furious."

Molly picked up the letter again, but saw that her aunts wanted more.

"Uncle Miles and Aunt Belinda went to dinner there and took Sophie. Sophie told me that the baron wore a kilt, and they had pink champagne for dinner."

Now Charlotte and Isabel were satisfied. Molly knew that there would be more questions about de Lecky at breakfast the following morning. Molly would have to apply to Belinda for additional information in her next letter home.

"As part of this new enthusiasm, Miles had the old donkey put down and sent to the kennels. He should have done it before, it would have been a kindness, but he couldn't bring himself to—though he'd never admit it."

229

Molly paused, but her aunts didn't comment. Their minds were too full of the de Lecky information to be distracted by the death of a donkey. Molly realized that in the past—before her father's death—she might have shed a tear for the animal. Once Sophie's beloved pet, now dinner for a pack of hounds who had themselves seen better days.

"Poor old Frank Paget's had a stroke. It's too soon to tell how much he may recover, but he's in a wheelchair. Miles went to visit him and says that the poor old boy's lost heart, and he doesn't think he'll ever walk again. He doesn't seem to have much interest in the present, but Miles said he became quite animated when he talked to him about point-to-points in the old days. Desmond's been running the place for a couple of years now, so it'll not make much difference in the day-to-day stuff, but there isn't enough land to make farming pay, and soon hard decisions will have to be made. I suppose it'll make him get a move on with marrying that rather common little McBride girl—Miles rather likes her and says she's 'a fine figure of a gerrel'—at least she might give him a prod and make him get on with it. I think the whole county will be watching to see how she and Lady Marjorie battle it out."

"You remember Lady Marjorie?" Molly asked, hoping not to have to answer questions about Desmond or to explain why he was thought to be a poor fish. Charlotte nodded without much enthusiasm or, more to the point, curiosity, and, grateful to the dubious baron, Molly felt it safe to continue.

"I'm sorry this whole letter is about everything falling apart—except for de Lecky, of course, who's never looked better. There isn't much news apart from that. And that they're having trouble with bats at St. Olaf's again.

Quite a heated vestry meeting with that on the agenda! I remember when your father and Miles were young men, and there was a similar infestation—they offered to go in one night and shoot the bats!"

"And then some stuff she wants me to get her at Harrods and bring back next time I go," said Molly. "And a P.S. about the hunt ball."

Aware that the hunt ball was a reference that might interest the great-aunts but no longer equal to their questions, Molly said she should do her homework before going out that evening.

By the time Gerald came to collect her, Molly had done very little homework. She had been thinking about the hunt ball. Belinda proposed to give a dinner party for it, and, as she assumed Molly would still be at Dromore for her Christmas visit and since Sophie, pregnant, would be spending Christmas in London, Belinda wanted Molly's thoughts on whom she should invite. Molly understood that her advice was not really being sought. Both the invitations and the placement would take care of themselves. Belinda wanted to know, without assuming the responsibility of a straightforward question, who should be invited as Molly's dancing partner. While Molly lay in the bath, picking at the flaking pink mask on her face, she decided that her choices were either to return to London with a convincing excuse before the hunt ball or to find a presentable dance partner so that the pain of seeing Desmond with Pauline McBride should not be compounded by the shame of dancing with someone embarrassing. It occurred to her that an invitation to Gerald might not be out of the question. He had come to Ireland cheerfully enough for Sophie's wedding, and the casual offer of a couple of days' hunting—whether accepted or not—tended to make any invitation more than respectable. He would be more than an asset. Not only would Gerald give Molly pleasure and confidence, his tall, handsome presence and casually worn well-cut clothes would reflect more than a little glory on her.

231

. . .

"I've brought a spare handkerchief."

Charlotte and Isabel, who were in the hall pressing Gerald to stay for a glass of sherry, looked startled.

"I thought we might go to the cinema. And in case Molly cries—"

"I'm sure Molly has a clean—" Charlotte started, but stopped when she saw her sister laugh.

"I have," Molly said, also laughing. Before the merriment had died down, Gerald had steered her out the door, across the wide marble landing, and into the antiquated lift.

"You like taking chances," she said.

"Bred for it." Molly remembered that Cynthia Sweeney's father, Gerald's uncle, was called the Chancer and that Gerald and Cynthia's grandfather was known as the Loose Canon. Such nicknames were not loosely bestowed in the west of Ireland. The definite article in both appellations was reminiscent of the older—pre-English—Irish titles such as the MacGillicudy of the Reeks or the O'Conor Don. "The most fun," Gerald continued, "is to tell the truth knowing that one won't be believed. At least not until it's too late."

Molly thought about that as they came out of the lift and walked the length of the red-carpeted lobby. She wondered if she had just heard a confession or received a warning. She also wondered where they were going but was reluctant to ask.

"I thought that we would actually go to the cinema. Especially since we both seem to be weighed down with spare pocket handkerchiefs."

"What a nice Beatrix Potter word that is," Molly said, hoping that Gerald was not planning to take her to a film that would actually cause her to weep. When she cried, it was hard for her to stop, and she did not want to snivel all through dinner. She also knew that she cried far too often for a girl her age.

"Don't worry, we're not going to a tearjerker. I have a tendency to get a bit choked up in the most embarrassingly bad

232

movies. Just imagine if *you* had to lend *me* your handkerchief. This is the plan—there's a Bergman festival at my local Classic— there is most of the time if truth be told—and we're going to see *Wild Strawberries*. We've plenty of time, so we're going to wait for a reasonably empty bus and sit in the front on top."

As he spoke, two buses drew up at the stop. Gerald and Molly got onto the second one, ascended the stairs, and took the front seats. Molly could feel a smile on her face; the evening was becoming an adventure. Not one that she could necessarily describe to everyone. "We went for a ride on a double-decker bus" didn't sound very grown-up, although she remembered Sophie telling her in the soft voice of amused pleasure of a suitor who had driven her through a car wash.

Gerald glanced back at the other passengers.

"There's quite a good game to play on buses," he said, "but I don't think this lot deserves it. You pretend to be a little girl fresh from the bogs of Ireland—you should be able to manage that, I expect—although it's better if you're foreign, if you could do an au pair without much English. I would point out the sights to you as we went along. Not always quite accurately. I would explain, for instance, that the Albert Hall was the Tower of London and recount the various people who had their heads cut off there. The other passengers would go mad, but being British wouldn't, of course, be able to say anything. I had one Indian Army type I thought would have a stroke when I identified the Ritz as the headquarters of the Brigade of Guards. Oh well, some other time."

Molly was relieved that she was not to be called upon to perform—and encouraged by the reference to future bus rides they would take together. She could feel that Gerald was enjoying her almost childish pleasure in the outing.

WILD STRAWBERRIES moved Molly without upsetting her. Her taste was toward the cool, the remote, preferring accuracy and observation over sentiment and color. She shied away from the warm, damp emotions that she tried to avoid in her own life and rejected Victorian landscape paintings, novels that had an animal as a central character, or anything with too much pale blue and pink in it. Bergman suited her very well; she felt exposed to a new view of the world and to the rhythm of an intellect that saw beauty with a calm, cold eye. She was silent when she and Gerald emerged from the cinema into a dusk a darker gray than the gray landscape of the movie. It had become colder, and Molly buttoned her coat to her neck.

"You liked it?" Gerald asked.

Molly nodded, not wanting yet to speak and knowing that he did not expect her to talk. He took her hand, the gesture less of romance than comfort to one whose emotions have had a good swirling.

During dinner she told him about the Lathams—she had worked three afternoons for Henry Latham since she had last seen Gerald—and how she had been to the library as well as the post office, had typed a letter to a poet she admired, and paid the gas bill.

"You do research for him?"

For a moment Molly considered making her responsibilities a little more grand, but a respect for Henry Latham's work and Gerald's worldly intelligence caused her reluctantly to shake her head.

"It's as much fun as real research," she said, "but in terms of his book, it's just checking things at the library. He told me when *he* goes to the library to look things up, he finds at least half as much again that is useful. Or valuable. Or beautiful."

"*L'object trouvé.*"

Molly looked blankly at him.

"Duchamp."

Molly shook her head and Gerald told her about Marcel Duchamp and on a paper napkin—for they were eating in a warm, cheerful, far from expensive Italian restaurant, not really much more than one of the great-aunts' coffee bars—drew a clumsy sketch of the milk-bottle rack. Molly thought about what he told her for a while.

"I understand, but I'm not quite sure whether it's cheating or not. I'm quite good at seeing what is good and original, although it's never something I would have thought up myself. In Sophie's house or something Caroline wears. Not grand and expensive things, things I could have done myself if I'd thought of it. An 'eye'—it's not the same as creativity. Of course, there is the element of wit—an element of wit is almost a legal defense in Ireland." Molly stopped, rather pink.

"You're a serious little thing, aren't you?"

"Do you think?"

"Serious and thoughtful."

"More fool you."

"Really?" Gerald laughed.

"I'm"—and she realized that Gerald still didn't know her exact age—"quite young, you know." She finished with a fair imitation of a precocious child.

"I need to know more about this."

Molly laughed, enjoying, she suspected, Gerald's teasing, affectionate tone, more than was quite normal. Feeling it fill a small corner in the huge void created by the deprivations of her strange childhood. A void of which most of the time she was ignorant. While missing her father, she did not think of herself as deprived as long as she had enough to eat and a roof over her head.

"Do you gaze into shop windows?"

"I spend most of my waking hours with my nosed pressed against the window of Mary Quant and Kiki Byrne."

"And you'd sell your immortal soul for what you see there?"

"Not in a general way—but maybe for the purple dress with hardly any back that I saw last week. But I don't know where I would wear it."

"Women's magazines?"

"Wherever I can find them. Sophie takes all the glossy ones, but I don't often see the other ones. I'd never actually buy them, of course."

"What other ones?"

"The kind we used to read at school. With advice columns and knitting patterns—though that was hardly the attraction—and soppy love stories."

"And advertisements for how to increase your bust?"

"They all have those."

"But you read them?"

Molly felt a blush rise. She avoided Gerald's eye, but she did not consider lying. Truth always seemed to her to be the point. It was something she and Sophie used to argue about. Molly felt that if enough people told the truth, some basic, hidden thing would gradually be revealed. Sophie held that the inevitable result would be the opening of Pandora's box.

"Yes," she said.

"They don't work, you know."

"Everyone knows that," Molly said, a defensive note of irritation in her voice.

"But you read them anyway?"

"Yes, I do."

"But you don't send away for what they advertise?"

"What do you take me for?"

"I take you for what you are. Adorable in every way. A flower. And the love stories? Do you read them?"

"Of course, although they're not satisfying. Not through lack of literary merit—though that, too—but because they don't evoke real feelings the way, say, music—especially cheap music—does."

"Film stars?"

"Yes, but not really. I can see it, but I don't feel it. Music works better. It's more accurate about feelings."

"Feelings. Sex? Desire?"

Molly didn't answer for a moment. "I suppose," she said eventually. "Although I think of it as love."

"You *are* a serious little thing." Gerald patted her hand. Again

236

Molly felt that her reaction to the pressure of his hand on hers held too much significance. It was dangerous for her. "Young, but serious. I live quite near here. If you come back with me I'm not sure whether to offer you brandy or cocoa."

Gerald's flat was on the top floor. The house was Victorian, close to the cinema, in a neighborhood Molly did not know. It seemed middle-class and safe, and she had the impression that it had once been more substantial, the breeding ground, perhaps, of successful merchants. The top floor would once have been the nursery. The rooms were too large and too light for either servants' quarters or an attic. The front of the house sloped inward toward the roof so that the windows were high and protruded over the broad street below.

Molly was a little shocked at the cheerlessness of the rooms. Her family and friends in London lived on a level of comfort that amounted to privilege. They had acquired or developed this standard of living in different ways. David was rich and Sophie had taste. The great-aunts were both frugal and comfortably off, the beauty of their flat based not only on architectural proportions, space, and light, but on objects that they had inherited and frequently enhanced or repaired with their own hands. Caroline's small, perfect flat was the substantial and comforting home with which she mysteriously assumed no man would provide her.

Although she had rarely visited the flats of her fellow students at the Queensgate Education Centre, Molly knew that most of them lived more modestly than Gerald did. Packed into flats with good addresses in South Kensington, they were waiting to find husbands. These girls shared bedrooms and quarreled in the kitchen, scrupulously tactful about rights to the late-night sitting room so that each of them might have a chance to land the young man who had brought her home that evening and who might rescue her from the temporary squalor in which she lived. Some of these girls wore engagement rings and counted the days until they had a home of their own. Others would bring a suitcase to the Queensgate college on Friday mornings and after classes take a train home to their parents for the weekends.

But Gerald was a man. He was supposed to provide the home. Molly had a momentary sense of a weakness in him, then berated herself for making a judgment based on material possessions.

"There is a high window set into the wall like this in my grandmother's house," she said. "In my room."

Gerald took a beer mug from the mantelpiece, fed an extravagant number of shillings into a meter, and lit the gas fire. The room was cold, and Molly, who had not yet taken off her coat, drew closer to the fire.

"I'll make you some cocoa, and by then it'll have warmed up a bit."

The kitchen was also very cold, and Molly was again shocked by its cheerlessness. The room, illuminated by one too-bright overhead bulb inadequately diffused by a cheap plastic shade, had not originally been intended as a kitchen, and the gas stove and stained sink seemed incongruous in the cheaply carpeted room whose only other furniture was a table and two chairs in front of an uncurtained window. It was a kitchen in which Molly could not imagine preparing even the simplest meal. As Gerald poured milk into a small enameled saucepan and struck a match to light the stove, Molly understood, for the first time, what people meant when they spoke of "love in a garret." In her daydreams, she had imagined herself married to Desmond, and even in fantasy she had not thought that they would be affluent. But she had set their impoverishment in a small, uncomfortable but well proportioned Irish house, and if told that they would have been really—as opposed to comparatively—poor, she would have imagined them living like the Irish rural peasantry in a whitewashed thatched cottage. Life in such a cottage would be hard, but it would not be as dismal as the shoddy, badly converted kitchen. Molly had watched women pump water in the yards behind their cottages and carry the heavy pails back to their homes. She had seen them cook meals in a large black pot suspended over an open turf fire. She had eaten the bread they made without yeast, cooked on the inverted lid of the pot. She had sat on the hob beside those fires and turned the wheel to encourage a

238

flame from the smoldering turf. She had watched those same women place one heavy iron by the fire and lift the other, hotter one to iron a husband's Sunday shirt. She did not really imagine that she would ever have to live like that—she knew of no Protestant who did—but, far from sentimental about the hardship of this way of living, she thought she could if she had to. What she could not do was to live in the depressing atmosphere of the hopelessly ugly, in one of the shoddy semidetached houses that were being built in Ireland and England. Jerry-built, thin-walled. She could not have lived in Gerald's flat. She had imagined that she could happily enslave herself to Desmond but not it seemed, not to her surprise, if she had to live with a stained and unhygenic carpet in an ugly kitchen.

"Needs a woman's touch, wouldn't you say?"

"How long have you lived here?" Molly asked, trying to avoid answering his question and realizing, too late, that she just had.

"It was the nursery when this house belonged to one family. Perhaps I should have emphasized that rather than tried to hide it. I thought of having a duck motif in the bathroom. Perhaps a Peter Rabbit frieze in the living room. But the kitchen would be a problem, and I'm not sure enough of my masculinity to have a Tom Kitten bedroom."

"Some girls I know do wonders with candles in wine bottles and bull-fighting posters," Molly said coolly. "Not Caroline, of course."

"Do you think this place is beyond hope, then? I'd love your help."

The living room was, as promised, much warmer. Molly carried their mugs of cocoa. Gerald followed with a bottle of brandy and glasses. Molly took off her coat and sat in the armchair. She was thinking about the flat; she supposed that if Gerald ripped up the carpet in the kitchen, put down linoleum, installed a heater, bought a tablecloth and a dimmer lightbulb, and put something colorful on the walls, the room might be a little less squalid. She was wondering how much such an alteration might cost and whether she should suggest it when Gerald, seating himself on the sofa, patted the cushion beside him.

"You're too far away. I want to show you something."

Molly took her mug and, crossing to the other side of the glowing gas fire, sat beside Gerald. She felt stiff and awkward, and, to appear more at ease, she slipped her cold feet out of her high-heeled shoes and tucked her stockinged feet beneath her.

Gerald took a photograph album from a shelf that ran the length of the wall. The shelves, which contained books, a record player, and a pile of records, seemed to be an addition to the original apartment, and since the paint had a dirty yellow tinge, Molly knew that they had been the effort of a previous tenant or maybe a rare concession from the landlord.

Gerald opened the dark-brown album and, with one hand covering the inscription beneath a photograph, asked, "Who's this?"

The photograph was of a little girl standing on a beach. She was wearing a woolen bathing suit that had lost its shape and sagged loosely around her body. She held a small tin pail in one hand and a little spade in the other. The wind blew her hair across her face, in no way concealing the fury and truculence of her gaze.

"Is it really? It is! Were you there when it was taken?"

Gerald laughed, enjoying Molly's delight.

"My cousin. Cynthia. Her character already fully formed—she can't have been more than three. We feared her even then."

Molly studied the snapshot for a moment longer, and then her eyes strayed to the other photographs.

"May I see?"

Molly took the album onto her knees, and Gerald turned on the lamp behind the sofa and switched off the harsh overhead light. He put a record on the turntable and poured them each a small brandy. When he returned, he sat a little closer than before.

"That's me," he said.

A photograph of a small boy—maybe four years old, wearing shorts, a striped pullover, and a white sun hat—on a donkey.

"I think I remember being there—but my parents tell me I only remember seeing the photograph when I was very young," he added.

A stiff family portrait. All except Gerald, the youngest, smiling in a determined manner at the camera.

"My family. That's my brother—the one who's a friend of David's."

"I've never met him."

"I don't think either he or David are very good at maintaining friendships." Gerald leaned in to turn the page.

"Wait a moment. That's your mother?"

Molly looked at the image of a pretty but clearly, even in a photograph taken more than twenty years ago, silly woman.

"The colonel's daughter. The regiment's pet. She still hasn't grown out of it."

"Is she—" Molly realized that her spontaneous "Is she still alive?" was not only inappropriate but had been answered by Gerald's bitter use of the present tense. She amended her question: "Where do they live?"

"Close to a regimental town. Far enough for weekend visits not to be expected."

He turned the page. Molly looked at the photographs. Gerald watched her as she searched for clues about his family. About families in general.

"I know about your father," he said after a moment. "But I've never heard anything about your mother. You must miss her."

"I don't know. There are photographs—not many. My father had one in his dressing room. And my grandmother has some. Of when she was young."

Gerald, bewildered, waited for Molly to continue. She saw his expression and smiled, a smile that contained no vestige of pleasure.

"I can't remember her, so I don't miss her. How could I? But I probably feel the lack of her. Or did when I was a child."

"How old were you when she died?"

"Eight."

241

Gerald opened his mouth as though to speak but then closed it again. Instead, he opened his arms and Molly, pushing the photograph album carefully to one side, went to him.

He was leaning against the back of the sofa, and she now turned to face him with her legs curled on the sofa behind her. The embrace was not particularly intimate—less so than it might have been were they standing or dancing. Molly gave a great shuddering sigh and relaxed her body against his. He held her and patted her back.

The warmth of his body and the comfort she drew from it caused her to remember again the feeling of comfort she had had carrying the pile of warm towels for her guests before Sophie's wedding, drawing from inanimate objects the pleasure and reassurance that should have come from love. At that moment she still had had hopes of Desmond returning her love, so the comfort was not as full of irony as it later became.

Gerald stroked her neck and shoulders, as though encouraging a baby to go back to sleep. Molly, to her surprise, felt no imminent threat of tears. After a moment, Gerald picked up the untouched glasses of brandy and handed one to her. Molly took a sip and relaxed against him, her head against his shoulder, his arms along the back of the shallow sofa and loosely around her shoulders. Neither spoke for a moment or two.

"What is the music?"

"Bellini."

Molly listened. A woman was singing; Molly had never been to the opera or, for that matter, heard a complete opera on a record or the wireless. Though moved by cheap and tinny music, she had thought classical music, like gardening, a middle-aged pleasure. Now she could feel a pleasure, accentuated by a hint of sadness, somewhat like the sourness of lemon in an otherwise sugary sweet, and she realized that she had begun to appreciate an acquired taste.

"This is *La Sonambula*," Gerald added. "The Sleepwalker."

Molly closed her eyes, enchanted by the music, pleased to have a new source of pleasure. Gerald drew her to him. His hand,

242

moving from her shoulder to her breast, did not alarm her. A feeling of recklessness, fueled by the two not quite understood emotions of sorrow and desire, overcame her.

Why not? she thought as his hand moved across her breast and rested and closed over her nipple. She felt a sharper wave of desire and heard her own involuntary intake of breath followed by a low moan.

IT SEEMED TO Molly, although she could not be sure—she had no experience of the sleeping habits of men—that Gerald was feigning sleep. She had shifted and rustled enough (not too much since if he were pretending, he would know what she was doing) to awaken anyone who was not an unusually heavy sleeper. For reasons not dissimilar, she imagined, to Gerald's own, she dreaded waking him. But it was late.

The window, set high in the wall, let in enough street light for Molly to be able to see most of the room. A large chest of drawers stood against the wall. It was the only piece of furniture in the flat that clearly had not been provided by the landlord. On top of the chest was a battered circular leather box, a small saucer, and an assortment of male accoutrements that reminded Molly of her father's dressing room. The leather box, she was sure, had been handed down from a grandfather or possibly, if he were not still alive, the father whose photographs she had been shown only an hour before. Two photographs hung over the chest of drawers, one of a team—cricket, Molly thought, or possibly tennis—the other of four rows of densely packed schoolboys.

The bed was warm. Gerald had turned on the electric blanket when he had come in to light the gas fire. The fire had gone out, having come to the end of the metered shillings, and the room was cold. In the next room the music continued; it was the second or third time that Molly had heard the record. If Gerald was actually asleep, the same piece of music would play until morning.

Although Molly knew in theory the principles of human re-

243

production, most of her information had come from novels that tended to describe the emotional rather than the physical aspects of the sexual act. No adult had ever discussed romantic love, let alone sex, with her, and the only firsthand account with which she had been favored had come from a girl at school. The girl was from Northern Ireland, and she had told Molly that some years ago a friend of her parents had exposed himself to her several times. Although she had never told her parents, she enjoyed a certain notoriety, a heroic status even, among the girls at Kingstown House. Reveling in their disgust and fascination, although not untinged by a shame that she had not felt until she had seen their reactions and fully understood the gravity of what had happened, she told the story often. There was another girl, one of five sisters, who had contributed the information that her father, once a week, used to take a bath with each of his daughters. This confidence, again only partly understood by the girl who made it, had been regretted instantly and never repeated. The girl was, by the time she was pointed out to Molly, a prefect, and could not be further questioned. The only erect penis Molly had ever before seen had been at some distance and belonged to the man who haunted the lane behind the hockey field and exposed himself, despondently masturbating, to two hockey teams and a games mistress.

Gerald, causing little pain and giving less pleasure, had humiliated himself with a premature ejaculation and fallen into a deep and unconvincing sleep. Molly had lost her innocence but remained technically a virgin.

The stairs to Gerald's flat were lit by a light on a timer. On the way up, Gerald had pressed the switch that ticked away for two minutes before returning the stairwell to darkness. Now she looked nervously at the appliance, worried that she might be about to press a doorbell by mistake, fearing that the light would bring the landlady, who lived on the ground floor, to her door. The light went out before she had crept down the final few creaking steps, and she reached the front door by the pale light of the streetlamp through the fanlight over the front door. There

244

were two locks to turn, and it took Molly a moment to understand that she had to open both simultaneously to leave the
house. A moment later she had closed the door behind her and
stood in the cold street.

When Molly reached the end of the short street of redbrick,
residential Victorian houses, she found herself on a wide, main
road lit by tall, modern lights that dispensed an unpleasant orange glow. She did not remember how she and Gerald had arrived at his flat, and she had no sense of where she now was. She
did not even know the name of the neighborhood. She did not
know how to get home. Turning left, not so much because she
favored the direction as in order to walk downhill, she trudged
along the deserted sidewalk. No car passed her. The cold bit
into her legs.

The road curved so that Molly could not see where it led. She
was fairly sure that when she came to an intersection she would
have a sense of her location. It was almost midnight, and the
buses had stopped running. She had missed the last underground,
but a station would let her know if she was heading in the right
direction. The road seemed endless and her footsteps loud. Once,
on the other side, a drunk, unsteadily wending his way home,
called out to her and, closer at hand, a rustling in the dead leaves
and discarded sweet papers in the gutter suggested the presence
of a rat. Molly ignored both; it was not that she felt brave, it was
merely that she was thinking about other, closer, more humiliating things. She had crept out of Gerald's bedroom, dressing in the
dark. She had not waited to find the bathroom and had not
washed or urinated. Now her bladder ached, and the crotch of
her knickers was wet. She knew that when she took her coat off
she would be able to smell the evidence of her recent sexual encounter. Both her great-aunts should be asleep by this hour, but
it was not inconceivable that either might remain awake listening for Molly to come home. If greeted, she would have to rush
past her dressing-gowned aunt to the bathroom to relieve herself,
to remove her semen-damp knickers and wash herself before returning to explain and reassure.

245

At the foot of the hill beside the barred gates of the deserted underground station, a solitary taxi waited at a cab rank. As Molly approached the taxi, she could see that the driver was asleep inside. She hesitated, unsure how to go about waking him, reluctant to give him a fright. Behind her the telephone began to ring; another potential customer for the solitary cabbie. He opened his eyes, Molly leaped forward to assert her claim and a moment later found herself in the back of the taxi. Immediately another cause for worry presented itself.

"How much do you think it will be?"

The driver pulled away from the curb and muttered something, "meter" being the only word Molly could understand.

"I know," she said, "but I may not have enough money. I may have to get out a little before."

"How much do you have?"

"Eight shillings."

The driver switched off the meter and said, "I'll take you for that, flat rate."

Molly did not know if she had been the recipient of a generous act or the victim of a petty fraud.

"MOLLY HASSARD, there's a telephone call for you. In the principal's office."

There was usually a reprimand, cheerfully ignored by repeat offenders, about telephone calls during class, but the principal's secretary changed her mind about delivering it. Molly's drawn face and a half-remembered sense of something sad in Molly's past caused the girl, only a little older than Molly herself, to hope that the telephone call was, in fact, of a frivolous nature.

"Hello," Molly said tentatively into the telephone. Her embarrassed fear that it might be Gerald was tempered by the dread instilled in her by two tragedies having thrown her life off course without a moment to brace herself in anticipation of either.

"I went to the park today. I'm allowed to get up for an hour or two if I want, and I went slowly. There were a lot of ducks—

maybe a hundred—all paddling in the same direction. Close to the shore, at the same speed, in a uniform way. Actually you couldn't see them propelling themselves; it was as though they were being drawn by a current. Or on a conveyer belt. They turned a corner so that I couldn't see where they were going— they were on the other side of the Serpentine—so I went along the path on my side. There was an old man with a bag of something—probably bread—who was feeding them. But he wasn't throwing the bread into the water. I can't think why. So the ducks came out of the water to go up the bank to him. First of all they were twice as big, and you could see how they moved. Clumsily, waddle waddle. They were going up a slope, which made them seem heavier. It was the strangest thing."

"Sophie, I'm meant to be in bookkeeping."

"The thing is, can you come over after school? David and I have had a fight, and he's gone off in a sulk. He said he would sleep at his club and I laughed. I need you to take care of me."

"What club?" Molly asked and earned a disapproving glance from the hitherto sympathetic secretary.

"Something to do with that exceedingly minor public school he went to."

Neither accurate nor, Molly thought, an attitude to buoy up an already extremely edgy marriage.

"I'll come right away," Molly said. She suddenly longed to curl up on the satin eiderdown at the foot of Sophie's bed and listen to Sophie talk about herself. After last night, after Gerald, she couldn't face the prospect of her bookkeeping class, of a dinner-table conversation with her innocently curious aunts, who would happily listen to a full summary of the plot of *Wild Strawberries* and then ask questions about the parts they hadn't understood or hadn't heard. They would expect to hear what Molly had eaten for dinner and where and to have a full enough description of the evening for them to live it vicariously. And Molly dreaded, too, the prospect of lying about something she did not yet understand.

"Good, I told the aunts you'd be sleeping here, so you don't have to call them. I'll lend you whatever you need for the morning if you insist on going to that dreary college of yours."

"We'll see," Molly said and put down the telephone. "My cousin is sick," she said to the secretary. "She's pregnant and she's alone at her house. She needs me to go over right away." Seeing the disbelief on the other girl's face, she added, "Not a nightclub. The other kind."

"WHAT DO YOU think he means when he says he doesn't want to see me anymore," Sophie said. It didn't sound like a question.

"Who doesn't want to see you anymore?"

"Almost no one wants to see me anymore. If you haven't noticed that, you're not very observant—why do you think I have to drag you out of school?"

"It's not school—" Molly protested.

"I know, I know. In this rare instance I wasn't talking about myself, I was doing an imitation. Were you asleep?"

"No," Molly said automatically. She yawned. "I suppose I must have been."

"I didn't realize. Usually when girls lie around silently in my bedroom, they end up asking, 'What do you think he means when he says he doesn't want to see me anymore?' As though there's anything complicated about men."

"No one has actually told me—to my face—that he doesn't want to see me anymore. Even if they're not so complicated, I sometimes find their silences a little hard to read. Especially if they're not in the same room," Molly said and added silently to herself, *Or if they're dead.*

"Indecision, cowardice, passivity accounts for more than ninety percent of that kind of silence. The other ten percent is probably a hangover."

"I expect you're right."

"Of course, if they're Anglo-Irish—"

"I was dreaming—"

Sophie, usually uninterested in what did not immediately affect her, took Molly's dreams seriously and was prepared to discuss them for as long as Molly wished.

"I don't remember the dream exactly, maybe it was just a fragment, but it was about my mother's mending basket."

"The one at Fern Hill, with the lid that kept all that tangle inside? Stopped it leaping out and incorporating the furniture and small animals and taking over the house?"

"Exactly. I dreamed that I wanted to sew on a button for Mr. Latham. To a knickerbocker suit—obviously in real life he doesn't dress as though he were going shooting—one of those woven leather buttons, do you know what I mean?"

"Like a chestnut?"

"That's how I think of them, too."

"My father has them on his tweed jackets," Sophie said. "Your father did, too."

"Yes. Obviously they don't have holes for the thread. They have a loop at the back which needs very strong thread sewn deep into the tweed or else it tears."

Sophie nodded, seeming more interested in the leather button than she had ever been in David's family or work.

"In this case I was going to sew Mr. Latham's button on with a piece of blue ribbon. Not shiny blue ribbon like a bow for your hair or on a present—narrow and ridged. Rather like the ribbon I have on my evening watch."

Sophie nodded again, and Molly felt grateful that Sophie could so effortlessly understand her references.

"I pulled a piece of it out of the workbasket clump. I don't know why I chose blue ribbon, but it was clear I had made a particularly good, an intelligent and original, choice. The ribbon came out easily, slipping through the tangle and—this was the particularly pleasing part—it didn't pull the thread and wool around it tighter as I pulled it out. The tangle was in some way simplified and diminished by one component being removed, as though the next time I needed a piece of brown wool to darn a sock it would come out just a little easier than it had before. I can't describe how satisfying it all felt."

"And did you sew the button on?"

"I don't remember, but I think I must have because there was such a feeling of completeness and satisfaction."

"Well, now that you're awake, how about a nice cup of tea?" Sophie said. Although reverting to character, Molly knew that she was still considering the dream. She was not, however, suggesting that she herself should make the tea.

Molly sat up and stretched. Outside it was quite dark. She wondered how long she had been asleep. If it had been any length of time, Sophie must have let her sleep, must have watched her. She had a feeling of physical well-being, of intense pleasure in the comfort of Sophie's bedroom. She thought how pleasant it would be to spend the remainder of Sophie's pregnancy with her, sleeping like a pet at the end of her bed, making a nest in— or under—the rich plump satin eiderdown. Eating the decorative fruit from the Chinese export bowl, which Sophie had bought from Mallet's when she had been told that she would have to spend most of her pregnancy in bed. To spend the autumn basking in the warmth of Sophie's flower-scented bedroom. Talking lazily about their family and waiting the arrival of the baby even now swelling beneath Sophie's satin nightdress. For a heady moment Molly didn't stop there. She imagined the baby lying on the bed, Sophie tickling it and laughing at its gurgles.

"Do you want anything to eat while I'm down there?"

"I'm not hungry." Sophie was never hungry. Molly was always willing to eat anything that tasted good. "Are you?"

"A little. I'll find something."

"I'm not sure. The last time I rooted around, there didn't seem to be much."

"That's the difference between Irish kitchens and English ones. If I went looking at Fern Hill, I'd find flour and lard and rashers and some horrible fatty cold mutton. Here I'm sure to find a tin of baked beans or tomato soup or something in the deep freeze. Baked beans on toast would be cozy."

"Tea," Sophie said. "Consider it an emergency."

Molly went down the thickly carpeted stairs. Heavy, nubby,

gray wool from painted wainscot to painted wainscot, fitted, cut and firmly attached—nailed? glued?—to the steps. No sign and less need of the brass stair-rods of childhood.

The lights were lit on the landing. It had taken Sophie about five minutes to forget or abandon generations of frugality. Hot water, heat, and electricity were squandered as though she needed reminding that by leaving Ireland she no longer had, in any way, to stint herself. They were, it occurred to Molly, more constant reminders of her wealth than the sometimes still-wrapped purchases in shiny, stiff shopping bags with the names of expensive shops on the outside. The expenditure on utilities had the advantage of not entailing bickering with David. Even more important, she did not have to leave home—or, in fact, even get dressed—to spend it.

Light, a faintly unpleasant fluorescent glow, came from the kitchen as Molly rounded the corner of the stairs. Someone had switched off the overhead light but neglected the lights that ran along the underside of the cupboards and illuminated the Formica counters beneath. Molly, on stockinged feet, silently entered the kitchen, not immediately noticed by two mice dining on the kitchen table. Molly froze, and a moment later the mice simultaneously, but without looking at her or communicating between themselves, shot off the table by way of a kitchen chair and bolted under the refrigerator.

The table was almost bare. An empty wine bottle lay on its side. On a plate was half a biscuit, perhaps what had attracted the mice. They had left a sprinkling of crumbs over the dimly lit table. The mice would, she thought, had she not interrupted them, have cleaned up their mess, ingesting the last crumb before returning to their underworld.

Molly was not afraid of mice. She would have considered squealing at the sight of them an affectation. She felt a vague affection for the occasional mouse to be seen at Fern Hill, particularly the field mice that would naively visit the house when the weather became cold in autumn, when the last gleanings of grain from the harvest had been eaten and pickings in the hedgerows became sparse. The mice, she had thought, were often unaware of the existence of humans and far more horrified than their domestic cousins by the sight of them. Like the heroes of the fairy tales she had listened to so rarely and so reluctantly as a small child. House mice were anthropomorphically depicted as miniature middle-class humans, while the voyaging field mice attained the heroic status of characters in the myths that Molly preferred and that never made her cry.

Molly filled a kettle and turned on the gas. Finding some rubber gloves under the sink, she carefully wiped the table, scrubbed the plate, and put the wine bottle in the garbage. The mice, the stuffy kitchen, the depressing pale light, made Molly lose her appetite. Loading a tray with a pot of strong tea, it was less from hunger than a wish not to have to return to the kitchen later that caused her to add a package of biscuits. Normally frugal, she would have taken the open package in the cupboard, but after seeing the mice, she put a sealed pack of wholemeal digestive biscuits on the tray and carried it upstairs.

November 1961

"VERY ANTHONY POWELL."

Molly was relieved by Sophie's tone. She had arrived at the Wigmore Street nursing home full of awkward dread and was grateful to take her lead from her cousin.

"What do you mean?"

"There are scenes in the corridors of a nursing home like this. Men comparing notes about their wives' insides. Mr. Widmerpool being treated for boils."

Molly had not read *A Dance to the Music of Time,* but as in the case of most books that Sophie admired, she was well acquainted with the plot and characters. *Casanova's Chinese Restaurant,* the fifth volume in the series, lay on the table beside Sophie's bed.

"There's more to come. That's something to live for," Sophie said and, without a pause, continued in the same not uncheerful tone, "Did you bring a sharp scissors?"

"Yes. Are you finished with those newspapers?"

And Molly spread out several thicknesses of that morning's *Times* and *Daily Express* on the floor and lifted the flowers from all Sophie's vases onto it.

"What are you reading now?" she asked when she returned with the last vase filled with fresh water. If Sophie was reluctant to discuss her physical and medical well-being, Molly was in the habit of fitting in with her cousin's mood.

"To the North," Sophie said, indicating the novel on top of the pile by her bed.

"Tell me," Molly said, cutting a new clean base on the stem of a chrysanthemum.

"It's about two young women, sisters-in-law—it sounds heavenly. Wouldn't you love a little house in St. John's Wood? Just the two of us and a cat and a garden. There's a bit where the one like me goes to stay in the country and takes a slightly *worn* evening dress—how long is it, do you think, professional entertainers apart, since anyone *wore out* an evening dress?"

Molly understood that Sophie was not seriously suggesting that she trade in her little house in Trevor Square for something farther unfashionably north, nor, as Sophie further unfolded the story, was she planning a career for Molly as a travel agent, nor, less still, hoping for her a spectacularly unsuitable lover. But there was a suggestion of an imminent change for Sophie; fantasy and discontent, as they had been so many times since childhood, were again in the air.

"All right," Molly said. "I'll come with you, but not forever. And you have to tell the great-aunts."

Sophie laughed.

"Not forever?" she said. "Whyever not?"

"Because it doesn't fit in with my plans."

"Plans?" Sophie asked. "You have plans?"

"Fantasies, wishes."

"Go on."

"I want to live in Ireland. I want to be married and have children—" Molly stopped, embarrassed, not only because Sophie

253

was not now going to have a child but also because she was not in the habit of showing her own hand so clearly.

"It's all right. You're still allowed to want children. To have children. Who's to father them is another problem."

Molly was silent. Had Desmond not been engaged to Pauline McBride, she might have hesitantly admitted her feelings, have sought Sophie's advice. But there seemed no point.

"Gerald told me he's going to Dromore for the hunt ball. I assume that's because you have no specific Irish male marked out for this ill-advised plan of yours. Or are you planning to marry Gerald and relocate him?"

Sophie did not ask this question seriously, and Molly did not feel the need to reply other than with a laugh. To her relief, Gerald had neither attempted to repeat nor ever referred to their unsuccessful attempt to make love. For a while Molly was awkward with him, but soon she gratefully accepted that Gerald was once again his easy, avuncular, ever flirtatious self. It was as though he had forgotten it ever happened.

"WILL YOU STILL go home for Christmas?" Mrs. Latham hesitated before the world "home" and Molly, as she was learning to do—at least while she was with the Lathams—addressed both the question and the whisper of unspoken meaning.

"Yes. Sophie may come, too, if she is well enough. She wants to—I think this Christmas in particular would be too grim in London. She and David are barely speaking. And Dromore is home. It's home now, but it was never not home. Like Fern Hill was sort of home for Sophie, although not ever quite as much as Dromore always was for me."

"And the dance . . . the hunt ball?"

"We're still going—not Sophie, but—"

"But tradition and ritual dictate the actions and words of everyone concerned until they're all on firm ground again," Henry Latham said, relieving the worn-down Molly from struggling to explain the nuances of Anglo-Irish behavior. Although

254

she was happier and felt a greater sense of her own value in the Latham house than anywhere else, Molly was not lazy there. Alert at all times to small, helpful things she could do—gestures that were for her minor, but for the Lathams, as they would be for her great-aunts, quite an effort, such as fetching hot water from the kitchen to top up the teapot and expressing herself clearly and accurately. It was not a household where a cliché would have passed unnoticed.

"Yes. After my father died—and the funeral—everyone knew what to do and what to say. And Christmas—it wasn't much fun, and Aunt Belinda had to work very hard, but eventually it was over and—"

"And traditions are preserved for when they are next needed."

"Exactly. We're all sad about Sophie's baby, but there are even conventions of behavior after a miscarriage."

"It seems a little cold-blooded. . . ." Mrs. Latham said tentatively.

"No, for us it's the only way. If we were Italian, or Greek—"

All three laughed, and Molly felt pleased with herself. For getting it right and knowing how to free them from talking about Sophie and Ireland.

There was a moment's pause, but Molly did not feel the need to break the silence. She was now used to the reflective moments in the Lathams' lives. Henry Latham might be quietly thoughtful for thirty seconds and then offer her some cake or give her a change in a letter he had dictated earlier. Or he might, as he did now, ask an abstract question.

"What do women want?"

His wife laughed.

"Freud's question. Let Molly answer."

Molly knew that she was allowed to think about her answer—the only thing that she should not do was to reply in a manner that was either glib or intended to deflect attention from herself. She smiled, again feeling a pleasure she had never experienced anywhere but in the Latham house. The pleasure of recognized truth. Of insight.

255

"They want," she said slowly, "to know where they stand."

"Not power over the finest of men?" Mr. Latham asked, and Molly, a little pink, understood that gentle teasing—a completely new idea for her—was slightly flattering.

"That, too, of course, but that is a bonus."

Henry Latham nodded, his wife looked thoughtful. The silence resumed. Molly gazed at the orange and gray embers of the fire and then, fearing Mr. Latham would feel the need to rise and add a piece of wood, she carefully placed two small logs in the grate. She could see, and feel, Alice Latham stiffen at the sound, making Molly, for the first time that afternoon, aware of her hostess's increasing blindness. After a moment's listening, and when Molly had retaken her seat, Mrs. Latham spoke.

"Sophie Spencer seems to me like a Hans Christian Andersen character—the child in *The Snow Queen*—the Ice Queen?—Little Kay, with the chip of ice in his heart. Is there a reason?"

Molly knew from her tone that she was not expected to betray a family secret. Nor, despite the recent reference to Freud, was she supposed to come up with a psychological diagnosis.

"When I was a child, those who criticized her in my presence thought she was spoiled. Blame was fairly evenly distributed between each of her parents. I had a nanny who used to call her 'bold' and 'brazen'—two words that don't mean quite the same thing in England."

"It seems," Henry Latham said, "that the chip of ice in her heart does not make her numb."

"No, she's brokenhearted and angry. She was willfully desperate to leave Ireland, and now she's beaten and homesick. And, of course, furious and blaming everyone else."

"You won't make the same mistake?"

"Marry someone like David? Mean-spirited and stupid? I should think not."

"Don't you think that you're meant to live in Ireland?"

Molly felt a pang that the Lathams should so carelessly suggest that she live in a country other than the one that they inhabited.

"Not this second," Mrs. Latham said, reading her thoughts again. Molly realized that the Lathams must have discussed her when she was not there, and she felt reassured. Timid and unsure of herself as she was, she knew that they would have spoken only with affection.

"We meant when you have finished your studies. Or later. Just that you shouldn't stop thinking of Ireland as home."

"May I ask you a question? Advice, really. It's something a bit embarrassing."

Alice Latham looked a little taken aback, but Henry Latham continued to smile.

"About money, I imagine?" And as Molly, startled, blinked and hesitated, he added, "That's surely the most private subject left. And I didn't suppose that you were going to ask us boyfriend advice. Although you could do worse than to consult Alice."

"It's not a boyfriend question," Molly said, aware that she was not quite telling the truth. "It's . . . there's quite a lot I would have to tell you first. Maybe we should do it another time." She glanced at her watch; it was already ten minutes after she should have left.

"I don't think so. Take your time."

Molly hesitated for a moment. Then seemingly without drawing breath she told them about the General's will and the deal carved to keep Dromore standing and about Uncle Jack and the trust fund and Vera's bitterness and Adele's tiny cottage, which she had chosen over Fern Hill as a dower house. She told them about entailment and death duties and about Miles making over Dromore to Sophie when she married.

She made them laugh several times, and when she came to tell them the new part, she found herself able to continue.

"What I didn't know was that Fern Hill was one of the properties that Uncle Miles had made over to Sophie. Sophie has already made a will—she did it when she married David, when she came into all the family property. She left me The Book." Molly explained the magical qualities of the fore-edged book. "Now, when I went to see her at the nursing home, she told me that the doctor had told her that she would never be able to have a baby and that—"

"Sophie's an only child?"

"Yes."

"And so are you. And there are no other cousins?"

"No. If Sophie has no children, the entail is broken. She and I are the same age, but if I have children—"

"Yes. The only other possible heir would be David."

"I think she's considering taking steps that would put David out of the running."

"Or if she married again, of course."

Molly nodded.

"So?"

"She wants to give me—make over to me—Fern Hill."

"Yes?"

"She wants to do it now."

"I see."

"But"—Alice Latham broke the short, thoughtful silence—"but you're only a child."

"That's what *I* said," Molly replied.

"Given our lack of interest in the claims of any husband Sophie may marry in the future," Mr. Latham said, "or of any children he might have with another woman after her death, the question is not whether you should have Fern Hill, but when."

"Unless she wanted, later, to leave it to someone else," Molly said.

"From what you tell me of Sophie, among her failings is not a lack of family feeling; she has a wish for continuity."

"Yes," Molly said.

"And there's another good reason. Do you think of Sophie as likely to outlive you?"

"We're almost the same age and—well, no. I don't."

"If Sophie died before her parents, they would be her heirs, and from what you tell me of death duties and their part of the destruction of the great Irish houses, Dromore itself might not survive."

"But can Molly just go back to Ireland and live at Fern Hill by herself—it is still furnished, isn't it?" asked Alice Latham.

"Yes."

"Sophie isn't planning to mount an Irish campaign of any sort, is she?"

"She said that the trick was to keep moving—but I had the impression she had somewhere warmer in mind."

"Palm trees, parasols, silk pajamas? A little roulette in the evenings."

"Something like that. There's one more thing. I'm not sure that I—that anyone—can keep Dromore going for another generation. It's probably not possible in the new Ireland. And if one did struggle on, for what?" And Molly found herself expounding Desmond's views. Opinions she had heard in the greenhouse at Moorestown House when she was eight years old, the day her mother died, holding a plate from which she had carefully scraped the remnants of gooseberry fool.

"What you're saying is that Fern Hill may be all there is when . . . when it comes to your generation?"

"I think so. I've never heard anyone say it. I don't think Uncle Miles has ever thought it—although he may now, now that he knows that Sophie can never give him a grandchild."

"Still, you can't live alone at your age." When neither her husband nor Molly replied, Alice Latham asked, "What will your great-aunts do with the baby clothes they were knitting for Sophie's baby?"

Chapter Eleven

"*I*T'S ALMOST STOPPED raining, and the dogs are desperate for a walk."

Sophie did not react to Molly's words, seemingly settled on the sofa for the afternoon.

"Or perhaps you are planning to prolong your Elizabeth Barrett Browning phase indefinitely."

"What happened to the little matinee coats the aunts were knitting?" Sophie asked.

Molly shrugged.

"This is not a morbid question. Think of it as social research."

"I never saw either garment again. They began tapestry backs for the dining-room chairs. I think they finished the baby clothes in their rooms."

"What will they do with them? Give them to the next baby? I can't quite imagine that."

"They'll send them to a sale of work or a church thing."

Sophie nodded and smiled, as though a small but irritating mystery had been solved. "Why don't *you* take the dogs for a walk?" she asked.

Molly hesitated. Belinda had sent her to shift Sophie off the sofa and get her out of doors. Help was required in the kitchen.

There was lunch to be served as well as preparation for a more elaborate dinner.

"I was going to help your mother. I'm doing the puddings for lunch and dinner." Sophie raised an eyebrow. Molly continued, "Apple pie and cold lemon soufflé, respectively. Plenty of cream."

"I see. So the walk was more about getting me off my bottom than getting the dogs off theirs."

"Well . . ." Molly shrugged and drifted into the hall. She could have raised Sophie by invoking the memory of Tibby putting his head around the nursery door at Fern Hill and inquiring of two lazy girls if they had no fear of bedsores. For the first time, Molly couldn't be bothered to indulge her cousin. The dogs, making the most of the fire that had been lit in the hall to warm the house for that evening's dinner party, thumped their tails on the carpet.

"No luck, boys, maybe later."

As Molly made her way to the green-baize door, Gerald, languid and loose-limbed in an old tweed suit, wandered down the stairs.

"Can I do anything?"

"Well, yes. These dogs are dying for a walk. Perhaps you could get Sophie to go with you. She's in the drawing room."

It seemed significant to Molly that Sophie was not hibernating in the shabby, warm study, sunk into a worn sofa facing the fire but looking out the drawing-room window onto the wet, misty lawn and the damp fields beyond.

"Leave it to me."

Sophie had her first fresh air since her miscarriage, and Gerald became a temporary hero. But only until lunch. Looking at the snipe on the saturated toast before him, he asked, "Are these the birds we shot yesterday?"

Sophie, silent until then, gave a yip of laughter, and Miles's eyebrows shot up.

"Certainly not," he said. "These have been properly hung."

"Several months in the garage," Sophie said helpfully.

Cutting into the tiny breast of the bird in front of him, Gerald found it to be rare to the point of bloody. As he hesitated before lifting the morsel to his mouth, he saw Miles pop the delicate, eyeless head into his mouth, loudly crunching the fragile bones. Molly thought of the story Desmond had told her about the girl who had brought her handbag down to breakfast in his parents' house. Gerald's inability to eat old, raw game was dissimilar in every way—having to do with masculinity rather than class—except in serving to illustrate the chasm between an almost extinct people, leftovers from a social and political system no longer existent, and the rest of the world. Molly thought of her first conversation with Desmond, about his description of the Anglo-Irish in the context of evolution; she thought about her father's flat statement that the entire English upper class had perished in the First World War. Her father spoke of the past, Desmond of the future. No one would have been more appalled than the squeamish Molly at the prospect of eating the snipe, but it seemed she would prefer the man she loved to consider them standard fare.

It was Molly's turn to be the heroine when the apple pie was brought in. She had made it in a deep, oblong bowl, and when the pastry crust was broken, the smell of apples, cloves, and cinnamon escaped. Gerald poured on the thick cream and ate two helpings. Even Sophie ate a little, slowly, pausing to savor the memories evoked by the sophisticated nursery fare.

Sophie, less pale than she had been that morning, returned to the drawing room. Gerald accompanied her; the perfect guest, prepared to spend a wet afternoon amusing Sophie and keeping from under the feet of the two more busily employed women.

There was no further cooking to be done that afternoon. The pheasants were plucked and cleaned and lay on a marble slab in the larder. The potatoes for the game chips had been sliced and now waited in a deep bowl of cold water. Molly had made a cold lemon soufflé. It, too, stood setting on the slab, a stiff wax-paper collar around the ridged soufflé bowl. Bridie would remove the collar before it was served, and the lemon pudding, several inches higher than the top of the bowl, would give the impression of having risen. Belinda's famous pig's liver pâté was in the larder; the old, discolored, three-pound earthenware marmalade jars sealed with melted butter. The pâté was a rare example of a sophisticated food that had crossed the cultural, social, and religious barriers between Anglo-Irish and, for want of a more accurate term, native or Catholic Irish. Michael Macliammoir, the actor and native Catholic Irishman, had given the recipe to Molly Keane, the Anglo-Irish playwright. She had, with a generosity not always met with in matters of recipes, given it to one or two others. Belinda, not acquainted with either of the two principals, had bartered her version of diplomat pudding for it with a third party. And now it would serve as a first course for that evening's dinner.

"What should I do now?" Molly asked.

Belinda consulted the envelope in her apron pocket.

"Flowers, I'm almost done with that. The table is being set— why don't you look at it, and put these candles in the candelabra? Then if you could do the place cards and put them on the table. After that, why don't you rest and get ready for tonight?"

Molly went into the dining room and, standing behind one of the chairs, mentally took herself through the meal. She mimed laying the large and heavily starched napkin on her lap and thought her way through the meal to the port being circulated, something that would happen after she and the other women had left the dining room. She counted the forks, checked salt spoons and butter knives, and took the placement, written on the back of an envelope from Miles's stockbroker, to Belinda's desk to make out the place cards.

With black ink and Belinda's fountain pen, she wrote each name on the stiff, white cards. First Sophie, then her uncle and aunt, then herself. With a sad carefulness she wrote Desmond's name. There were to be ten people to dine that evening, and it was not until her pen wrote the ninth name on Belinda's list that she realized that Pauline McBride was not one of them.

"I CREPT INTO the dining room before dinner and moved my place card so that I could sit beside you," Sophie said, laying one of her slim, soft hands on the arm of Gerald's dinner jacket. "I hope you're flattered."

"'Flattered' isn't the word for it. I'm bowled over, and, since I'm not quite myself"—Molly, Gerald's official dinner partner, heard him murmur to her cousin, his words just loud enough for them not to be limited to an audience of one, however appreciative—"I'll tell you a trade secret. Provided that you promise not to use it to sit beside anyone but me."

Sophie laughed.

"I mean it," Gerald said. "You have to promise."

Molly would have hesitated, but Sophie laughed and said, "I promise." She did not take her hand from his arm.

"The trick is not to move your own card to improve your placement—that just maddens your hostess. What you do is stay where you are and change the cards on either side of you. It plays havoc with the table, of course, but *you* are not bored."

Sophie looked at him with, for once, unfeigned admiration. "I never thought of that."

It seemed to Molly, who was well aware that both Gerald and Sophie were seated exactly where she had placed their cards, that Gerald and Sophie were the perfect pair. Both could enjoy the nuance and manipulations of a love affair without ever calling the other's bluff with a demand that it be consummated.

She turned, dutifully rather than with enthusiasm, to Oliver Ross, who sat on her left. Desmond sat on the other side of Sophie, the curve of the table allowing Molly to look at him almost directly, but putting him outside the range of her conversation. He was looking at her. Sophie, on his left, was engaged in flirtatious banter with Gerald, and April Banville, knowing Desmond to be a man who didn't hunt, had turned to Miles. Desmond was isolated between two conversations. He showed none of the anxiety Molly would have felt if the conversation around her had gone off track so early. Desmond, unselfconsciously, looked at Molly; she could not quite meet his eye. She smiled weakly at him as she turned to Oliver Ross, but not so quickly that she couldn't see that Desmond did not return her smile. But his glance did not waver, either.

Oliver Ross was not more than twenty-six years old, but his thin hair had receded to an extent that might justify the word "bald." Or, perhaps more charitably or even more accurately, "balding." He was home on leave from somewhere in Africa— Molly could not quite remember where, although she knew that it was close to a lake from which emanated a disease with an uncertain and painful cure—for the first time since he had gone there straight from Cambridge as a district officer. Molly cast about for something to say. A prolonged stay on the shores of— was it Lake Victoria?—had not fostered the never remarkable social skills of the Ross family. Acutely aware of Desmond, she could think only of subjects she should avoid. She and Sophie had once been taken to tea at Dark Hill, the Ross's house. To her delight, and Sophie's, Miles had sat heavily in an armchair, unaware of a sturdy clump of gorse, camouflaged by an ugly green-and-yellow cushion and further concealed by the fading light of the winter afternoon and the frugal policy of the Ross household toward the premature switching on of electrical light. After Miles had leaped up with a startled oath, it had been explained that the gorse was kept on the chair to discourage an old water spaniel from napping on it. *Don't talk about gorse—the Rosses are famous for their lack of humor,* Molly told herself, but she could think of nothing else to say.

"Hunting tomorrow?" Oliver eventually asked her. Molly felt foolish. It was a question that had, in all likelihood, broken more than one silence that evening.

Molly rode well, but not beautifully. She was neither imbued with the desire to show off nor with unlimited courage when it came to jumping over things without knowing what lay on the other side. Hunting was also expensive. Expensive in a way that few of the Anglo-Irish ever had the honesty or self-knowledge to calculate to its fullest extent. The price of the subscription to the hunt would be acknowledged, also the capital outlay for a horse and the inconvenient ready cash for the "cap" collected at each meet. Less often admitted were wages for the groom, feed, vet's bills and, in Molly's case, the necessary clothes. A woman who would wear a baggy skirt for years and mend her stockings would be ashamed to appear on the hunting field less than perfectly outfitted. Molly, the following day, would wear her own boots, now slightly tight—a Christmas present from Miles and Belinda two years before—a jacket that had been Sophie's, and a bowler that had been Belinda's. Her britches were also Belinda's but had been altered by the local tailor. If she grew an inch or put on more than two pounds, her very occasional hunting days would be over.

Molly had been given—mainly because a mount had to be provided for Gerald—Sophie's mare, Lil, for what would be little more than half a day's hunting. Lil was getting old and wasn't entirely fit. Nor was Molly. A brief appearance, the first cover drawn, and maybe a good run with a couple of smooth banks, and she and Lil would go home. Like many things, it would be enjoyed most in retrospect. She knew this was not Oliver Ross's idea of hunting.

Desmond didn't hunt. For reasons, Molly imagined, not only of economy but as a way of stating his attitude toward his own future and that of the entire Anglo-Irish. His father, Frank Paget, used to hunt. Lady Marjorie still, occasionally, did. The following day she would be mounted on a horse that, as Tibby once remarked, had nothing wrong with it that an adequate supply of oats wouldn't cure.

Molly glanced at Desmond a little guiltily. She wondered if he disapproved of her hunting. He was still looking at her. Molly fought an instinct to avert her glance. She invoked not Sophie, whose brazen attitude toward men would not provide a useful example, but Henry Latham. He had never specifically directed advice to her, but he sometimes mentioned general principles as though they were maxims that she already knew and approved and of which she was merely being reminded. She held Desmond's gaze. There was nothing flirtatious about his look; it was fascinated, sad, defeated. As though he were thinking, *In another life, at another time . . .*

Gerald, sensing Molly's silence, although not her preoccupation, turned to her ready to compensate for his attention to Sophie.

"You're saving the first dance for me?"

Molly, still transfixed by Desmond and searching her mind for what Mr. Latham would tell her to do at this moment, suddenly remembered, as clearly as though she could hear his steady low voice, him once saying, "So far there seems to be remarkably little evidence to support the theory that the meek shall inherit the earth."

"I'm afraid not," Molly said with a gentle smile, turning a little toward Gerald, but not taking her eyes from Desmond. "I've already promised it to Desmond."

"IN LONDON, EVEN during the height of the season, this would be past my bedtime," Gerald had remarked as they drove into the courtyard of the castle.

It was important not to arrive at the ball too early; the parties coming from the grander houses would show up at half-past eleven or midnight, having allowed the room to fill in an inverse proportion to their social status.

The Dromore party had enjoyed a leisurely dinner. Port and cigars for the men; the women had lingered over coffee in front of the drawing-room fire before they had wrapped themselves warmly and set off for the ball. The dinner party itself had been so complete an event that Sophie—now that it was no longer a possibility—had remarked while they were being rowed across the river that it was a pity Vera and Adele had not come to dine. Belinda, in the pleasantest possible voice, had said that she had hoped for a Dromore evening at which some of the participants, at least, experienced pleasure. Miles frowned; Sophie laughed;

Molly failed to work out whether some reproof had been offered or received during the exchange.

When Molly had gone upstairs to her room after doing the place cards, she had had several hours to get ready for the dinner party and hunt ball. A pale-green dress, again once Sophie's, hung on the outside of her wardrobe. Belinda had offered Molly a new dress for Christmas, but Sophie had intervened and said that Molly should, instead, have a new coat. Molly, grateful, had agreed. The green dress, worn by Sophie only once or twice in London, was limp and beautiful and was, Molly imagined, the kind of dress women had worn at house parties between the wars.

Molly washed her hair, set it, and did her nails. She could easily have asked Belinda why Pauline McBride was not coming to dinner that night. She had not asked, for reasons of superstition more than inhibition. As she waited for her hair to dry, she struggled with the spark of hope that Pauline's absence had ignited— and that her own longing was fanning to a small flame. Regarding herself in the dimly lit mirror, she could see that hope had lit up her face. It made her afraid.

Eau de Nil, the woman at Hardy Amies who sold the dress to Sophie had called the delicate green. When Tibby had been a young man, girls had worn stockings of a pale gray called Elephant's Breath. Molly slipped her stockinged feet into her evening shoes and pulled the dress over her head. The silk lining against her skin excited her. She wriggled around to fit the dress to her body and looked at herself in the long mirror. Molly thought that she looked beautiful. She felt tall and powerful. Looking herself in the eye and still trying not to hope too much, she thought that a brief lifetime spent in self-effacement, thoughtful of others, modest and undemanding, had not saved her from any of the devastating losses that had shattered her childhood. And why should it have?

Now once again she was dancing to the music of Major Archdale's band, again close enough to breathe in the dark scent of Desmond's dinner jacket.

"Where is Pauline?" she asked coolly.

"Pauline and I are no longer dancing partners," he eventually said, sounding as though he had revealed more than he had intended. Molly looked at him steadily, her eyes insisting on more. "She left me."

"Oh. And . . . do you mind very much?"

"Not as much as I am supposed to."

The music stopped, and she could see Gerald standing not so far away looking, perhaps for her, among the dancers. Before he saw her, and before the music started again, Molly drew Desmond through the crowd. On the far side of the room, away from the band, were three deeply set windows with window seats. The throng of tightly packed dancers looming over them provided a kind of privacy, which was further enhanced by the heavy, dark, velvet curtains drawn back loosely to either side. The castle was built on a rock overlooking the river, and the Blackwater flowed below. Light from the ballroom shone onto the river and the shadowy trees on the farther side and the wet rocks and shiny fragments of ice on the edge of the bank. An almost-full moon illuminated the river downstream as far as the next bend. Upstream, shadowed by the height of the cliff and the trees that grew on it, was in darkness.

Molly could feel the cold through the window glass. Her dress, the wine she had drunk at dinner, and, above all, the music gave her an aggressive energy she had never felt before.

"I thought that you were going to get married?"

"So did everyone else, so did—there's something about you or maybe it's this island of calm in the middle of the West Waterford mayhem that makes me feel that for a moment I don't have to be a gentleman—so did Pauline. With no action on my part, there were assumptions, and we became thought of as engaged. My parents occasionally used to refer to her as my fiancée. When that happens once or twice in public, it tends to make it official."

"But, didn't you love—"

"I'm afraid it was more about apathy and convenience and how we were all going to muddle through the rest of our lives

269

than a great love affair. It doesn't reflect well on anyone. Particularly me."

Molly tended to agree, but she said nothing.

"I felt as though there was no reason not to. Pauline wanted it, my parents weren't wild about her—if we had married, she and my mother would have fought like cats—but they could foresee a future with some kind of structure. I had to choose between a gloomy, practical existence full of irritation and compromise or a kind of limbo. Looking after my parents when they got old—you know my father had a stroke?"

"Belinda wrote and told me. I'm sorry."

"A dreary way to live one's life but imaginable if one has a competent wife. And Paulie was efficient." He hesitated and added: "And an only child."

Angered less by Desmond's veiled allusion to Pauline's money than by his apathy and passivity, she said, a little more sharply than she intended, "If it was all so convenient, why didn't you marry her?"

Desmond moved a hand as though to touch her, then changed his mind.

"If I were Gerald, I would tell you that it was because of you, and you would laugh, but you wouldn't press the question."

"I wouldn't laugh."

Desmond paused, struggling against a lifetime habit of unspoken feelings.

"When we danced together—at Eithne's dance—do you remember?"

Molly nodded. It chilled her to think that Desmond asked this question seriously, as though she might have forgotten—that the moment might have been trival for either of them.

"And that afternoon at Fern Hill, when we sat in your father's study . . . I had the sense that there was something else, something I would never have but—it made it harder for me to imagine the rest of my life as—" He broke off, glancing at someone over Molly's shoulder.

"Molly, my angel, it is necessary for you to dance with me.

270

Your absence is causing me to compromise your cousin. The old biddies think I'm her fancy man."

"But I'm trying to compromise Desmond," Molly said, astonishing herself with the lightness of her tone. She hoped that Gerald would leave, but he held out his hand, and she rose reluctantly and allowed him to draw her into the passing dancers. She looked back over her shoulder; Desmond had half risen as she stood; now he sat back, watching her go. His face was expressionless.

OLIVER ROSS HAD been detailed to "bag seats" in a small, dark room that had a good fire and was convenient to the bar. It was not clear to Molly for what purpose this room was used. The castle itself was only lived in six weeks a year when the duke came from Scotland to fish his stretch of the Blackwater and the duchess wandered through the well-kept gardens, strolling under apple trees whose blossoms she always missed and whose fruit would not be quite ripe by the time they left for London. "Perhaps next year," she would say regretfully. Each summer she would admire her beautiful gardens, make small suggestions about planting, and choose bulbs for a spring she would not witness. Her old hunter was brought in from grass each morning, and she would ride every afternoon through the castle's woods and the new government-owned forestry plantations that adjoined their estate.

It was considered very sporting of the duke and duchess to allow the hunt ball to take place each year in the castle. It would be even more sporting, Miles had once remarked, if they were to show up one year and join the conga line that was now noisily forming in the ballroom.

When Molly and Gerald entered the room—it had been agreed that the whole party would meet for a drink when it began to get rowdy, a moment recognized by the Dromore party as accurately as though watches had been synchronized while they crossed the river—they could hear behind them the sounds of hunting horns amidst the noisy, good-natured, drunken shouts and laughter.

"Take a look at Carew's teeth." Oliver Ross greeted Molly and Gerald with a gesture toward Freddy Carew. Freddy Carew—only recently "young Carew," great-great-great-grandson of the Carew girl who had danced at the Duchess of Richmond's ball on the eve of Waterloo; young Carew in the hand-me-down dinner jacket making up the numbers at Eithne's coming-out dance—was now a good-looking young man with a Jermyn Street haircut and a dazzling white smile. All eyes were turned toward that smile, more specifically the teeth. "It's his third set. His third set—the second fell out when he was twelve. Did you ever hear of such a thing?"

Carew laughed, enjoying the attention. He had grown into the dinner jacket—if it were indeed the same one, and Molly thought it probably was—and one arm lay loosely along the shoulders of a pretty girl about Molly's age. One of Nona Bellew's five daughters—five daughters so beautiful and unpredictably spirited that no schoolboy had to be press-ganged to make up numbers at their hunt-ball parties; undergraduates from Oxford and Cambridge traveled at their own expense to stay in the unheated, drafty house.

Even Sophie seemed animated, as animated as anyone in a *La Dame aux Cameilles* pose on a saggy sofa can appear, her face alive and flirtatious.

Two bottles of champagne, one almost empty, stood on a table in front of the fire. Miles poured a glass for Molly and one for Gerald.

"You certainly know how to have a good time," Gerald said, raising his glass. It was not clear whether he was referring to the entertainment provided by Carew's teeth, the exertions of the dancers, or even the decent but no longer cold champagne they were drinking.

"This part doesn't last forever," Belinda said. "Archie is like a nanny. At this stage he's trying to tire them out; then there will be slow music to calm them down, and then home they'll all go."

"A quick nap, and they'll all be at the meet at eleven. In good spirits if a little green about the gills," Miles said. "I among them."

Molly slid into the small space on the sofa not completely occupied by Sophie. "Move over," she said. Sophie made room for her. Sophie was not by nature physically affectionate, and Molly had learned, not only from her cousin, to restrain her impulses. When Molly kissed her lightly, Sophie turned her head, smiling, a little surprised. Molly saw that she was as surprised at her own reaction as she was pleased at Molly's gesture.

"You might encourage Gerald to dance with you," Molly said in a low tone less carrying than a whisper.

"Are you mad?"

"Not now, you fool," Molly laughed. "When the music is slow again. Take "Smoke Gets in Your Eyes" as a cue. Can't you see he's dying to dance with you?"

"And who will you dance with? Not Carew—the Bellew girls would eat you alive."

"Desmond."

Sophie raised her eyebrows. The noise from the other rooms suddenly started to abate.

"Here we go," Molly said. "Or do you want to argue about it all night?"

Sophie was less surprised by Molly's choice of dancing partners as by the note of impatience her little cousin had used to address her. She turned toward Gerald and raised a languid arm.

"You've been neglecting me, Gerald," Sophie said.

As MOLLY HAD known, the band played "Smoke Gets in Your Eyes." The red-faced men in pink coats and their wives retreated, their evening clothes damp with sweat, to the bar. The dancers were younger now, the atmosphere romantic.

Molly danced with Desmond. They danced silently, close together. Not cheek to cheek; Desmond did not hold her tightly. Molly felt a sudden sense of relief, as though she had been lost and, after a long period of helplessly trying to attract the atten-

273

tion of those searching for her, had finally been found. She felt as though Desmond had, at last, recognized her. A tear ran down her cheek. Desmond wiped it away carefully.

"Are you sad?" he asked.

"No."

"Are you happy?" His smile was gentle.

Tonight she would tell Miles that she would not hunt in the morning. Tomorrow she would take the keys to Fern Hill and meet Desmond there. Although she had known for a long time that anything one has to ask for is not worth having, he was what she wanted.

"Yes," she said. "I am."